Short of Glory

Also by Alan Judd

A Breed of Heroes

Short of Glory

Alan Judd

HODDER AND STOUGHTON
LONDON SYDNEY AUCKLAND TORONTO

With thanks to J.G.

British Library Cataloguing in Publication Data

Judd, Alan
   Short of glory.
   I. Title
   823'.914[F]   PR6060.U3/

   ISBN 0-340-34653-1

For all have sinned, and come
short of the glory of god (Rom. 3:23).

Although the setting of this book is obvious the towns and regions mentioned are amalgams of various places. There is, for instance, no city that is both the administrative and commercial capital. In order to avoid charges of inaccuracy, therefore, I have invented names; and, to be consistent, I have altered the name of the country itself.

A.J.

1

Patrick did not read the letter again until after take-off. It was from Clifford Steggles, head of chancery in the British Embassy in Battenburg, Lower Africa. Clifford and his family were staying in the house that Patrick was to move into; a house normally occupied by the consul, Arthur Whelk, who had disappeared. It was a letter of welcome, probably well meant.

"Dear Stubbs,

Greetings from a cold but sunny Battenburg. It will still be quite cold comparatively speaking by the time you arrive but not long after summer will begin and it should be warmer. Summer lasts for nearly eight months with the other seasons taking up the other four. I am sure you will enjoy being in this idyllic climate.

This house is large with many rooms. We are sorry to be moving out just as we are getting used to it but it will nevertheless be good to get back to our own now that the roof is back. Yours is an ideal family house but I am sure that as a bachelor you will enjoy it. Of course, you are over-housed for your grade and will soon have to move into something smaller and more appropriate. The admin officer hasn't yet been able to find anything small enough, all the houses here being so big, so make the most of the space while you can!

It has a delightful lounge, a dining room, kitchen, study, scullery, three bathrooms, four loos, six bedrooms, a double garage, extensive outbuildings and not least a veranda and bar. It stands in an acre of walled garden with trees and a swimming-pool. No tennis-court, I'm afraid. We're trying to get funds for that as in this country it is essential for entertaining to have all facilities.

The main problem that we – Sandy, my wife, and I – think you will have is in finding enough paintings, sculptures, bric-à-brac etc. to fill it up with. At present it still contains Whelk's effects but they will go eventually presumably, even if he reappears in which case he will doubtless be rapidly posted elsewhere. Therefore bring all your objets d'art. It is of course furnished and decorated by the Property Services Agency (PSA) via the embassy but you are nevertheless responsible for seeing that it is kept in good order and maintenance. I trust you will find nothing to complain of in our 'housekeeping'.

Sarah is the maid who lives in the outbuildings and goes with the house. She is in her late 40s/early 50s, a regular church-goer, teetotal and as honest and loyal as can be. She is in all ways an excellent housekeeper and a good cook. In fact, she is better than our own maid and we would take her with us if we could. She is also a passable waitress. We cannot recommend her too highly. A maid is essential for your entertainment.

There is also Deuteronomy, the gardener, who is also hard-working, reliable and honest though he is not teetotal. He does not live in the outbuildings but comes to us for two days a week. Again, you are advised to permit him to continue in your employment. Your allowances should cover this sort of thing.

How do you feel about dogs? Snap is a ridgeback. He is loyal and affectionate and an excellent deterrent to would-be burglars. He is like Sarah and goes with the house. Arthur was particularly fond of him, I believe. I should, however, warn you that, like many Africans, Deuteronomy does not get on well with Snap, being a ridgeback, and though it was hoped that relations would improve after he had been doctored, they did not. Sarah, however, continues to get on well with both and this is not a serious problem.

I am unsure as to what else I can tell you. Battenburg is a large and impressive city offering all the luxuries of a highly-developed consumer society (cinemas, theatres etc.) as well as a complete availability of everything needed to make life comfortable. Prices are lower than in the UK except for electrical goods.

Please don't forget to write the usual courtesy letter to the ambassador if you haven't already done so. He is greatly looking forward to hearing from you. Also, if there is anything I can do from this end to ease your passage I should be very happy.

Yours ever,
Clifford E. Steggles

P.S. I don't know what car you plan to bring. Nearly everyone here has a Ford."

It was the second time Patrick had read the letter. The first had been some weeks before. He had tried to convince himself that it was merely the threat of unaccustomed domestic responsibility that he found so depressing. He could not imagine conducting diplomatic entertainments. He was to be the third secretary in the embassy and Steggles, as head of chancery and first secretary, would be his boss. He was to take on some of Steggles's work as well as some of the missing Whelk's, though in neither case had the work been defined.

A stewardess announced that they could unfasten their seatbelts, then apologised for the late take-off. Other stewardesses sold drinks and headphones. The film was a comedy.

2

Patrick had applied to the Foreign Office because it sounded interesting, even glamorous, because it was said to be difficult to get into and
because people admired it. He often sought what he thought was most
desired by the rest of the world so that he could then feel more a part of
it; but it did not always work.

He had passed the written papers and then attended the two-day
Civil Service Selection Board. This was not the weekend in a Cotswold
house of popular imagination, where the skill was to know how to cope
with the peas, but a two-day battery of tests and interviews in London.
It was a bureaucratic adaptation of the wartime selection courses for
military officers. Assault courses and initiative tests were replaced by
committee meetings and drafting exercises. Patrick soon learned that
no one in the Civil Service ever wrote; instead, they drafted then sent
their papers to someone else for redrafting.

There were several other candidates, one a woman from the University of Sussex with a CND sticker on her handbag. Patrick had most
contact with a tall, thin, fair-haired man a few years older than himself.
This man hunched his shoulders and clasped his hands behind his back,
like a crow folding its wings. When he walked his head nodded from
side to side and he grinned nearly all the time as at some private joke.
He shot out keen, inquisitive, sideways glances at whoever he was
with. He said he had been in the Army and looked a little mad.

"Fancy a drink?" he said at lunchtime on the second day. "I can't
bear staying in offices all day. Have to get out."

"Why are you trying to be a civil servant, then?"

"Tell you outside."

They stood in the corner of a crowded pub, drank beer and ate
tasteless steak and kidney pies. "Point is, I'm not really trying to be a
civil servant," said the Army man. "They won't have me, I know that.
I just thought it might be good interviewing practice."

"Why won't they have you?"

"Isn't it obvious?" The man was unable to continue because his
mouth was full. He chewed energetically and swallowed some beer.

10

"Well, Army for a start, you see. They're suspicious of the military, especially when I said I was leaving because there weren't any more wars. Then Cambridge – got the Army to send me there for a while" – he hesitated – "before leaving. Well, you know what it's like these days. Oxbridge backgrounds count against you now. They're all leaning over backwards to prove they're not biased in favour of their own kind. I went to a public school, too. You'll be all right with a state school – am I right? Thought so. University?"

"Reading."

"Subject?"

"Economics."

"You'll be home and dry as long as you can spell your name. Same with that woman. Sussex and sociology – she'll get through. My only hope is if I could convince them I'm black." He grinned. "Perhaps I should've worn camouflage cream."

"I suppose you weren't in the ranks?"

The Army man shook his head. "I thought of saying I was. It would help but they'd check up and when they found I was an officer they'd probably chuck me out, always supposing they'd let me in, of course. No, it would've been better if I'd been wounded." He looked thoughtfully at his right knee. "I've got a pretty good limp on occasion."

Patrick looked at the knee. "What happened?"

"What? Oh, nothing. Pretty convincing limp, I should've said. More so with the right than with the left for some reason. I say it's shrapnel moving round the body in damp weather, you know. That way I'm covered in case I forget." He lifted his leg a little and cautiously wriggled his foot as though it was unused to movement. "Got me out of some pretty nasty situations, the old instant limp. Husbands, traffic-wardens, that sort of thing. What do you use?"

The question seemed to be serious. Patrick smiled. "Nothing, I'm afraid. I've never had a car and I know only one or two husbands. I haven't yet felt the need for a disability."

The Army man nodded. "Worth bearing in mind, though. Better still if you have a stick."

They walked back through the lunchtime crowds. Patrick tried to imagine the Army man as a diplomat. Perhaps he had what it took, whatever that was. "D'you think you'd enjoy being in the Foreign Office?"

"Don't know. Might be fun. Get around a bit. Doesn't strike me as a ball of fire, though. Still, I'm surprised I got this far, really. Perhaps I should've applied to the Min of Ag and Fish or something." He

11

laughed with disconcerting abruptness, then frowned. "Mind you, I reckon they're having us on with all this guff about needing high quality candidates for the Foreign Office and the Treasury. I mean, what are the two great areas of British failure since the war? The economy and foreign policy. The rest of the country works all right. I reckon they must send all the wets and no-hopers to the Treasury and the FCO and all the good guys to the Inland Revenue and the bloody Customs and Excise. They work well enough."

Patrick was not put off. He wanted a career. The Foreign Office sounded fine. It turned out that only he and the woman from Sussex were selected to go forward to the final board, a long and testing interview at the end of which he was asked by a lady novelist – one of a panel of co-opted outsiders – whether his late father, a vicar, had ever preached a sermon in Wigan on the need to sin boldly. He did not know but thought it sounded likely. His father had had many parishes. The lady had once heard such a sermon and had incorporated it into one of her books. It had been a remarkable message, preached with fervour, and much needed in Wigan.

Patrick was surprised and very pleased when he heard he was successful. His delight survived even the first few days of his contact with the Training Department but it began to fade on contact with Personnel. There he was received by a big flabby man with an unhealthy complexion and an irritable manner. The man shuffled papers slowly on his desk as if looking without hope for one in particular.

"It is the Secretary of State's pleasure," he said dolefully, "that you should serve in" – his podgy hands continued shuffling the papers and he did not look up – "The Republic of Lower Africa. You will be third secretary in chancery. Are there any questions?" He gave up with the papers and clasped his hands limply, staring at the wall behind Patrick. His eyes were grey and watery, as if the colour were running out. "Normally you'd serve on a desk here for a time but they need someone as soon as possible. LAD – Lower African Department – are very keen to get you out there."

Patrick would have liked time to go away and think about questions. When he joined he had wanted to go abroad but now that he was faced with the prospect he did not know whether he really wanted to or not. It was also strange to think of someone being 'very keen' to have him. He wondered for what. "Don't I need to learn Lower African?"

"They all speak English as well, you know. Of course, LAD may think otherwise but it's not for me to say. I would only point out that it is essential in our work to maintain a certain detachment from the country one is in, otherwise one's reporting suffers. People sometimes worry too much about languages."

"How long is the posting?" asked Patrick.

"Normally four. Two two-year tours with leave in between. To start with you'll be doing some consular work as well as your chancery work because of that man Whelk going off like that or disappearing or whatever he's done. You know all about that, do you? No? Well, LAD will tell you. Whelk was or is the consul – deals with passports, rights of British subjects, visas, that sort of thing. He has an assistant there so it won't be too onerous for you." A gentler, more reflective look came into the man's watery eyes. "Comfortable posting, Lower Africa. Good allowances, too, twenty years ago. Don't know what they're like now, of course." His podgy hands resumed their slow shuffling of papers and he replied to Patrick's farewell without looking up.

The more Patrick thought about it the more he liked the idea. Lower Africa was an exciting controversial country, a place where things happened, a place of sun and storm. Four years was a long time, though, and the knowledge that he was leaving them for so long lent the grand shabby corridors of the Foreign Office building a surprising charm.

LAD was said to be two floors, three corners and two wings distant from Personnel. The lifts were out of order and he was soon lost. He passed numbers of busy geographical department offices where through the huge half-open doors people could be glimpsed drafting, dictating, discussing and – presumably – deciding. He had never seen so much paper nor so much earnest busyness. The Foreign Office began to recover some of its appeal.

He asked for guidance in the Heads of Mission Department, an office whose purpose was to administer ambassadors and high commissioners. Following their directions led him to the Secretary of State's Private Office where he almost collided with a young male clerk who wore a gold ring in one ear. The clerk directed him towards what had been the old India Office.

The post-war history of the Foreign Office – indeed, its twentieth-century history – was one of remorseless bureaucratic expansion. It had grown in inverse proportion to the decline in Britain's overseas responsibilities. The India Office, the Colonial Office and the Commonwealth Relations Office were swallowed up as soon as they became dispensable. This expansion of function could be read in the building: obsolete signs remained in inaccessible places; statues

13

brooded in scruffy corners; imposing staircases were neglected and led nowhere, holes had been knocked through the walls of conquered departments. He went through one. It was a small hole, reached by steps, and it was necessary to stoop. Through the dirty windows of the final corridor he saw a neglected glass-roofed courtyard, its walls bearing in faded lettering the names of forgotten viceroys, victories and campaigns.

Next came a library of old documents and beyond it a corridor reached through a pair of heavy doors. The end of the corridor was obscured by billowing clouds of dust, from which came the sound of a pneumatic drill, shockingly loud. The first door on the right bore the letters LAD, beneath which were written the names of those who worked within. He guessed that this would be what in nearly all departments was called the Third Room, housing the three desk officers. The next two doors would house the head of the department and his secretary. They were more obscured by dust but on one he could make out the name of Mr E. J. W. P. Formerly, Head of LAD. When the pneumatic drill stopped the sound of sledge-hammers hitting brickwork came from within.

While Patrick hesitated the door was thrown open by a bespectacled middle-aged woman who rushed out and slammed it behind her. She struggled with an armful of files covered in brickdust and drew back with a hostile glance as he stepped forward to help. He introduced himself.

"You've come at the worst possible time," she snapped. "The Home Office has broken through the wall and the Third Room has been dispersed. Mr Formerly had to abandon office the moment he arrived. If you want him you'll have to go back the way you've come, up the second stairs, through the hole in the wall on the next floor and then keep turning right until you can't any more. Now, if you'll excuse me I must get on. We've got to save the files."

Mr Formerly's retreat was in the roof. A small square window set deep in the wall looked down into yet another neglected courtyard. The room was furnished with an old wooden desk and two plastic chairs. Near the middle of the floor was a telephone which was prevented by its flex from reaching the desk. On the desk was an open copy of *The Times*.

Mr Formerly looked up reluctantly from his reading. He had a pale cadaverous face and large dark eyes. His expression was sensitive and listless. They shook hands gently.

"Mozambique?"

14

"Lower Africa."

"Of course, yes." He indicated that Patrick should sit and slowly folded the paper, lingering for a moment over the Test match report. "Dreadful business."

"I'm afraid I haven't seen a paper this morning."

"What?"

Patrick leant forward in the uncomfortable chair. "I'm sorry, I wasn't sure whether you meant Lower Africa or what's in the paper."

It seemed for a few moments that the question had robbed Mr Formerly of power of speech. "I mean the Home Office coming through on us like that. They started yesterday afternoon before anyone knew what they were up to. Lot of banging and drilling and whatever but nothing untoward. I got in this morning and I'd just got my coffee when a drill came through the wall behind me. Then another came through from the back of a filing cabinet. Made an awful mess of the Angolan aid policy files. Next thing was chaps started knocking the wall down. I lodged an immediate protest but they didn't even pause. Then another chap came along and said it was all a mistake. Wrong wall. Load-bearing or something."

Mr Formerly stopped speaking. It was not clear what response was required. "Must've been pretty alarming," Patrick said eventually.

Mr Formerly continued as if he had neither expected nor heard the response. "Of course, we knew there were alterations in progress but not that we were to lose anything. In fact, I thought we were to take over some of them. I'm sure we should be. It's always been an anomaly having bits of the Home Office in that wing. Not that we had relations, but there you are, it never works." He paused again and looked at the backs of his hands. "So the Third Room are God-knows-where – having an early lunch if they've any sense – and all the safes and cabinets and furniture and files have got to be carted up here. No idea where we'll put them. Not even room for my secretary." He looked moodily at the telephone. "And that thing won't reach the desk."

They both looked at the telephone. "I suppose you could move the desk," said Patrick.

Mr Formerly shook his head slowly. "No, I like it here. I can see out. Anyway, the phone has no number. It'll be days before they get one." He spoke in a quiet monotone, without bitterness, and gazed placidly out of the window. Both the sill and the brickwork of the outer wall still bore the pock-marks of wartime shrapnel.

"When do I leave?" asked Patrick.

15

Mr Formerly's gaze tacked slowly back. "Personnel seem to want you there right away. All to do with Whelk, I suppose. They explained all that, did they?"

"They said you would."

"Ah." There was another pause. "Well, there's nothing much to say, really. He just didn't turn up for work one day. After a few days people began to think it was a bit odd and so at the end of the week someone telephoned his house. His maid said she hadn't seen him all week and thought p'raps he'd gone on holiday. He does that sort of thing now and then. Odd chap. There was nothing missing except his car and no sign of a struggle but the police keep saying he might have been kidnapped. They don't think it was accidental, anyway, probably because they don't like to admit that diplomats can simply go missing in their country without good reason, as it were. But there's been no ransom demand. Not that any would be paid, of course. It's not policy. In fact, it's the ambassador who's the keenest on the kidnap theory. The police aren't doing much but the ambassador wants to move heaven and earth." Mr Formerly looked at the backs of his hands again. "The ambassador suspects you-know-who."

Patrick had to ask.

"LASS," said Mr Formerly quietly.

"LASS?" asked Patrick, also quietly.

Before Mr Formerly could reply, four men, apparently foreign, struggled through the door with a large metal filing cupboard. They manoeuvred it into the middle of the room, knocking the telephone on to its side, and departed in a multilingual clamour.

Afterwards Mr Formerly raised his dark eyes to Patrick's. "Lower African Security Service. The ambassador is convinced that they kidnapped Whelk."

"Why would they want to kidnap him?"

"To learn our secrets."

"Our secrets?"

Mr Formerly looked again towards the window, nodding very slightly. "I know it does seem rather bizarre but I suppose LASS have secrets of their own and that leads them to think that everyone else must have them too. The ambassador thinks this explains why the police don't seem to be doing very much about Whelk. He's rather got the bit between his teeth, I'm afraid, and so it's at his insistence that we're calling in L and F. They're a sort of insurance outfit that advises people on how to negotiate with kidnappers. Lots of chaps travelling round the world advising grieving relatives and anxious companies on

16

how to get the ransom down a bit. Call themselves Lost and Found. Rather quaint, isn't it? Most irregular for HMG to get involved with such business, of course. Unfortunately the junior minister got a whiff of it at an early stage and became frightfully keen. He supports the ambassador. It's all terribly hush-hush. We mustn't let the Lower Africans know we're doing it."

The pause allowed Patrick time to think. "Why not? If it is them we won't have lost anything because we won't be able to find him anyway, and if it's not they might be able to help."

Mr Formerly shook his head as though he had been asked whether it were true that someone long dead had recently returned to life. "Possible embarrassment."

'Embarrassment', Patrick soon learned, was what the Foreign Office feared most. Questions as to who would be embarrassed in whose eyes and how much, or whether they should be or whether it mattered if they were, were rarely asked. Save on those occasions when ministerial or prime ministerial will was directly imposed, like the personal interventions of Yahweh in the Old Testament, it was better that Britain should do badly in negotiations than that she should be seen to be obdurate and judged responsible for their breakdown. The worst case of all was to be 'out on a limb', 'out of step' or 'odd man out'. It was better to lose the argument than risk being thought ill-mannered by persisting.

It was acceptable, however, to try to win by deceit provided one could do so without being caught. Mr Formerly explained the case of Whelk in these terms. To inform the Lower Africans of the involvement of L and F would imply that HMG did not trust the Lower African authorities. This was in fact the case, but it was important to pretend otherwise. If, on the other hand, the Lower Africans discovered that L and F were trying to make contact with the hypothetical kidnappers then HMG could plausibly claim that they must have been hired by the family. Actually Whelk had no family but that was neither here nor there.

"But might he not simply have fallen off a cliff?" asked Patrick. "Or thrown himself?"

"He might." Mr Formerly's gaze returned to the window, where it was most at rest. The window was spattered by raindrops. "I doubt it, though. I know Arthur Whelk of old, you see. Not the sort of chap who drives over cliffs. Most likely he's simply gone off and got himself another job without telling anyone. In the Middle East he was working for a sultan the whole time he was there. Procuring something or other, it was never clear what. Actually had a desk in the palace. Used to drop into the embassy in the mornings for his mail and then disappear. Bit of a fuss when the ambassador found out but the sultan sent a message to London saying he'd rather have Arthur in his country than the whole of the rest of the embassy and so that was that. Very embarrassing if we'd all been declared persona non grata – png'd. Arthur served out his time." He turned wearily back to Patrick. "Point is, the ambassador wants you to liaise with the police about this but also with the L and F chap when he gets there in secret. Keep him in the picture and so on without letting the police know. Sounds a recipe for disaster to me. Arthur will turn up when it suits him, I'm sure."

A sudden commotion announced the return of the four men, this time with a security cupboard which had a combination lock. They dragged the second cupboard across the floor and banged it heavily against the first. Its one door came open and a file fell out. The men left.

Mr Formerly gazed at the file which was marked 'CONFIDENTIAL'. "Not that I imagine you'll be in a hurry to find Arthur. At least not while you're living in his magnificent house. You'd otherwise be in a flat for a Grade Nine in a noisy part of Battenburg. I should get on with your personal admin if I were you. Awful lot to do and all very boring. Make sure you claim your full allowances." He reopened *The Times*. "Anything I can do, don't hesitate."

Patrick stepped carefully over the file. The rain beat steadily against the small window.

Mr Formerly looked up. "Couldn't switch on the light on your way out, could you?"

Patrick flicked the switch. Nothing happened, but Mr Formerly was already reading.

Not all Foreign Office briefings were like Mr Formerly's. Some were lengthy and thorough, even energetic. The longest and worst was the two-day Going Abroad course for those on their first postings.

They were issued with a booklet describing diplomatic life overseas. From this Patrick learnt that he should always, whether walking or in a car, keep to the left of his Head of Mission; that he should acquire a stock of superficial topics and gambits for use in diplomatic conversation; that he should prime himself before going to a party with useful and effective small-talk; that if he had to speak a foreign language in which he was not fluent he should, before attending a function, learn a dozen or so new phrases and try to bring them into the conversation;

that he should pay attention to placement at table and be prepared to take advice on dress. The handbook's stated purpose was to make social intercourse easier.

Most of the fifty or sixty people on the course were clerks, guards, telex-operators and wives. The other dozen or so were of diplomatic rank, like Patrick. They were given a lecture on security and another from a doctor who warned against the dangers to health of unhealthy climates. A titled lady, wife of a former ambassador who was now a very senior man in London, spoke of how spouses could contribute to their husbands' careers and advised strongly against complaining. By the end of the course the audience was bored, bemused and mutinous. Patrick fell asleep during the second afternoon and awoke only when the two books on his lap slipped to the floor with a double bang.

What Mr Formerly had called personal admin was indeed very tiresome. There were medical and insurance formalities, clothes to be bought, allowances to be claimed and spent, even a will to be made. The allowances seemed very generous and it was soon clear that they were for many people the crucial aspect of any posting. Accommodation was furnished at public expense but each person was given money for the tax-free purchase of washing machines, fridges, cutlery, crockery and any other necessary or unnecessary household goods. This applied only to the first posting but shipping costs were paid for all postings. There was an allowance for moving, an allowance for being abroad and an entertainment allowance to be claimed once there. Petrol would be tax free. Patrick's bank account swelled overnight to undreamt-of proportions.

He had also to buy a car. For this there was an interest-free loan based on grade and repayable over two years. There was also diplomatic discount, no tax and no VAT. Shipping was free provided the car was British. Patrick had never owned one and had never seriously thought about which kind he would like. He determined to avoid Fords because of the implication in Clifford Steggles's letter that he ought to have one. He tried Vauxhall but the model he wanted was not available in time; Talbot had something he liked but although theoretically British it had in fact been made in Europe and was therefore ineligible for the loan; the Leyland man was still at lunch at half-past three and so, one wet afternoon, he slunk into the Ford export office and signed for one, still unsure what it looked like.

During the last few weeks in London Patrick went to as many plays and films as possible on the mistaken principle that experience was entirely quantitative, to be stored and drawn on later, like nuts. Since his father's death his mother had lived in Chislehurst, a suburb of London flush with estate agents, riding schools and new Jaguars. He did not stay with her, though, because at home his impending departure felt like an intimation of mortality. She was sad and anxious and he was tense; neither could enjoy the last few days because of the knowledge that they were the last. He stayed instead with a friend in Southwark who worked for an American bank and spent half his time in New York.

On the last but one night he had dinner in Clapham with two other friends from Reading, Rachel and Maurice. He knew them through his former girlfriend, Susan. The acquaintance survived his break-up with her probably for no better reason than habit. Rachel was on a BBC trainee producer scheme which, she said, took men and women in equal numbers no matter how many or what quality of each applied. Maurice was training to be a solicitor. He hoped to specialise in trade union law and intended to stand as a local councillor at the next election. Rachel said that they would start a family in due course but they were determined not to marry.

They sat on the bare floorboards of the large main room. The furniture was sparse and plain. Maurice was proud of a sofa with a broken arm which he had taken from a rubbish skip in the street. He said he liked it because the colour of the stuffing matched his beard. A friend of Rachel's had painted an abstract mural on one wall – angular shapes of black and white with a red sun or football in one corner – which was reflected in a large Victorian mirror hanging above the bricked-up fireplace. Rachel explained that this came from her parents' Cotswold home.

They ate rice with meat of some sort, tired lettuce and wrinkled tomatoes. They drank a large bottle of sweet white wine. The claret that Patrick had brought was left unopened.

Rachel balanced her plate on crossed legs and dug in with a fork, her brown hair falling forward over her face so that the fork had to be manoeuvred towards her mouth as if through curtains. "To be honest, Patrick, I don't know how you can do it," she said, with energy but no annoyance. "I mean, you must be really determined or thick-skinned or something. Perhaps you're a racist under the skin. Perhaps that's what it is."

Patrick paused in his eating. "Under the skin?"

"Yes. Daddy is. Above the skin too now because he's been corrupted by all those dreadful Lower Africans until he's come to agree with them. He says it's the best thing for everyone. We had a blistering row about it over Christmas lunch and I left before the pudding and came back to London he was so awful. Mummy was in tears.''

"I'll have to see for myself."

"But the trouble is you've already put yourself on the side of the status quo by joining the Foreign Office. You've sold out just as much as if you'd gone into business or something. You're committed to a point of view, like it or not.'' She negotiated a piled forkful through her hair. "I don't mean it personally, you know. It's just the position you're in. Really I don't think we should even recognise them diplomatically."

Patrick was still uncertain as to what exactly he had committed himself to in joining the Foreign Office. He hesitated. "Well, diplomatic recognition doesn't signify approval or disapproval. It's simply the way of dealing with the acknowledged power in a country." It sounded like one of his briefings. He wondered how long it would be before he ceased to notice such changes in himself.

"They're bound to get at you in one way or another,'' said Maurice. "I mean, look at LASS. They're as bad as the KGB."

"Worse,'' said Rachel. "They're really really bad. They'll probably get you in bed with a black woman then photograph you and then you'll be tortured."

"Why should they do that?"

"Or they'll corrupt you with their point of view, which is more likely,'' continued Maurice.

"Why is that more likely?"

Maurice looked embarrassed and touched his beard. "Well, no, I mean, I don't mean it's actually likely or anything. It's just that you're more sort of naturally Establishment-minded. You're more a part of it. I mean, you don't mind having to wear a suit every day – I have to wear one too, but – well – you know what I mean. Not that there's anything wrong with it but it's just an aspect which in your case you embrace more willingly." He poured more wine.

Patrick did not like arguments. He smiled. "Does that mean I'm more corruptible than lawyers?"

Maurice shook his head. "No, no, 'course it doesn't, nothing like that. It's just a statement about the sort of people you're mixing with, you know, the whole scene."

"Perhaps I'm already corrupted." Patrick smiled again and Maurice began to look less awkward.

"You must write and tell us all about it, anyway,'' said Rachel, scraping her plate. "Except that they might get our address and then get on to us if they wanted. You could send letters via Mummy and Daddy. They're more respectable, only better not use the title because it attracts attention."

"I could send it in the diplomatic bag."

"Is that safe?"

"I think so."

"Really, what you're doing is incredibly brave," Maurice resumed with more confidence. "I mean, going to a racist totalitarian state, even as a diplomat. You'll have to live with censorship and imprisonment without trial and all that. But if you find out any interesting information we could pass it on to the freedom fighters. We've got contacts."

"What kind of information?"

"Well, you know, secret information." Maurice seemed no clearer about his secrets than Mr Formerly had been about his.

"Two gorgeous blacks," continued Rachel. "They were in the studio last week and they came to dinner. I think they're incredibly brave. What they're doing takes real courage."

Patrick's briefings on black movements had not been comprehensive. "What are they doing?"

"Oh, sort of organising and stuff." She glanced at Maurice before resuming in a self-consciously offhand tone. "Actually, there is something you could do. We're members of a group that helps a school out there, a black school in Kuweto. We send teaching materials and things. If you could take some out for us it would save an amazing amount of time and money. It could go with your heavy baggage."

"Teaching materials," Patrick repeated.

"The black schools are really poorly equipped compared with white schools," said Maurice. "They don't get enough textbooks or anything."

Rachel laughed briefly and pushed her hair back from her eyes. "Don't worry, it's not bombs. We're not going to blow you up. We'll write to people out there who can come and pick up the stuff from your house when it arrives. You don't have to do anything. But I mean don't do it if you don't want to. We don't want to pressurise you."

Patrick was entitled to take nearly three times as much heavy baggage as he possessed. He did not feel guilty about going to Lower Africa but being the object of moral questioning produced in him a desire to be conciliatory. Anyway, if the school needed textbooks he was happy to help. He agreed.

Later, he helped with the washing-up. Rachel made a point of being boisterously indifferent to household matters but Maurice came from a middle-class nonconformist background in Northamptonshire and was punctilious about everything domestic.

"I suppose you'll have a servant out there," he said.

"Yes, a lady called Sarah."

"A black lady?"

"Yes." Patrick stopped drying the plate in his hand. "At least, I assume so. It wasn't actually said."

When he left the kitchen to go upstairs to the lavatory he saw Rachel sitting on it. Her jeans were round her ankles and she leant forward, elbows on knees. The spread of her plump white thighs made the lavatory look small. He looked to see what had happened to the door but there was none.

She smiled at his surprise. "We don't believe in hiding anything. There's no point. We're all alike, aren't we? Nobody's got any secrets. If we have sensitive visitors I hang up a blanket for them."

Patrick leant against the wall, shuffling the loose change in his pocket and talking energetically about mutual acquaintances.

"We might come out and visit you," Rachel continued. "It would be really interesting to see how the blacks and coloureds live and staying with a diplomat might give us protection from the police. I suppose you'll have a big house with servants, will you?"

"Something like that."

"God, how awful, I couldn't stick that. Anyway, we'll send these teaching materials to your packers if you give us their address." She finished. "You can go after me. I won't pull the chain."

He went, wondering if she would stay to make sure he had no secrets, but she did not.

3

It was dark as the plane came in to land and the orange street lights of Battenburg were ranged in straight lines like an illuminated chessboard, though all the squares were black. Dawn broke while the travellers queued at immigration. The startling clarity of the light showed up the pallor of their faces.

The immigration officer was plump and serious. He looked closely at Patrick's passport, where 'student' had been crossed out and 'HM Diplomatic Service' substituted in Biro. Most other countries issued their diplomats with special passports.

Patrick wore jeans and a crumpled shirt. "What is your purpose in visiting our country?" the immigration officer asked dully.

Becoming a bureaucrat had not increased Patrick's liking for officials and lack of sleep had left him disinclined to make an effort. "To work."

"You have a job here?"

The clipped accent was familiar but still it grated. "Yes."

"Where?"

"At the British embassy."

"Do you have evidence of that?"

"Yes."

"Will you show me?"

Patrick produced a Foreign Office document addressed to the Lower African government. The immigration officer read it slowly more than once before reluctantly stamping the passport.

The arrivals hall was busy, sunlit and clean. All directions were in Lower African and English. Patrick looked in vain for someone from the British embassy. There were a few people holding up placards but none with a title that was remotely official. Perhaps the entire embassy had disappeared along with Arthur Whelk and he was about to discover the *Marie Celeste* of the Diplomatic Corps. It was not at that moment an unpleasing thought. More likely, though, the plane had arrived so early that no one had wanted to meet it. He headed towards an empty bench.

He had no sooner sat on it than he noticed another some distance away on which there was a woman with such startling blonde hair that he could not understand how he had not seen her on the plane. She shook her head and pushed some hair back behind her ear with a quick thoughtless movement that was obviously habitual. Her forearm was bare and she glanced up. For a moment he thought she smiled at him but then he saw that she was talking to a little girl, also with very blonde hair, who stood beside her. She adjusted the little girl's dress, talking and smiling.

Patrick's view was interrupted by a dark-haired man in a blazer. The man hugged the woman and stood talking for a while before lifting the girl on to the nearby luggage trolley, where she clapped and laughed. The woman slung a bag over one shoulder and a red coat over the other and all three left. She walked freely and confidently at the man's side. Patrick leant back on the bench. The sun warmed his face.

He was awoken by a white policeman with polished black boots and holster. The policeman spoke first in Lower African, then in English, explaining that Patrick's was a bench on which it was not permitted to sleep. Patrick felt like arguing but did not.

He went next to the gents to wash, where he was greeted by a smiling black attendant who seemed to be hoping for a tip. This reminded him that he had no Lower African currency. He waited until the airport bank opened at seven, cashed some sterling and telephoned Clifford Steggles, the head of chancery.

Steggles's voice was heavy with sleep. "Are you at HE's?"

"Where's that?"

"The residence."

"Whose residence?"

"The ambassador's." Irritation dispersed the sleepiness in Steggles's voice.

"No, I'm at the airport."

"You shouldn't be. You should be at the residence."

Whilst still six thousand miles away Patrick had known that he and Clifford Steggles would not get on. The letter had been sufficient. Whatever trouble was to come, there was some satisfaction in these moments of confirmation.

"The ambassador's driver was supposed to take you to the residence for breakfast," Clifford continued accusingly. "He was sent to pick you up specially."

"Well, he doesn't seem to be here."

"He ought to be."

Patrick said nothing. He was too tired to care.

"Chap with a placard with 'British Embassy' written on it," Clifford said eventually.

"There wasn't one."

"There should've been."

There was another pause.

"Stocky chap with a cap," resumed Clifford. "He might have forgotten the placard."

"I'll have a look." Whilst Patrick was looking the line went dead. He dialled again. "Chap with red hair?"

Clifford sighed. "No. He's black."

"No blacks with caps."

There was a further long pause and then, "I suppose I'll have to pick you up myself. I'm not up yet. Stay by the phone booths."

Clifford Steggles was in his late thirties, short, balding and pot-bellied. The bald patch on his head was burned brown and he wore a moustache that made him look cross. They shook hands unenthusiastically.

"Is that all the stuff you've got? No need for a porter, then. The car's in the place reserved for diplomats. One of the perks." They loaded Patrick's bags into the back of the big Ford estate. "Why have you brought so little – thinking you won't stay long?"

"I haven't got much."

"But you've got some heavy baggage coming?"

"Oh yes. It was shipped last week."

"Makes no difference. You won't see it for months. That's why you should've brought more now. Thought they'd have told you that."

They were soon on the motorway, heading for Battenburg. Despite the sun and the blue sky it was a cold, sharp morning. The motorway was lined by new buildings, many of them petrol stations. Beyond these were low hills covered with dry grass and scrub.

"When it rains in the summer all this is green," Clifford said. "We've had no rain for weeks. Watch the altitude, till you get acclimatised. Makes you tired at first. Are you tired?"

"Yes."

"Busy day ahead. Why was your flight so late?"

"Engine trouble."

"Fly British Air you never get there."

It was soon apparent that the more Clifford spoke the more he pleased himself, and so the more he liked whoever was with him. He described how the dry air would crack lips and burn nostrils and how

26

good the wine was and how quickly it went to the heads of the unacclimatised. He wondered aloud a dozen or so times what on earth could have happened to Simon, the driver. The ambassador himself was admittedly rather forgetful but it hadn't been up to him to remember. The drivers sometimes got things wrong but there was only one airport and they were there once a week to pick up the bag, so they should know it. He had telephoned the ambassador's residence and spoken to one of the maids but could get no sense out of her, not even whether or not the ambassador was actually there. He did sometimes spend the odd night away, no one knew where. But he should have been expecting Patrick for breakfast because Patrick was to stay at the residence a day or two until Clifford and his wife moved into their own house. Things only really worked at the residence when the ambassador's wife was there but she was back in Surrey. She was mad, anyway. They spent most of the time apart, quite understandably.

"You've been briefed about this Whelk business, I take it?"

"Yes. I'm told I'm to liaise with the police and at the same time maintain secret contact with the Lost and Found man."

Clifford looked offended. "I'm not supposed to know about the Lost and Found side of it. You shouldn't have told me. Breach of security but we'll say no more about it as you've not been here long. Of course, I do know about it because the ambassador can't help mentioning it but it's not generally known around the embassy." He pulled out to overtake, then quickly back in again to a chorus of hootings from behind. "The whole thing's a lot of fuss about nothing, if you ask me. Whelk probably got drunk and drove off a cliff. Sort of thing he would do. All this unofficial investigation nonsense is improper, in my opinion. The Lower African authorities are quite able to sort it out without us blundering around freelancing. The ambassador hardly thinks of anything else these days. It's his last post, you see, and I think he's gone a bit over the top on this one. Very able man, mind you, but rather too much of an enthusiast sometimes. And London don't help. I hear now that the junior minister's been bitten by the same bug. Is that right?"

"Mr Formerly told me he was."

"Well, Formerly wouldn't know it if you hit him on the head with it but I think he's right in this case, all the same." There was a pause while Clifford successfully overtook the petrol tanker he had been stuck behind. "What gets me though is the house. Arthur's is the best one after the residence. Better than the counsellor's. All right, he is theoretically senior to me in terms of length of service so I can't object;

but he's a bachelor and I have to live with a wife and two small children in a smaller house. Also, as head of chancery one does have certain responsibilities, to put it mildly."

He looked at Patrick as though seeking agreement. Patrick nodded.

"And now because London can't decide whether or not Arthur's coming back they're going to let you live in it, which is bloody outrageous. A lot of people here are rather upset about it, to speak plainly. Nothing personal, of course. If Arthur does come back he's hardly likely to be kept on here after this so they might as well reallocate the house now. And to have let us live there whilst ours was being done up just rubbed salt into the wound." He glanced again at Patrick. "Of course, you could always claim it was too big for you and not move into it. Doesn't make much difference where you live when you're single."

Patrick's tiredness made him proof against threats of even universal unpopularity. "Are we going to the residence now?"

"No, we're going to our house – Arthur's. Yours. I'll find out what's happened at the residence later." They drove on for a while in silence.

There were familiar makes of car on the right side of the road and familiar advertisements on hoardings except that some were styled differently. The Marmite advertisement was a big black jar held before a big black face. From a distance Battenburg appeared to be built upon hills with the highest in the centre, crowned by tower-blocks that were brilliantly white in the early sun. Above the city there was a dirty haze.

"That's always there in the mornings. It's called inversion. All the smog gets trapped." Explaining made Clifford feel better. "The smog clears off as the air gets warmer. It's caused by the warm air being trapped by the cold."

"Is it really?" Patrick tried to sound impressed but his tone was wrong.

Uncertainty and irritability returned to Clifford's face. "Well, that sort of thing. Or the other way round. Makes no difference."

In the city the pavements bustled with people, black, brown and white. The shops were busy. Clifford drove with aggressive incompetence, swearing most of the time. Everyone else was doing the same. The distant sky showed in vertical strips of blue between the tall buildings, while that above was still hazy.

They stopped suddenly at a corner crowded with pedestrians. "You have to give way to them at junctions though they're only supposed to cross when the lights say they can. It's bloody inconvenient for everyone. Cars can't go round corners without stopping and pedestrians can't cross until the lights say so. The police keep cracking down so most people obey." The next sudden braking was at traffic lights which Patrick had not seen because they were high and insignificant. "They call them robots," said Clifford.

Soon they were in the northern suburbs where opulent houses were set amidst spacious grounds behind high walls. Elaborately-wrought iron gates showed swimming-pools and tennis-courts. There were large shopping centres but no small shops. New cars, mostly Mercedes or BMWs, cruised with quiet ostentation along broad tree-lined avenues. The only people were a few black servants and gardeners who walked slowly or sat in small groups on the wide sunburnt grass verges. They gazed without apparent curiosity at the cars that passed, much as they might have gazed at the wall opposite when there were no cars.

Clifford waved a hand. "Jacarandas."

Patrick looked at the group of blacks. The word was familiar, possibly a tribal name.

"Bloom in the spring. Bloody nuisance for the pool, though. Fill it with leaves."

Patrick looked at the trees.

They passed by a long white wall before turning abruptly into the drive. It was lined by trees and shrubs and had a well-watered strip of grass running up the middle. The house was large and white with a red tiled roof. Broad gleaming white steps led up to the front door.

Clifford drove into the double garage and was soon locking the car. "You have to. Must lock everything all the time. Lots of thieves."

Inside it was cool and dark, the rooms large and high. The furniture was an uneasy mixture of the standard PSA issue and the accumulations of someone who had travelled and collected promiscuously. The mounted heads of wildebeest, stags, tigers and one polar bear competed for space with South American wall-hangings, Chinese jade, Japanese prints, Flemish reproductions, encyclopaedias, dictionaries, works of reference and a set of boleros. There were some old chests and sturdy chairs which went ill with the PSA living-room suite. In the dining-room was a solid PSA table which seated twelve and smelt of polish. Fastened to the underside was a bell for summoning the maid. French windows led from the dining-room to the veranda, beyond which the lawn undulated down towards the sparkling blue swimming-pool.

Clifford had the air of a man who had made it all himself. "Not bad, eh? Thought you'd like it. Some of it belongs to Whelk, of course, but even so it's not bad." His tone was warmer and more approving. "Come and meet the wife."

The wife was sitting in a cane chair below the veranda, hidden from the dining-room by one of the creeper-covered pillars. Because Clifford was unappealing Patrick had unthinkingly assumed his wife would be similar. Instead she was slim and lithe with close-cropped brown hair and a sharp quick face. She looked momentarily harassed, as if annoyed with herself, but smiled as she extended her hand. "Sandy," she said before Clifford could introduce her. "Coffee?" Patrick accepted gratefully. She went into the house to tell Sarah.

Clifford eased himself into one of the cane chairs, loosened his belt and undid his trousers so that his stomach could expand. He surveyed the garden and pool. "You're bloody lucky. Battenburg is a marvellous place for a bachelor." He glanced in the direction of the house. "Wouldn't mind a few months unaccompanied myself, I can tell you." He nodded and smiled so that his eyes nearly disappeared.

Patrick was still trying to imagine Clifford and Sandy making love when she returned. "You look exhausted. Was the flight awful?"

"They always are," said Clifford. "Flying's always awful. He's not used to the altitude yet."

Patrick described the flight and the mystery of his not being met. She laughed abruptly and loudly, one hand on her breasts and the other shielding her eyes against the sun. "The ambassador's such a fool. He's probably forgotten all about you. You'll have to get used to that sort of thing."

"He is not a fool," said Clifford slowly. "He is sometimes absent-minded. I daresay on this occasion it was his driver who forgot."

"He is a fool, he's a silly old buffoon."

"He is an intellectually distinguished man."

"All right, he's a clever fool. That's worse. And he's completely helpless without his wife. But the less said about her the better." The sudden petulance made Sandy's face look thinner.

Clifford frowned. "Darling, the less said the better, full stop. He is not a fool and he is not helpless. He is our ambassador."

"He's also a husband and he's as helpless as most."

Patrick stared at the clear blue water of the pool.

Clifford folded his arms, crossed his legs and turned half away from his wife. He spoke with weary finality. "The ambassador is an intelligent man and he's good at his job. I don't think we should say more than that in front of a newly arrived member of staff."

"Pity he's not so good at real life." Sandy seemed cross with herself now and her petulance made her plain. No one said anything for a while but then she remarked quietly that the children had been playing up with Sarah that morning. Clifford grunted. She glanced coldly at him, then looked over Patrick's head and smiled.

Aware that someone was approaching from behind, Patrick stood. His shoulder caught on something, there was a cry and a crash of china.

A stout black lady was on her knees before him, picking crockery from the grass and putting it back on the tray. Her round face creased with anguish as she looked up at him.

"Massa, I am so sorry."

Patrick bent to help but almost made her stumble again as she got up. "Is all right, massa, is all right," she said quickly. She wore a clean blue dress and a white apron. Her heavy spectacles were askew and she straightened them hastily with one hand. Patrick had not realised that black people could blush. "It was my fault," he said. "I'm sorry, I didn't see you. I'm very sorry."

Sandy put her hand on Patrick's arm. "It wasn't anyone's fault. Only one cup and saucer gone. Sarah saved the rest."

"I am very sorry, madam, I am very sorry."

"You did very well to save them, Sarah. They're not Mr Whelk's best so we can call it fair wear and tear. They're easy to replace."

Sarah turned away with the tray. "I get another cup."

"That's right but leave the tray here. I'll sort it out."

Sandy spoke simply and clearly as though to a child. When Sarah returned Patrick was formally introduced to her as Mr Stubbs.

They shook hands and Sarah curtsied. "I am very pleased, massa. I am very sorry for the cup."

"It's not important. It's my fault for being so clumsy. I'll buy another cup." He tried not to speak with the same obvious care as Sandy.

Sarah smiled broadly. "Yes, massa, another cup." She backed away towards the house, glancing at Sandy to see whether anything else was wanted. Her bow legs seemed too thin for her wide body. She held her hands before her as in prayer but she was still smiling.

Sandy poured the coffee. "She was very nervous about your coming, quite worked up about it. She's never looked after a young man before. Arthur was different, of course. I keep telling her that young bachelors are all right" – she glanced up as she handed him his cup – "that, in fact, they're no problem really."

Clifford shovelled several spoonfuls of sugar into his coffee. "Ever had servants before?"

31

Patrick hesitated. It probably looked as if he was trying to remember. "No."

"Thought not. You'll get used to it. Never apologise to them."

"But it was my fault."

"Doesn't matter."

"It seems to me that it does."

Sandy took the sugar bowl from Clifford. "Sarah's very good, not like some. I was brought up in Kenya and I've never known anyone as good as her. She'll look after you well. I'm sure you'll get on."

Snap, the dog, was next to be introduced. He looked like a large black labrador but the ridgeback breeding showed in the distinct line of raised fur that ran from head to tail. Clifford took an immediate and obvious pleasure in being stern with him, which was not difficult because he had been well trained by previous occupants of the house. He sniffed suspiciously at Patrick but permitted his back to be patted.

"He's getting on a bit but he's a very good guard dog," said Clifford. "Once people know you've got a good dog you tend not to be burgled. But watch him with guests. He's all right if he sees them introduced into the house but if they just walk in he has them. Really has them, not just barking. Whites as well. Doesn't discriminate."

Patrick stopped patting. "Do dogs normally discriminate?"

"A lot do, ridgebacks especially. They only go for blacks. I don't know whether they're trained to do it or whether they just pick it up, you know, sense it. Blacks smell different to us, anyway."

Patrick imagined Rachel's and Maurice's reaction.

"What are you smiling at?" asked Sandy, smiling herself. She now looked more pretty than plain.

"I was thinking of some people I know. Is Snap safe with Sarah?"

"No love lost but they tolerate each other. I don't think Africans like dogs in the way we do."

"I'll show you the pool," Clifford announced, doing up his trousers as he walked off.

Patrick had an idea that swimming-pools needed some sort of maintenance, but no idea of what was involved. Clifford was quick to display both knowledge and enthusiasm. He detailed the required chemical balance, demonstrated how to use the chemical test kit without getting cancer, how to get leaves (jacaranda) off the surface, how to work the pump and how to flush the dirty water out of the system.

"It leaks," he explained, "so you need to top it up every day and readjust the chemical balance. The PSA won't pay to have it repaired because they're cutting the pool budget but you buy the chemicals out of another budget so they keep paying for them quite happily. Actually, it's easier than it sounds to look after. Deuteronomy, the gardener, can do a certain amount like getting leaves out and topping up but flushing and vacuum-cleaning is a bit complicated for him."

"Vacuum-cleaning?"

"No problem. I'll show you." Clifford energetically assembled poles, suction-pads and hoses, then demonstrated. "There you are. Simple. Have a go."

Patrick had a go. Nothing worked and he got his sleeve wet.

Clifford took the pole. "There's a knack. Let me show you."

He demonstrated deftly again. As he pulled the fourteen-foot pole from the water he caught Patrick in the mouth with the rear end. "Sorry. You okay?"

Patrick nodded whilst groping for his handkerchief.

Clifford continued his demonstration. "There you are, you see. Do it as often as it needs it. A lot depends on the weather."

"And on the jacarandas?"

"You're learning already." He made a few more sweeps of the pool whilst Patrick dabbed at his lip. "Mind you, you're going to be too busy in the embassy to spend much time playing around like this, what with Arthur's consular stuff and your share of the chancery work. Up to now Philip Longhurst, the second secretary, has been having to do what you'll be doing. I do the more important stuff myself, of course, because the ambassador's a bit of a stickler in some ways. Don't run away with the idea that because of all the Whelk business you're going to take off and play the detective whenever you feel like it. The work of the embassy must go on. There's not much room in the Diplomatic Service for this sort of extra-marital stuff with Lost and Found and what-have-you."

There was a sudden furious barking. A small black man in baggy green overalls sprinted across the lawn with Snap ten yards behind and gaining. The man reached the wall that divided the backyard from the garden and scrambled over. The dog's jaws closed a few inches behind the trailing trouser-leg. Snap stood on his hind legs against the wall, barking furiously. Sandy was on her feet and calling to him, ineffectually.

Patrick hastily stuffed his handkerchief back in his pocket and was about to set off in pursuit of the supposed burglar when he noticed that his host was in no hurry. Clifford switched off the pump and rested the vacuum cleaner carefully against the iron fence that surrounded

33

the pool. "You mustn't let Deuteronomy and Snap into the garden together. Snap won't have it."

They walked up the lawn. Sandy and Clifford argued as to which was more at fault in not telling the other of Deuteronomy's arrival. Clifford ignored his wife's repetitions and pointed at a tree. "Said to be one of the oldest jacarandas in Battenburg," he told Patrick.

Snap was still barking when they reached the wall. Clifford shouted to him to stop. The dog barked twice more before trotting off towards the rubbish-heap looking pleased with himself. The ridge of hair along his back bristled like a boar's.

Deuteronomy stood in the far corner of the whitewashed courtyard. He was small, wizened and wiry, no longer young but not obviously old. He grinned shamefacedly and rubbed his hands.

"I am sorry, massa."

Patrick was introduced. Deuteronomy clung to his hand and greeted him with a prolonged smile and a long-drawn-out, admiring, "Massa." It was as if Patrick were endowed with great beauty or fabulous wealth.

"Deuteronomy will always do precisely what you tell him, neither less nor more," said Clifford.

Deuteronomy nodded and grinned enthusiastically. "Yes, massa, you tell me and I do. Not more, massa. Always what you tell me."

Patrick knew nothing of gardens. He smiled and nodded confidently. "Good."

Deuteronomy grinned even more enthusiastically. "I am happy for you, massa."

"Good. I'm pleased." They both nodded and shook hands again.

Clifford pointed to the single-storey building that formed one side of the courtyard. "Sarah's quarters. They can be inspected at any time by the Native Administration Board and you can be fined if they're not up to a certain standard. Sarah's are all right, bigger than most. Bedroom, bathroom, sitting-room. She uses the house kitchen."

From within the house came the sound of a protesting child followed by Sarah's scolding voice. She appeared at the kitchen door, wiping her hands on her white apron, and addressed Deuteronomy in another language. He nodded and replied, smiling uncertainly now. She looked at Clifford. "I give him his tea now, massa?"

"Yes, yes, then put Snap away so that he can get on with his work. I'm going to take Mr Stubbs to the embassy."

Patrick waited in the large kitchen whilst Clifford went away 'to make himself comfortable', as he put it. Sarah introduced the two

34

fair-haired little girls, one aged seven and the other three. Sandy had disappeared.

"Are they a lot of work for you?" Patrick asked.

She laughed and shook her head, ruffling the hair of the smaller one who stood staring solemnly at Patrick. The other swung on Sarah's arm, as if trying to pull her over. "Not bad work, massa, they are nice piccaninny. But sometimes they are heavy pull."

"Heavy pull?"

She nodded. "Sometimes when they are difficult with each other."

Clifford shouted for Sandy from somewhere within the house. Sandy called out that she was in the bar, adding quickly, "I'm just getting them ready for later, that's all."

Clifford walked through the hall and said something angrily. Then he called peremptorily for Patrick.

"Time to start your first day," he said.

4

Patrick had imagined embassies the world over to be stately buildings set in parkland or at the very least in Georgian terraces. The British embassy in Battenburg occupied the ninth floor of a twenty-one storey block in the centre of the city. Clifford drove into the underground car-park beneath and they descended several levels, turning sharp corners past rows of parked cars.

As they turned the last corner he braked hard enough to make the tyres squeal. A black Jaguar was slewed across their front, its nose against a concrete pillar and its tail against a parked car. A little to the left of it was an empty parking space.

At the wheel was a man of late middle age with wild white hair. He had a tanned wrinkled skin and large watery brown eyes. He stared as if the arrival of another vehicle in the car-park was an inexplicable phenomenon.

"The ambassador," Clifford said in a low voice. "I can't think what he's doing with the Jaguar. He's normally driven in in the Rolls. Never drives himself unless he has to. Perhaps something's happened to Simon and that's why you weren't picked up."

Clifford got out and hurried forward, his body slightly bent and an expression of barely restrained admiration on his face. Sir Wilfrid Eagle got out of the Jaguar, a slow operation for so tall a man. A few strands of hair flopped against his cheek. His grey pinstripe was well cut to his lean figure but hopelessly crumpled, the pockets bulging. As he walked away from his car he raised one hand in its direction as though tied to it by a string. This action lifted his jacket so that his shirt-tail was revealed. His other hand went through the motions of smoothing his hair.

"It's got stuck again," he said in a loud drawl. "Won't fit anywhere."

Clifford was eagerly deferential. "Shall I have a go, sir? It's sometimes easier if someone else does it."

"Would you? Awfully kind."

Clifford got briskly into the Jaguar and moved it backwards and forwards several times, but the few inches between the concrete pillar

36

and the next car gave him little room. It was not clear how the Jaguar could have got into this position. There was a great deal of revving. Clifford's brow puckered and his lips compressed.

Patrick thought he had better introduce himself. He approached the ambassador with what he hoped was appropriate deference. The ambassador glanced at him quickly then fixed his gaze resolutely on the Jaguar. It looked very like a physical manifestation of what newspapers called a diplomatic snub. Patrick wondered what rule he could have transgressed and then remembered what he had read in the handbook in London: he should always be to the left of his ambassador. Or was it the right? Whichever it was, he must have approached from the wrong side.

The ambassador continued to stare at Clifford, who was beginning to sweat with the effort of twisting and turning. Patrick took a couple of steps backwards and approached from the other side. He was about to say good day when Sir Wilfrid spoke quietly out of the side of his mouth.

"You decided to come after all, then?"

The tone was enquiring rather than sarcastic. The ambassador did not look angry. He did not look at Patrick at all. Patrick hesitated. "There was a little confusion at the airport, sir."

There was no response. Was he waiting to be called Your Excellency? To relieve the awkwardness Patrick signalled Clifford to stop as the boot of the Jaguar just touched the car behind. Clifford edged forward again. The silence continued.

"Takin' a chance, ain't you? Blowing your cover and all that?" Still the ambassador did not look at him.

"I'm sorry, sir, but I don't understand."

The ambassador fished in his jacket pockets and pulled out a pair of spectacles. One arm was Sellotaped to the frame. He slowly turned towards Patrick. "Lord. Thought you were the other chap. Who are you?"

"Patrick Stubbs, sir, the new third secretary. I arrived this morning."

"Did you, by Jove? Well, that explains it. I thought at first you were the chappie I had breakfast with. Wondered why he'd turned up here when we'd agreed he should keep away." He tapped his spectacles. "I should wear these things more, you see. Always take them off for driving. Pleased to meet you at last." They shook hands. The ambassador bent his head conspiratorially and spoke quickly. "Chappie I had breakfast with was the one from Lost and Found who's come out to find poor Arthur. The driver picked him up at the airport in mistake for you. Same plane, you see, and a young chap like yourself. Easily done. White faces look alike to Africans, like black ones to us. Or like white ones to me without my specs. Nice young chap, cheerful, determined, not short on confidence. Halfway through breakfast before we realised we were talking at cross-purposes. Problem then of what to do, of course, bearing in mind we have to keep him a secret from the Lower Africans. Had him smuggled out in the boot of the Rolls in the end. Just have to hope he wasn't spotted on the way in but with luck they'll have made the same mistake as me and thought he was you. Simon then went back to the airport to find you. Must be still there. That's why I drove myself in."

There was a screech of metal on concrete as the front wing of the Jaguar jammed against the pillar. Clifford's face was red and angry. "Look what you made me do. I thought you were supposed to be directing."

His anger was so great and so obvious that it was almost unconvincing. Patrick was careful not to smile. "I wasn't watching," he confessed.

"That's right, he wasn't, he was talking to me," said Sir Wilfrid.

Clifford's fury was constrained by his desire to be respectful. He got out to inspect the damage. "It could be worse, I suppose."

Sir Wilfrid regarded the vehicle without interest. "Perhaps we'd better leave it as it is and call the garage."

However, a few minutes more shunting, twisting and turning saw the car parked. "Thank you, Clifford," said Sir Wilfrid, slamming the door twice before it would shut. "I'm sure there's something wrong. It ought to be easier to park than that."

Clifford was further annoyed to find that the ambassador and Patrick had already introduced themselves. The confusion at the airport was explained to him, with whispered references to the Lost and Found man. He shook his head and exhaled noisily through his nose. "Sometimes I despair of these African drivers, sir."

Sir Wilfrid raised his eyebrows. "Very understandable mistake. After all, I made it myself."

When they were safely in the lift the ambassador put one hand in his jacket pocket and held his glasses with the other, scratching his jaw with the Sellotaped arm. "Told the L and F chap to go to earth. He must lie low for a while to make sure no one's on to him, otherwise he'll disappear, too. Damn shame he was brought to the residence like that. Good idea for you to lie pretty low as well, Patrick."

Patrick was not sure what this involved. "Does that mean I stay at home, sir?"

"No, no, nothing like that. Just keep a low profile. Try to act normally. Don't do anything to make LASS take an interest in you or you'll lead them to the L and F chap. You'll have to meet him eventually, of course, to hear how he's getting on, but not yet. I've every confidence in that young man. He's bound to turn up something sooner or later."

They got out of the lift. Sir Wilfrid put his spectacles back on and his hands fluttered over his pockets. "Briefcase. Damn. Must've left it in the car. Or at home. Got to have it because it's got all yesterday's telegrams."

"Patrick will get it," said Clifford.

Sir Wilfrid turned to Clifford, his hearing apparently no better than his eyesight. "Would you? Most kind. I'll give Patrick his introductory lecture."

As the lift doors closed on him Sir Wilfrid remarked that Clifford would need the keys. "Never mind. I'll leave them with Jean, my secretary. Come in and have the welcome chat. I always give it to newcomers. Don't s'pose it does any good but does no harm, anyway."

They walked quickly through reception, a shower of respectful glances falling upon Sir Wilfrid. The receptionist pressed a buzzer to open a door marked 'Private', which led into a corridor at the end of which was another door marked 'Chancery'. This was normally opened by pressing buttons in a secret sequence but for the ambassador it was held open by his secretary who had been warned by reception. She was a slim, severe-looking woman in her late thirties with dark hair and thin lips. She held out a cold bony hand to Patrick when they were introduced and smiled with a sudden, desperate friendliness.

"*So* pleased to meet you," she said.

Sir Wilfrid gestured at the heavy door. "All this in case of terrorist attack. Chap came all the way out from London and said we were at risk. God knows who they think is going to get at us here. Not easy to carry out a terrorist attack in a police state."

The ambassador's office had a conference table at one end and a desk and leather armchairs at the other. It looked across the city to the great slag-heaps outside, produce of the gold mines, levelled, squared-off and neat. The conference table was polished and had pencils and notepaper set out. On the desk was a confusion of books, papers, inkwells, newspapers and pipes. To one side of the desk stood a tall grandfather clock showing ten past four. The door of its front hung open, revealing an immobile pendulum, weights and chains.

Sir Wilfrid waved at a chair. He put his hands in his trouser pockets and gazed out of the window, his back to Patrick. Patrick removed a crumpled brown tie from the chair and sat down. There was silence.

"Real problem here is heartlessness," said the ambassador firmly, without looking round. "Lack of heart. People don't care for other people. The evil that this country is so rightly condemned for is not the essence of the problem but its symptom. They're self-righteous, obdurate, thick-headed, hard-hearted. They don't want to feel. That's one side of the pioneering coin, you see. They're also determined, loyal, resourceful, brave. They've set their faces against the world and told themselves they're hated. And so they are, now. They themselves have brought about that which they feared and it need never have happened, that's the tragedy. They pretend they don't care but they do. They feel guilty. And so they harden their hearts and pretend they don't."

He turned to face Patrick, jingling the loose change in his pockets. The seriousness and urgency with which he spoke contrasted sharply with his relaxed manner. "'Course, you haven't been here for five minutes. After a while you'll see what I mean. Perhaps you won't, though, p'raps you won't. Depends how sensitive you are. Are you sensitive?"

Patrick smiled, partly from embarrassment. "Not at the moment. I'm rather dull."

Sir Wilfrid laughed loudly and stamped one foot. "We all are, we all are, blunted by habit. The immigrants are often the worst but also the short-stayers like us, so watch it. In fact, the sensitive are sometimes the worst of all. Because they won't admit to feeling guilty they're filled with self-hatred, which is unbearable, and so they externalise it and hate other races, creeds, opinions instead. Poisons everything. Their whole lives become one long monotonous excuse, an attempt at self-justification which becomes less consoling the longer it lasts." He shook his head. "I know you probably think I'm an eccentric old fool, going on like this, but no one else will say it if I don't."

He picked up a pipe from the desk, put it in his mouth, removed it immediately and examined the mouthpiece, which had been bitten through. He tossed the pipe into the open interior of the grandfather clock and picked up a stained meerschaum from another part of the desk. Patrick shifted in his seat and was about to attempt a remark about self-deception when the ambassador continued. "The other sort are less passionate. They cut themselves off and pretend they don't see and in the end perhaps they don't. They're the majority. Kind, decent, honest, ordinary, indifferent. You will meet them in this embassy." He lit the pipe, which billowed smoke, then took it from his mouth and examined it again. "I say this to all new arrivals. They laugh behind my back but never mind. It ought to be said."

Jean came in with coffee and chocolate biscuits. "Clifford is in my office asking for your car keys." Sir Wilfrid gave them to her and she went out, another smile drawing a thin line across her face in the direction of Patrick.

Sir Wilfrid sat in an armchair and crossed one long leg over the other. He waved to Patrick to help himself. He swallowed his first cup of coffee and poured another, took two biscuits and then, whilst he was talking, took the last.

"Read much?" he asked, his mouth full.

Patrick nodded and swallowed. "A fair bit. Not as much as I'd like."

"Novels and what-have-you?"

Patrick nodded.

"That sort of thing?" Sir Wilfrid waved at the books scattered on his desk.

There was Josephus's *History of the Jewish War*, volume M-S of the Battenburg telephone directory, David Jones's *In Parenthesis*, three books in Lower African and two of Evelyn Waugh's early novels.

"I've read most of Waugh," Patrick said.

"That's what this country needs, a humorist, someone to show them themselves. It can't come from outside, it has to come from within and he has to stay here. He mustn't leave. He's got to see it through."

The ambassador talked enthusiastically until Clifford returned. He put the briefcase reverentially on the desk then sat quickly on the nearest empty chair to the ambassador. He glanced at the coffee pot.

"Just telling Patrick here what this country needs," said Sir Wilfrid.

Clifford nodded. "Oil."

The ambassador had been running his hand slowly through his white hair and now stopped, his palm on the top of his head. "Oil? Why?"

"Well, sir, the country has virtually none of its own and although they turn coal into oil that isn't very efficient."

"And what would having oil do for them?"

"It would make them wealthier and less dependent upon the outside world."

41

"What a bizarre suggestion." Sir Wilfrid kept his hand on his head.

Clifford looked bewildered and wretched, like a dog that does not know what is expected of him.

"The very last thing we want," the ambassador continued slowly, "is for this country to become independent of the outside world. Then they'll be impregnable, they'll never compromise, they'll be impossible to influence. No, no, what we'd decided they really need is a Waugh."

Clifford frowned. "With whom?"

Sir Wilfrid tipped the coffee in his saucer back into his cup and gulped it. "Well, I won't keep you." He picked up his pipe and stood so abruptly that the others were left sitting. "You've got plenty to do, no doubt, settling in and all that. But remember" – he lowered his voice and pointed his pipe at Patrick – "low profile."

Once away from the ambassador Clifford began to reassert his authority. He spoke of the importance of trade with Lower Africa and of the extent of British investments. "No doubt HE gave you the usual ear-bashing, did he? He always does. Perfectly correct in its way – from the point of view of policy, that is – but not always practical for those of us down in the boiler-room. You'll find you just have to get on with things as they are. No point in theorising about them, trying to change what's beyond your control." He hesitated, perhaps thinking he was on the verge of impropriety. "Mind you, he's a very clever man."

"Yes, he seems it."

"Not that you'll be seeing much of him. You'll be working through Philip Longhurst to me. It's pretty demanding for a first post, quite apart from the complications that have been foisted upon you. In fact, I'm surprised they sent you. Lots of paper to move, you'll be up to your ears. The important thing is not to let yourself be distracted by this other business of yours. London expect a very high level of political reporting from this post as well as a lot of it and if they don't get it they'll soon start shouting."

It was hard to imagine Mr Formerly shouting for anything but Patrick nodded his agreement.

He was to share Philip Longhurst's office. Philip was a slim, pale, worried-looking man with brown hair. His handshake was limp and brief and the arm so far extended that he appeared to be trying to dissociate himself from whatever the hand might do. Clifford asked after someone's health – either Philip's or his wife's or both, it was not clear – and from Philip's answer it seemed that there was either no improvement or some improvement or that it didn't matter very much anyway.

Philip looked and sounded clever, and after initial coolness was quietly friendly. They talked about the altitude, Patrick's journey, how long Philip and his wife had been in Lower Africa, how they had preferred Vienna, what it was like in the mountains and whether or not there would be cuts in allowances as a result of the forthcoming visit by the inspectors of posts. Philip's speech was careful and some words and phrases were spoken as if in inverted commas. This had the effect of distancing him from them, suggesting they were not his first choice and might carry with them implications for which he would not wish to be held responsible.

"Your desk," he said, looking at the empty one opposite him, "carries a heavy work-load, though it has been known to fluctuate."

"Heavy to very heavy," said Clifford.

Patrick was not sure about paperwork. He had imagined when joining the Foreign Office that there was an activity called diplomacy that was conducted by people talking to each other. This may have been true for some but there was a depressing amount of paper on Philip's desk. Patrick felt tired.

"It's a matter of identifying priorities," Philip continued. "You have to know what needs action this day and what to put on the back-burner, as it were. Not everything demands or can be given immediate attention."

"You can't do it all at once," said Clifford. "You have to sort it out."

Miss Teale, the administration officer, was a harassed-looking lady nearing retirement. Her cheeks sagged so much that when she shook her head they wobbled. Her mouth was small and cross. Patrick later heard stories of her having had affairs with men who had gone on to become senior ambassadors, leaving her behind. She now had the manner of one who considered herself frequently put-upon.

"Things were bad enough with Arthur Whelk here. I never thought they could be worse when he isn't. It's hopeless trying to administer someone's accommodation and possessions without the someone. But it's even more of a problem with you coming in and using them for however long it's going to be. As for your own heavy baggage – d'you know what ship it was on?"

"The *Limpopo*."

She looked through the mass of papers on her desk. "No record," she said with satisfaction. "It probably hasn't been loaded yet."

"What about my car?"

"I've heard nothing about any car."

"Well, I ordered one in London. It was supposed to be delivered directly to the docks."

Miss Teale shook her head with her eyes closed. "If I haven't heard about it it can't be coming."

"You'll need a car to get to work," put in Clifford. "Don't know how you'll manage until it gets here."

"Aren't there any buses?"

They both looked surprised. "There are," said Miss Teale, "but they're not usually taken by diplomatic grades."

"What about trains?"

"There are no suburban trains. Now, I'll have to come and do an inventory of your house after you've moved in. God knows how I'm going to do it with all Arthur's things still there. Not that it's your house, anyway, so I shouldn't call it that. You may have to move soon whether or not Arthur returns so I shouldn't make yourself at home if I were you."

"It's all wrong for his grade," said Clifford. "Ridiculous."

"Wouldn't it be better to do the inventory before I move in?" asked Patrick.

Miss Teale turned away. "I'll do it when I can. I haven't time to go chasing here and there at everybody's beck and call. You're only at the residence for a night or two, aren't you? Well, then. One thing I shall have to do, though, is to remove the double beds. Single people aren't entitled to them."

Patrick was shown round the library, the consular section – where he was to take over an undefined portion of Whelk's responsibilities – and the registry. He shook hands with everyone and remembered no names. Clifford looked bored and distracted. Ignoring his earlier promise of a long day ahead, he suggested Patrick should go back to the residence to rest. There was nothing he could usefully do at the embassy that day so he might as well catch up on his sleep. The only essential fixture was the party Philip was giving that evening – "at which your kind presence is required." Clifford would call at the residence to take him to it. They parted with mutual relief.

The residence was a 1930s mansion set in acres of garden in the most expensive part of the northern suburbs. Built of red brick, it had castellated wings and a double front door painted white with gleaming brass fittings. House and gardens were festooned with security lights and devices.

A woman servant led Patrick to the guest wing while a man carried

44

his baggage. The three walked in silence along polished corridors and up and down carpeted stairs. In one hall they met the ambassador's new guard dog, a young doberman that ran whining into the garden and hid among the bushes. Patrick was given a twin-bedded room overlooking the swimming-pool and tennis-courts. Across the corridor was a bathroom in which someone had recently showered, leaving a soggy white towel in the middle of the floor. The woman servant hastily tidied it, explaining that it must have been left by the other gentleman that morning, the one who had had breakfast with Sir Wilfrid.

It was blissful to be alone at last. He drew the curtains and pottered about in the semi-darkness, unpacking some of the items he did not need and failing to find those he did. He soon gave up and ran a bath in which he wallowed, dozed and dreamt vividly for a few seconds about vacuum-cleaning a lawn. He dried himself on a fresh towel the size of a blanket.

As he slipped gratefully between the sheets he noticed from the state of the pillow that the other gentleman had also rested there, but he was too tired to mind. Something fell from the bed and rolled along the floor. It sounded like a coin but he was too tired to look. He was not aware of his head touching the pillow.

5

A woman was standing in the doorway, silhouetted against the electric light in the hall. She was saying something he could not understand, although he knew the words. He propped himself up on his elbow and recognised the female servant. He remembered he was in Lower Africa.

"The lady has come for you." She had already repeated the statement twice. He thanked her and she went out, leaving the door ajar.

He sat on the edge of the bed, staring at his bare feet whilst the events of the past twenty-four hours were marshalled by his memory. It was quite dark. No light came through the curtains. It was evening and he had gone to bed during the day, in the morning. Before lunch, therefore. He could not recall lunch, so it must have been in the morning. He could not think what lady could be calling for him. Perhaps he had misheard.

Something metallic on the floor gave off a dull brassy gleam in the light that came in from the hall. He picked it up and found it was a bullet, small and solid, cold at first but warmed quickly by his fingers. He remembered something falling from the bed when he got into it, then that the L and F man had been there before him. He stood the bullet on its base on the bedside table, wrapped the big white towel around his hips and stepped out into the corridor, blinking.

At the far end stood Sandy, Clifford's wife. She leant against the wall, her arms folded and a black handbag over her shoulder. She wore a pleated black skirt with a cream blouse and her short hair shone from recent washing. He remembered that Clifford was supposed to have picked him up to go to the party.

She smiled. "You look awful. Are you all right?"

"Yes." He heard his voice as if from outside. He was possessed by a feeling of dreamy unreality.

"How long have you been sleeping?"

"I don't know. What time is it?"

"Gone seven. I've come to take you to the Longhursts. Clifford was

46

late back from the embassy. We'll pick him up on the way. There's no one here except the servants."

"Right." He stood without moving. He had a strange feeling he had forgotten something.

She laughed, looked down, then up, then laughed again. "I don't want to embarrass you."

"No." There was definitely something.

She looked down again, shaking with laughter. "Your towel."

He was clutching it to his hip but had inadvertently let go of one corner so that only his left thigh was concealed. He looked at himself, as if it were important to know what she could see. "Thank you." He rearranged the towel.

She pushed herself off the wall and after a momentary unsteadiness began to walk towards him. Her step was heavy and uneven. "Have a bath. It'll wake you up. I'll scrub your back."

She did not follow him into the bathroom but walked past the door and along the corridor. Perhaps she had not meant what she said. It was the kind of remark people often made without translating it into action, whether or not they'd meant it at the time.

He turned on the bath, then searched for the flannel he knew he must have had when he'd had his first bath some hours before. He found it tucked into one of his shoes. The hot water gushed, filling the room with steam.

Just after he had lowered himself gently into the water Sandy returned with two large gin and tonics. She put one on the soap-rack for him then sat on the stool which she pulled up to the side of the bath.

"When did you last wash your hair?"

"Yesterday, or the day before. I'm not sure. It was in London."

"Where's the shampoo?"

"I don't know."

She found it in a cupboard. "Wet your hair."

"The water's too hot."

"Then we'll make it colder."

She leant across him and turned on the cold tap. She smelt of perfume and drink. Desire and the sense of reality returned together. He wanted to touch her but feared to make her clothes wet. She briskly washed and massaged his head, then scrubbed his back with a loofah.

"Would your husband mind?" he asked, his eyes closed. He enjoyed having his head pushed from side to side.

"Of course he would."

"Did he mind your coming here?"

"Probably. I didn't give him time to object. He's quite jealous."

"Already?"

"Anyway. Not of you particularly. But he's more jealous than he has reason to be." She squeezed the sponge over him once more and then flung it aside. "Come on."

He dried himself in the bedroom whilst she went off to refill her glass. The bullet was still on the bedside table and he wrapped it in his handkerchief just before she returned. Presumably she was not to know about the L and F man. She entered the room as if walking on wobbling floorboards, touching the wall with her fingertips. She sat on the bed and watched him dress.

The silence made him awkward.

"D'you enjoy being a diplomatic wife?"

"I don't enjoy being a wife."

"You don't have to be."

"True."

She crossed her legs and leant back on one arm, pressing her glass so hard against her bottom lip that the lip was flattened. "You'd better take those off."

He paused in zipping up the flies on his jeans.

"Everyone else will be in suits."

Even now he frequently forgot he was no longer a student. Fortunately he had a suit with him but the search for a tie was fruitless. "I know I've got one. More than one. I brought them with me. They must be somewhere."

"You'd better borrow one of the ambassador's. He'll be there but he never notices."

She went down the corridor and returned with a blue and white checked tie.

"That looks odd. It's like a duster."

"It'll be even more odd if you don't wear one at all."

When they were outside she walked towards the Cortina estate with careful deliberation. "If the keys aren't in it I've lost them. Clifford's always telling me not to leave them in. I hope they are."

They were. "Would you like me to drive?" he asked as they were about to get in.

"No. Think I'm drunk?"

"Yes."

"I can drive. I do everything better when I'm slightly drunk except walk. Don't know why, it's just walking. I even knit better. Not that I do that often, mind you."

48

She drove steadily through the wide avenues. Street lights were few and the headlamps picked out secluded gateways, high walls and the inevitable jacarandas in slow succession. Occasionally there were blacks walking, or sometimes simply standing.

Either the sense of unreality or the gin had left Patrick light-headed and confident. "Why don't you leave him if it's so bad?"

She pouted briefly. "The girls, really. I don't want to bring them up by myself. Also, both families would be horrified. It's a lot to break up for no obvious reason, nothing dramatic, you know. And he's not always that bad. He makes an effort sometimes. It's just boring."

"Is he faithful?"

She smiled as she looked past him at a road junction. "Sometimes I think it would do him good to have a fling. But he's frightened of women, really, and he doesn't get much chance, poor thing."

"So why did you marry him?"

"It seemed a good idea at the time. Isn't that what they all say, the married ladies you ask? I had a boring job and I was sharing a flat with three other girls in Paddington and he was in the glamorous Foreign Office and made a fuss of me. Adventure, travel, all this, you know. Why haven't you married?"

Patrick was still feeling pleased with himself. "How d'you know I haven't?"

"Come off it."

"Too young."

"So's everyone when they marry."

"I've never been in love."

She laughed, took a cigarette from the packet on her lap and pushed in the dashboard lighter. "D'you think you ever will be?"

Patrick had always assumed that love and marriage would come to him as they came to others, separately or together but inevitably and in an apparently indefinite future, like his death. "Why not?"

"I don't think you will. I don't think you care enough. You seem remote, you keep yourself back from everything. You probably don't care about anyone else or anything else and never have. You might do it out of boredom or for money, I suppose."

He was surprised. He thought of himself not only as approximately normal but also as what was normally called 'nice', more or less. Her accusation suggested coldness and detachment, qualities which he did not greatly like in others. The dashboard lighter popped out. He took it and she held his hand during the lighting, without taking her eyes off the road.

"Watch out tonight for Pat Eliot, the military attaché's wife," she said, exhaling smoke. "She might not be there but if she is she'll be drunk and after anything in trousers. There's nothing personal in it so don't get conceited. She grabs anything new."

"Is the party going to be awful?"

"Anything to do with the Longhursts is awful. Actually he's okay when you get him alone. She's a pain. Don't repeat that to Clifford. He thinks it's all good experience for you. I suppose it is in a way. Gives you a taste of what you're in for."

Clifford was angry because they were late and insisted on driving. The younger of the two girls was coughing again but Sarah knew what to do about it. To her husband's further annoyance, Sandy said she would go and see anyway, and go to the loo as well.

Clifford turned the car round and sat with the engine running. Patrick was about to get into the back. "No need," said Clifford. "I'd rather have her in the back when I'm in a hurry."

"I suppose it's safer."

"What? Oh, yes, I suppose so." Clifford opened the window and sat with his elbow on the door, drumming his fingers against it. "You mustn't think tonight is going to be typical. For one thing, there's some sort of entertainment and for another there'll be Lower Africans as well as dips – diplomats, that is. Businessmen mainly, more commercial section contacts than chancery but it doesn't hurt once in a while. We don't see as much of the Lower Africans as we should, really. So damn busy. Now you're here, though, I'll be able to get some systematic entertainment going. HE will be there for a part of the time – quite improperly since there's no one else of his equivalent seniority and most ambassadors would never come to a thing like this. Sir Wilfrid's very keen on doing his bit with his staff, you see, and when he heard about this he just invited himself. Feather in Philip's cap, of course, but don't read too much into it. At least the presence of HE will give things a focus. Social occasions need a focal point, don't you think?"

"They need some point."

"Precisely. Exactly what I think."

Clifford gave a prolonged blast on the horn that brought Sarah to the door but no Sandy. Sarah had to be waved back. Sandy made a brief appearance, then retreated to get some more cigarettes. When she reappeared Patrick again offered to get into the back.

"Don't. I'd rather go there." She got in clumsily and slammed the door.

Clifford glanced at her in the driving mirror. "Darling, what did I tell you last time about that door?"

"What you always tell me."

Clifford drove fast and no one spoke. Once, when Patrick turned to look at a group of blacks who were sitting huddled in wraps beneath a street lamp arguing, he noticed Sandy sitting very still and staring straight ahead. She looked small, crumpled and unhappy. She clutched the packet of cigarettes in her lap but did not smoke. He wondered if she felt ill. She did not appear to notice his looking at her.

Philip's house was an extensive bungalow spread like a small motel along grass terraces. His wife, Claire, was short and chunky with small hard brown eyes like buttons. She greeted everyone with a determined smile.

"I heard all about your arrival," she said to Patrick. "It must've been simply awful and you must be dying for a drink. Did you have one at the Steggles's? Well, you must be dehydrated by now. Philip will take you in and see that you get one but mind the altitude till you're used to it. We must talk later."

Philip smiled automatically at Patrick, then reached forward to stop a servant who was attempting to relieve Sandy of her handbag. "I must introduce you to some people. It's going to be rather awkward because with the ambassador coming and no precise equivalent for him we're going to have to make up in numbers what we lack in rank. We'll have to provide him with a series of guests, as it were. That might not leave many for you, I'm afraid – nor for anyone else, of course. Red or white?"

"Red, please."

"I'd advise white. The red's rather strong and should be treated with care until you're used to the altitude. Particularly at your first function." He beckoned to a waiter and handed Patrick a glass of white wine.

When Philip turned away Patrick substituted it for a red. Clifford was talking seriously to the commercial officer, nodding thoughtfully without lifting his gaze from the carpet. Sandy was standing with two other wives who were apparently talking about a third. She still looked subdued.

There were three camps in the room. The British were entrenched before a table and were seemingly so absorbed in each other that they were unaware of anyone else. They talked with the nervous excitement and boredom that usually afflicts people who have nothing to say but are forced to talk on their feet in a small space, clutching their glasses like tickets.

The foreign diplomats were grouped in a solid defensive position in the far corner, complacent but watchful to see who came in. The Lower Africans, outnumbered but resolute, had formed a laager in another corner from which they fired mistrustful glances as if expecting a trap. They said little and observed a lot.

Patrick sipped his wine and tried to avoid catching anyone's eye. When he glanced in the direction of the door he saw Philip enter with the blonde woman he had seen at the airport. She had her hair pinned up in a bun, showing her face to be sharper than he had remembered it, and she smiled as she said something in reply to Philip. She wore red again – her blouse, this time – with a high-shouldered black jacket and matching skirt and boots; a Spanish effect. The dark-haired man with her was the one who had met her at the airport. He was stocky, tanned and fit-looking and wore a brown leather jacket with tight white trousers. He nodded to one or two people in the Lower African laager then looked round the room, calm and unhurried.

Clifford abandoned the commercial officer and made a determined diagonal sortie from the British corner. He obviously knew the couple and began chatting with proud assurance whilst Philip hesitated uneasily. Everyone's eyes were on the group since they were in no man's land, the centre of the room. Philip's eyes flickered around the other groups seeking a home for this rogue one.

The wine was already having an effect. Patrick could feel it brimming in his eyes though his head felt clear. He would have to talk to someone soon. Better someone he wanted to talk to. He crossed no man's land quite steadily but a little quicker than he intended. Clifford broke off from what he was saying and with ill-concealed irritation performed the introductions.

The man was Jim Rissik of the Lower African Police Force and the woman was Joanna McBride, no explanation. Hands were shaken and there was a polite show of interest in how long Patrick had been in Lower Africa, where he had been before and how long he expected to remain. Philip went off to greet more newcomers.

Jim Rissik was in charge of that section of the LAPF that dealt with the protection and problems of diplomats. "Every now and again someone remembers us and I get invited to a few functions. At Christmas we give a ball round a pool somewhere but not many of you dips turn up to that." He grinned.

They talked about the difficulty of protecting diplomats, of terrorism in other parts of the world, of the line between protection and infringement of liberty. Rissik was robust and four-square. He looked Patrick in the eye whilst talking and stood very close as though the

better to push his points home. The clipped speech and the thick
Lower African accent were harsh on Patrick's unaccustomed ear. He
thought of Arthur Whelk. He guessed that Rissik must be the man he
was to deal with and wondered whether Rissik knew that. Perhaps
Rissik already knew of the presence of the L and F man. He had
remarked with a slight smile that in protecting people you got to know
a lot about them and that not much escaped the protectors.

"D'you follow us around all the time then?" asked Patrick.

Rissik hesitated, still smiling. "We look after your physical security
for some of the time."

Patrick smiled back. "So we're safe, are we?"

"So long as you're sensible." Rissik took another glass of wine from
a passing waiter, making it clear by his posture that he wanted to
continue talking. "What did people tell you about us Lower Africans
before you came? Did they say we're a bunch of racists and fascists?"

"They told me I had to learn to make small talk."

"Less dangerous than big talk, eh?"

"Easier than big talk."

"Well, maybe we are a bunch of racists and fascists but you'll get
used to that, I reckon."

Joanna McBride laughed at something Clifford said. Her lips lingered over the smile some time after the laugh had ceased. Patrick
caught her eye fleetingly but she showed no recognition. Sandy joined
them. Jim talked about how unfairly Lower Africa was dealt with in
world news. Other countries in the continent escaped criticism because
they were black though they were every bit as bad, often worse. It was
because the liberal conscience was unconsciously racist, expecting
better of white men than of black. Also it was weak and mistrustful of
itself and sought to denigrate its own. Patrick tried to see a way of
swapping partners so that he could talk to Joanna.

"What annoys us here more than anything is that we get criticised
and others don't," continued Jim. "Even the liberals get annoyed by
that." He turned to Sandy. "Even your husband and he's not Lower
African."

Sandy was looking livelier than when in the car. "He's not exactly
liberal, either."

"Compared with me he is." They all laughed. There was an appeal-
ing frankness in Rissik that bordered on the brutal. He turned to
Clifford. "What d'you think of our wines, Cliff? Better than all that
French plonk, eh?"

"Not bad," said Clifford.

"'Not bad,' he says. Damn good, that's what they are. Damn good.'"
Jim put his hand heavily on Patrick's shoulder. "This one's plonk,
though, so watch for the kick-back. You'll be able to take more when
you're used to the altitude. The best wines come from the coast. This
doesn't. I'm going down there this weekend to stock up with a few
crates."

Patrick had an idea that the coast was a thousand or so miles away.
"That's a long way to go for a weekend, isn't it?"

"I'm borrowing a plane from a friend. Fly it myself. That's how we
live here. He's seen nothing yet, has he?" Clifford made a remark
about the economy and the wine industry which Jim followed up
enthusiastically. Joanna listened, saying little. She had grey eyes
speckled with green. She watched Jim talk.

Patrick did not like it. He turned to Sandy, who was coquettishly
touching the rim of her wine glass with the tip of her tongue. "A
healthy interest for you if you're not too detached to take one," she
said quietly. "At least she's unmarried, though that wouldn't bother
you either way, would it?"

"What makes you think I'm interested?"

"It's obvious. Everything about you is obvious. D'you really think it
isn't? Don't worry, I'll see if I can dispose of your rivals. It'll give me a
vicarious thrill."

"Are they both rivals?"

"Mine would be if he could, except that he'd be frightened to death,
poor thing."

She turned to Jim and asked him abruptly where he came from.
Interrupted in mid-sentence, he told her and she turned to Clifford and
asked him if he had not been there. He said he had not, she said he had
and Jim began describing the area for Clifford's benefit.

Patrick raised his glass to his lips, partly to hide his smile, but
managed the matter rather clumsily. When he took his handkerchief
from his pocket something fell to the floor and rolled. He looked for a
coin and saw the bullet he had found in his bedroom. It rested against
one of Joanna's black boots. She looked down, then up at him, her
eyebrows raised slightly and an amused questioning light in her grey
eyes. No one else had noticed.

He bent and picked up the bullet. The action was enough to remind
him that he might be slightly drunk. "There is an explanation." He did
not know what he would offer.

She looked at the bullet as he turned it in his fingers. "Don't some
people make beads and necklaces with them?"

"I don't know." He had been keen to hide the bullet from Sandy but with Joanna he had an impulse to do the opposite, wanting to show off. He held it out. "Have it."

"Don't you want it?"

"For what?"

"In connection with your 'explanation'."

"It's not mine. Have it."

"What do you think I should do with it?"

She had the same clipped speech as Jim but the tone was softer and there was a slight lilt. Patrick had the bullet in the palm of his hand, aware that at any moment the others might see it. He particularly did not want to explain it to Jim. "Keep it for luck."

"Is it a lucky one?"

"It has been so far."

She smiled and took it, fingering it for a few moments before putting it in her bag. "I'd assumed it was for your gun."

"I don't have a gun."

"A lot of people do. Some carry them all the time."

"Does Jim?"

The question came out more abruptly than he had meant. She turned her head a little to one side. "Some of the time he does, yes."

There was a pause. He had introduced a wrong note and the conversation had lost impetus. He needed to restore it quickly before one of the others noticed they weren't talking and included them. "It was a tiring flight, wasn't it?" he said lamely.

She looked at him before replying. He had assumed that she had seen him at the airport simply because he had noticed her. Now he felt unsure and foolish.

She smiled. "You looked so lost I felt quite sorry for you. You didn't know where to put yourself."

This cheered him. The fact that she had noticed him and had not said so suggested a hint of complicity. "It made it worse when you smiled and then went off with someone else."

She laughed now. "I'm sorry, I couldn't help smiling. You looked so tousled."

Further conversation was prevented by an eddy of people surrounding the ambassador, who was now moving through the room. His presence and those attracted to it destroyed the defensive lines of the three main groups. Taller than anyone else, Sir Wilfrid nodded continuously and courteously, saying "Yes, yes, quite" very frequently. He shook hands, attempted to smooth his wild white hair and

55

occasionally touched the knot of his tie. Seeing this last gesture caused Patrick involuntarily to do the same.

Philip startled everyone by announcing in a high voice, "Your Excellency, ladies and gentlemen, if you would be pleased to go through now."

After some hesitation the ambassador proceeded on the arm of the German counsellor's wife. Jim said something to Joanna and Sandy walked on ahead of Clifford whilst he was talking to her. Patrick was separated from them by a troop of Lower Africans. He had not in any case imagined that he could remain talking to Joanna for much longer. Perhaps there would be a chance later so long as someone else talked to Jim. He was grateful to Sandy and would have thanked her had she not walked off as though everyone was a stranger. However, the prospect of food reminded him that he was very hungry. He entered the next room with a sudden excess of saliva in his mouth.

Instead of food, though, there were rows of government-issue metal chairs. They faced a piano, beside which stood Clair Longhurst, her hands tightly clasped and her smile fixed with the rigidity of rigormortis.

There was a discreet race for the back of the room which was won by the British, able to make use of the national characteristic of self-effacement in order to be more craftily pushy. The Lower Africans seized the front and middle rows to the right of the gangway while the foreign diplomats shuffled disconsolately to the left. Sir Wilfrid was shown to a low armchair on the front right, which meant that his head was on a level with the chairs on either side of him. Patrick and a sulky Frenchman who would not speak English hovered near the door until directed to a row of three chairs at the side.

The entertainment consisted of Philip playing humorous records as examples for 'our foreign colleagues, friends and guests' of what he called English humour. One piece was a recording of Hoffnung's speech to the Oxford Union which was so crackly that it was impossible to hear what was said and not easy to tell when it was finished. Everyone sat with expressionless faces, except Sir Wilfrid who twice turned to Claire to say that it would do no good to play the record with a broken needle. In order to reply to him Claire had to bend her head to his, on a level with her own knees, causing her skirt to creep up her thighs. She maintained her smile throughout.

At the end of the records there was silence until the Japanese commercial attaché began to clap briskly, forcing nearly everyone else to join in.

Philip next read a speech about how the origins of jazz were said by some experts to be found in nineteenth-century martial music and introduced Mr Johann Botha who was to demonstrate on the piano. Mr Botha was a short, bespectacled, bearded man who bowed stiffly and unsmilingly, once to Sir Wilfrid and once to the audience. His spectacles glinted. The Japanese attaché again stimulated applause. Mr Botha looked vainly for the piano stool and bowed again. Philip stepped back, leaving the floor to the pianist. Mr Botha made several silent expostulations. Claire jumped from her chair and whispered to her husband, who looked with surprise at the piano and then at Mr Botha, who looked back indignantly, his hands clasped behind him. Claire put Philip's chair by the piano. Mr Botha sat with his back to the audience and his shoulders not far above the key-board.

Before Mr Botha could start the ambassador clapped several times, loudly and quite slowly. He told Claire he had enjoyed the comedy. Others joined in the clapping. Mr Botha turned in his seat and bowed his head. He then played rousing martial tunes such as *Rule Britannia* and *The British Grenadiers* for about twenty minutes.

When Philip announced that there would be a break the applause was genuine. Patrick tried to get near Joanna but such was the rush that there was no point in waiting. In the reception room two black servants stood anxiously holding trays of drinks. He ignored them and made for the nearest peanut dish. He next found some crisps. The ambassador appeared, flanked by Clifford and Philip. Patrick went in search of Joanna.

He found her queuing with other women for one of the lavatories. Her grey eyes showed faint surprise when he stopped. For a moment he was almost reduced to complimenting her on her black jacket and skirt but a happier inspiration came.

"Is Jim getting you a drink?"

She shook her head. "I don't think so. There's another loo somewhere. He's probably gone there."

"Would you like one?"

"Red wine, please."

"Large?" He was not aware that there was any choice and had asked only because he felt self-conscious before all the women.

She smiled. "Very."

Back in the reception room people talked and drank with boisterous relief. They formed three camps roughly as before, but common adversity had brought about some mixing. Patrick lifted two glasses of wine from a tray of four that a servant was taking to someone. He

57

planned to intercept Joanna in the corridor so that they could talk away from the others.

"Kind of you, Patrick, thank you." Sir Wilfrid took a glass from him. Clifford was about to take the other but Patrick held it closer. Sir Wilfrid waved his pipe whilst complimenting Philip on the mime show at the start of the piano-playing. "Takes an awful lot of rehearsal, that sort of thing."

Philip smiled awkwardly, caught Patrick's eye and looked away. Clifford stared uncomprehendingly at the ambassador, then resentfully at Patrick's wine. Sir Wilfrid said it was time he did his bit of mixing and moved off towards the Lower African camp. Philip redirected a waiter towards the Lower Africans as Clifford was about to take a glass from him.

Jim was talking to some Lower Africans. Patrick met Joanna as she came through the door. They stood by a sideboard.

"Aren't you having any?" she asked.

"I was but the ambassador took it. He thought it was for him. I'll get another."

"Does that sort of thing often happen to you?"

"Quite often, yes, but I usually overcome it somehow." He was the only person in the room without a drink but if he went for one someone else might talk to her. "Actually, I'm more interested in food at the moment."

"You'll be out of luck there. Diplomats have a reputation for not being over-generous when it comes to entertaining the natives. Despite handsome entertainment allowances, I'm told." She smiled as she looked round. "There were some peanuts on this sideboard earlier – or did the ambassador take those as well?"

"No, I got them – and the crisps. It's all right, I'll nip round the corner and get something afterwards."

She laughed as at something quaint. "No one 'nips round corners' in northern Battenburg. There's nowhere to nip. There aren't any pubs or fish and chip shops or Chinese take-aways like in England. Everyone drives to restaurants. Why don't you come back with us and have something? We're going to eat anyway."

This was more than he expected but the implied cohabitation was a setback. Jim was already watching when she turned to wave him over. "Patrick is starving. I said we'd feed him afterwards. He can come back with Sandy and Clifford."

Jim clapped Patrick on the shoulder again, like a father trying to put some gumption into his weakling son. "Needs feeding up, does he?

Well, you'll get it, Pat. It'll be a good old Lower African fry-up, nothing fancy. We'd go outside and have a braii – barbecue in your language – if it weren't so damn cold. What d'you reckon of the show? I don't get it at all. Is this really how people entertain in England?"

Patrick did not hesitate long over the question of loyalty to diplomatic colleagues. "No. I've never seen anything like it."

"Then what the hell are they doing it for?"

"Haven't a clue."

"So what do people like this do in England?"

Patrick thought. "I've never met people like this in England. Perhaps they're only like it when they're abroad."

Philip announced 'round two' and there was a rush to top up glasses. Jim yet again put his hand possessively on Patrick's shoulder. "I'm glad you're coming back. We must get to know each other. I'm sure we'll have a lot to talk about, you and I."

His friendly manner had an unasked-for complicity about it. "What things?"

Jim grinned. "Just things."

Philip told his audience that Mr Botha would now demonstrate how the American musician Scott Joplin had adapted early jazz rhythms to his own use. Mr Botha, seated on a higher chair this time, demonstrated with precise severity. Between tunes Philip read aloud from a potted biography of Joplin, at one point getting the pages wrong so that Claire was halfway to her feet and gesturing with her braceleted arm before he corrected himself and inserted the missing decade. A plume of smoke from Sir Wilfrid's pipe became a slowly revolving cloud which enveloped the piano, causing Mr Botha to cough twice and look round. Philip stepped forward to see where the smoke came from, saw and stepped back.

At the end the Japanese and his wife again led the company in quick-fire applause which was prolonged by relief and embarrassment. When Mr Botha bowed Philip clapped more vigorously than before and the applause was renewed. It had already gone beyond what was polite or credible and was beginning to die away when Sir Wilfrid, who had been groping for his pipe after it had fallen from his mouth during the first barrage, began to clap loudly and widely as if to make up for his tardiness. Those whose hands were slowing then speeded up. Mr Botha bowed twice more, smiled nervously and hurried out.

The ambassador left immediately afterwards, which permitted everyone else to go. Patrick travelled with Sandy and Clifford. They argued about whether or not the evening had been good for him.

Clifford thought it had been a useful experience "in itself" and also because it enabled Patrick to be seen.

"Why's that important?" asked Sandy.

"For his job, of course. It means that people will know him. They'll take him more seriously."

"More likely the opposite. People take diplomats less seriously the better they know them. You'd all be better thought of if none of you ever met anyone. Though since most diplomats spend most of their time talking to other diplomats I don't s'pose it really makes much difference." She turned and smiled at Patrick. "Like your tie."

Patrick touched it again. "Thank you."

"Where did you get it?"

"A girlfriend gave it to me."

"You should be so lucky." She laughed, then argued with Clifford about the route he was taking. From this it became apparent that Jim and Joanna had separate houses and did not live together.

6

Jim's bungalow was small compared with diplomatic housing. Patrick looked automatically for the pool and was not disappointed. It was green and kidney-shaped, with a springboard. Inside the bungalow almost every wall and most shelves, sideboards and tables bore some reminder of hunting, either in the shape of antique weapons or the heads of shot beasts. Hunting prints and pictures abounded.

"Did you shoot all these?" asked Patrick.

"Wish I had."

Both women and Clifford disappeared to various lavatories. Jim led the way to the veranda. "Wait, I'll settle the dogs. Otherwise they'll have you."

He whistled and two black Alsatians padded out of the darkness. He directed them to sniff Patrick. "Beautiful beasts, aren't they? Dangerous and beautiful. Sometimes I wish I was one. D'you ever think like that?" He glanced at Patrick, then continued without waiting for a reply. "They'll be okay now that they've seen you with me. I'm going to the bar to fix the drinks. What d'you want?"

The effects of the earlier wine had still not worn off. "A tomato juice."

Jim looked at him scornfully. "I was offering you a drink."

Since meeting Jim he had sensed there would be a confrontation but this was as absurd as it was unexpected. "And I asked for a tomato juice."

Jim hesitated, then grinned and shrugged. "Your choice."

Patrick stepped out on to the veranda and the two dogs slipped into the house behind him. He could hear Jim talking to them in encouraging, friendly tones. It was a clear evening with a touch of frost, the kind of night he loved in England. He walked across the grass to the pool, in which was reflected the garden light of the house on the other side of the road. He had been in Lower Africa a little over twelve hours. It was impossible to believe that he would actually last the full four years. Rachel had been in his mind throughout most of the day, which was curious because he did not often think of her. He kept imagining her

61

reactions, perhaps comparing them with the lack of his own. Maybe Sandy had been right in saying he did not care about anything. He wondered if he would care about that, if it were true; or whether Joanna would think the same, if she were interested in noticing. Perhaps he was just tired. Even so, it was always the women that he thought of.

He heard Joanna's footfall on the grass behind him a moment before she spoke. "Dreaming of England?"

It was not easy to see her features against the house lights but he thought she smiled. She had probably noticed that he was startled. "The weather reminds me of it," he said.

"A lot of people here dream of England."

"Do you?"

"I used to. I lived in Lincoln until I was nine. I used to dream of it all the time but I don't any longer, not now that I can go back to it whenever I like. That's why I was on the plane. I'd been visiting my family."

"Did you enjoy it?"

"England?" She walked towards the pool, her arms folded. "Not much, no. I was disappointed. I hadn't been back for some years, you see, and it was not – I won't say not as I remember it, but not as I wanted it to be. It was shabby."

Patrick tried to defend his country, partly, he suspected, because her Lower African accent and her criticism made her seem more independent of what he knew, and therefore of himself, than he wanted. She thought London dirty and the people pale and unhealthy-looking. Everyone hurried and looked miserable. The whole place felt as if it were running down and no one seemed to care.

"Did you go outside the cities?" he asked.

"Not much. Should I have?"

"No, no, I just wondered." He argued that the shabbiness was in fact ordinariness, a reassuring normality, that the people were kind, that Britain was an easy, peaceful, civilised place to live.

"The quality of life, you mean?"

He had been trying to avoid the phrase. "Well, yes, sort of."

"Perhaps you're a romantic after all."

"After all?"

She knelt by the pool and felt the water. "He never heats it, you know. It's always like this and he always goes in every day, even in winter. More of an English than a Lower African habit, I should think."

"How do you know him?"

"He was a friend of my husband's."

"I see."

"Do you? What do you see?" She smiled again and walked slowly round the edge of the pool. From somewhere nearby a bird made several perfunctory cheeps. A shrub gave off a heavy sweet smell. "I'm divorced and I'm twenty-six and I have a little girl, the one you saw on the plane. Does that answer your next few questions?"

"Yes, I think so, thank you." Short of asking if she would ditch Jim and have an affair with him instead he could think of nothing more.

She laughed quietly. "Are you always so polite?"

He thought. "Probably. I usually am, yes."

"And do you probably usually mean it?"

"Sometimes."

She laughed again and began unpinning her hair as she walked. There was a careless intimacy in the way it fell and in the way she shook it. "Where else has the Foreign Office sent you?"

"Nowhere. I've just joined. I was at university before this." He saw her glance at him with raised eyebrows. "Why, do I look older?"

"No, but you seem older. A little bit – well, ragged around the edges." She smiled. "I don't mean that unkindly."

"There you are." Sandy walked down the lawn towards them, rubbing her arms. "We've been wondering where you both were. You'd better come in if you want some food. Aren't you cold? I'm freezing. I'm sure the blood gets thinner out here. Yours will after a while, Patrick."

"When I get used to the altitude?"

"That's just what I said to Jim. He's worried about you because you wanted a tomato juice. He thought there might be something wrong with you, like principles. I told him that whatever it was it wasn't that."

Inside the house Clifford and Jim were discussing Lower African wines. Clifford insisted that some of the dry were sweet. Joanna went in ahead and Patrick reached to close the door at the same time as Sandy.

She smiled. "Don't say I don't give you a chance. You were making a meal of it, though. I thought you'd run off to a bedroom together."

"We were only talking."

"Keep it that way. She ain't your sort, love. Too conventional."

He was not sure he had a sort. If he had he wanted it to be Joanna. She was, by all the conventions, unusually attractive.

Sandy gave a look that was exaggeratedly arch, then steadied herself before walking carefully into the sitting-room.

Refusing all help, Jim cooked fried eggs, tomatoes, mushrooms, sausages and toast. It was his servant's day off and on that day he always looked forward to a fry-up of anything he could find. The others sat talking in the sitting-room, Patrick by then almost wholly absorbed in the smells of cooking. He finished his food before anyone else. Afterwards they drank hot chocolate and whisky. Jim nodded his approval at Patrick's having whisky, then talked to Clifford about the blacks. He was drinking a lot. Joanna and Sandy discussed local schools.

Patrick felt drowsy. He asked a few questions of Joanna and Sandy then listened to the other conversation. He was interested but was sinking gradually beneath a rising tide of alcoholic tiredness until the awareness of growing anger on Jim's part cleared his head.

Jim stood by the fireplace. "They'll never get it together," he said, interrupting Clifford suddenly, "not in a million years. Well, in a million maybe but that's because I'm an optimist. They just don't have what it takes, you know?"

Clifford glanced uncomfortably at Patrick. "I don't think you can say that, really. I mean, it's all a question of environment. As they become industrialised – "

"Environment my arse. It's in their heads, you know, in here." He tapped his forehead several times. His dark eyes were hard and glistening. "Look around you if you don't believe me. Look at black Africa. Corrupt, inefficient, brutal, lousy dictatorships. And the farther they get from colonial rule the worse they get. Look at Zimbabwe and Kenya – the great black hopes. Where are they headed? Down the plug-hole with the rest. Straight down the plug." He jabbed his thick forefinger downwards. Clifford's eyes followed it. "You say we should leave them to make up their own minds how they live. All right, supposing we walked out of here – not that there's anywhere for us to go, mind you – what do you think would happen? I'll tell you. For twenty years they'd tear each other to pieces, then they'd have so-called peace and slip back to what they were before the white man came – a lot of tribes living without the wheel and dying off because of diseases the white man taught them to conquer. Left to themselves they can't even keep the bloody mosquitoes down. Their only hope would be if the Japs took them over."

The room seemed to reverberate for a second or two with Jim's energy. Clifford started to say something about democracy but Jim cut in again, slicing the air with his hand.

"They don't give a damn about democracy. A few do – all right, but only when they're in Europe or America, not when they come home to rule. They're not interested. Your African wants food in his belly, many wives, many children and stable government. He wants a leader, not a vote. Anyway, that's not the point, is it?" Jim smiled and glanced round. "The point is not what they want but what we want. We, the ones who are in control." He pointed at Clifford. "The point is whether you'd want to live under black rule, like you say we should. Do you? Do you want to bring up your two little girls in a black one-party state? Well? Do you?"

Clifford appeared awkward, almost shifty. Joanna, no longer talking, looked at the toe of her shoe. Sandy stared at Jim as if hypnotised, both hands clutching the empty glass in her lap. Patrick tried to avoid catching anyone's eye. He said nothing, but felt he was being involved against his will.

"The point is, Jim," Clifford began slowly, "you can't expect progress in decades that took centuries for Europeans or – or Arabs. I mean –"

Jim thrust the whisky bottle towards Clifford. "The point is, you haven't answered my point. Never mind, let's stick to yours. Centuries for Europeans and Arabs, you say. Centuries also for Indians, Chinese, Japanese, even the Goddam Incas. And why do we know about them? Because they all developed civilisations that lasted, they all had some degree of mastery over their environment instead of being slaves to it, they all learnt from other civilisations and fast, too, in decades often. The survivors, that is. All except the blacks."

He held the bottle at arm's length and stared at them all. Patrick looked out from beneath half-closed lids. Jim's gaze rested upon him for a moment, then he relaxed and refilled his glass.

"Even the bloody Eskimos turn out to be natural mechanics," he continued quietly. "It didn't take them centuries either. So what is it that's missing?" He tapped his glass against his forehead. "Why don't people admit it? They admit that blacks are better athletes or that Japanese work harder or that Jews are cleverer but no one admits that blacks as a whole don't seem to have it up top. Why not? If we have the same kind of evidence for or against physical abilities and we all admit them, why not mental ones?"

"Because it's more important." Sandy blurted out the remark like an eager schoolgirl, causing everyone to look at her.

Clifford breathed in deeply. "You must admit, Jim, that they haven't had much of a chance."

"Haven't had a chance?" Jim turned and almost shouted. Joanna said his name quietly but he did not look at her. He held up his hand before Clifford's face, the fingers splayed. "How many millions of them are there in America? How long have they been there? What have they done? Nothing. No thing. Don't tell me it's all because they've been kept back, downtrodden. Look at the Jews. No race in history has been more downtrodden than them. Look at what they've done, in America or anywhere. They run this city, I'll tell you that, and good luck to them so long as they make a good job of it. And what about the Puerto Ricans in America, or the Mexicans? Or the Chinese – sweated labour who were no better than slaves, there and here? They've all adapted better than the blacks. Why won't everyone admit that for some reason the blacks don't seem to be able to make it in the way that other races make it? Eh? Why won't everyone admit that?"

He downed his whisky and poured himself another. A small vein throbbed on the side of his temple. He looked at each of them in turn. His gaze rested on Patrick.

Patrick was tired, he did not want to have views, but he was the newcomer and they were all waiting, Jim especially. Joanna glanced at him and looked away. "It doesn't matter whether what you say about blacks is true," he began. "The point is that people should be given equal opportunities, equal resources and freedoms. They should at least be equal before the law. You could argue that different races don't get on with each other and that therefore they should have separate development. All right, so long as no race is put at a disadvantage to any other."

Jim stood with his legs apart. He was holding his whisky glass in one hand and pressing the palm of his other on top of it. He rubbed the glass with a backwards and forwards movement of his palm and smiled with self-conscious deliberation. "You only came today," he said quietly. "This is your first day. You haven't seen anything."

"My point's the same whether or not I've seen anything. It's a moral point."

Jim nodded and held up his hand. "A good liberal moral point. Maybe even a true one. But not relevant, not important, not to us. We're not moral. No one is, really. It's just that with us it's more obvious because our choice is starker. It's dog eat dog in this life. You either rule or be ruled. Either the white tribe rules or another tribe. It's the same for you in Britain ultimately but for us it's more dramatic and immediate. In Britain you have the luxury of not having to decide, not yet, anyway. You can afford to be liberal. You don't have to choose whether or not you'll be ruled by another tribe. We do. We live with that choice. It's us or them."

Joanna spoke his name again but he ignored her. She pushed back her hair and looked away.

Patrick could feel Jim's stare upon him. "In oppressing others you oppress yourself," he said without looking up. "You become less than you were. It's not just the blacks, it's you that's diminished. The oppression of one diminishes all." He knew he must be quoting someone and hoped no one would ask who.

Jim was still smiling but his eyes were nearly closed. "So what?"

"You don't mean that."

"What do I mean?"

Patrick could feel his heart beating. "You say the moral point doesn't concern you but you know it does."

"What makes you think that?" Jim was still quiet but was no longer smiling.

"You. You keep trying to justify your attitudes, justify yourself. You wouldn't do it if it didn't matter whether or not you were just. You've been trying to justify yourself all evening. You say 'so what' but you don't mean it."

Seeing Jim's raised arm and feeling the glass whistle past his right eyebrow were almost simultaneous. The glass broke on the floor and someone, probably Sandy, gasped. Jim crouched, his left arm holding the edge of his jacket. No one spoke or moved. There had not even been time for Patrick to flinch. He and Jim stared at each other. He remembered Joanna had said that Jim sometimes carried a gun and it occurred to him that he could be shot as he sat in the chair. It was more a ridiculous than an alarming thought.

Joanna was on her feet tugging at Jim's shoulder and saying something but he continued to stare. His eyes had lost their depth and showed only rage, impersonal and unselfconscious. As Joanna tugged at and spoke to him his stare softened. His eyes were still fixed on Patrick but showed growing awareness and recognition. He relaxed and straightened. She spoke quietly, her hands on his arms. For a moment Patrick thought he was about to grin, perhaps actually had grinned. He almost grinned himself.

Everyone started to move again. Sandy began to pick up the glass, Clifford stepped decisively forward but then stopped and simply watched Sandy. Patrick remained where he was. He wished Joanna wouldn't touch Jim so much.

The door at the far end of the room opened and a middle-aged black woman appeared. She wore a light pink dressing gown which she held together with one hand. Her feet were bare and on her head was a white nightcap. Her face was creased with concern. She addressed Jim in Lower African. He replied, she nodded and asked a question. He spoke again, this time in Zulu. She laughed, replied in Zulu and went away chuckling.

Jim looked at everyone except Patrick. "She said she heard noises – shouting, things breaking, was I looking for food? Just smashing the crockery I told her. Did I want her to wash up the dirty plates? Wait till the morning, I said, see which ones I break." He laughed. "She's a good one, Alice."

Clifford asked Jim where he had learnt Zulu. Jim had learnt it on his father's farm. He spoke some dialects as well. Conversation began again.

Patrick went to the study next door. It was filled with model aeroplanes, target-shooting trophies, antique firearms, photographs of police training courses and a framed police award. On a table by the desk was a small screen with buttons and connections that, had he been certain of identifying one, he would have said was a small computer. There were no books. He was interrupted by Joanna.

"I'm sorry about that," she said.

He smiled. "No damage done."

"I could see it coming. He was very angry."

"Is he often angry?"

"A lot of the time."

"Why?"

"He's unhappy."

"Why?"

She pursed her lips, shrugged and raised her eyebrows. "He's not at ease with himself. I don't know why. He never is."

He felt elated and confident. "Why are you with him?"

She turned away. "That's a little premature."

"May we meet?"

There was an amused light in her grey eyes. She nodded. He asked for her telephone number, found he had no pen, then that he had no paper. He used one of Jim's pens and a sheet of Jim's notepaper. He sought for something to say during the necessarily bureaucratic action of folding the paper and putting it in his wallet. "I thought for a moment he might shoot me."

"He's capable of it."

"It struck me it would be an absurd way to die."

68

"I suppose any way is to the one who's dying."

"I suppose it is, yes." It was not the ideal note on which to finish. They were interrupted by Clifford who had been sent by Sandy to ask where the vacuum cleaner was.

Sir Wilfrid was still up when Patrick returned to the residence. He wore a dressing-gown and nothing else, having just had a bath. His white hair sprouted riotously. His long thin legs were almost as white.

"Have a nightcap." He poured two large whiskies. "Less said about the party the better. Who is this Joplin character, anyway?"

"An American negro musician. He's become fashionable again. He's been dead for some time."

"Dead, is he? I didn't catch that bit. Many more parties like that will kill off the fashion, too. Lucky he didn't live to see it, poor chap." They sat in armchairs. Sir Wilfrid crossed his legs revealingly. "Saw you talking to that Rissik chap. He has the reputation of being a police whizz-kid. Looks after all the dips – he told you that, I expect? Probably spies on us all, too, though what for I don't know. He's also the chap you'll be dealing with over the Whelk business. How d'you get on with him?"

Patrick described what had happened at Jim's bungalow. Sir Wilfrid was unsurprised. He commented that Jim sounded an excitable sort of chap and that Lower Africans were a red-blooded lot with plenty of spunk who, whether right or wrong, were always passionate. The British, on the other hand – in public life at least and particularly since the Great War – had become timorous, dilatory, spinelessly selfish and inward-looking. The Lower Africans never paid any attention to anyone who wasn't as red-blooded as they.

"Not that I mean you should've thrown something at him. I was making a more general point. But you don't think he suspects anything about the L and F man, do you?"

"No, I don't." Patrick was less confident than he sounded. Jim's manner early in the evening had suggested complicity of some sort but could have meant anything or nothing. It could have meant he was aware of Patrick's interest in Joanna.

When eventually they stood to go to bed Sir Wilfrid pushed some of his damp hair away from his eyes. "Didn't realise you were at the House."

Patrick stopped. "The house, sir?"

"You know, the House. Christ Church. The college. Just noticed the tie."

For the third time that evening Patrick involuntarily touched it. "Ah, yes, no, sir, this is a borrowed one. I couldn't find mine – I mean, any of them."

"I see. Where were you, then?"

"Reading."

"One of the new ones, I s'pose? 'Fraid I've not kept up with them. There've been one or two new colleges since my day, I believe. Good night to you. Sleep well."

7

The move into Arthur Whelk's house was easy for Patrick but moving out seemed hard for Sandy. It was twice postponed and when the day came she was fraught almost to the point of incoherence. Clifford lost his temper and shouted at her that they were moving only a couple of miles down the road, not to Peking. She ignored Patrick until they were about to leave with the last carload.

She turned to him in the hall while Clifford tried to fit two lamp-stands into the car. She looked drawn and irritable but smiled for the first time that morning. "Have a good time here. I expect you will."

"I hope you enjoy being at home again."

"There's no need for hypocrisy. It doesn't suit you." She stopped smiling and stared at him.

Clifford reappeared and asked bad-temperedly if there was anything else. She walked out past him without answering. Patrick felt awkward and so asked more questions about the payment of Sarah and Deuteronomy. Explaining things improved Clifford's temper, as usual. He spoke repetitively and at length until Sandy called him from the car. As they drove off she glanced at Patrick, then purposefully away as if catching his attention in order to demonstrate ignoring it.

Patrick was as self-conscious about having Sarah as a servant as she clearly was about having him as a master. It took very little time for her to sort out his possessions and put them in the appropriate cupboards and drawers; rather longer for him to learn where they were. Dirty clothes were washed – by hand, since the embassy did not provide a washing-machine and it had not occurred to him to buy one – dried and ironed within a day. Sarah was so anxious to be doing things that she followed him around the house, wanting to clean up wherever he went. One day he stripped in order to have a shower and returned to the bedroom to find that his clothes, clean that day, had already been removed for another washing. After that they agreed that he would put all dirty clothes in the laundry basket and that Sarah would not wash any not in the basket.

At first he tried to cause as little work as possible but he soon found

71

that this increased her anxiety. She became puzzled, then bored and after a while started on unnecessary reorganisations of the kitchen. Used to looking after families, she felt that she was not doing her job properly unless there were always more things to be done. Patrick next tried to create as much work as possible. He took his meals in solitary state at the head of the highly polished dining-room table, his tea and coffee on the veranda or in the sitting-room. He left everything where he had put it down and cleared up nothing. He even took to smoking the occasional cigar, without much pleasure, so that she would have ashtrays to clean. He encouraged Snap to roll on the sitting-room carpet.

The tactic worked in that Sarah was busier and so more cheerful than before but it was nothing like enough. It crossed his mind to import some children for one or two days a week. The young Steggleses were not a good idea, with Sandy in her present mood, but perhaps Joanna could be persuaded to lend her daughter and thus make herself more available.

However, the announcement of a visit by Miss Teale, the administration officer, caused Sarah days of real worry. Miss Teale was to check the inventory. Embassy possessions, Arthur Whelk's and Patrick's, had all to be identified. Miss Teale would also comment on the state of the house. Sarah feared her and, despite Patrick's reassurances, spent hours checking and rechecking.

In the event Miss Teale had no comments to make on the state of the house and reserved for Patrick her dissatisfaction with the inventory. She spoke with sharp displeasure. Her sagging cheeks wobbled.

"It's quite the wrong house for your grade, as I've told you before. The inventory is a hopeless mess with all these comings and goings. Just look at it. How am I supposed to keep track of the items when the people themselves disappear?" She pointed at the large double bed in Patrick's bedroom. "That will have to go to start with. As a single person you're not entitled to a double bed. Unless you find a wife to put in it – one of your own, I mean." She looked tartly at him.

Perhaps Sandy had been giving people the impression that they were having an affair. He ignored the remark. "Supposing I were married but unaccompanied?"

"Only if your wife were coming to join you. And I can't imagine your being in that position."

It was some time before he realised that Miss Teale was not naturally or even personally unpleasant. She was as she was partly because she had been left behind by those who had enjoyed her, and wanted to no longer, and partly because she had to administer the domestic detail of other people's lives. For this she was unthanked, resented and sometimes abused. Patrick gave vent only to his curiosity. "How was it that Arthur Whelk, a bachelor, had a double bed?"

"Mr Whelk was not a bachelor. He had a wife who was coming to join him."

Patrick knew there was no wife recorded under Whelk in the ubiquitous Green Book which adorned every office. It listed all British diplomats, their wives, offspring and professional records, like a stud-book. Also, Mr Formerly had said there was no family. "Was she always coming to join him? I mean, did anyone ever meet her?"

Miss Teale looked down at her clipboard. "What Mr Whelk did with himself is none of my business. He assured me he was married and that his wife was to join him from Tunbridge Wells as soon as her ailing mother died. That was enough for me. Mr Whelk was – is, because I'm sure he still is, you know – a gentleman. I wish you'd met him."

As they left the bedroom she handed him a PSA booklet entitled *Guide to the Care of Official Furniture*. Illustrated by cartoons, it gave instructions on how to install, fit and maintain such items as curtains, pelmets, loose covers, divans, rugs and underlays. There was an appendix on how to remove stains.

"And you know all about locking the rape-gate," she added, pointing at it.

He had not heard it called that before. It was a solid iron grill, painted cream, like those that protect secure areas in banks. It spanned the landing at the top of the stairs and reached from floor to ceiling. The part by the stairs was a gate and could be locked by a heavy iron key.

"You do understand," continued Miss Teale, "that the PSA pay to have these installed as a protection against theft of government property, not as protection for you. If you don't lock it at night you're not insured – as well as being more at risk yourself, but that's by the by – so if you take my advice you will. The only other thing is your car and your heavy baggage." She leafed through her notes. "Yes, here we are, they're either still at Tilbury or they're on their way to Oslo. There's been a mistake. It doesn't much matter either way because it'll be some time before we hear anything more. The ship they were meant to be on is halfway here now. Sign here for the inventory, please."

After this visit he locked the rape-gate at night. He did not want to because it seemed cowardly, especially as Sarah was outside it. She had several times mentioned the legendary brutality and ruthlessness of 'black men thiefs' and was visibly relieved that Patrick at least was safe. As when any emotion came upon her, her English deteriorated.

"I am pleased you lock the gate, massa," she said. "It feel better now."

"Only for me, surely, Sarah. You're outside the gate."

She shook her head. "But I worry. Now I stop worrying. Anyway, there is Snap. Also, Mr Whelk keep a big gun in the cupboard."

"Where? Which cupboard?"

"A cupboard in the bedroom which he always lock."

"Show me." There were thirty-seven fitted cupboards, wardrobes and drawers in the master bedroom. The locked one was unlocked and empty. There were no guns in any of the others but beneath the bed there was a truncheon of a sort commonly sold in hardware shops. "Did Mr Whelk ever use this?"

"Sometimes he take it to the embassy."

"What for?"

"For the difficult people, he say."

"For Miss Teale?"

Sarah shook her white apron as though she were fanning a fire, dabbed at her eyes with a corner of it, then walked away, shaking her head and muttering, "Oh, massa, massa."

It was not difficult to get used to being waited upon. Although his conscience was not seriously troubled, Patrick tried daily to remind himself that he should not be seduced into accepting this as the natural order of things. It was simply that being brought tea in bed in the morning was so natural and pleasant a way to start, or delay starting, the day. Everything else followed from that.

After the locking of the rape-gate, though, tea could no longer be delivered to his bedside since the one key to the gate had naturally to be kept out of reach of it. Sarah woke him by rattling the gate and would leave the tray on the topmost stair. Summoned like a zoo animal by the noise of the bucket banging against its cage, he would creep from his room, unlock the gate and take the tea back to bed. Snap became more friendly and would often venture up the forbidden stairs to beg a biscuit. Sometimes, as a sign of growing affection, he brought with him a dead mouse or vole.

Whilst sipping his tea Patrick would listen on the radio to the Lower African version of the news. Though he had never before lived where there was censorship it was not this that most struck him. More noticeable was the provinciality. This showed itself in a detailed concern for local events and people and in a selective interest in world events. Although they were taken seriously they were reported as though they were happening so far away that they could not possibly affect Lower Africa. This gave the impression that everything important happened somewhere else, a distancing effect heightened by the 1950s BBC tone of the announcements. At the end of the news there was a commentary on some aspect of it. This was never attributed but appeared to be the Lower African Government's view on how the chosen item should be regarded. Often it was the weather forecast, though, that was most interesting. Here Patrick learned that to be drenched referred not to rain but to sun and that 'good rain' falling, itself a newsworthy item, was a matter for prayer, hope and gratitude.

Patrick wanted to ring Joanna but was afraid of appearing too keen, though he sensed that his enthusiasm must be obvious. It was in any case difficult to ring from the embassy because Philip Longhurst never left the office. He was there when Patrick arrived, ate sandwiches for lunch and was there when Patrick left. Barricaded behind files, he never ceased from writing, though something about the angle of Philip's head, an ostentatious concentration, made Patrick suspect that his every word and movement were observed. Occasional wry comments that Philip made about people who rang confirmed this impression. He did not want to be heard talking to Joanna by anyone who knew Jim.

He finally rang her on the Saturday morning after the move. He had a confused conversation with her maid which began with the maid's thinking that he was Jim Rissik and ended with her repeating, "Madam will come back on Saturday."

About ten minutes later the telephone rang. He picked it up eagerly but it was a woman asking for Sarah. Sarah spoke for some minutes in Swahi. Her plump face unusually solemn, she then thanked Patrick rather formally and went back to her quarters.

After that he played with Snap, looked at the prices of second-hand cars in the local papers and sorted through Arthur Whelk's books before finally settling down with Clive Barry's *Crumb Borne*. Sarah reappeared but did not cheer up. When she served lunch at the head of the polished table he asked her whether all was well.

She nodded solemnly. "Thank you, massa, everything is well."

He did not know whether she took such enquiries as an unpardonable intrusion or whether she regarded them as one of his rights as master. When she brought him his coffee in the sitting-room he asked her again, referring to the telephone call. She stood holding the empty tray before her, her head bowed.

"You must tell me if there's anything wrong, Sarah," he said.

Her eyes were dull. "Massa, my son is a bad boy."

"I didn't know you had a son."

"His name is Stanley."

"What has he done?"

"He has gone from home again." She paused, assuming Patrick knew she had a home and where it was. He had to ask. "In Swahiland. He live with my sisters and my daughters."

"Where do you think he's gone?"

"Maybe he come here. It is not permitted. He has no permit for here. If the police catch him he will go to prison. He come once before when Mr Whelk was here."

"What did Mr Whelk do?"

"He send him home."

Patrick imagined himself and Stanley being arrested by Jim Rissik as Joanna arrived for lunch. "How old is Stanley?"

"He is fifteen."

She was waiting to be told what to do. He tried to think of something useful. "Well, let me know if he arrives and we'll find a way to get him home again," he said with an attempt at cheerful confidence.

Her eyes brightened. "Yes, massa, thank you, massa. I tell you right away." She went out swinging the tray.

The weekend stretched ahead, empty and threatening. There was nothing he had to do and little enough that he could. Without a car he could not explore the city, apart from the area where he lived. Even there he could not, apparently, take Snap for a walk. Snap had neither collar nor lead and so far as Sarah knew had never been for a walk. She was puzzled by the suggestion and did not at first understand what Patrick meant. Snap lived in the house and garden, which he guarded. He knew nothing else; nothing else was necessary. Patrick postponed the walk but resolved to buy collar and lead.

The only thing he wanted to do was ring Joanna again but the farther into the weekend he left it the more likely, he thought, that Jim would be there. However, knowing that he would definitely ring some time gave purpose and tension to the weekend, if not content. During the evening he would write to his mother and the following morning to Rachel and Maurice. He was not used to spending time alone and remembered with something approaching alarm that Sunday was Sarah's day off.

Dinner was a meal which she had not yet learnt to scale down to the needs of one person. Snap had been trained not to expect food from the table but soon discovered that he could with advantage steal into the dining-room when Patrick was alone. Replete and heavy, as well as a little guilty at the amount he had given Snap, Patrick tried that night to help with the washing-up. He did it really because he wanted to talk rather than because he expected her to let him help, but nevertheless was surprised by the vehemence of her opposition. She was at first uncomprehending, then offended, almost angry, then embarrassed.

"Please, massa, no, please, no," she said, holding up her hands as if to prevent him from hurling himself into the sink. "I can do it. I can do all for you. There is little and it is done. Please."

Patrick desisted and asked instead about Arthur Whelk's catering arrangements. Looking after Arthur was apparently very much like looking after a family. There were many guests who ate and drank much and played cards. Sometimes they would stay all night. Before Arthur, she had always looked after families. He asked how many children of her own she had.

"I have three children, a son and two daughters. Also, three who die when they are young." She nodded and smiled. The elder girl was twenty and worked in the post office in Swahiland, a good job. There was a young man who wanted to marry her but Sarah did not like him. "Many young people are not good now. They want bad things and not work." Stanley, the missing son, had just left school and she did not know what to do with him. He was always a worry. The younger daughter was very young.

"How young?"

She gave an embarrassed smile then suddenly giggled and hid her face in her apron. "Massa, I cannot say."

Patrick laughed. "Three years?"

She shook her head.

"Two?"

She lowered her apron, trying to compose her face. "Massa, I am so ashamed by that. I am too old for piccaninny."

"How old are you?"

"I don't know, massa, I don't know. My mother tell me but it is so long ago and I forget."

"Not too old, anyway."

"I was very surprised," she said, dabbing at her eyes.

She laid the table for breakfast, refusing without offence this time his half-hearted offer of assistance and talked cheerfully about herself.

77

She had been born and bred in Swahiland and had spent all of her working life in service. She had worked for one family for twenty years – "until the madam kill herself with a gun in the summer house" – and now went to the weddings of the children she had helped bring up. The same madam, the one who had shot herself, had bought her a plot of land in Swahiland and had paid for the house to be built. That was where her children lived, brought up by aunts and neighbours.

"Don't you mind not seeing them?"

"Twice a year I go home."

"Do you mind seeing them so little?"

"It is normal for us. The women must work and so the children are with the old aunts and the neighbours."

"But what do the men do?"

She shrugged and smiled. "If they must work they go away to the mines or the city. If they are not away they talk and eat and drink and talk, always they talk. They do not work in the fields like the women. That is not for men."

"Do they help bring up the children?"

She laughed. "Oh no, no."

In the second family she worked for the madam suddenly returned to England, leaving the husband with a girl of three and a baby boy of six months. She remained with them for four years until the man remarried and reared the baby herself.

"That was heavy pull, massa," she said, shaking her head slowly and grinning. "That piccaninny was heavy pull. But now he is fine boy."

For the first time in his life Patrick could afford to take wine with his meals. He soon found that he took it before and after his meals, too. Following his conversation with Sarah on the Saturday night he had another glass, then another, and then felt bold enough to ring Joanna again. He knew whilst dialling that Saturday night was probably the worst time: she would either be out with Jim or in with Jim, but he dialled nonetheless.

It was she who answered. When he said who he was she said "Yes" sharply as if he should have known it was obvious. He asked if she would like lunch some time and she again simply said, "Yes." He began to suggest dates but she cut him short with, "It's difficult at the moment." When he asked if he should ring back she said, "It's just a bit difficult at the moment." He asked if he should ring the following day and she said, "Yes."

78

He put down the phone and poured another glass, feeling drunk and miserable and farther than ever from recalling the reason why it seemed so important to ring her there and then.

On the Sunday morning Sarah went to church with two other women of about her own age. They all wore black skirts, stockings and shoes, red long-sleeved blouses with wide white collars, like a sailor's, and round white hats. They each carried a bible.

The day stretched ahead but he was not now depressed by it. Some time he would ring Joanna and whether that brought good news or bad was, as regards coping with the time on his hands, immaterial. It was as if he had to go and fight at a moment of his own choosing; for the time being he was content to keep the event in the future. There had been no frost and the day was warm and bright, the blue sky vivid and exhilarating. He sat reading on the veranda and occasionally patrolled the garden wall with Snap. Once or twice he netted leaves that had fallen into the pool. Already, after only a few days of his tenure, it was not quite the colour it should have been. He decided to put off vacuum-cleaning or adding more chemicals until he could see which colour it was becoming.

Sarah returned from church before lunch which she ate in her quarters whilst he laboured over a tin of soup. After lunch she slept, as did he, but after that she came to him on the veranda. She still wore her church uniform and carried her bible. He thought for a moment that he was to be subjected to a conversion attempt or ticked off for not having been to church.

"Are you going to church again, Sarah?"

"Yes, massa, and again this evening."

She looked solemn. He waited for the criticism.

"Massa, I have a man called Harold."

He nodded, waiting for more. She waited for him. "Your husband?"

"He is" – she moved her shoulders awkwardly without taking her eyes from him – "the father of my children."

"Ah, yes. And his name is Harold."

"Yes, massa." She became more confident and went on to explain that although Harold worked in a Battenburg mental hospital he was not allowed to spend the night with her because he had no permit to stay in the northern suburbs. She had no permit to stay in his area. With repeated promises of discretion, she asked if he could surreptitiously spend the occasional night with her. He was a quiet man, not drunk, and would leave his car round the back of the garage and out of sight from the road. Mr Whelk had allowed him to do that.

Patrick agreed. She clasped her bible in both hands and thanked him effusively.

He invited her to sit. After a brief hesitation she sat carefully on the edge of one of the wickerwork chairs. "Do you think it is bad that you can't spend the night together whenever you like?" he asked.

She frowned. "Bad, massa?"

"Wrong, not right. Do you dislike it?"

She opened her eyes wide. "No, no, not bad. To be every night with a man, that is bad. When you are young maybe is all right but when you are older" – she closed her eyes and shook her head, smiling – "when you are older once every two, three weeks maybe is enough. Anyway, he is a lazy man. Every time I have to do his washing and he never go to church, never."

"Do you ask him to go?"

"Yes, but he sleep, always he sleep. He say he is too tired and will go next week. He is lazy man."

She laughed and he noticed for the first time that one of her teeth was missing. He could not understand how he had not noticed it before and thereafter never saw her laugh without wondering how he could have missed it. She went to church that afternoon and went again, as she had said, that evening.

It was also evening when he rang Joanna, his now customary glass of wine by the telephone. She sounded friendly and relaxed and began by apologising. Jim was there when he rang before. They were having a sort of row and it was a bit awkward. Patrick apologised without meaning it and, encouraged by her manner, suggested dinner rather than lunch. She agreed.

"Did Jim know it was me?" he asked.

"Yes. Well, he asked who it was and I told him."

"Did he mind?"

"I don't know. He didn't say much. Perhaps he did. I was just glad of the silence." She laughed and he imagined her turning her head and pushing back her hair.

He put the phone down, his feet up and poured himself another glass. With effortless accuracy he tossed the empty bottle into the wastepaper basket and described Joanna to Snap.

8

The telegram was addressed to the British Ambassador and marked Personal. It read: FUNDS LOW STOP NO COMMS LONDON STOP SEND MONEY HOTEL STOP PROGRESS SOON STOP MACKENZIE END. It had been sent from a well-known hotel on the coast. Sir Wilfrid pushed it into Patrick's hand as staff gathered for the ambassador's weekly meeting.

"Come to my room afterwards," he murmured.

During the meeting Sir Wilfrid sat at the head of a long table with everyone else ranged along it in order of consequence. There was an empty place next to him where the counsellor, who was on mid-tour leave, normally sat. On the other side and slightly lower was Clifford, next to him Philip. Opposite Philip sat the defence attaché and next to him the commercial officer. At the far end of the table there was a silent jockeying for position between the security officer, the senior registry clerk, Miss Teale, the press officer and the commercial officer's assistant. The British Council representative who was always invited through either courtesy or habit sat on a chair at one side as if to preserve his political virginity. Patrick sat next to Philip.

Sir Wilfrid wore a baggy tweed suit with a large red handkerchief billowing from the top pocket and breadcrumbs on the waistcoat. He smoked a curved pipe which would not stay lit and he had a new pipe stem behind his left ear. His manner was businesslike, almost tetchy.

"Expenses and allowances," he said. "Inspectors are coming, as you know. Looks like allowances will be cut." There was a perceptible stiffening around the table. Sir Wilfrid paused, put his forefinger inside his collar and looked up at the ceiling. "Heard from poor old Joe Slingsby in Tripoli. Anyone know him? Married one of the Dalton girls – Lord Dalton's. Went all wrong years ago, of course. Then married his secretary like everyone else." He pulled his finger out of his collar and examined it. "Point is, he's had the inspectors at Tripoli and there and elsewhere they've cut both allowances and establishment. I reckon they'll do the same here."

Most people stared at their notepads. Someone dropped a pencil.

"How big a cut, sir?" asked Clifford.

"About twenty-five per cent, according to old Joe."

It was as though it had been announced that twenty-five per cent of staff were to be shot. Sir Wilfrid dug into his pipe with his knife, manifesting an unconcern so obvious as to suggest he was in fact relishing the effect of his words.

Philip leaned forward. "Surely, sir, across-the-board reductions on such a scale are inapplicable here?"

"Don't see why. Our allowances are probably too high, anyway. After all, they're supposed to compensate for being abroad and to enable us to live at a properly representational standard, nothing more. We're not meant to make money out of them though people do, of course. I worked for an ambassador once who banked his entire salary and his entire ambassador's fund, which was as much again and tax-free. He never entertained anyone to more than one glass of sherry. Bloody awful stuff that was, too. Also, this isn't exactly a hardship post. We're not like those poor devils in Angola, scratching around for a bit of cabbage leaf to see them through the day." He knocked out the scrapings from his pipe, carefully closed the knife and began to refill. "Next, the forthcoming visit by our junior minister. Is that in hand, Clifford?"

Clifford was making calculations on his notepad. "Ah, yes, sir. All in order. I'm finalising the plans. It's going to be quite a fuss, this one." He laughed.

"Of course it's going to be a fuss. He's a minister."

Clifford laughed again and nodded. "Exactly. I'll get Patrick to help with the final stages." He looked significantly at Patrick, who was surreptitiously rereading the telegram.

"Patrick has other business, don't forget," Sir Wilfrid replied in a tone that was probably meant to be discreet but which sounded sinister and caused everyone to stare.

"Is the ministerial visit before or after the inspectors, sir?" asked the commercial officer.

"Before. No good looking to him for help. He's only a junior minister. It's nothing to do with him." He relit his pipe, waving away the smoke with wide sweeps of his arm. "We'll discuss the visit nearer the time when I've seen your proposals, Clifford. Now, what about these riots down south?"

There was some uneasy shuffling. Clifford leant forward, his expression pregnant with news. "Up to a thousand rioters. Two dead and a number injured. It's all quiet now. It was on the radio this morning."

"Yes," said Sir Wilfrid mildly. "It was in the papers, too. That's how we know about it. But London will expect us to have an opinion. We have to decide now what it should be."

There was a pause. The main effect of the rioting, so far as the embassy was concerned, was that it generated paper. Various opinions were put forward as to the cause of the riot, including the unusually warm weather in the south, the unpopular increase in bus fares and the extent to which terrorists had infiltrated Lower Africa. The fares issue was thought to be the most important.

Sir Wilfrid nodded. "Yes, that's what the papers say and they're often right. But of course people in London may question whether they want to maintain an embassy just to tell them what they can read in their papers on the way to work. They may expect their embassy to contribute more than that, though sadly I doubt it. But that's by the by. It shouldn't stop us from trying."

He spoke crisply. The faces round the table were puzzled and fearful. Philip leant forward and tentatively scratched his right ankle, usually a sign that he was about to speak.

"The radio also said that hand grenades had been found in a servant's quarters in the northern suburbs," he said.

"Indeed it did, Philip. I listen to the radio too. But if we're going to say anything about it we should try to assess whether, for instance, this was an isolated incident or whether it might be part of a campaign to radicalise the domestics in the northern suburbs." There was a little awkward laughter. Sir Wilfrid looked at them all. "Well, has anyone any suggestions?"

The security officer, seated at the bottom of the table and generally ignored because he dealt with security, cleared his throat and began to speak in a quiet Midlands accent. He mentioned the forthcoming trial of some terrorists who had attacked a police station. If they were sentenced to death as was expected there could be widespread trouble. Grenades could indicate preparation for trouble, just as the finding of them might indicate pre-emptive action by the police. Whatever the present cause of the riots, if they continued until the trial they would inevitably become associated with it and might lead to further disorders.

He spoke slowly, with several nervous glances at the ambassador. When he finished Sir Wilfrid took his pipe from his mouth. "Thank you, Bernard, that was an excellent suggestion and the first this morning not to have appeared in the press. It may soon do so and thus I

83

think an early telegram to London today is called for – will you draft something, Clifford, and let me see it before it goes?"

"Right, sir." Clifford nodded and looked at Philip, who nodded bleakly, moving his lips as he made notes on his pad.

"Good," continued Sir Wilfrid. "Any other business?"

Harry White, the commercial officer, pulled up his chair and read a report of a visit he had made to a machine tool factory, the manager of which had said that he would have bought British rather than German and Japanese machinery had it been less expensive, delivered on time, more reliable and easier to service. Harry was an earnest man who the previous year had had printed two thousand copies of a twenty-page document entitled, 'Redistribution of Greater London Industrial and Office Employment during the past Ten Years'. The blank sides were now used, without his knowledge, as rough drafting paper in chancery. Philip had said that the paper was in fact rather well written but he was the only person who had bothered to read it. When Harry finished reading his report everyone nodded sagely and the ambassador thanked him.

After the meeting Clifford asked Sir Wilfrid if they could have a word about the British-Lower African Trade Association lunch at which Sir Wilfrid was to speak. The ambassador nodded and said, "Patrick, come into my office. Time we got cracking."

Patrick followed, feeling Clifford's glance at his back. He closed the door as Sir Wilfrid rooted noisily among the pipes in the grandfather clock. "God, these meetings drive me mad. I hope you'll be spared them by the time you get to my position though frankly I doubt it. Mind you, there might not be a Foreign Office by then because someone one day will wake up to the fact that if you don't have an aggressive foreign policy you don't need a large foreign service. Cut your overseas representation and leave just enough to handle consular matters and to transmit dictats from London. They'll say that's all we'll need and they'll be right. It could so easily be otherwise, that's the tragedy of it. The machine is excellent but there's no one to make it work. We need heart, belief, will." He came away from the clock with a well-chewed pipe and changed the mouthpiece for the one behind his ear. His eyes were hard with conviction.

"D'you think I'm mad?"

"No, sir."

He smiled suddenly and his gaze softened. "I bet you do but I'll go on. You see, I think we are the tentacles of the octopus, London, but the heart of the octopus isn't pumping out enough blood any more and we are going to die. D'you see what I mean? One day we'll wither and drop off. Of course, I shouldn't be talking to you like this, a young man at the start of your career, but one has to let off steam sometimes." He threw the discarded mouthpiece back into the clock, then faced Patrick, his hands in his jacket pockets. "Now: Whelk."

He was in no doubt that the telegram was from the L and F man, though MacKenzie was not a name he recalled. It didn't matter because it could only have come from him. Mind you, he shouldn't have sent it because the Lower African authorities were likely to get on to it. They might think it odd and so sniff him out. Embarrassment all round, accusations about British spies and so on. Fortunately the minister approved – which was about the only good thing one could say about this minister – and so the mud would be spread widely and thinly. The point was that the poor chap must be desperate to have done this. He must really need money and was clearly out of touch with his own people in London. Equally clearly, he was on to something. It would be asking for trouble, foolhardy, for the embassy to send him anything, nor could he himself, for the same reason. That left Patrick: could he see his way to forwarding something from his own account to tide the chap over? He would get it back all right – that was guaranteed.

Patrick did not know how much he had but assumed he could afford it. Sir Wilfrid, pleased, then suggested he should visit "our friend Inspector Rissik" before doing so, partly to see if Rissik dropped any hints about knowing what was going on – in which case, better not send the money – and partly because it was high time Patrick got on with the official liaison anyway.

Patrick agreed, although he wanted to avoid Jim Rissik almost as much as he wanted to see Joanna. Clifford tried to prevent him going by claiming there was important work in chancery for him that day. Patrick would happily have done it if Clifford had been prepared to argue with the ambassador, which he was not. He was in fact interested to try some political reporting since it was supposed to be one half of his job. He did not, of course, know what he would have reported and was already beginning to suspect that the amount of original political thought, insight or opinion was so small that it had to be jealously guarded.

"Don't be more than an hour," said Clifford crossly. "We've got to talk about the arrangements for the ministerial visit. You'll probably have to work through lunch."

85

Patrick nodded obediently. "When is the visit?"

"No date's been fixed. That's why we have to be on our toes, in case they spring an early one on us. Can't have people swanning off all over the city. One hour, remember."

Clifford spoke in the tone he used when he was annoyed with Sandy. Patrick felt less obedient. He nearly asked if they could synchronise watches but thought of Sandy and the bath, and minded Clifford less.

The police headquarters was a twenty-two storey building near the city centre. It was notorious because of the number of people alleged to have fallen or thrown themselves from twelfth-floor windows whilst assisting the police with their enquiries. Others had hanged themselves in their cells.

It was like the headquarters of a large company but rather easier of access. A young white policeman behind a desk in the spacious entrance hall gave curt and monosyllabic directions to the sixth floor. Patrick walked unescorted and unchallenged through clean bare corridors but there was no sign of Jim's department. All the office doors were unmarked and the rooms empty. He met a woman with dyed black hair and a well-formed face. Her skin was hard and wrinkled.

"Jesus, what a bloody place," she said. "I've come to see about my driving licence. D'you know where that bit is?"

They had each been directed by the dour policeman. She glanced irritably up and down the corridor. "It's these bloody old Lower Africans. They're carved out of the veldt. The Police Force is stuffed with them, and the Civil Service. That's what's wrong with this country. Lot of boneheads in charge."

In the next corridor they found a helpful black man with a mop and pail who told them that they should be on the sixth floor of B block, not A block.

On the way out Patrick said to the young policeman, "The floor was right but the building was wrong."

The policeman looked up from the booklet he was reading. "What?"

"You should have directed us to the sixth floor of B block."

"Yes."

"Boneheads, carved out of rock," said the woman.

The policeman stared and then continued reading.

In Jim Rissik's outer office there were two more young white

86

policemen, no older than Patrick. They were smart and looked fit but their eyes and mouths were sullen. When he asked to see Jim one of them told him he would have to wait and pointed to a chair. He explained that he had tried to ring and make an appointment but the line had been continuously engaged. The policeman pointed again to a chair. When Patrick said he was from the British embassy the other got up slowly, knocked on Jim's door and went in.

Jim came out with his hand outstretched. His naturally strong and regular good looks were enhanced by his uniform. He looked spruce, competent, confident and friendly.

"I'm glad you came. I wanted to get in touch with you anyway. It's time we had a talk. Maybe we should make it lunch next time." He smiled.

They went into his office, and were soon talking about Philip's party. "I still haven't got over that," said Jim. "It just about burned me out. Joanna coped with it better than I did. Maybe I've seen too many diplomatic functions. I mean, what was Longhurst trying to do? What does he think we are, for Christ's sake? I mean, what do you dips think we're like if that's what you think we like?" He laughed, picked up the phone and ordered coffee.

References to Joanna made Patrick uncomfortable. After a few more remarks about the party he raised the subject of Whelk. Jim went to a combination-locked cupboard and took out a blue folder.

"I keep all my dip files right here. Pretty undiplomatic crowd they are too, some of your colleagues – in other embassies, of course. The British are pure as the driven snow." He grinned and dumped the file heavily on the desk. "All I have are the basic details, which you know. One day Arthur Whelk, British Embassy consul, didn't turn up to work. He left the house at the usual time and did not reappear. The evening before he had spent in and the afternoon before that he had been prison-visiting. Checked in and out, no trouble there. If it was an accident or amnesia we'd expect something of him to turn up some-where, or at least his car. If he'd been murdered, reasons unknown, we'd still expect to find something. As for your ambassador's kidnap-ping theory – he's been going on about that ever since it happened, hasn't he? – well, where's the ransom demand or the blackmail? My guess is your Arthur's done a bunk, found himself a wealthy widow and a new life." He let the file fall closed.

"Surely he'd have resigned?"

Jim shrugged. "People do funny things sometimes."

"Perhaps he was running away from something."

"From what?" There was a slight edge to Jim's voice. This time it was Patrick that shrugged. "Are you taking over his duties?"

"Partly, until something permanent is sorted out."

"But not his hobbies?"

"Hobbies?"

"Playing, you know. He liked to play a little, your Arthur."

"Playing?" It was only when Jim smiled at what he took for disingenuousness that Patrick realised he meant gambling, which was illegal in Lower Africa. He then remembered that Sarah had mentioned that Arthur played cards but he didn't want to involve her. He said nothing about the gun that Arthur had apparently kept.

"I didn't know he played."

Jim's brown eyes were warm and friendly. "How is Miss Msobu?"

"Miss Msobu?"

"Sarah, your maid. Don't you even know her name? You should, you know. She has to be registered annually with the Native Administration Board. Don't trust the embassy to do that for you. If they can't keep track of their own diplomats I wouldn't put money on the state of their records of domestics."

"We have a lady called Miss Teale who administers constantly. I'd put money on her having done it." Jim's manner when he had asked about Sarah had been smug, as if he were flaunting his knowledge of her. "D'you know Sarah well?" Patrick asked.

"It's my job to keep an eye on all you people, you and your premises. To keep you safe. She's a good maid, isn't she? Let me know if you ever want to get rid of her. I could easily find her a place."

Patrick tried to get Jim to talk more about his job but Jim took his questions as applying to promotion prospects. "If I'm really going to go places I have to do two things," he said, leaning back in his chair and holding a red pencil delicately upright between his thumb and forefinger. "I have to go on from this to a good stint on counter-terrorism which is the growth area now and then I have to do another crime job in a senior position. That way you get known. Then you just have to make sure your face keeps fitting." He laughed. "I'm not really very ambitious, though. I'm not stupid but I do stupid things. If I like a job I stick with it even if it's a no-no. I've never done a job I didn't like just to get on. I'd rather sweep the streets, so long as I liked it. You ambitious?"

Patrick thought for a moment. He had never asked himself the question. "Not yet."

"Still playing around, eh?" Jim flicked the pencil on to the desk and stood abruptly.

Back in the outer office a black man and an Indian lawyer were arguing with one of the taciturn policemen about whether or not something had been delivered. Jim put his hand on Patrick's arm. "If you're looking for somewhere to have dinner," he said pleasantly, "try the roof restaurant of the Lion Hotel. It's in the Battenburg Centre near where you work and it overlooks the whole city. Try it."

"I shall."

Jim clapped him on the shoulder. "Do that."

When Patrick arrived back he found that Clifford, far from being annoyed that he had been away nearly two hours, was affably concerned.

"Everything go all right?" he asked in an undertone.

"I think so, yes. We're none the wiser, though."

"Shouldn't worry about that. Just keep plugging away, that's the thing. HE wants you."

He later discovered that whilst he was out Sir Wilfrid had thanked Clifford for the help and supervision in the matter of Whelk that he assumed Clifford was giving Patrick. Henceforth Clifford was in Sir Wilfrid's eyes joint beneficiary with Patrick in any credit due, and so Clifford was generally content.

When Patrick went in to report to Sir Wilfrid his opening remarks were halted by the ambassador holding up his hand. Sir Wilfrid then tiptoed with elaborate caution across the carpet, took a transistor radio from the bookcase, lowered it carefully on to his desk and turned it on full volume to a pop music station. He put two chairs alongside the desk and beckoned Patrick to sit. They faced each other with the radio blaring between them.

Sir Wilfrid cupped his hand to his mouth and shouted. Patrick put his hand to his ear. Sir Wilfrid shouted again and Patrick made out the word 'microphone'. He went to turn the radio down but Sir Wilfrid pushed his hand away and moved closer so that their knees were touching. He bellowed directly and wetly into Patrick's ear.

The gist of what he shouted, rendered yet less comprehensible by the obscure telegraphese that he adopted, was that he was worried that his room might have been bugged by LASS. Therefore when discussing the L and F man they should have the radio on to cover what they were saying. It did not matter that they had previously discussed the subject without the radio because past lapses did not excuse present.

Patrick gave a staccato account of his meeting with Jim. Sir Wilfrid did not know that Whelk had gambled, a serious matter. Had he been running an illegal casino? Was he the victim of gang warfare? The fact that the police knew about it merely increased his suspicions that they knew more than they were letting on. It was just as well that the L and F man was 'playing it long'. This last phrase had to be repeated to Patrick several times.

Jean, Sir Wilfrid's secretary, came into the room. She stopped when she saw the two men sitting knee to knee before the radio. Sir Wilfrid waved her away with a sweep of his arm. Thereafter she treated Patrick with frosty politeness.

Those of Whelk's consular duties that Patrick had to assume were light. He did not understand them and neither did anyone else in chancery – at least, no one admitted to any knowledge. It was soon clear that consular matters, like trade and foreigners, were the sort that some chancery officials did not wish to understand.

He relied entirely upon Daphne, Whelk's conscientious spinster assistant. She was plump, middle-aged and bespectacled, with a round mouth that was never still. She appeared to be a friend of Miss Teale's, in that they went about together, although Miss Teale constantly complained behind Daphne's back about her being neurotic, not up to her responsibilities and a burden. Patrick found her quietly, almost formidably competent. He authorised what she told him to authorise, signed where she said. She was fully capable of running the consular department herself but was not allowed to because of her grade. She had no prospect of promotion because she was too near retirement. She did not respond to any of Patrick's remarks about Arthur except once, when she said that whatever had happened to him she was sure he would be all right.

"He may have run off and got married," she said. "It'll be something like that. There'll be a reason behind it, whatever it is."

"Someone said he was married already to a lady in Tunbridge Wells."

She shook her head. "He had a wife in Bangkok but that was a local matter. I believe he sold her."

"To whom?"

"The man who bought his car."

Daphne had the manner of one who could be surprised by nothing, acquired perhaps through years of dealing with British subjects. The only area about which she briefed Patrick in detail was on his responsibility for DBSs – Distressed British Subjects. They were to be found in all countries that admitted British nationals. Mostly they were holiday-makers who had lost their passports and money, or were ill. Some were people who had settled locally and then had family problems in Britain. A few were deportees. Another, fortunately small, class was formed by those who were British by birth and who lived abroad not very successfully. They were usually convinced that the British govern-ment owed them lifelong assistance in whatever form they wanted. They were easily the most troublesome group.

"Nevertheless, the ambassador is very keen that all British subjects who come to us should get a fair deal," Daphne explained. "Arthur was rather sharp with them but I don't think the ambassador knew that. You have to be particularly careful with DBSs because if things go wrong there they go dramatically wrong and you get the newspapers involved. Then everyone's up in arms and we always get the blame, rightly or wrongly."

After his visit to Jim Rissik Patrick's reading of the monthly digest of Lower African trade figures was interrupted by the sharp tap of Daphne's footsteps in the corridor. Her worried face showed round the door.

"McGrain," she said urgently.

Patrick thought he knew the name. He tried to pretend he wasn't at a loss.

"In one of his states," continued Daphne. "He's got young Cather-ine by the wrist. You'd better come quickly."

He joined her in the corridor.

"Our most troublesome DBS, I told you about him," she said as she clicked along. "An awful drunkard who comes to the embassy de-manding money and support and makes scenes if he doesn't get in. You know, molests the girls, starts fights, all that sort of thing. Violent man. Every post has one."

"Starts fights?"

"Yes, and swears dreadfully, it really is quite shocking. Upsetting for the girls. He gets in because he has the right to come to the consular department and the ambassador won't let us call the police to throw him out because we could then be accused of denying access to British subjects. Anyway, it would set a bad precedent to have police on the premises. Arthur was dead set against it. He said we should keep the police away at all costs. That's why he used to evict McGrain himself. Such a small man, Arthur, and McGrain's so big but I suppose judo helps. Can you do judo?"

"No."

"Never mind, you're young and fit, I daresay."

They walked briskly towards the visa office. Patrick had no idea what to do. He wanted to slow down and discuss the matter but his legs carried him towards the double doors at Daphne's speed. He noticed for the first time the careful workmanship of the panelled walls. He would have liked to discuss that.

"This is the first time he's been since Arthur went," Daphne said. "He really is drunk, though you can never tell what that means. The last few times he went quite peacefully without Arthur's having to use the truncheon. Have you found Arthur's truncheon?"

"Yes, it's at the house." He considered whether he could get away with suggesting he went and got it.

"Oh well, you don't need it really, I'm sure. It's just a frightener. In fact, I've noticed recently that Arthur seemed able to exert some sort of authority over McGrain. It's strange, he just keeps turning up. Is that what you'll do?"

"What?"

"Exert your authority."

"Something like that, I expect, yes."

Daphne nodded. "Good, I was sure you would. That's what I told the visa girls when I said I'd fetch you. It's just as well it's you and not Mr Longhurst. I don't think he'd have been much use, do you?"

Patrick was in no mood to denigrate Philip. He wished it were Philip in his place, or Clifford who at least was stout, if that was a help. His stomach felt light and empty. The double doors were very close now. Daphne's unwarranted confidence did nothing to boost his own.

"We had a man like this in Tripoli. He was called Fraser, another Glaswegian. They nearly always come from Glasgow, I don't know why. He broke the head of chancery's jaw."

She pushed open one of the doors and stepped aside as though Patrick were a bull entering the arena. He felt there was something else he should say to Daphne, even if only goodbye. The door closed behind him.

McGrain was a burly, grizzled, grey-haired, red-faced man. He was leaning across the counter saying something to the frightened girl behind it whose wrist he held. He wore a dirty white shirt which hung loose. His ragged jeans were stretched by his bulging belly and broad haunches. When he moved, the shirt came apart from the jeans which stretched so low across his backside that they exposed the crack between his fleshy white buttocks. He had an old jacket slung over one shoulder. The broad forearm holding the girl was hairy and tattooed.

Three or four visa applicants sat on a bench as far away as possible from McGrain. They looked shamefaced and frightened and at the same time tried to look as if they weren't noticing what was going on. They glanced hopefully at Patrick as he entered. He glanced hopefully back, considering and then dismissing the possibility of assistance. McGrain continued talking to the girl. His thick speech was quiet and incomprehensible.

Patrick walked slowly towards him. The visa girls looked out from behind the screen on the other side of the counter. The captured girl threw him a glance of relief. He had no plan. A surprise attack from behind whilst McGrain was not looking would be best in purely tactical terms but was no doubt the kind of incident that the ambassador was most anxious to avoid. An unprovoked assault upon a British subject by a diplomat paid to help him would be hard to present in a favourable light. More importantly, it might not work. He could easily imagine himself the bloody loser of an unequal contest.

Still without any constructive thought, he tapped McGrain on the back. McGrain gave no sign of having felt anything and continued talking to the girl, who stared with wide eyes from him to Patrick. Patrick put his hand on McGrain's shoulder, recalling the polite but authoritative way in which a policeman had once done it to him when he was trying to start his motor-scooter. McGrain's conversation, which growled like a dredger in an estuary, slowly ceased and he heaved himself awkwardly round, still holding the girl. His unshaven cheeks were red and purple, his blue eyes small and clouded. He said something that might have been, "What do you want?"

"I must ask you to leave the embassy now. We're closing the visa section."

McGrain let go of the girl and Patrick let go of his shoulder: it would be better to have both hands free. The girl ran off holding her wrist. McGrain said something about Mr Whelk.

"Mr Whelk isn't here. I must ask you to leave." Patrick sounded to himself like the caricature of a stiff and embarrassed British official.

"Ah'm no goin' till ah speak wi' Mr Whelk," said McGrain. He turned back to the counter and leant his elbows heavily upon it, adding that he was British, that he knew his rights and would have them.

Everyone looked at Patrick. He tried to imagine what Whelk would have done.

"He owes me money," mumbled McGrain. "Ah'm no goin' till ah have ma money."

"He's not here at the moment."

"Where is he?"

"I'm afraid I don't know."

McGrain nodded towards the screen. "You sure he's no' hidin' in there?"

"Yes, quite sure." He imagined McGrain climbing the counter and tearing down the screen like an enraged bear. "If you have a complaint you could write a letter," he added, not optimistically.

McGrain muttered again, lurched away and walked unsteadily towards the swing doors. Patrick reached them first and held one open for him, a gesture that he hoped would make it appear to McGrain and to the onlookers that everything was under control.

Shambling, smelly and incoherent, McGrain swayed along the corridor. He continued to mutter about Whelk and money but showed no sign of aggression. Patrick now felt bold enough to begin to question him but McGrain stopped and leant against the panelled wall. It opened and he fell through it, sprawling on his back on the concrete floor. Patrick was as surprised as he and looked beyond McGrain to a clean and well-kept gents' lavatory. McGrain growled, swore incomprehensibly and struggled to get up. Patrick bent to help, perhaps making it appear to McGrain that whoever had pushed him down was now following up the attack. He swung his fists wildly. One crashed into the door, making him shout with anger. The other caught Patrick a glancing blow on the right eye. It did not hurt; he had seen it coming and had turned his head away. He stepped out of range and McGrain, ceasing to struggle, lay on his back breathing heavily. Patrick waited a few moments, then stepped cautiously behind McGrain and tried again, talking softly. McGrain grunted and allowed himself to be helped. As they walked slowly down the corridor Patrick noticed the visa girls looking on open-mouthed through the windows in the double doors.

They had to wait at the lifts for some minutes. McGrain was almost comatose. He stood by the opposite wall and stared at it.

When the lift arrived Sir Wilfrid stepped out. "Ah, Patrick – " he began, but stopped on seeing McGrain.

Patrick held the lift door. "That's Mr McGrain, sir, I'm just taking him out."

"Isn't he the DBS?"

"Yes, sir."

94

Sir Wilfrid continued to stare past Patrick. "Who's been looking after him?"

"I have. He hasn't been here long. He's on his way now."

"Are you sure he wants to leave?"

Patrick looked round to see McGrain resting his forehead against the wall and fumbling with his flies. For the first time he regarded him with real hostility. "Yes, sir, he's in a hurry. He's been telling me all about it." He went to McGrain, took him by the shoulders and steered the unresisting figure towards the lift. The door attempted to close but the sudden buffeting aroused him. He shouted, staggered into the lift and swung his fists again. Patrick pushed him further in and closed the door. He pressed the button for the ground floor but saw from the indicator board that the lift stopped at the third, occupied by the city's largest and most fashionable hairdressing salon.

Sir Wilfrid looked on, pulling thoughtfully at his white hair. "Are you really sure he wanted to go?"

Patrick was panting slightly. "Yes, sir. He was a little excited, that's all."

"I've seen him before. Didn't he used to come and see Arthur?"

"He seemed to think that Arthur owed him money."

"I know what that must have been." They walked towards chancery. "Arthur was always terribly good with these DBS chaps. I expect he used to give him some cash when he was hard up and that's why he's come back. Certainly poor Arthur never had any trouble with them. He always knew what to do. It's most important you should, too. We must ensure that any British subject who comes to this embassy leaves it less distressed than when he entered." They waited for the chancery door to be opened. "Something in your eye, Stubbs?"

"No, sir, just a knock."

"Must be more careful. You've only got two, remember." Sir Wilfrid laughed. When he stopped he kept his features still composed for laughter and said in a low urgent voice, "Have you sent that money to the L and F chappie?"

Patrick had forgotten. "Just about to, sir."

"Better get on with it. You never know, he might be in a tight spot. Let me have a note of the amount." He relaxed his features and walked briskly to his office.

From this time on it was believed throughout the embassy that Patrick had fought and overcome McGrain. In the consular department he was accorded more respect than anyone except the ambassador and was remembered for long after he had left as a great liberator, a toppler of tyrants. His own description of what happened was put down to modesty and he soon stopped trying to persuade anyone otherwise. Besides, the slightly swollen eye he was left with was taken as eloquent testimony to the contrary. Whenever he visited the consular department Daphne would bring him tea and cakes.

He later discovered that the gents' lavatory door was unmarked and deliberately concealed so that it would remain known only to embassy staff: it was thought that otherwise it would have been abused every day by waiting visa applicants and loitering DBSs.

Waiting at the bus-stop on the way home that evening Patrick felt for the first time that he was regarded with mute hostility by the black people around him. It was the second occasion he had taken the bus and there had been no queue before. What struck him as hostile was the way they avoided looking at him. When the bus arrived he went to pay his fare but the driver, a big black of middle age, would not take it. He shook his head, said something and pointed at the back of the bus with his thumb. Patrick thought he was meant to pay there but could see no conductor. The passengers, all black, stared in silence.

"Not for white," the driver said, with heavy emphasis.

"Oh, sorry – is there another one for whites?"

The people waiting to pay pushed through and the driver began taking their money. "This bus for black people." He did not look up.

"Yes, I'm sorry." He was unable to get off because of those still getting on. "Could you tell me which is the white bus?"

At first it seemed that the driver was going to make no reply but after taking another fare he pointed again with his thumb. "Back there for white. Next stop."

Patrick thanked him and got off. He noticed then that there was another stop twenty yards or so up the road at which whites were queuing. They had seen him get on the wrong bus and they too avoided looking at him. He learned later that buses were driven by whites or blacks regardless of the colour of the passengers. The way to distinguish was to read the notices in the windscreens which said Whites or Non-Whites.

When the silver BMW drew up at the bus-stop he did not at first recognise the tanned driver with curly brown hair and dark glasses. He thought it was the person next to him who was being addressed in Lower African. It was only when the driver smiled and snapped his fingers for having used the wrong language that he recognised Jim Rissik. He was no longer in uniform.

"I've been arguing in Lower African with my boss," Jim said as they moved slowly into the traffic stream. "It stays with you. What are you doing at a bus-stop? I thought all you embassy guys had your own Mercedes."

"All the British have Fords," said Patrick confidently. He explained his own lack.

"Jesus," said Jim with a dismissive wave of his gloved hand. "No wonder no one buys British any more. You can't even get the stuff here." He put a cassette into the tape-deck. "Who banged your eye?"

"It was an accident."

"The embassy must be a rougher place than I thought. McGrain, I guess?"

Patrick looked at him. "How did you know?"

"He's been a problem for years. We could put him away if you wanted. You've only got to say the word. Looking for Arthur, was he?"

There was no point in concealment. It was, at least, some relief that they were not talking about Joanna. "Yes, he was. I don't know why though."

"Mixed up in Arthur's playing, I reckon. That's how McGrain makes his living. Funny how everyone's looking for Arthur, isn't it? All of a sudden."

He grinned as he made the last remark. Patrick waited for him to mention the L and F man but he asked instead about Patrick's background.

"I suppose yours is pure Lower African?" said Patrick after a while.

"Not all that pure. On my father's side it is – they go back to the early nineteenth century, all settlers and farmers – but my mother's different. Maybe you wouldn't know it but she's very different." He paused as if waiting for a response. "My mother's Jewish."

"Is that so different?"

"It is here. There's a lot of white tribes here as well as the others – Lower African, British, Italian, Portuguese. They all have different clubs, different jobs, live in different areas. They don't like each other and they don't mix but they unite when they have to. That's the name of the game here."

"D'you like the game?"

Jim lifted both hands from the steering wheel for a moment. "Yes, I

97

like it. Everyone's out for himself in this world. That's exhilarating. I'm one of the lucky ones, I know – I could be one of those guys." He pointed at an open lorry they were overtaking, in the back of which black labourers were crammed like watercress in a box. "Mind you, they're lucky compared with all those starving millions in India. That's what really gets me. The whole caste system has its origins in discrimination on account of colour. The whiter you are the higher you are. They persecute the untouchables, shoot hundreds in race riots and elections and no one says anything. Three lines in a newspaper. We shoot a few who get wound up on beer and it's headlines the world over. Makes me sick."

"At least they have elections."

"That's a polite name for them. How many untouchables in the government? Can you tell me that, eh?"

Jim's face and voice became harder as he spoke. His mood changed as rapidly as the surface of water in wind. Patrick did not want a row. "D'you think it's made a difference to you, being half Jewish?"

"It's made me very Lower African. Also, I rationalise being Lower African. Thoroughbreds don't. They just are." He accelerated through the traffic with aggressive competence until turning off the motorway towards the northern suburbs. "You've got to do something about this car business, you know. You can't live here and not have a car. How d'you get around the neighbourhood?"

"Walk."

"No one walks here. I've got an old bakkie, what you call a pick-up. Borrow that."

Patrick said he didn't like borrowing cars, Jim said he was being too damned British. They compromised on Patrick buying it. It was old and battered and Jim was thinking of selling it anyway. Patrick could buy it cheaply and would sell it when the Ford arrived. He thought he should pay more for it but Jim became all the more insistent on the low price as the sense of his own generosity took hold of him. By the time they reached the house they had agreed that Patrick should see it that weekend.

Jim turned the car round in the drive. Snap barked and Sarah stood in her blue uniform at the front door. Jim leant across the passenger seat as Patrick got out. "When are you seeing Joanna?"

Patrick tried to pretend that it had not been to the forefront of his mind. "Oh – er – tomorrow, I think. Yes, tomorrow night." He knew he sounded unconvincing.

"You'll need the bakkie for then. She's miles from here."

"I'll get a taxi."

Jim shrugged, waved at Sarah, who raised her arm mechanically, and accelerated away with a spurt of gravel.

"D'you know him?" Patrick asked as she put the lid on the kettle for his tea.

"He come here sometimes."

"What for?"

"To see if everything is all right."

Her tone and expression were flat and reluctant. "Have you heard from Stanley?"

"No, massa."

"Would you like to go home, to see if you could find him? I'll pay your fare."

She shook her head. "Thank you, massa. Is not worth that. I have my holiday later. One day he will come."

"It must be very worrying."

She looked at him for the first time. "Thank you, massa, I am well."

9

It was not easy to get to know Deuteronomy. He lived and worked somewhere else in the neighbourhood and appeared on only two days a week. Patrick's first attempt at conversation was noisily interrupted by Snap who, seeing the target, leapt from the study window. Deuteronomy escaped over the garden wall leaving a glove, a burning cigarette and the garden fork where he had been standing. He did not reappear that day.

A remark of Sarah's suggested that Deuteronomy could most easily be found on pay-days and so on those days Patrick made a habit of talking to him. They had amiable conversations. Deuteronomy grinned broadly at Patrick's every remark, closed his eyes as though with sublime understanding, said "M-a-s-s-a" in an adoring manner, then reopened and rolled his eyes before once more letting them rest, glistening with admiration, on Patrick. The result was that he continued to do what he liked with the garden, which looked presentable, while the swimming-pool became greener and murkier either despite or because of Patrick's daily attentions.

On the day when he was to have dinner with Joanna, Patrick took the temperature on the veranda after breakfast. Already he had an energetic interest in the detail of the day. Deuteronomy was in the corner of the garden beyond the swimming-pool trying to prune a young tree with a pair of shears. Patrick crossed the neatly cut lawn. There was the usual exchange of smiles, nods and greeting noises. "Isn't it difficult with the shears, Deuteronomy? Wouldn't it be better to use a saw?"

Deuteronomy smiled. "Saw better, yes, massa."

Patrick had bought the shears for him only the previous week. He pointed at them. "It will make them blunt. Also, they won't cut through the bough."

Deuteronomy nodded enthusiastic agreement. "You buy me shears, massa."

"Yes, but they are not good for the tree."

"Bad for tree." Deuteronomy pointed at the few ineffectual cuts he had made. "No good."

"No, very bad."

"Very bad, massa."

"Why don't you use the saw?"

Deuteronomy rolled his eyes and smiled again. "You buy me shears, massa."

Further conversation was cut short by the telephone. It was Clifford, speaking as though from a bunker under shellfire. Everything was happening, he had no time to waste, Patrick was to come in early that morning because a meeting had been moved forward. Also, a lot of people had dropped out of the European Community buffet lunch that was being hosted that day by Sir Wilfrid. There was a possibility of serious embarrassment. Patrick would have to come in and make up the numbers. Of course, all the drop-outs were far senior to him and he mustn't expect to be invited in future. In fact, he needn't stay for the whole thing. He just had to appear, that's all. Clifford could not waste time talking. He would brief Patrick fully on arrival.

Back on the veranda Sarah and Deuteronomy were standing together. She pointed solemnly at the shears in Deuteronomy's hand and said that there had been a misunderstanding. Deuteronomy had not wanted shears at all but a bow-saw. When Patrick bought shears Deuteronomy had assumed that he was unwilling to pay for a bow-saw and so had tried to manage with what he had been given. Sarah apologised, saying she should have realised, Patrick apologised and then so did Deuteronomy. Patrick said he would get a saw before Deuteronomy came again. They all three smiled. Deuteronomy went back to the tree and continued to hack at it.

The meeting that morning was one of a series involving what Clifford called the Ministerial Task Force. It comprised himself, Philip, the commercial officer and Patrick. Its purpose was to arrange the forthcoming ministerial visit. As the series went on minutes were drafted, redrafted, lengthened, filed, rewritten, lost, found, abandoned, resurrected and superseded. Programmes were drawn up, revised, split, merged, provisionally accepted, provisionally rejected and filed for ever. Clifford spent longer in the embassy with every day that passed. Philip was walled in behind ever-rising stacks of files. He would not go home whilst Clifford was there. His responsibility was to draft the ministerial political briefing in a form that could be sent to London and combined with whatever was drafted there. He took as his starting point the discovery by Europeans of that part of the continent.

101

Clifford allocated to himself the statistical presentation of UK-Lower African trade and financial dealings – what he called "the hub and centre of good relations" – and nominated the commercial officer to prepare the figures. Patrick was responsible for transport arrangements.

Clifford was incapable of delegation. Every decision taken at each meeting was overturned by subsequent memos which were themselves altered at subsequent meetings. He had never got on with Harry White, and soon reached the stage of communicating only by memo, save when they argued at Task Force meetings.

"The man's a buffoon," he complained, red-faced and pulling at his shirt-collar as if to widen it. "Doesn't understand the first principles of anything. I sent him a memo yesterday making the point about invisibles and he sent a ridiculous piece of paper back saying he couldn't see the point at all. Either he was being facetious and therefore daft or he can't follow a logical argument and is therefore more daft. It's Personnel I blame really. They're at the root of most of our problems."

Harry was older, hard-working and not very able. He resented not having been promoted. Like Clifford and Philip, he saw the ministerial visit as a chance to shine and like them wished to prevent anyone else from shining more brightly. Patrick was too new and too junior to be a threat and so Harry took to ringing him several times a day to complain about Clifford and to find out what was going on. He had a morbid and just suspicion that Clifford was trying to prevent him from even meeting the minister. One day, in a rage, he stormed unannounced into chancery to complain that Clifford was attempting to remove all references to the commodity futures market from the brief.

"It's only because he doesn't understand futures himself," he said, lowering his voice to a whisper and leaning across Patrick's desk. "He can't see that they're the biggest new thing in the financial market since – well, since the wheel – and because he doesn't understand them he doesn't want them in the brief. It might mean that someone else would have to present them. He's a schemer, nothing but a schemer, but I see his little games." He nodded in agreement with himself and pointed at the stack of files behind which Philip normally sat. "And that one, he's a snake in the grass. You want to watch him from where you're sitting. I've seen his sort before. He'll bite you as soon as look at you, he will."

Patrick eased one of Philip's files on to his own desk so that Harry should not see the use that was being made of his paper on the deployment of Greater London office accommodation.

Most of the time Philip preserved a passionate silence that was as much a wall as the files around him. He stayed later, grew paler, came in earlier and nibbled at Ryvita biscuits which he kept in a locked drawer. Once, when waiting for some files from registry, he sat back in his chair and pressed his hands against the sides of his face. "Makes you wonder if it's all worth it, doesn't it?" he said.

Patrick put down his pen. "I've been wondering that since I got here."

"Some of it is, I suppose. One works hard, does what one can, hopes people appreciate it and so on but I can't help wondering how often the national interest really is served. I mean, what difference would it make if we simply didn't do most of what we do? I doubt it would even be noticed. I'm not sure whether it's because we're all doing the wrong things or whether we're doing the right things wrongly."

"D'you ever think of doing something else?"

Philip smiled. "Daily. What worries me is that I might end up asking myself the same questions whatever I do. Every post I've had has been busy, demanding and largely irrelevant. I've a horrible feeling it might be the same with all bureaucracies. There are exceptions of course but there's so much wasted time and energy. Perhaps that's the only way we can do things – perhaps all human endeavour is like natural selection, a very wasteful process." He shrugged. "I suppose you could argue in defence of the Office that at least it's trying to serve the national interest and trying to demonstrate a way of doing things that would make the world better if more countries did the same. What I suppose I mean is, at least we're trying."

The missing files arrived and Philip withdrew behind them. During the next few days he had no time for further conversation.

Within a week Sandy and the commercial officer's wife found it necessary not to get on. "Not that I give a damn about trade figures or the minister or the whole boring business," she said when she came to pick up Clifford. "But the silly little b. decided she couldn't – simply could not – get on with me and so I thought right, darling, have it your own way." She shrugged. "Why don't you do her a favour? She needs someone. Not that I'd fancy it, I must admit."

At the very first Task Force meeting Clifford detailed two or three times to Patrick his responsibility for seeing that there were enough cars to take the ambassador and the reception party to the airport to meet the minister, then to take them to the residence, then to bring the minister to the embassy, leaving his wife with transport, then to see that there were cars for all the visits that would be made as well as reserve cars in case of mechanical breakdown or 'driver failure', as well as to see that cars continued to be provided for normal embassy business.

"You might have to use your own, of course," Clifford concluded.

"I think it's still in England."

"You'd better organise something else, then. It reflects badly on everyone if people don't keep up to certain standards."

Every possible arrangement turned out to be unworkable. Patrick was at first worried but became less so as Clifford passed him ever more memos, each more unworkable than that which it amended. Because there was no possibility of ensuring that it was all right beforehand it would have to be all right on the day. Clifford's interventions were so frequent and peremptory that he soon learned to keep all memos in a folder, adding new ones as they came in and waiting to see how long it was before Clifford arrived back at the programme he first thought of.

The meeting that morning was already in progress. The other two were seated but Clifford stood by his desk, tapping it with the edge of his clipboard to add emphasis to what he was saying. His belly bulged threateningly against the lower buttons of his shirt and he kept passing his hand over his bald patch. He had just received the unwelcome news that the inspectors were to come within a few weeks of the ministerial visit. He went on about this until Harry White asked if they could get started on Task Force business as he had another meeting to attend. Ignoring this, Clifford then explained why Patrick was invited to the EC buffet lunch that day. It wasn't the normal monthly lunch at which EC heads of mission entertained each other but the occasional buffet lunch to which wives and members of staff were invited. The purpose of the lunches was the maintenance of 'good relations', a widely quoted phrase referring less to the real relations between states and peoples than to the reciprocity of congratulation obtaining between a very small number of officials.

However, there had been so many regrets this time, that "Patrick and people like him" were being invited to avoid embarrassment. "It'll be at the residence. You won't need to stay till the end."

Most of the time Clifford's rudeness was not annoying: it seemed personal to Clifford rather than to the victim. Patrick was more concerned with what he would say to Joanna that evening. It was odd that he could form no clear picture of her. The idea of her filled him with warmth and excitement but when he tried to picture her face he could see clearly only her hair and her arms when she folded them under her breasts. Her voice, though, was as clear as when she was with him.

After another intemperate intervention from Harry, Clifford turned to the purpose of the meeting. He first revised the ground rules of Philip's political briefing. Philip frowned but said nothing. He then made new suggestions for Patrick's transport arrangements, changing everything that had been decided at the previous meeting, only quoting the reasons he had given then. Next he argued with Harry about how much time should be given to precious metals other than gold.

Patrick mentally rehearsed his own arrangements. He had booked a table at an Italian restaurant not far from the city centre. This meant they would have to travel and could thus have more time together. He had not taken up Jim's suggestion of the roof garden restaurant since he would have felt that Jim was then controlling the evening. Jim's remarks on parting had sounded deliberately casual, a sign of unease that now made Patrick more confident.

Clifford's and Harry's argument was as inconclusive as most. When Harry stood to go he fired a parting shot about signs that one of the cipher clerks was operating a currency fiddle. Clifford said he had no time to worry about that sort of thing and demanded a shortened version of the brief on precious metals other than gold by close of play.

He turned to Patrick as a way of turning his back on the commercial officer. He held out his hand. "Message for you."

It was a telephone message taken by the receptionist saying he should ring Joanna. His first thought was that she wanted to postpone or even cancel the evening. Perhaps Jim had caused trouble. Then he persuaded himself that she more likely wanted to check on the time he would call for her.

"Friend of yours?" asked Clifford.

"Well, I know her. We met at Philip's, remember?"

"You're fishing in deep waters there, you know, with Jim Rissik on the scene. Which reminds me, have you spoken to him about any police arrangements for the visit?"

"No. I'm saving it till I see him again about the Whelk business." There was no point in discussing the visit until it had been decided where the minister was going and what he was to do. He turned to go.

"Where are you going?"

"Back to my office." He intended to ring Joanna.

"No, you're not. You're coming to the residence with me. We've got to organise this lunch. Make sure everything is there. Come on."

Patrick imagined shooting Clifford. Not in anger or hatred but neatly, calmly, with a single loud shot. "All right," he said. He would ring from the residence. He now felt as anxious as he had been secure some minutes before.

At the residence they found Sir Wilfrid's staff, supervised by his cook, in lethargic disarray. One was missing, another had cut his forearm in the garden and bled all over the veranda, two were with the cook peeling potatoes, the only thing they could find to do. There was little food because Sir Wilfrid had warned the cook a few days before but had not named the day until he left for work that morning. As in any diplomatic house, there was plenty to drink.

Clifford fumed. "As if I didn't have enough on my bloody plate without having to play the ambassador's wife. If I'd known it was going to be such a shambles I'd have got Sandy to come along and do something. As it is, she's at the bloody hairdresser's."

Organising food, drink, tables and servants prevented Patrick from getting to the telephone. At first he felt a malicious pleasure in Clifford's exasperation. "There's no meat," he said, after talking again to the cook.

Clifford put his hand to his head. "What do you mean, no meat?"

"No meat to eat."

"Has he ordered any?"

"The cook thinks not."

"Oh, Christ All-bloody-mighty." Clifford put both his hands to his head and turned away. When he turned back his arms hung limply by his side and there was the same hopeless expression on his face as on the servants'. "You know what the sodding problem is, don't you?" he asked quietly. "He works off last year's diary. He won't throw it away because there are so many things in it he always wants to remember and never does. Jesus. It's all very well being eccentric and brilliant and all the rest of it but if you don't know what sodding day it is it makes you bloody impossible to work for. I mean, I am the head of chancery." He prodded his chest with his finger and wrinkled his brow in plaintive appeal. "This is an important embassy. I have a lot of responsibility. I shouldn't be my ambassador's surrogate wife. He could have got his secretary to do this, or contractors, anyone. Trouble is, he doesn't think about practical arrangements. Always with his head in the clouds worrying about policy or principles. It's all very well for him." He sat heavily at the table. "There's no time to cook any meat. Just have to serve them with chopped-up potatoes and salad, I suppose."

Insensitive and pompous as Clifford usually was, he seemed at this moment an honest trier, unfairly let down. Patrick even forgot for a while about Joanna. "Why don't I take your car and go to the hypermarket and buy up all the cold meat that's ready to eat?"

Clifford's expression was hopeful but wary. "That sounds like a good idea. At least, I can't see anything obviously wrong with it, can you? But it seems too simple to work."

"It does seem rather simple, yes." They both thought, then reminded each other that there were such things as cold hams that needed only to be carved.

Clifford held out his car keys. "Buy as many as you can find. I'll ring the embassy and get all available women out here. Thank God there aren't many people coming."

It worked in the end. Female help arrived, the food was simple but plentiful and wine did the rest. Those who knew Sir Wilfrid well were pleasantly surprised to find anything. Clifford received a fair amount of jocular credit. There were not too many guests, and ambassadors, fortunately, were thin on the ground. The Dutch ambassador had died of a heart attack some time before and had not yet been replaced. The French ambassador had been recalled because he had gone on safari with his Spanish mistress during the visit of his own foreign minister. The Italian ambassador was at the coast visiting Mafia relatives. The Greek was said to be in Kenya with the French ambassador's wife.

Sir Wilfrid talked to everyone. He had bursts of energy, towards the end of each of which he became abstracted and would suddenly remove himself, only to reappear ten minutes later fully charged. Patrick began to wonder whether he was an alcoholic.

"D'you know what he's doing?" asked Clifford in a low voice as they squeezed past each other in a crowded doorway. "I caught him at it accidentally on the way to the loo. He's got a telly in the study and he's watching cricket. England v. Australia, highlights from yesterday at Lord's. Crafty old bugger."

Because there was no disaster Clifford's manner with Patrick was now friendly and conspiratorial. His eyes brimmed with alcohol and good nature as he introduced him to a Danish first secretary and a German counsellor – "bit senior for you, but never mind." The Dane talked about how a doctor visiting a hospital in a black township outside Battenburg had found it so ill-equipped that some patients had to sleep on the floor with newspapers as sheets. There were rumours of sinister medical experiments.

"At least there are hospitals, unlike in the rest of Africa," said the German in careful but faultless English. He swallowed his ham, drank more wine and changed the subject to the topic of the day. This was the story that the body of the Dutch ambassador, a very large man, had been too big even for the outsize coffin and there had been some unseemly compression of the corpse. Someone said that one of the crew of the plane that took it back had talked of amputation but this the German did not believe. He laughed heartily and took more ham. The Dane looked serious and shook his head.

A servant summoned Patrick to the telephone, saying that the embassy wanted him. When he reached it whoever it was had hung up. He assumed it was Joanna again and rang to see if there was a message. The girl in reception said it was the other girl, now gone off, who had been trying to get him. A man had come to see him, she did not know who but he was very insistent, the other girl had said. He said it was urgent. Patrick thought of McGrain and said he would come in, in case the man returned. He was grateful even for this excuse to leave the lunch, having discovered he had left Joanna's number at the embassy.

On the way out he met Sandy. "It hasn't finished already, has it?" she asked, touching her neat hair. She wore a blue trouser-suit which made her look older and less feminine.

"No, I'm leaving early. They're all enjoying themselves."

"Has Clifford noticed I'm not there?"

"I don't know. He hasn't said anything. He seems fairly pleased with life."

"Thank God for that. How've you been able to skive off already?"

"I've got to see someone in the embassy." He told her about McGrain. As he spoke he was aware of himself trying to charm. It was not so much that she appealed to him now as that she had before; also, he was carried along by the momentum of his own speech.

She laughed. "Come on, I'll give you a lift."

"You can't. You're late now. You'll be later still. I can take the official car."

She opened her bag and took out the keys. "No, I'll run you in. It won't take long and if they haven't noticed yet it doesn't matter. Anyway, I never see you these days. Come on."

She drove jerkily when sober. "Why don't you come to see me?"

He tried to respond playfully. "Should I?"

"How's your lady-love?"

108

"Who?"

"Don't play the innocent, it doesn't work with me."

"I'm seeing her for the first time tonight."

"I thought you were a quicker worker than that."

"I thought you were."

"Shows us both how wrong we can be, doesn't it? Light me a fag."

He took one from her packet, lit it and puffed at it himself a couple of times. She took it in her lips without touching his hand.

"What about Jim?" she asked.

"He knows I'm seeing her."

"Does he mind?"

"I don't know."

"He must do. We're not all like you."

"Wouldn't I mind, then?"

She looked at him. "I don't know. P'raps you would. It's hard to imagine."

As she left the motorway she swore at another driver who cut in front of her. Patrick decided he was attracted to her again because she was paying him attention.

"I don't know Joanna very well," she said. "I don't know what she wants. I mean, she's got her kid and she's got her man. Maybe she wants something else. She seems very nice."

"Yes."

She laughed. "God, you're passionate."

She asked about Sarah, Snap, Deuteronomy and the house before dropping him near the embassy in a no-stopping area, causing traffic to pile up behind. He got out quickly. She pouted coquettishly. "Don't worry, I wasn't going to kiss you goodbye. You don't have to run."

The caller was not McGrain. He was described as young, presentable and English. He had asked first for the ambassador, then for Patrick. He had said something about being on to something and needing more money. He had left no name but would call again some time.

Patrick did not want to encourage speculation. "Perhaps it was someone I knew at university. Messing about, you know."

"He was very serious," the receptionist said. "Perhaps he was a DBS, I don't know. He didn't seem very distressed. I'll call you the moment he comes in again, if he does, but he said he was going away tonight." She giggled. "You could throw him out, like you did with that other one. I'd love to see it."

His office was empty of Philip for once. He rang Joanna but she was out, the maid didn't know for how long. He said he would ring back.

Sir Wilfrid returned from the lunch before anyone else. Patrick followed him into his office and began to tell him about the L and F man's visit but realised that the radio was not on. He stopped. "England are seventy-four for six," Sir Wilfrid said abruptly. Patrick continued his story in a whisper but Sir Wilfrid was not pleased. He interrupted sharply. "Don't murmur, Patrick, it's a very bad habit. People normally acquire it after they've been around the office for a few years. It's useful then but I'm distressed to find it in one so young. Now start again and speak properly."

Patrick described what had happened and Sir Wilfrid said "damn" several times. The L and F man must have been desperate, that was clear; Patrick should not have gone to the lunch, that too was clear; the L and F man was no doubt chasing up a lead – that was a good thing. A great pity he was missed. He must not be missed again.

The ambassador turned the pages of his desk diary. "Difficult with leap years. The days are the same but not the dates. Or the dates but not the days, I'm not sure which. One of them is always wrong, anyway. Important to get them right. Today is Kuweto day, I think. I'm almost certain. Very important to get that right. Might be useful if you come with me. Show you how the majority live."

The embassy maintained a library and community centre which was normally visited once a week by Miss Teale or by Clifford, when he felt it necessary to demonstrate concern. Patrick's first thought was that if he went it would be hours before he could ring Joanna again, but Sir Wilfrid regarded the matter as settled.

"I occasionally go down myself, you see. Take the British newspapers. Good for morale and that sort of thing and keeps me in touch. I'd like more people to go but it's hard to interest them. Trouble is, many of those who join foreign offices the world over are unsuited for dealing with foreigners. They dislike them. They don't like their own countrymen, either. In fact, they like only other diplomats. The same applies to teachers and policemen. Both professions are filled with people who by temperament and ability should be barred. Also, I make a point of driving myself when I go there. Means it's slightly less formal and does no harm to show people we take a serious interest. Some of us, at any rate. Good for the Lower Africans to see that."

Patrick later discovered that Sir Wilfrid's driving himself mortified Simon, his driver, who felt rejected. He lost face in front of his colleagues and sometimes went into a decline for days.

They took with them three heavy piles of old British newspapers.

"Only proper news they get," explained Sir Wilfrid.

Patrick took two piles and Sir Wilfrid one. When they reached the lift Sir Wilfrid put his down and rummaged through his pockets. "Must've left my keys in the office. You hang on here and keep the lift when it comes."

The next lift was occupied by Clifford and Philip. They got out, discussing a teleletter that had to go to London that afternoon. Clifford stopped on seeing the bundles of newspapers.

"He's going himself? Taking you?" His earlier good mood had gone. "It's not the ambassador's job to deliver newspapers and there are better things for you to do than go swanning off all afternoon. He's not carrying this one himself, is he?"

"Yes."

"He shouldn't. He's got his position to think of."

Clifford's irritation prevented him from noticing the same in others. "I've only got two arms," said Patrick. "I haven't yet learnt enough of the local customs to carry things on my head."

"It's a question of status. It will lower his standing in the African eye if he's seen bearing burdens himself."

Sir Wilfrid reappeared. "Must've left them in the car. Really should tie them round my neck. What are you doing with my bundle, Clifford?"

"I thought I'd carry it down for you, sir."

"Really, Clifford, I should have thought that the head of chancery in an important embassy would have had better things to do than lug bundles of old newspapers about the place. Now give them to me and call the lift."

Clifford walked away without a word. Philip held the reception door for him and smiled briefly at Patrick. "That's the first we've heard of the African eye," he whispered. "It could be the next fashion."

In the basement they nearly collided with one of the African drivers who was waiting to get in the lift. He carried a stack of clip-files in both arms.

"Good day, Simon," said Sir Wilfrid. "How are you?" The driver was just able to nod and grin above the topmost file, which he held in place with his chin. Sir Wilfrid put down his newspapers. "All well, eh? A good load there. You work hard, Simon." He spoke slowly and loudly.

The driver maintained his grin and, with teeth clenched said, "Not Simon, sir, Harold."

"Harold?"

"Please."

Sir Wilfrid turned to Patrick as though it were he who had been speaking. "Harold, yes, of course. Simon's the other chap." Harold was trying to edge himself into the lift without spilling the files. "Are all those for chancery?".

"Sir, for the embassy, please."

"Yes, yes, I know that. I bet they're going to the commercial office. Who ordered them?"

"The embassy, please, sir."

"Who told you to bring them?"

"Simon tell me."

Sir Wilfrid turned again to Patrick. "Look into this, will you? We don't want to appear profligate when the inspectors arrive. Can't have them wading through piles of empty files to get at the full ones. Mention it to Miss Teale and Clifford."

Harold stepped unsteadily into the lift. The doors closed on him as he was turning. The top few files began to fall.

"Always important to talk to these chaps," continued Sir Wilfrid as they walked towards the car. "They appreciate it. Most people ignore them, I'm sorry to say, but when you're doing menial jobs like that you feel a little better if people notice you. It's even more important here than it is in London. We're representative, remember."

10

When driving, Sir Wilfrid's awareness of other traffic was intermittent, like one whose delirium is interspersed with brief periods of consciousness and clarity. He talked all the time. Was it true that Patrick's baggage, so far from having left London, was probably not even loaded? In which case he had a favour to ask.

It was another minute or two before the favour was made known because Sir Wilfrid turned into a one-way street. Once out he explained that Mrs Acupu, a member of the black Kuweto council that was elected by a tiny proportion of the Kuweto electorate, was on a sponsored tour to Britain. The trip had not gone well. After spending thousands of pounds on getting her there the Office was messing it up by not getting the little things right. Sir Wilfrid was particularly upset because the trip had been his idea. Of course, she was aiming a bit high in expecting to be met by the Queen at Heathrow and he had told her so, but the Office might have done a bit better than just sending old Formerly from the department. Apparently they hadn't hit it off at all. Then there'd been some sort of row about racism with the chief of the Metropolitan Police and after that the Office arranged for her to stay in a place in Brixton. She hadn't liked that and the next morning they'd moved her to some other place in Mayfair. There'd been other things as well but now it seemed that she was overweight. It was all quite ridiculous.

Patrick assumed that Sir Wilfrid meant her baggage, though the description applied equally to her person. He remembered newspaper photographs showing a vast voluble woman with a huge grin. She was known for taking enthusiastic advantage of government-sponsored visits to Europe and America. This pleased governments because by entertaining her at the expense of their citizens they were able to persuade themselves that they were doing something for the black people of Lower Africa – at least, to persuade other countries that they were – and it pleased her because she became well known and therefore apparently important. In fact, it appeared from the Lower

African papers that she was better known in Europe and America than amongst her own electorate.

Sir Wilfrid went on to explain that she'd bought a few things in Harrods or somewhere and was a few pounds over. The Office were getting shirty about paying for it. No doubt that Formerly chap was sticking his oar in but even so it was ridiculous that they should spend all that money then spoil the ship for a hap'orth of tar. It was the little things that people remembered, not the big things. Those they took for granted.

"The point is," he concluded, "it would do a lot for Anglo-black Lower African relations, Patrick, if her excess could be included in your baggage. If you reckon there'll be room I'll send a telegram when we get back."

"There's certainly room." Patrick would happily have agreed for the lady herself to be a part of his baggage. His mind was more on whether or not it would be possible to ring Joanna from Kuweto. Similarly, he might also be able to invent a reason for getting a bus back rather than risk his life again with Sir Wilfrid. But perhaps there weren't any white buses.

Sir Wilfrid said that despite the million and a half or so people in Kuweto, it was still not marked on some maps. The main road led past army camps well sited to act as a barrier between the township and the city. After leaving it they drove through an unmanned police checkpoint. Sir Wilfrid missed a bollard by an inch or two. "The police sometimes stop you because whites aren't allowed in without a special pass, unless they're on an official tour. We don't need passes, of course, and there's never any trouble once they realise who we are. In fact, they're very polite. Make an effort because it's me, I daresay."

Kuweto was thousands of small bungalows ranged in lines over low hills. Most of the roofs were of red corrugated iron and the buildings appeared to be identical, like so many Monopoly houses. Each had four rooms with an outside toilet at the back and was set in its own large garden. There were few attempts at cultivation. The predominant colour of the ground at that time of year, whether garden, road or sidewalk, was reddish-brown.

People walked slowly in all directions. Some stood in groups in the roads, squatted at one side or walked without apparent purpose across large tracts of bare dirt. The few shops were so boarded and barricaded that it was impossible to tell what they sold. No one took any notice of the two white men in the black Jaguar.

"Big business is only just discovering the black African market," Sir

114

Wilfrid said. "A million and a half people here and they're only now building a supermarket. One of the two big chains that cater mainly for blacks. Odd. You'd think simple commercial sense would've brought them here before. Perhaps the blacks didn't have enough money to spend. They're richer now." He pointed at one very large area of wasteland and called it a park. On the far side was a police station, well fortified and surrounded by a high wire screen. "That was put up after the rocket attack last year."

Beer halls and liquor stores were almost as heavily fortified. What looked at first like exceptionally grim barracks turned out to be hostels for migrant labourers. Most of these came either from the neighbouring black African states or from the tribal homelands. They were single men and travelled into Battenburg each day by train. Protection rackets were operated on the trains, and gangs competed for the pickings when the workers arrived at Kuweto station on pay-nights. Most of the drunkenness, tribal rivalries and fights occurred in the hostels.

The town rambled incoherently over the hills with no definable centre unless it was that the centre was elsewhere, in Battenburg. It was neither sinister nor hostile, simply indifferent and scruffy. Abandoned cars and other twisted and broken metal objects lay here and there, pushed away from the houses as a dog will scuff away the old newspapers amongst which it sleeps.

The British cultural centre was a library attached to a room about the size of a village hall which contained a table tennis table. Next to it was a small bungalow occupied by the curator, Mr Oboe. He was a plump, jovial black man who smiled all the time he was speaking but composed his face into an expression of exaggerated seriousness, almost of mourning, whenever anyone else spoke.

"The British are very big in Kuweto," he told Patrick, grinning hugely as they shook hands.

He would not permit Patrick and Sir Wilfrid to unload the newspapers but summoned instead a gaggle of youthful helpers, many of whom were his offspring. In the enthusiasm and excitement two of the bundles were dropped in the dirt. Mr Oboe shouted at the culprits in shrill Zulu.

The library was a small room with two electric heaters and a fan, despite what seemed to Patrick a warm day. Half a dozen adolescents sat reading at a table, meek and solemn. Mr Oboe introduced the two visitors and said that they had brought more newspapers from the embassy. Since no one responded he added, "Many, many more," and

115

pointed at the bundles being brought in. The adolescents nodded, smiled and looked embarrassed.

"Good afternoon to you, good afternoon." Sir Wilfrid's loud greeting reverberated in the small room, startling everyone. He nodded for some seconds after speaking as if his head had been unbalanced by the effort. One of the boys mouthed "Good afternoon" and looked quickly down at what he was reading. The bundles of newspaper were carried amidst bobbing black heads and a welter of competing instructions into an adjoining room.

"We have many papers. Very good," said Mr Oboe with a smile. He pointed at the bookshelves around the walls of the room and turned to Patrick. "Would you like to see our books? They are from the embassy and the British Council."

"Some jolly good books there," Sir Wilfrid said, still speaking as if in a gymnasium.

"Many jolly good books," added Mr Oboe. They all three looked at the shelves and nodded at the unremembered novels, the nearly complete sets of Dickens, Trollope and Shakespeare, The British Isles tide-table, the English-Hebrew dictionary and the back number of *Field*.

Sir Wilfrid walked around the table and peered over the backs of the young readers like a benign school inspector. Patrick did the same. Mr Oboe looked on contentedly.

A tall slim girl was reading calculus. "What are you studying?" asked Patrick.

Her dark eyes were big and trusting. "For my examination."

"You have to do calculus for your examination?"

"Yes, for medicine."

"You want to be a doctor?"

"Yes."

He felt like inexperienced and reluctant royalty. He wished her luck. She smiled shyly, turned over a couple of chapters and began reading in the middle of the page.

"You are a man of education, Mr Stubbs," said Mr Oboe, almost ecstatic. He picked up the nearest book. "Please accept this jolly good gift from the British cultural centre, Mr Stubbs."

Patrick was alarmed. "No, please, I have many books. Your need must be greater than – "

"Please, to remember the British cultural centre. The embassy gives us many books and newspapers. This gift is for you."

Sir Wilfrid nodded enthusiastically. Patrick accepted the 1926

116

Secker and Warburg edition of Lion Feuchtwanger's *Jew Süss*.
"Thank you, I am very honoured."

"Yes," said Mr Oboe, his eyes wide with delight. Everyone smiled.

Four teenage boys played table tennis in the hall. Their movements
were quick and graceful, their play inexpert. When the ball bounced
on to the floor they turned to pick it up with eyes resolutely downcast as
if determined not to notice the spectators. Mr Oboe explained that
when they had more money he would have a stage built at one end of
the hall and a volleyball court marked out at the other.

"Volleyball, that's good," said the ambassador enthusiastically.
"They'll enjoy that. Do you play volleyball, Mr Oboe?"

"Yes, I play volleyball. I like it."

"Good." They nodded and grinned at each other.

There was no sign of a telephone. Mr Oboe told Patrick smilingly
that there was one, then that it was in the office, then how to get
to the office, then that it had broken the day before.

"D'you know Mrs Acupu?" Sir Wilfrid asked.

Mr Oboe looked solemn. "Mrs Acupu? No, I don't know her."

"The councillor. She comes from Kuweto. Patrick is helping with
her luggage."

"She come from Kuweto?"

"Oh yes, yes. She's a very nice lady."

Mr Oboe grinned. "A nice lady. I like to meet nice ladies. You like
nice ladies?" He laughed.

Sir Wilfrid took refuge in smiles and nods. Mr Oboe, delighted,
turned to Patrick. "You help with her luggage? When you finish, may I
help?"

"I would like you to," said Patrick. Mr Oboe put his hand to his face
and giggled. For the rest of the time that they were together he turned
to Patrick every so often, nudged him with his elbow, winked and
giggled. The table tennis continued. It was hard to tell whether Sir
Wilfrid was absorbed in the play or whether he was day-dreaming.
Patrick turned again to Mr Oboe. "Do all the people here live in
bungalows, apart from those in hostels?"

Mr Oboe looked surprised. "Oh yes, very many people live in
bungalows."

"One family in each?"

"Yes. Sometimes the family is very big." He laughed. "But not all
are lucky. When the floods come all the people have to leave their
houses in that part of Kuweto and they are put into army barracks, old
ones, huts, you know? But it is many years ago and still they are there."

117

He continued to smile. "And there are many more people who are moved from a town where the government say black people must not live any more and they come to Kuweto. These people do not want to move because they own the land, it is theirs for more than seventy years, but the government takes it from them and they are moved in one day only in army lorries. In the morning very early the lorries come suddenly and they take them to hostels where they must stay and where they own nothing. That was years ago but still the people feel hard about it."

The ambassador had bent his head and listened. "I know, I know, I know," he intoned. "It is truly, truly terrible. But such injustice must end. It cannot be allowed to continue."

"The people are used to it."

"But they don't like it, surely?"

"Oh no, sometimes they are very angry." Mr Oboe laughed.

"It must change. It cannot go on like this."

"Yes, must change."

The table tennis ball bounced again on to the floor.

"D'you think it will change?" asked Patrick.

Mr Oboe looked puzzled. "Will change?"

"The government and the black people – d'you think it will change?"

"Will change one day, perhaps." He grinned, put his hand to his face and nudged Patrick.

There were effusive farewells from the gaggle of children and several minutes of shaking hands with Mr Oboe. They left by a different route so that Patrick could see more of the township. He saw the same rows of bungalows with corrugated iron roofs and acres of the same brown land. There was far more space than in European towns. Sir Wilfrid talked about Mr Oboe's enthusiasm and helpfulness, how he did much for children and how it was better to do something for only a tiny minority than to do nothing at all.

"Of course, it can't go on, people living like this and the rest of us in luxury. It has to change."

"Yes, I suppose it does." Patrick was calculating at what time he would now have to ring Joanna.

Sir Wilfrid looked at him. "But isn't it obvious that it does? How can it possibly go on?"

Patrick only ever thought about the problem with reluctance. It could very possibly go on for a very long time. "You mean, civil war and – "

118

"No, no, I don't mean anything like that. The whites would always win unless the blacks had truly massive help – white help – from outside. The Rhodesians would never have given in in Zimbabwe if their white supporters abroad hadn't threatened to turn off the taps. And even if the blacks did win a civil war that wouldn't improve matters much. You'd simply substitute one form of tribal domination for another. No, what I mean is that people must be made to see that they're wrong and then helped to put things right. It's our job to hammer that message home every minute of every day. Don't you agree?"

Patrick thought of Jim Rissik. "D'you think it makes any difference if they do see they're wrong?"

"You mean that to know the good is not necessarily to desire it? Plato wouldn't have liked that at all, not at all. You must have a pretty gloomy view of human nature, Patrick. Surely one always feels one wants to do something to improve the world – don't you feel that?"

"Well, if possible." Patrick had never seriously considered improving the world any more than he had considered improving himself.

The ambassador banged his hand upon the steering wheel. "The point is not 'if' – we have to make it possible," he said energetically.

He did this at a point where the road dipped to cross a thin brown stream which had several feet of dried mud on either side. Having approached the stream slowly he accelerated and overcorrected the steering-wheel. Patrick felt the car go and grabbed the door handle. The rear wheels spun, slithered off the road and sank into the caked mud.

Sir Wilfrid banged both hands on the steering-wheel. "Now we're stuck again. Every time I take this car out something goes wrong."

Patrick was every bit as angry. He could see both his telephone call and his dinner sabotaged. Night would fall and breakdown lorries would fail to arrive. They got out.

"Can we push it, d'you think?" asked Sir Wilfrid.

The wheels were deep in the mud. Patrick pointed at a group of men standing some way off the road. "We could ask them to help."

Sir Wilfrid paused with his hand to his head. "I wonder if we should? On the other hand, why not? You wait here."

He walked over to the group and when a few yards from them began to beckon and cry, "I say!" as if they were still a hundred yards away. He made pushing motions with his hand, pointed at the car and shouted loudly enough for Patrick to hear. "We are stuck – car stuck – you push please, okay?"

The men ambled good-naturedly over, some of them laughing, and after a few seconds of heaving the car was back on the road. Patrick joined in and everyone laughed when his foot went into the mud. Sir Wilfrid distributed banknotes which were accepted with no sign of humiliation.

"Jolly helpful, these chaps," he said as they drove away, leaving the men standing much as they had been before. "Don't think they minded, do you? Very willing. People say they don't work but it's not true. They jolly well do."

On the outskirts they passed some large and expensive-looking bungalows with appropriate cars. "Indians, mostly," said Sir Wilfrid. "One or two wealthy blacks. Businessmen, gangsters and so on." He appeared to make no distinction. "They don't get up at four-thirty to get to Battenburg like the others. They drive in or stay behind and make their money here. It's dreadful that people should be forced into such behaviour. It can't go on, it really can't. That must surely be clear to everyone, even to pessimists like yourself."

Patrick stared at the bungalows and said nothing.

Philip was head-down over his desk. His pen moved inexorably over the green drafting paper. There was no alternative but to ring Joanna in his presence.

She spoke quickly, gushing in a way Patrick had not heard before, eagerly, insistently apologetic. Her daughter Belinda was ill and she would not leave her even though the maid was there. They would have to rearrange dinner.

This was bad but not quite as bad as Patrick had feared. His urge to see her was stronger than ever. He asked questions about the little girl while he tried to marshal arguments and to think of alternatives that would still mean he saw her that night. His desire to do so was concentrated, almost cruel.

Describing the child's symptoms and answering questions about sleep and diet relaxed her. He suggested a quick pizza or something but no, she couldn't go out, really, not even when Belinda had gone to sleep; she would feel awful if anything happened and would worry all the time anyway. He stopped trying to persuade her but kept the conversation going, acutely aware of Philip's listening, until she talked herself into feeling guilty because he would have had no meal prepared for that night. Neither of them mentioned that Sarah could easily do it. Eventually she suggested he came round and had scrambled eggs. It wouldn't be much but it would be better than nothing.

Patrick left the office as a cheerful registry clerk brought in another memo from Clifford about transport arrangements and another three files for Philip, who barely had time to look up.

The taxi dropped him in a cul-de-sac of small bungalows with neat lawns, their borders wet from recent watering. Joanna wore jeans and a blue guernsey, her blonde hair loose upon her shoulders. She was shorter than he remembered. There was a momentary awkwardness at the door when they might have shaken hands or kissed but did neither. She talked to him as if he were the doctor. Belinda was asleep, it was a sort of cold or flu, probably nothing much but it was worrying and had to be watched. He was introduced to the maid, a tiny, exquisitely formed young woman called Beauty. He stared to see such elegance in miniature and shook her slim hand very carefully. Beauty smiled demurely and Joanna told her she could go back to her quarters.

"She's very sweet but she will gamble. They hide amongst the trees and play a game of their own. Sometimes the police have a crackdown and round them up and send them back to the homelands or to prison. I keep telling her she'll get into trouble but she still does it when she thinks I don't know. The other problem is her man. He beats her up and he's such a great brute I wonder he doesn't kill her. I suppose he's jealous because she's such a little flirt and if he knows she's even talked to another man there's trouble. The last time was when she brought him back here whilst I was away, otherwise it wouldn't have happened. He took all her money and left her unconscious. She had fourteen stitches in her head."

She talked quickly and impersonally, a mode with which he fell in because it was neutral and easy although it offered no clear line of advance. He was encouraged when he saw on the mantelpiece the bullet he had given her, polished and gleaming.

"Beauty cleans it nearly every day. I was thinking, I can't really put it on a bracelet, can I? It would be dangerous, wouldn't it? And probably illegal, too. Where did you get it?"

"I found it."

"Where?"

"On the floor."

He turned it over in his fingers and handed it back. She stood it again in front of the clock. "Why did you give it to me?"

"You looked as if you'd like it."

"I was curious, that's all. Not everyone has a bullet in his handkerchief."

"Also, I was embarrassed."

"You seemed very calm."

"That's how I am when I'm embarrassed."

She smiled as she turned away. "That sounds rather convenient."

They ate scrambled eggs, mushrooms, tomatoes and toast, and drank the wine that Patrick had brought. All subjects were interesting. They talked of marriage, the Foreign Office, having children, ageing, Kuweto and Joseph Conrad. She asked about diplomatic life and he replied with an authority he didn't know he had. She was impressed which at once pleased and disconcerted him. Although he wanted to be admired he did not want to be closely identified with a job which he felt did not express himself. At first he was confident that he was untypical but after hearing his own explanation of the Foreign Office he was less confident.

He explained how he had spent the year after leaving university travelling and working in America. When he told her his age she put her hand to her breast. "How awful. You're so much younger than me. This has never happened before. It's embarrassing."

"You seem very calm."

She laughed. "It's not calmness, it's confusion."

After the meal they sat on the floor and faced each other across a white rug. The rug was no man's land. To attempt a crossing early on and to be repulsed would be a serious failure; it would preclude later, prepared assaults. They talked and found each other intelligent. "You seem to say a lot about yourself but you don't really," she said. "You talk about what you've seen and what's happened and the people around you but you don't actually say anything about yourself. You do ask rather a lot of personal questions, though."

He smiled. "Well, you could do the same."

She laughed and tossed back her hair, needlessly pushing it with the gesture he had noticed when he first saw her. "No need for that. Some people tell you enough about themselves in the questions they ask."

He never once relaxed. He would like to have said or done something affectionate since that was how he wanted to be with her, but it was not possible to cease trying to be entertaining.

"What about Jim?" he asked eventually, having stepped round the subject all evening.

"What about him?"

"Do you love him?"

She looked down at the carpet, then moved her shoulders very slightly. "No, it's simpler than that."

He felt himself becoming tense. "In what way?"

"The simplest." She picked at something in the carpet. "Not what you might be thinking. We get on. He's complicated and difficult sometimes but we just get on."

"Do you have much in common?"

"Not very much. It's not really necessary. You can be close to someone just the same."

It had seemed a crass question even as he asked it. He felt he had to go on quickly. "In a funny sort of way I like him."

"Why funny?"

He wasn't sure. "Well, he's slightly sinister."

"Sinister or not, he likes you."

"Does he?"

She smiled. "In a funny sort of way you're very naive."

It was gone midnight when he left. She stepped outside the door with her arms folded beneath her breasts, as when they had talked by the pool. He was determined not to leave without arranging to see her again. He suggested lunch on Wednesday. She laughed. "So soon? Are you sure you want to?"

"Thursday, then."

"Belinda permitting." Her eyes were still smiling but her expression was softer. When he turned to go she added quietly, "Thank you for coming."

As he walked to the waiting taxi he began to relax. On the way back he exulted. His mind wandered over the evening, sampling impressions which now that they were memories could be properly tasted for the first time. He tipped the driver extravagantly. Snap barked as he walked up the drive. Illuminated by the porch light was a big red Toyota pick-up. Jim Rissik got out as he approached and then another man. Jim wore jeans and the other, who was very tall, a blazer, tie and flannels. It looked like a film set for a beating-up.

Patrick slowed.

Jim smiled and stretched out his hand. He indicated the other man. "Piet." Patrick shook hands with Piet, who nodded and did not smile. Jim slapped the bonnet of the pick-up as he would the rump of a horse. "Served me well, this bakkie. I wouldn't get rid of her if there wasn't such a damn good deal on new cars. Have a go."

The bakkie was big, battered and rugged. Patrick knew immediately that he would like it and agreed to try it out then and there. Also, having come from Joanna, he wanted to humour Jim. Piet sat on the steps and did not come with them. During the short drive Jim painstakingly pointed out features and faults but it was enough for Patrick that the vehicle was solid, red, friendly and powerful, higher than other cars, almost like a lorry. He kept talking about it in the hope of avoiding any mention of Joanna.

When they got back they argued about the price. Patrick wanted to pay at least the trade-in value but Jim wanted less. "If I'm selling to someone I know I sell for less in case something goes wrong. That way there are no recriminations."

"But I can afford it. I could sell it for what I'm giving. Anyway, with my allowances I bank half my salary."

Jim leant against the side of the bakkie and folded his arms. "I don't want your money."

"Then I don't want your vehicle."

Jim stared as if considering, then dismissing, the idea of action. "Suit yourself." He nodded at the house. "You going to offer us a drink?"

Patrick shut Snap in the kitchen. Remembering that they were policemen, he hastily explained that the wires stretching from the radio on the mantelpiece across the back of the sofa and out of the window were an extended earth and aerial for picking up the BBC World Service. No radio or part of a radio could be purchased or repaired in Lower Africa without a licence giving details of the set and the owner. He had no licence and did not know whether Arthur Whelk had had one. He added nervously that Sarah dusted round the wires each day without comment, regarding them, perhaps, merely as evidence of eccentricity. Jim took no notice but Piet stared at the radio for a long time before sitting on the sofa by the wires. They drank Arthur's lager from Arthur's fridge in the bar. It was the first time he had entertained anyone.

"Are you going to stay in the Foreign Office?" Jim asked abruptly.

"I don't know. I've only just joined. I've no idea what else I'd do."

"You don't want to kill tigers, go into business, be an engineer, run a farm?"

"Yes, I'd do them all if I could. I'd live a dozen different lives."

"But you won't?"

"Probably not."

Jim drank from his can. "I don't reckon you will stay in. You're not the type."

"What's the type?"

"Wet-arsed old women." Jim's tone was matter-of-fact.

"What makes you think I'm not one?"

Jim put his can to his lips again. His Adam's apple bobbed slowly and when he lowered the can he wiped his lips on the back of his arm. "Have you seen Joanna today?"

Patrick felt his stomach tighten. Piet sat impassively on the sofa. "Yes. Have you?"

"Not today."

Jim's tone was affectedly offhand. It irritated Patrick. "D'you see her nearly every day?" he asked.

"That's my business." Jim's face looked heavy and brutal but he said nothing. They drank in silence until Patrick made a self-conscious remark to Piet about World Service reception.

"You heard anything about Whelk?" asked Jim.

"No. Have you?"

"Not a squeak."

"D'you have any more theories?"

"I never had any. He hasn't telephoned you – or anyone on his behalf – no funny calls?"

"No, nothing." His denial sounded glib and unconvincing. They were probably tapping the embassy phones or had perhaps seen the L and F man when he called or had read the exchange of telegrams.

"You normally expect something by this time," Jim continued. "You would let me know, wouldn't you, if you heard anything?"

"Of course I would." Patrick had no real compunction about lying but felt he did it badly. He was relieved when they left although regretful as he watched the bakkie pull away. He would certainly have to get a car now that it looked as if he would be seeing more of Joanna.

He was unable to sleep at first, and then only fitfully. The encounter with Jim and Piet discoloured his memories of the earlier part of the evening and made it impossible to recall them untainted by Jim's heavy brutal expression, or by his quiet tense voice. He was awoken very early by the sound of a vehicle but assumed it was Sarah's man, Harold, and went back to sleep. When he got up he found the red bakkie parked in the drive. The keys and documents had been pushed through his letter-box.

"The man bring it, massa," said Sarah. "The policeman who was here before. He tell me not to wake you." She smiled listlessly. "I thought he was here about Stanley but he go away. I was happy for that."

Before going to work that morning Patrick sent Jim a cheque for the trade-in price.

11

It was Saturday morning. The murky green of the swimming-pool had become opaque and was now sinister, possibly fecund. The sun was warm and the rest of the garden cheerful and busy with birds, but the pool looked dangerous and sullen. It had absorbed all the chemicals in all the right combinations but with none of the right effects. For some minutes Patrick stared at a patch of water where he thought he saw something move.

"Massa."

Sarah's face was screwed up against the sun. She held one of his shirts by the collar, not pressed and folded as usual when she had finished them but limp and open. He glanced anxiously at it, expecting to be told that it was of such poor quality and so worn it would have to be thrown away.

"Yes, Sarah?"

"De shirt has come off de button."

It was clear from her English that she was embarrassed. "Ah. Yes. Right, Sarah, I'll get some more buttons."

"Yes, massa."

She remained standing, holding the shirt. He had known for two days that the house was short of nearly everything and that a major shopping expedition was necessary. He had hoped that by doing nothing a solution would occur naturally. However, there was now the bakkie in which to take Sarah to the supermarket. This was another excuse to drive it. "We must go shopping together this morning."

Her face brightened and she folded the shirt over her arm. "Yes, massa, we do big shopping."

In a large and deliberate hand she wrote a list of food and household items and brought it to him to inspect. He felt he was expected to comment and pointed at the two unfamiliar items.

"For me, massa, for my food," she said of the first.

"But you can share mine."

She smiled awkwardly. "I like to eat mealie-meal. It is better for me."

126

He pointed at the other item.

"For killing de noo-noos," she said.

"Noo-noos?"

She pointed at the floor. "Noo-noos." She stamped her foot several times, laughing. "Noo-noos. What you call" – she struggled for the word – "ants," she said, triumphantly.

They both laughed. "Noo-noos is a good word for ants."

"Swahi word, massa, from Swahiland. Also there are cockroaches."

"In Swahiland?"

"No, here, but also in Swahiland, yes."

"I've never seen a cockroach."

Her eyes were wide with surprise. "There are not cockroach in England?"

"No – well, yes, there are but I've never seen one."

"When it rain there are many cockroach in the house."

"They don't like the rain?"

"No, they come in the house when it rain." She frowned. "My first madam when I first begin my work say to me it rain all time in England."

"It rain – rains – quite often, yes."

"But still there are no cockroach in the houses?"

Patrick thought for a moment. "There are but they hide so that it is hard to see them."

She went into her quarters to put on a clean blue maid's dress and white apron and cap. When she came back she stood in the kitchen tying the apron. "Are there black people like me in England?"

"Yes, Sarah, there are many black people, just like you."

She smiled a little shyly, looking down as she smoothed her apron. "Ready now, massa."

It was a great pleasure to cruise in the bakkie through avenues of jacarandas but the journey was not long enough. He had hardly got into top gear when Sarah directed him to a large car-park in front of a low new building. He drove unnecessarily right round the car-park before choosing a place. As he was locking the vehicle two small black boys approached wearing trousers and shirts that were torn. One had a sore on the side of his head.

"Guard car, massa, guard car," they said peremptorily, holding out their pink palms.

They looked very needy. He gave them some of the loose change that was in his pocket. "Guard it well and I'll give you the other half when I come back."

Sarah frowned across the high red bonnet of the bakkie. "Mr Patrick," she said firmly. "I am sorry. Please excuse me." She walked round to his side of the vehicle, dignified and offended. "Excuse me, please," she said again, then turned to the two boys and delivered herself of a torrent of debased Zulu. Her voice was shrill and her speech rapid. The two boys scampered away behind other cars. She turned rather formally to Patrick. "Massa, please, no money for them. They are bad boys. It is bad to give money to bad boys."

"I thought they would look after the car."

"No. They steal. But now they will not come back."

The supermarket turned out to be an underground town on a scale beyond anything in Britain. Escalators led down through several levels, and opening off each of these were arcades and avenues of shops. They radiated like spokes from a central well about thirty yards across. At the bottom a great chess-board had been painted on the ground. The pieces were four or five feet high and the two players, young whites in jeans and T-shirts, moved them around by pushing or by lifting them with both arms. They walked around and between the pieces, gesticulating and talking. Captured pieces were laid on their sides off the board, like forsaken gods. A few other young men sat or straddled them, giving advice or laughing.

Everything in the underground town was clean. There was piped music and air-conditioning. Most of the staff were black and most of the customers white, and the majority of these were women. Uniformed guards sauntered about, the blacks armed with truncheons and the whites with revolvers. Some had Alsatian dogs.

Sarah led the way to the supermarket. There was a bewildering acreage of shelves. Patrick, unaccustomed to shopping, found it difficult to pick out particular items from amongst the whole. The profusion glazed his eyes. Sarah consulted her list whilst he tried to extract a trolley that was stuck inside three others.

Sarah was used to shopping with experienced, interested madams. She was reluctant to make decisions herself and treat Patrick as a porter. He therefore attempted to make up in system for what he lacked in knowledge and interest by ordering one of each where there was a choice of two brands and by choosing the largest or most colourful when there were more than two. He went for bold primary colours.

"Is that it?" he asked after about twenty minutes, when the trolley was nearly full.

"Meat, massa. There is no meat. I don't know what you like."

128

"I like all meat."

"All?"

"I like all food."

She put her hand to her mouth. "But you have to choose. I don't know what you want."

He chose steak, a pound of each kind. This principle worked equally well with fruit and vegetables. He bought eight toilet rolls, two for each toilet, and a couple of big sacks of mealie-meal for Sarah. He discovered that she usually had her own tea, sugar, milk and coffee.

"Why not share mine?"

"Because it is yours, massa."

"Then we'll share it."

Sarah never feigned reluctance. "Thank you, massa."

Dog-food was all that remained and Patrick, determined to find something for himself, suggested they leave the trolley by the fruit shelf and each set off in search.

She was to look for meat, he for biscuits. He soon returned in triumph with two sacks, one of each kind. Having seen Sarah crossing the lanes near the check-out counter he took the trolley and set off after her between the gardening tools and the boots and shoes. She was gone by the time he reached the top but he thought he glimpsed her crossing lower down. Eyed by a dour white security guard, he went rapidly down between the household utensils and the soap powders. Near the bottom the lane was blocked by an attendant who was restacking and by three women talking. Patrick turned his trolley round and headed quickly back. At the corner he collided with another trolley, catching it broadside-on. It toppled over, quite slowly. Bread, meat, tin foil, washing-up liquid, Marmite, butter, potatoes and apples spilled on to the floor. Some of the apples rolled as far as the check-out counter. A bag of self-raising flour burst over the shiny black boots of the security guard.

"Oh, Jesus bloody Christ!" shouted the woman who had been pushing the trolley.

He recognised her as the woman he had met at the police headquarters. He started to apologise but she turned angrily to the guard.

"Did you see him do that? Did you see what he did? Downright bloody criminal stupidity!" She stepped over the rubble so that she was closer to the guard and turned to face Patrick. "Coming straight at me as if I wasn't there. Haven't you got any consideration for other people? Are you blind or something?"

"What are you doing speeding about like that?" asked the guard.

"You've no business speeding like that in here. This is a shop, not a race-track."

Patrick held up his hand. "I'm sorry. It was entirely my fault. I wasn't looking where I was going."

"That's no excuse," said the guard.

Patrick got down on his hands and knees and began picking up the woman's shopping. His own trolley had remained upright and nothing had fallen from it. "I'll pay for everything that's broken."

"Me or the shop?" asked the woman.

He looked up at her. "Whoever claims it."

The guard stamped his feet to get the flour off his boots and then stepped back, crushing some biscuits. "You are responsible," he said as if the point were in dispute.

"Yes, I am," said Patrick.

"You should look where you're bloody going in future," said the woman.

He ignored her. A few seconds later a pair of black hands joined his in rapidly picking up the goods. Sarah was on her knees beside him, gathering tins and packets with submissive haste. She did not glance at him but worked quickly, almost fearfully. After stacking tins in the trolley she put in a packet of Oxo cubes that was intact though battered. The woman stepped forward, took it out and flung it back to the floor by Sarah's hand, causing it to break open.

"That's no use, that's damaged."

Sarah did not look up but humbly pushed the packet towards the pile of damaged goods.

"Dumbo," added the woman, under her breath.

Patrick took the broken packet and stood. He saw his own anger reflected in a look of alarm on the woman's face and a sudden watchfulness on the guard's. "What did you say?"

The woman hesitated. "I said – I said it was damaged, it was already damaged."

She was frightened but still hostile. The sight of Sarah's bowed head fired his anger for a few seconds more. "It wasn't but it is now. By you. You pay for it." He tossed the broken packet at her feet. She stepped back.

The guard put one hand on the belt of his holster. He pointed at the mess. "We want this cleared up."

"It will be." Patrick's anger evaporated as he became more aware of the absurdity. It seemed he only ever got angry in ridiculous circumstances and his anger never lasted because he was never more than

130

fleetingly unaware of its uselessness. He and Sarah were joined by a cleaner with a broom and then by a supervisor who said that no one need pay for anything. The woman had simply to replace the goods she had lost and take them out in the normal way. She left without a word as soon as her trolley was loaded.

At the check-out Patrick paid for Sarah's mealie-meal, for which she thanked him in a subdued voice. The bill was so large that he decided to abandon his system of buying at least two of everything in future even if it did mean they would have to shop more often. Sarah still looked chastened and so he attempted to cheer her by buying a women's magazine like one he had seen in her quarters.

Her face brightened. She flicked through pictures of pretty white women in exquisite houses. "Is my favourite, massa."

Two assistants loaded the shopping into bags and carried them through the town, up the several escalators and out into the car-park. Patrick paused to look down the well at the game of chess. He saw Black's remaining bishop carried off and laid across two pawns so that one of the spectators could use him as a bench.

The assistants loaded the bags into the bakkie. Patrick did not tip them, recalling Sarah's outrage. "Should I have given them money?" he asked as they drove away.

She looked round at the departing assistants. "It depend on you, massa. If they are good boys and they do good job. They are not like this children. But I don't know them boys. Zulu."

"Not Swahi, like you?"

She shook her head seriously. "No, massa, not like me. I don't know many Zulu."

At work that week Patrick drafted and redrafted, made and remade transport arrangements, read and reread files. It did not bother him because he could look forward to Thursday's lunch with Joanna. There were no cancelling telephone calls and he grew more confident as the day approached. Several times he was called in by Sir Wilfrid to confirm that nothing more had been heard from the L and F man. He was instructed to check that his bank had sent the money the L and F man had asked for. By Wednesday the ambassador had begun to suspect that the Lower Africans had got him. He considered telling Patrick to ask for Jim Rissik's help in finding the man but decided that so drastic a departure from present tactics should await discussion with the minister. After all, there was still a chance that the chap might turn up. Patrick was relieved. He particularly wanted not to see Jim before Thursday.

He wore his new lightweight suit to work that day with a new and sober tie. He was a little late because he nearly ran out of petrol and had to make a detour. By the time he arrived there was a palpable atmosphere of alarm and urgency. The ambassador was to be guest of honour at a luncheon given by the Progress Association, a group of leading local businessmen, with a few journalists and one or two of the more liberally-inclined politicians. The lunch was to be in the Gold Club, the bastion of wealthy English-speaking Lower Africans, and the ambassador was to read a paper prepared some time before by Philip, subsequently amended by Clifford and called, 'Lower Africa: Gold and Good Intentions.' Philip was ill, though, and could not be contacted because he was at the doctor's. Only an unamended copy of the paper could be found, and this would not do.

Clifford lost his temper with the registry clerks who were trying to help him find the final draft and later slammed the telephone down on Philip's wife. He could not remember all the alterations he had made and could not possibly sit down and do them all again in time for the ambassador to have the final draft in his hands at least an hour before the lunch. Then, with an abruptness and an illogicality that gave grounds for the prevailing suspicion that he was actually unsure about his own drafting, he declared that Patrick should rework the paper and that he would look it over before it went to the ambassador. Sir Wilfrid, unaware of the drama, was said to be at the pipemaker's.

When Patrick heard this he at first feared for his own lunch but, realising that his task, however rushed and confused, would have to be over by then, he relaxed. A minute or so after the paper arrived on his desk, though, he was interrupted by Daphne from the consular department. She looked worried and attempted an unconvincing smile.

"There's something rather urgent," she said.

"Really urgent?"

"Well, yes, but not McGrain." She explained that Mr Whelk, as consul, had as one of his responsibilities the duty to visit British subjects in Lower African gaols. The hard won right of consular access was something that the authorities accepted fully but it was essential to maintain regular visits within the time-limits agreed because if they were allowed to lapse, if even one visit were missed, there might be difficulty in re-establishing the routine. The Lower Africans were punctilious and one had to keep up to the mark oneself. Unknown to her, Mr Whelk had some time ago arranged to visit a prison that morning, the last day in the present period when a visit could be made.

The prison had telephoned just an hour previously to confirm. Knowing how important it was not to miss a visit, she had said that Patrick would come in Mr Whelk's stead. She hoped that that would be all right. She knew he was busy but there was no alternative.

"How long does it take to drive to the prison?"

"About an hour, I believe. Mr Whelk usually spends an hour or so there, sometimes more. It's a question of seeing that there are no complaints or problems, that's all. There usually aren't."

Patrick calculated that he could get there and back by lunchtime provided he didn't do the speech. He picked up the papers. "We'll have to talk to Clifford."

"Would you like me to come with you?"

"I think you'd better."

Daphne smiled consolingly. "I know Mr Steggles can be awkward but he's no McGrain. I'll do the talking if it gets difficult."

Clifford was in his office. "You can't," he said before Patrick finished explaining.

"Someone has to and it has to be this morning."

"It's a question of priorities. You're always gallivanting around. Daphne can go."

"It has to be someone of diplomatic rank," said Daphne mildly.

It looked for a moment as if Clifford might offer to go himself but he thought better of it. "Look, the ambassador's paper has to be amended. There's no question about that. You're the only person available with the time to spare, so that's that. I'm not going to go and tell him he'll have to speak from a rough draft. For one thing, I'm going to be there with him and it must sound good."

Daphne shrugged. "Oh, very well then, I'll go and explain why we've jeopardised our consular access."

He looked as if she had stung him. Her tone was gentle and there was no trace of hostility on her face. He turned bad-temperedly towards Patrick. "I wish someone would either bloody well find Whelk or get the office to send a proper replacement. Don't think you're getting away with anything, Stubbs. I want you back here by lunchtime. Someone will have to hold the fort while we're away."

Patrick handed over the draft. "You might find there's not much to alter."

Clifford glared for a moment before sitting down.

It was an exhilarating drive. The days were getting warmer but this was the first really hot one. The tar glistened, there was a heat haze on the road, the rolling veldt was brown and parched. The red bonnet of the bakkie was too hot to touch. Around the prison site, though, the land was green and well watered. There were playing-fields, a supermarket, workshops, newly planted trees and rows of new detached houses, each with rectangular lawn and garage. The perimeter of the prison itself was formed by a high wire fence, some fifty yards inside of which was a high wall. All the buildings were brisk, clean and new; none, save the watch-towers, was more than single-storey. Despite the impression of openness and space it was a maximum security prison for long-term prisoners. Because it was near Battenburg it also housed a number of men on remand.

Patrick showed his diplomatic identity card. A warder wearing khaki shirt and shorts and a Sam Browne and holster took him through the wire to the main entrance. The warder's thick pink legs bristled with fair hair. He stamped and saluted in the office of the administrative commandant, Major de Beers, a fat jolly balding man with red cheeks and a smile that was cheerful and complicitous. His small brown eyes shone like his holster.

They shook hands. "Very good of you to find time to visit, Mr Stubbs. Mr Whelk was always very regular. That's how the prisoners like it and that's how we like it. Has Mr Whelk gone back or has he moved on to another job? I didn't know he was leaving."

"He's away at the moment. He'll probably go to another post when he comes back. I'm just a stand-in."

Major de Beers smiled. "Stand-in or not, you're very welcome, Mr Stubbs. Please sit down. Coffee?"

Over the coffee and ginger biscuits Major de Beers went through a typed list of a dozen or so prisoners, commenting on their crimes, lengths of sentences and years left to serve. Some he expanded on, sipping his coffee with his plump little finger tightly curled. The younger and more dangerous of the two psychopaths had been quiet for some time now and was getting on well with his daily therapy sessions. The other had attacked a warder and had lost some remission but was back in his classes and responding well. The rapist was due for release soon. The homosexual thief had had to be put in a cell on his own again. The embezzler, a former liberal journalist, had become even more convinced that everyone was against him and was now a fervent evangelist as well. He refused to work and was unpopular with the other prisoners. He was still refusing to visit the psychiatrist. Major de Beers thought that he should because he was getting worse. He would be grateful for Patrick's opinion since it would be necessary to force him. The major regretted that the other embezzler had been moved to another prison; they had been good friends and had had some good talks together, but it was necessary to move him in the end. There was one other, a remand prisoner called Chatsworth, recently arrived; he had no details to hand but could get them. Patrick said he would get them himself.

He was led along cool polished corridors to a visiting room divided by a glass partition from an outer office where there were two more armed warders. The prisoners would arrive at ten-minute intervals although he could have as long as he liked with each man. Except for the psychopaths and the remand prisoner they would be unescorted. The warders could be summoned by a button on the underside of the desk.

The prisoners looked like soldiers. They wore olive-green overalls, had short hair and were tanned and fit. They worked in the mornings and in the afternoons took exercise, usually football or weight-lifting. Most had no complaints about the prison except that they were in it nor about the food except that it was monotonous. Their mail arrived regularly and they wanted to continue receiving the old British news-papers that Arthur Whelk salvaged from bundles destined for Kuweto. Some had not been in Britain since childhood or infancy. Nearly all were to be deported on release and all wanted to stay in Lower Africa. Most had kept their British passports in order to avoid conscription.

The unofficial leader was a former corporal of light infantry who had won a Military Medal in Malaya. He spoke of the others more than of himself. They were all well apart from the journalist who complained continually and made life difficult. It was just as well that the major's embezzler friend has been transferred recently as there were several who very much wanted to meet him again. The man spoke quietly, his manner confident, shrewd and reassuring. When he left Patrick felt he had been talking to a doctor.

A tall, blond, powerful man had two of a ten-year sentence to run. He had robbed and beaten people whom his prostitute wife lured back to his flat. He sat leaning forward, his elbows on his knees, his hands clasped, talking man to man. He had made trouble earlier in his sentence but realised now that it wasn't worth it; he wanted out. He had no complaints.

The elder of the psychopaths was strongly built and formidable looking. He was calm and rational. He regretted his attack on the warder and would try hard not to do it again; it was simply that prison got at you every now and again, knowing that year in year out you'd be eating the same food with the same people, hearing the same voices saying the same things and all in the same place. It was then that the little things got at you. Outside you could always walk away from what made you fed up, here you couldn't. He would be thirty-eight when he got out.

The man who had raped two black maids was small, courteous and careful, with mild eyes. He had no complaints and planned that when deported to Britain he would go into the hotel trade. The journalist embezzler complained about the prison administration, the food, the other prisoners, the work and the godlessness. He was discriminated against because he was British. He would not see a psychiatrist because there was nothing wrong with him.

The younger psychopath had a fresh complexion, curly brown hair and an attractive, shy smile. He had no comments about prison but spoke of fishing and golf, having come close to winning a competition in the latter. He was near the start of a long sentence for the attempted murder with a shotgun of a girl bank clerk, whom he had blinded. His own glacial blue eyes were disconcertingly wide open as though in perpetual surprise. He said he would like to have been a farmer.

The last man was the remand prisoner, Chatsworth, escorted by a warder who remained behind the partition. He was tall, fair and gangling. He walked with his shoulders hunched, his hands clasped behind his back and his head nodding like a bird's. It was a moment before Patrick realised why he was familiar. He was the Army man from his Civil Service Selection Board, the one who had predicted his own failure and Patrick's success. The habitual grin that then had made him look slightly mad had been replaced by a thoughtful compression of the lips. On his brow were three horizontal lines. His eyebrows were raised as in permanent query. He recognised Patrick and advanced with his hand outstretched.

"What on earth are you doing here?" he asked.

"I might ask you the same question."

"Bit of a misunderstanding."

Patrick saw the warder looking on in surprise. "Better sit down."

Chatsworth's grin returned. "You got through, then?"

"Yes, in the end. I'm third secretary here and temporary part-time consul."

"So you're Stubbs? Well done."

"Well, yes. How do you know my name?"

Chatsworth held up his hand. "Don't worry, no need to act dumb. They can't hear from out there. I couldn't hear what you were saying to

136

the last bloke. I'm Mackenzie, the one you sent the money to. L and F, remember?"

"You tried to see me at the embassy?"

"That's right. I needed some more."

"So you're not really Chatsworth?"

"Yes, I am. It's only Mackenzie that I'm not. Pays to use another name when you're dealing with kidnappers."

Patrick leaned forward. "Were you dealing with kidnappers?"

Chatsworth held up his hand again. "Explain later. Main thing is, what's your plan? No good swapping clothes because they can see us. You'll just have to take me with you. Bluff your way."

Chatsworth looked cheerful now, recovering his former self-confidence. Patrick wondered at first if he'd misunderstood but decided he hadn't. "Look," he said slowly, "I haven't come to get you out. I can't do that. I've just come to see who you are and to check that you have no complaints. I didn't know you were here, you see. That is, I didn't know it was you."

Chatsworth looked aggrieved. "I thought that's what you consul blokes were for. Especially bearing in mind what I'm doing for you."

Patrick recalled Chatsworth's advice about adopting a limp on certain occasions. He also remembered the abrupt laugh and reference to a mysteriously short time spent at Cambridge. He picked up his pen and spoke carefully. "You'd better tell me how you came here."

"No time for all that now. Be more use if you'd tell me how I'm going to get out."

"I can't do anything about that until I know what you're here for."

"Well, I'm not sure I know myself, to be honest. All a bit of a cock-up. Not really my fault. Problem of money and identity."

"What kind of problem?"

"Not enough of either." Chatsworth laughed and folded his arms. "Pity, 'cos I got off to a good start. Picked up by your car at the airport and all that. Stroke of luck. I liked your ambassador, by the way. Not as stuck-up as some of them. Does he know I'm here?"

"No. Look, unless you tell me why you are here there's no hope of anyone doing anything. It's three months before the next consular visit." Patrick knew that this tone of calm bureaucratic implacability was one that he could not have adopted six months before. Chatsworth sighed, crossed his legs, refolded his arms, glanced over his shoulder at the warder, shook his head as if at the world's foolishness, and began in a roundabout way to explain.

His story was rambling and incomplete. The theme was Chatsworth's struggle against a corrupt, uncomprehending and ungrateful world. Major events were mentioned in passing while certain details received extravagant attention. It was not clear why he had left the Army. He had decided to "chuck it in and let them stew in their own juice" as a result of persecution. Getting a passport in the name of Mackenzie was glossed over by reference to someone who had died. On the other hand, an angry encounter with a hotel porter was described at length, as were the circumstances of an insult allegedly received at the hands of British Airways in a dispute about the validity of a ticket. He was considering legal action.

The job with L and F, who employed a lot of ex-Army people, had started well enough but he'd been let down of late. He'd handled a negotiation in Bogota – an old stamping-ground – concerning a kidnapped banker but it had all gone wrong before he got there and the chap had been done in. No one's fault but the office couldn't be expected to see that. They'd got even more upset when he'd done the decent thing and stayed on for a few days to comfort the widow.

He'd been thinking of chucking it all in again when they'd asked him to do the Whelk business. Probably had no one else with the experience, though if he'd known what a dog's breakfast it was he'd have left them to it. Anyway, having arrived he'd decided to lie low and wait for the kidnappers, if there were any, to make a move. Like the ambassador, he had from the start suspected the Lower African authorities. He suspected them even more now that they'd framed him. Anyway, he'd pushed off down to the coast for a week or two to blow away the cobwebs, get some new ideas and so on and had booked in to what seemed a reasonable sort of hotel. Everything had been okay until L and F had started to get a bit sticky about the expenses and he'd had to ring them a few times. They wouldn't understand that you can't expect quick results when you don't even know whether there's been a kidnap. The hotel got suspicious – perhaps they'd listened to the calls – and had demanded cash down. That's why he'd had to telegraph the embassy. He was grateful to Patrick for coughing up so quickly and would see him all right in due course though there wasn't much he could do from where he was, quite frankly.

Then on his last night the hotel staff must've taken it into their heads that he wouldn't be able to pay the remainder, and called the police. Unless it was all a put-up job, of course, and it looked increasingly like one. They said at the time that it was because he'd been doing a bit of entertaining in his room during the previous few days. No harm in that, but as luck would have it there was one with him when they burst in.

138

She happened to be black – dark brown, to be exact. He knew the law, of course, but he'd assumed it was one that everyone broke and that it wasn't taken too seriously so long as you did it discreetly, like fiddling the income tax. He'd never had a black – or, rather, a dark brown – before and though he could easily have done it in London, it felt safer in Lower Africa. They were friendlier here.

Anyway, there was the most God Almighty fuss. Room suddenly filled with Keystone cops, the girl screaming and dancing about like a scalded cat, vase of flowers knocked on to yours truly who was flat on his back, naked. Frog-marched out through the hotel lobby at light infantry pace wearing only a blanket and in front of a pack of bloody Nippons, all with cameras whirring. Blanket then got stuck in the swing door and he was left starkers at the top of the steps with all the fuzz inside trying to get out. Absolutely bloody, the whole thing, and all for being friendly.

The discovery that he had two passports really put the cat among the pigeons. They took that more seriously than anything. Kept asking what he was doing here but he hadn't told them because he knew from the ambassador that it would embarrass HMG. He damn soon would though if HMG didn't do something about getting him out. Also, if the police were so worried about hotel bills and who you were and who you had if off with they'd probably say looking for kidnap victims was a hanging offence. As it was they were accusing him of being a terrorist and infiltrating the country in order to stir up the blacks. That would be funny if he weren't in prison for it. When he'd heard he was going to see the consul from the embassy he'd assumed HMG was playing the white man and was getting him out. What Patrick had said had not cheered him, frankly. On the other hand, he was sure the ambassador would do something. He was a chap who had his head screwed on and his feet firmly on the ground. Also, Patrick knew the background, so everything should be all right. It had to be.

Patrick was not so sure.

The warder peered through the partition again. Chatsworth looked glum. He leaned forward and rested his elbow on the desk and his chin on his hand. "You've got to get me out, you know. I can't stay here."

Patrick nodded. "I would if I could but I don't know how. We've no authority. If you've broken their law it's up to them what they do about it."

"Lock up one of them in London."

"That works only with diplomats. I'll try to find out what you're

139

going to be charged with. You haven't been charged yet, have you?"

"Not properly. Only some bloody silly thing about impersonating someone else, just so that they can hold me. Though how I'm supposed to be impersonating someone else when both people are me I'm blowed if I know."

"I'll try to find out what they're planning to charge you with and then I'll speak to the ambassador."

"But what should I tell them I'm doing here? They keep asking."

"Say you're looking for a job – you want to be a mercenary or join the Lower African army or something. If we're lucky we might be able to persuade them to deport you quietly. I'll try to come again as soon as I've got some news. Anything I can bring you?"

"Nothing I'd be allowed."

"Any complaints?"

"Only the fact that I'm here." Chatsworth sat back in his chair, looked around the room and sighed. "It's a bit like being back at Sandhurst, really, only not as bad. They're more polite here." A truck-load of black prisoners was driven past the window. They all wore standard olive-greens. "Working party," he continued. "We don't have anything to do with them. Strict segregation."

They stood and shook hands again. "You didn't by any chance leave a bullet in the ambassador's residence, did you?" asked Patrick.

Chatsworth's eyes opened wide and he retained his grip on Patrick's hand. "My little nine-milly, yes. That was my lucky charm. Take it everywhere. Why, has the old boy found it?"

"No, I did."

"Have you got it?"

"Well, no, but I know where it is. I gave it to someone. I can probably get it back."

"You must, you must." Chatsworth was pulling on Patrick's arm and the warder was looking suspiciously at them. "That's why it's all gone wrong, you see, because I lost it. Everything was all right up till then."

"I'll see what I can do."

"You must get me out."

"Yes." Chatsworth was led away, frowning again, his head nodding like a pigeon's as he walked. Patrick said nothing about him to Major de Beers, asking only to be kept informed of any charges likely to be made. Major de Beers said it was a police matter but he would pass on the message. They agreed that the journalist should see a psychiatrist and the major undertook to send the report to the embassy. Patrick was shown out with the same punctilious formality as had welcomed him.

He did not at first realise that it was a police car parked next to the bakkie. The driver sat with the window open and his elbow on the door. He got out as Patrick approached. It was Jim, uniformed, smiling very slightly, his regular features wrinkled against the sun. For a few moments the gleam from his polished belt, the red shine from the bakkie and the bright prison wire behind lent to the scene the detailed unreality of film.

"Seems I can't go anywhere without stubbing my toe on you," he said.

Patrick forced a grin. On first seeing him he had felt that he was himself about to join Chatsworth. "You don't have to follow me around."

Jim pressed down the lower flaps of his jacket. "How's your friend?"

"My friend?"

"The one you've just seen. The man with two names."

"The remand prisoner?" He knew that his pretended puzzlement would sound affected but pretence was too instinctive a reaction for him to avoid it. "He had no complaints."

"Just as well. He could be in serious trouble."

"What's he being charged with?"

"Depends what he's doing in our country." Jim looked up at the prison roof, stretched and yawned.

Patrick unlocked the bakkie. The handle was hot to touch. He stood back to let the heat out. "Looking for work, he said."

"Looking for Whelk, did you say?"

"No, I didn't."

"Maybe he's an accomplice of Whelk's."

"In what?"

Jim looked at him. "Perhaps you really don't know."

Patrick said nothing. Jim began slowly grinding a stone into the hard earth with his polished boot. A working party of white prisoners was marched out of the main gate and towards the married quarters. They were bronzed, fit men, all young. Those in the front rank marched with unseeing eyes past the policeman and his friend, their faces closed and brutal.

"What d'you think will happen to him?" asked Patrick.

"Dunno. Depends on the British embassy. He could be granted bail or surety if you were interested in someone involved with Whelk."

"Involved in what way?"

141

"You tell me." Jim kicked away the stone he had been burying. "If you are interested you'd better move fast. He can only be held until tomorrow without being properly charged and if he's done under the anti-terrorist laws, as he could well be, that's it. No bail, no remission, nothing."

"Is this your opinion?"

"Let's say I speak with authority." He smiled again. "I think you and me understand each other well enough, Pat. For all our differences."

Patrick nodded. "I'll speak to the ambassador."

"When I say move fast, I mean fast. Headquarters will need a letter guaranteeing his good conduct by early this afternoon. Otherwise by late afternoon the papers will have gone across to the prosecutor and then we can't do anything."

Patrick thought immediately of his lunch with Joanna. Also, that the ambassador would soon be out. "I'll see him as soon as I get back."

"Good." Jim straightened his uniform. "No sign of Stanley, Sarah's boy?"

"No." Patrick decided to proceed with their new-found frankness. "Why d'you ask?"

"Wondering where he is, that's all."

"How d'you know he's not back home in Swahiland?"

"He left there a while ago." Jim got into his car but paused before closing the door. "How's the bakkie?"

"Going well."

"You're pleased?"

"I'm pleased."

"Be nice to her." He looked away as he spoke, started the engine and accelerated suddenly, leaving a small cloud of dust where Patrick stood.

12

"He's gone," said Clifford.

Patrick didn't believe him. He knew Clifford was to go to lunch with the ambassador. "When?"

"As good as. He's reading through Philip's paper – with my revisions. He hasn't got time for anything else now."

"He's still in his office?"

Clifford stood in the corridor, a file under his arm, barring the way. "He's leaving in two minutes. So am I. You can tell me. Make it brief or let it wait till this afternoon."

No explanations to Clifford were brief. Besides, Patrick had been forbidden to discuss the L and F man. "It's about the British prisoners. There's something urgent."

Clifford scoffed and made to move off down the corridor. "Well, it can't be that urgent – they're hardly going to run away, are they? That can easily wait till this afternoon. Anyway, it's a consular matter. If they're being tortured report it on the normal channels. You don't bother ambassadors with that sort of thing."

Patrick stood aside as if he were going to follow but when Clifford turned the corner he slipped up the corridor. In the anteroom Jean paused in her typing. "He's very busy. He's reading his speech for the Progress Association."

"I have to see him about the British prisoners."

"You can't. He's reading his speech."

Sir Wilfrid appeared in the doorway to his office, holding some loose papers in one hand and untidying his long white hair with the other. He was in his shirtsleeves and one of his braces was half undone. "Seen my jacket anywhere, Jean?" He yawned.

Jean got up to search. Clifford reappeared, glaring at Patrick. Sir Wilfrid thought the jacket might just possibly be in the car.

"Patrick will run down and see," said Clifford.

Patrick tapped his breast pocket as if he had papers in it. "I've got something we should talk about, sir. News."

Sir Wilfrid's eyes opened wide. "You've got news? How wonderful.

Come in, come in." He looked around for Jean, not seeing her because she was behind him. "Er – yes, worth trying the car, Clifford. Let me know if it's not there, won't you?"

Once in his office Sir Wilfrid closed the door and picked up the radio. He placed it carefully on the desk and switched it on. There was no sound. He switched it off and on again and twiddled the tuning knob, with no result.

"Must be the battery, damn it," he whispered. "Is it very important? Right, well, whisper." He sat on the edge of the desk while Patrick bent to his ear. At the end of the explanation Sir Wilfrid said aloud, "They've got them both, then? Whelk and this other chap?" Patrick whispered again. Sir Wilfrid nodded, then resumed his own whisper. "So we still don't know what's happend to poor Arthur, although this Rissik friend of yours seems to know all about it?"

"I don't think he does, no, but I'm sure he knows something and he's very keen to find out more."

"Told you the police knew more than they were letting on."

"They think we do."

"LASS are behind it all, mark my words. They'll know the minister's coming and they could be planning to embarrass us."

There was a solemn silence. Mention of embarrassment was like mention of plague in a medieval city. "What would LASS want with Whelk?" asked Patrick in an undertone.

"They'd want to find out our secrets."

Patrick wasn't sure there were any. "Does he know any secrets?"

"He must know some, don't you think?"

"I suppose so, yes."

Sir Wilfrid stood and began pacing the room, his fists pressed down into his pockets. He talked in his normal voice. "On the one hand, if this chap spills the beans in court to get himself a lighter sentence there'll be frightful embarrassment all round. The Lower Africans will get publicly indignant and will laugh like drains in private and we shall look very foolish indeed. On the other hand, if they really are prepared to release him on our surety to see if he leads them to Whelk – well, doesn't that suit our book too? It seems to me it does. Either he leads us all to Whelk or, more likely, he doesn't and is quietly deported in the wake of a successful ministerial visit." He stood still and nodded to himself. "I must say I dislike being bounced into taking action like this without being able to get a view from London but there's no other way. We'll accept your friend Rissik's offer and I'll look to you to see that the chap behaves himself once he's out. You know, lives a quiet life, gives them no cause to embarrass us. You'll have to draft a letter of guarantee now and bring it to me at this lunch for signing. No, better still, come to the lunch yourself and draft it on the spot in the club library, so that I can amend as necessary. Tell Jean to ring them. They're bound to be able to squeeze in an extra one."

Sir Wilfrid picked up his jacket from the floor behind the armchair as Clifford, redder in the face and still cross, came in to say that it was not in the car. "What? Oh, no, it was here all the time. I've just found it. Look, Patrick's coming to lunch with us. Can you get Jean to ring and tell them?"

Clifford momentarily forgot himself. "But he can't – he's not invited. It's heads of mission and – and important people only."

"Never mind that, he's invited now. He's my guest. I can have guests if I want, can't I?"

Patrick was determined not to postpone his lunch with Joanna. It was not until one-thirty. If necessary, he would run away, feign the falling sickness or start a fight; get there he would.

The Gold Club was the elder and grander of the two that emulated London clubs. It was an architectural copy of the Reform and its membership was drawn mainly from the English-speaking business community. The rival club dated from the turn of the century when it had been founded by Jews who were forbidden the Gold. Inside brass gleamed and woodwork darkly shone. Black servants, called boys, wore white shirts and long baggy white shorts. They polished, cleaned, fetched, carried and served with slow decorum. Outside an armless and legless black beggar sat in a wheelchair at the bottom of the steps. He had a round wrinkled face and a battered brown trilby so large that it rested on his ears. Another trilby was placed where his lap would have been, upturned to collect coins. Someone said he was put there every day. Patrick wondered who collected the money.

They were ushered into the bar for drinks. The company, all male, was made up of prominent Lower Africans, a few journalists, a visiting German professsor and a dark-jowled Argentinian general. Drinks were served. Patrick asked a plump lawyer where the library was and received in reply a sermon on the liberalising effect of international trade upon political and legal institutions. Because he had entered with the ambassador people assumed it was important to talk to him and it was not until the arrival of the second glass of chilled white wine that he was able to escape.

He was still thirsty after his drive from the prison and the sudden intake of alcohol did not help his concentration. After two attempts at the letter he got up and walked around the library. Through the sash windows he could see modern Battenburg, concrete, glass-plated, automated and hurried; within were deep leather armchairs facing the shelves, all the major international newspapers and hundreds of well-kept first editions ranging from Stanley's account of how he found Livingstone to new novels by little-known authors. The only sound to break the silence was the regular breathing of an elderly sleeper who sat facing the drama section. Outside the armless and legless beggar was propped like an unfinished Guy Gawkes in his chair.

Patrick's third attempt produced a document stating that the embassy would take responsiblity for Chatsworth. It did not imply that it had any prior knowledge of him, nor did it say that it had not. He did not see how he could improve it further and so made a fair copy since there was no time to take it back and have it typed.

He was guided to the private dining room by the swelling noise of male voices and the clatter of cutlery and china. The main course was being cleared away. Sir Wilfrid sat in the middle of the top table with the chairman of the chamber of commerce on the one hand and a leading opposition politician on the other. Clifford sat alone at one end of the table, an empty place beside him. He looked as if he were clinging to an overcrowded life raft, wanting to pull himself farther on but sensing that his best interest was to stay where he was and not be noticed.

He was gratified to have someone to be angry with. "Where the hell have you been?"

"In the library drafting something for the ambassador."

"Your coming has thrown out all the placement. They thought I was bringing you. That's why I'm stuck down here. Then you don't even turn up." He pushed away his plate and suppressed a belch. "I wish to God they'd find Whelk's body somewhere. He's causing more trouble missing than when he was here. You'll have to make do with pudding. They won't bring the main course again just for you."

"It's all right. I've got another lunch in forty minutes."

"Two in one day? What on earth for?"

"One. I haven't had this one. Excuse me." He walked to the top table and hovered respectfully behind Sir Wilfrid, holding the folded letter. It was some time before he could get himself noticed. Sir Wilfrid was talking rapidly and drinking quantities of claret. He sprawled in his chair. When he noticed Patrick he half turned in his seat. "What's that – ransom demand?"

Patrick showed him the letter. Sir Wilfrid nodded. "Ah, right. Right you are. Leave it with me. Wave you over when I'm ready." He put the letter in his pocket.

Patrick stood for a few moments without moving. He resisted the impulse to snatch back the letter and run off with it only by closing his eyes and imagining himself doing so. He had assumed that the letter would be read immediately but Sir Wilfrid was raising his claret again and saying something to the politician beside him.

Clifford tucked into apple pie and custard. "He didn't want to be bothered by it now, did he? I could've told you that."

"He's going to read it as soon as he can." Patrick spoke with more determination than confidence.

"More likely he'll forget about it altogether. I should say goodbye to your next lunch if I were you."

Clifford allowed the waiter to fill his glass to the brim and gulped half of it. "Wish they'd hurry up with the port."

Patrick sipped at the wine before him, more for the sake of doing something than because he wanted it. Sir Wilfrid lounged in his chair and talked good-naturedly to the head of the chamber of commerce, swilling the wine in his glass and occasionally emptying it. An attentive waiter saw to it that the glass was never empty for more than a second or two.

"You're not thinking of getting married, are you?" asked Clifford. His voice was thick and he leant heavily forward with both elbows on the table.

Patrick started. "Who – me?"

"No need to look as if it's never occurred to you. It must've."

"Well, yes, but only in principle. Not with anyone in particular." He instantly felt guilty about Sandy, almost as much as if he had done something with her.

"Know what my advice would be to anyone who was thinking of getting married?"

"What?"

"Don't." Clifford delivered this with emphasis. He held his empty glass by the stem and stared at it.

Patrick waited for an explanation. "You don't like it?" he asked eventually.

"What?"

"Marriage."

"I didn't say that, did I? I never said that. Nothing wrong with Sandy. What's wrong with Sandy?"

147

"Nothing's wrong with Sandy."

"What I say, exactly what I say." Clifford nodded ponderously. The perspiration showed on his bald patch. "It's marriage that's wrong. Marriage and kids. Not Sandy. Nothing wrong with her."

"No."

"Bloody inspectors don't help."

"No."

"Cut our allowances, make us diplomatic paupers. Laughing stock of the international community. Not right when you've got wife and kids. Can't hold their heads up in the street." He dithered over the choice of white and red port, tried the white, didn't like it and called back the red. "No thought, you see. Same with the minister. London don't want any briefing papers yet. Don't want him to come, I reckon. It's him who's insisting, or the Prime Minister. They'll want them in a mad rush in the end. Lot of extra work for all of us, specially you and Philip. Laughing stock again, you see. Work all for nothing. Like today, Philip gets the credit for the paper. I don't. Same with the minister. Ambassador gets medals. I don't. Never had a medal. Have you?" His eyes bulged towards Patrick. "No, me neither. Bloody, isn't it?"

"Bloody," said Patrick. It was already one. He watched bitterly as Sir Wilfrid dawdled over the cheese and chatted to the wine waiter about the white port. Clifford mumbled on for a while before subsiding into gloomy silence. Eventually the head of the chamber of commerce stood and laboriously introduced Sir Wilfrid, listing all his previous postings, referring in passing to his many virtues and to his charming though absent lady wife and emphasising the ambassador's untiring efforts to improve British-Lower African relations. He ended with a triumphant declaration of the title of Sir Wilfrid's talk – 'Gold and Good Intentions' – and sat down to hearty applause.

Sir Wilfrid spoke with unhurried ease, one hand in his jacket pocket and the other holding, sometimes waving, the sheaf of papers that comprised his speech. He frequently departed from his text and did not always rejoin it at the right point. No one seemed to notice. There were grunts of approval during pauses and a few "hear hears" during the longer interludes while Sir Wilfrid refreshed himself with more port. Cigar smoke curled overhead. Clifford slumped in his chair, his eyes closed, one hand resting on the table. Patrick watched every minute on Clifford's watch.

Owing to his many departures and frequent asides, the nearest that Sir Wilfrid came to sustained argument was a passage which sought to demonstrate that rising economic expectations amongst black miners would lead to rising political expectations, a favourite theme of Philip's. "There is," he read, "a clear correlation between economic achievement and aspiration on the one hand and political awareness on the other. It is not simply the case that workers in the mines will demand as a matter of course tomorrow what they can only hope for today, but that this very climate of expectation creates" – he turned the page but digressed again before looking at the next. Smoothing his hair with one hand, he reminded his audience that such general truths sometimes stumbled and broke themselves upon the rocks of contrary particulars; in this case, possibly, upon the expectations of different groups. For instance, the nearest that Lower Africa had come to full-scale civil war in this century had been in the 1920s when white miners had forced the white government to drop its plan to give more rights to black miners. In the end it had taken an artillery bombardment of Battenburg to quell the white uprising. Whatever expectations the blacks had had – if any – must have been altered as a result of this.

"And so," Sir Wilfrid concluded, now staring aggressively at his audience, "we must not forget that at the very time when one set of expectations is coming into being, another, opposing set may be created amongst those who seek to protect their own superior positions." He emptied his port glass to grunts of approval. The wine waiter stepped forward and filled it. Sir Wilfrid looked again at his papers. "I must emphasise," he read, raising his voice a little, "that although the British embassy guarantees the continuing presence and the law-abiding behaviour of Mr Chatsworth pending investigation of his alleged offences and pending also developments in other areas of current concern to the Lower African government and to the British embassy, the British embassy is not in any way to be held responsible for offences that Mr Chatsworth may be found to have committed before he was placed under the charge of the British embassy."

Patrick reached for his wine.

Sir Wilfrid turned the page and continued reading the next, which dealt with the extent to which political expectations could be bought off, delayed or even stilled by the prospect of yet further economic advance.

Patrick stared at his empty plate, waiting for the expected interruption or apology, but none came. The ambassador continued reading in the same effortless and confident voice. Clifford was still slumped in

149

his chair, his jowl bulging over his collar. The Progress Association did not react. Some members pulled on cigars and gazed dreamily at the smoke, others fiddled idly with any small objects on the table. Many were comatose. Patrick lowered his empty glass.

Sir Wilfrid ended with a moving and sincere appeal for understanding, economic justice, legal reform and action now – above all, action now – before it was too late. His raised voice, sweeping arm and evident seriousness roused the audience to sit up and glance at their watches. The applause was loud and prolonged. Some men clapped ostentatiously, cigars in their mouths. Others banged the tables with their palms. Clifford clapped and called, "Hear hear" several times. There was a toast of thanks, a renewed hubbub, a scraping of chairs and a rush for the toilet. It was one-thirty.

Patrick touched Sir Wilfrid on the elbow. "I must have the letter now, sir. They want it immediately."

"Letter? Lord, haven't had a chance yet. Better do it. Where is it?"

Patrick extracted one of the sheets from Sir Wilfrid's speech. The other was discovered by Sir Wilfrid in his pocket. His pen was by the pepper. He nodded as he read. "Yes, yes, this will do. You're learning, Patrick. The essence of good drafting is to be both clear and comprehensive which is never easy. This isn't bad. The essence of good diplomatic drafting is where possible to avoid saying anything that admits of only one meaning. That's why good diplomatic drafting is bad, but you have yet to learn that, fortunately."

Patrick ran from the room while the ambassador was saying something about the need to keep the whole business under wraps. He took the steps outside four at a time, dodged the beggar's chair, then hesitated. He went on, hesitated again, started, stopped. He was suddenly superstitious. The motive was unworthy but it was the money not the thought that counted. He put all his loose change and a couple of notes into the empty trilby. The beggar barely nodded.

The same two earnest young policemen were in the outer office. Jim was on the telephone but put one hand over the receiver and beckoned Patrick in. He was clearly busy, which was good because it would save explanations.

He took the letter. "Okay?"

"Okay, all agreed." Patrick backed towards the door. "Let me know when you want us to pick him up."

Jim nodded. "Have a nice lunch."

They were to meet in the roof restaurant of the Lion Hotel. She rather than Jim had suggested it this time. Patrick sprinted through the streets and arrived in the busy foyer panting and sweating. The lift elevated him so quickly through the thirty or so floors that he was still breathing deeply when the doors opened. His hair was tousled and he felt hotter than ever. It was ten to two.

The restaurant was filled with plants and foliage, some of it twelve to fifteen feet high. White tables showed between the leaves and some-times waiters and waitresses, dressed all in white. There was a high domed roof of tinted glass, the two halves of which had been opened a few feet at the centre to let in the breeze. The room was shades of green, sunlight and shadow. Patrick made his way warily through the foliage but found it much thicker on the outskirts than within, where there were a large number of tables clustered around a sparkling green pool. Like all pools it reminded him for a moment of his own, because it was so unlike it.

At first he could not see her. The Lion was famed for having no colour bar but it happened that day that all staff and customers were white. His eyes slid from table to table, narrowed against the bright-ness and failing to pick out features. The tables nearest the pool had glass tops and it was noticing the swift dexterity with which a waiter passed between her table and the pool that made him see her. She wore tight white jeans, a cream silk blouse, a black belt and the black boots she had worn at the party. Her blonde hair was caught up in a bun and held in place by a black comb. She was reading a book and did not see him approach.

"I'm sorry," he said, grinning with relief that she had waited.

She smiled. "I thought you might be busy at the embassy, whatever it is you do there. That's why I brought a book."

"What is it?"

She dropped it into her handbag. "It's rubbish. You wouldn't approve."

"What makes you think that?"

"Because you're a snob. You'd think it was beneath you."

"You mean it isn't really beneath me?"

She laughed. "Of course it is. Why d'you think I'm hiding it?"

He told her why he was late, omitting only any mention of Chats-worth and Jim.

"You mean you've already had lunch in the Gold Club?" she asked.

"No, I didn't eat anything."

"Wasn't that a bit difficult?"

151

"Well, no, I was only there to give the ambassador a paper he wanted."

"Why did he need a paper at lunch?"

"Well – he needed to read it. It was his speech."

"Tell me about the Gold Club. I've never been in. Women can't, can they?"

He described the club, then the beggar who sat outside. He did not mention his offering.

"How awful," she said.

"I'm told he's put there deliberately. Someone's making a rather obvious point."

"Rather obvious." She mimicked his accent and laughed. "Very British. Overdone, would you say? A little crude, perhaps?"

"Unsubtle."

"You're worse than I thought."

"At least that's possible."

She laughed once more, and smoothed the sides of her hair with her hands. Her uplifted arms stretched the blouse tightly across her breasts. "We've got a whole lunch to get through. It may not remain possible."

The waiter appeared between their table and the pool almost as if from the water. They chose seafood salad and a light white wine from the coast. Patrick suggested oysters, having once been told that they were an aphrodisiac, but she wouldn't have them. The wine came first. Following the drink in the club, it soon made him feel pleasantly light-headed. The sun warmed his back. He took off his jacket and tie and rolled up his shirtsleeves.

"Getting down to business?" She smiled.

They talked about the embassy, about diplomatic life again, her marriage, childbirth, crime, Battenburg, censorship, the prisoners he had met that morning and, because the interest that two people have in each other may for a while be reflected in even the most opaque of subjects, the problem of chemical balance in his swimming-pool.

With the second bottle of wine they spoke about the problems of Lower Africa and agreed on the need for something to be done.

"I could join a civil rights group or something like that," she said, "but it's only tinkering with the problem, really. You're permitted so long as you're not a serious threat and the moment you look like becoming one they sit on you. And that's not so easy to contemplate when you have a child to look after."

"Jim wouldn't be very happy if you did, would he?"

152

"Jim doesn't mind other people having their views."

"It didn't strike me that way."

She picked at something on the glass table with her fingernail. "He feels threatened by you. That's why he threw the glass."

"How do I threaten him?" He recalled his remarks about Jim's need to justify himself but they were not the answer he wanted. His heart was beating faster. He hoped it wasn't obvious.

She stopped picking at the table and smiled. "You tell me."

He was not ready to do that. Not having thought how to put it, he did not know what to say. "He seems to want everything to be bad. He was trying to tell me that racial problems in Britain would end up by being as bad as here. Then I discovered he's never even been there."

She shrugged. "Well, I daresay he's wrong. I hope he is. I think he might be wrong quite often but he's not wrong about everything. He's nobody's fool, you know, Jim."

He talked energetically about Lower Africa, about how it had to change if only because the world itself was changing and no country could hold out for ever. The sun and the wine lent urgency to his seriousness and she eagerly quoted examples and incidents. They competed in establishing claims to right-minded views. From this the conversation moved back to diplomatic life, in which she was more interested than he. He put this down to his knowing it better. As they talked scenes from the embassy, snippets from the ambassador's speech, echoes of Clifford's complaints, a picture of the serious expression on Chatsworth's face as they parted bubbled through his mind and burst harmlessly on contact with the pleasure of being with her. Nothing else mattered at that moment. He was vividly aware of enjoying himself.

Nervousness disappeared with the wine. He poured the last of the second bottle. He felt lucky. "Are you and I going to have an affair?"

She smiled and looked away from him. "Why do you say that?"

"I suppose I'm drunk enough to say what I think."

"Perhaps it's the altitude."

"I don't think so."

"So what do you think?"

"I think we are."

She lifted her glass to her lips. "You're very sure of yourself, Mr Third Secretary Stubbs."

He was less sure than he appeared. He tipped back on the hind legs of his chair, balancing with his knee against the table, and smiled whilst

153

he tried to think of what to say next. His smile broadened as the pause lengthened; as also, imperceptibly at first, did the angle of his chair to the ground. The moment of helplessness at the start of the fall was actually pleasant, though short-lived. Awareness and alarm returned as his feet came up hard against the underside of the table. There was a crash and a muted cry that might have been hers.

The water struck him like a prolonged slap. It was particularly cold after the warmth of the sun on his shoulders. His backward somersault was completed beneath the surface. It felt a slow, even graceful movement. He would have preferred to stay under for some time.

He heard nothing as his head broke the surface but when his ears cleared he heard laughter and applause. Fortunately, he had gone in at the deep end. He swam a circuit of the pool. When his trousers and shoes were beginning to feel heavy he heaved himself gracelessly on to the side. A smaller pool immediately began to form on the floor. People at the farther tables stood on their chairs to see him. Waiters joined the applause, their trays tucked under their arms. He waved an acknowledgement, which provoked good-humoured shouting and encores, and walked back around the edge of the pool. The table had not toppled although a plate and his wine glass had slid off and were broken. A waiter and two waitresses, brisk and delighted, were clearing up.

Joanna was still laughing, one hand over her eyes and the other holding her stomach. He sat carefully on the edge of his chair so as not to touch his jacket. "Don't tell me that was the altitude, too."

It was a few seconds before she could speak. "I'm sorry. I was worried at first, really worried. I thought it might be shallow and you'd cut your head open or cracked your skull or something awful like that. Then when I saw you swimming I just – " She put her elbows on the table and her hands over her eyes. "I'm sorry, I must stop. It's not funny for you. Shouldn't you get changed?"

"I didn't bring a spare set of clothes. Let's have coffee."

"You really should go home and get changed."

"Come with me and we'll have coffee there."

"By your pool?"

They made their way out between the plants and tables. The restaurant manager would take no money for breakages and facetiously invited Patrick to return and perform at any time, clearly pleased with himself for having thought of saying this. A small puddle formed around Patrick's feet in the lift.

154

They took the bakkie as the embassy was nearby and Joanna's car was parked some distance away. She was to pick it up when he drove back to work later.

Being wet made him feel carefree at first. It did not matter that he was less than sober. He felt capable enough but his limbs, his voice, even his skin seemed to be someone else's.

By the time they reached the house it was no longer refreshing to be wet and he felt thoroughly himself again. Sarah would be having her siesta, which was just as well since although he was reasonably confident she would be asleep, he felt uneasy at bringing another woman into the house. Sarah did, after all, go to church regularly. Not even the occasional presence of Sarah's man, Harold, made him feel entirely free to claim the same indulgence for himself.

Snap met them noisily at the front door but was quickly quietened and introduced to Joanna. Patrick was aware even then of something different about the house but paid no attention. With Snap sniffing his wet trousers he followed Joanna through the hall and into the sitting-room.

She stood by the sofa and looked around. "Do you always live like this?" There was an echo to her voice.

"Like what?"

She held up her arm. "Like this."

It was then that he noticed that all the paintings, all the ornaments and most of the furniture had gone. One carpet remained but the expensive rugs did not. The PSA tables and chairs were there but none of the old chests, none of the shooting trophies, none of the books. He went into the kitchen. Crockery, cutlery and cooking utensils had gone, save for a few bits and pieces stacked on a shelf in the larder. The fridge and stove remained but all trace of Arthur Whelk had disappeared.

"No, not usually," he said eventually. "At least, not until today." He wished he were more imaginative. "It was fully furnished this morning with stuff belonging to the last chap but they must've come and packed it."

"Strange you didn't know."

"Yes, it is, rather."

"Where's he gone?"

"I'm not sure." She looked disbelievingly at him. He wondered whether Jim had told her about Whelk. "I mean, I don't know exactly where he is at the moment."

"Where's he going next?"

"I don't know."

"Well, where are they sending his things?"

"I don't know that either. You see, it's nothing to do with me. I never actually met him."

She shrugged and turned away. "Anyway, it's a lovely house. Wasted on a bachelor."

"Yes, it is." He pulled at his trousers where they were sticking to his thighs. He was reluctant to wake Sarah but wanted to know whether Whelk had been there. "Look, hang on here a moment and I'll have a word with Sarah."

She was dozing in the armchair in her bedroom. He waited outside while she fumbled for her slippers and glasses. "The men come and take it away this morning, massa," she explained.

"Which men, Sarah?"

"I don't know. I never seen those men before. They say the embassy send them for Mr Whelk's things. They have a list and a big lorry."

"Was anything written on the lorry?"

"I don't know, massa. I don't see it because it is parked on the road and they take everything down the drive to it."

"Did they give you a receipt, a piece of paper?"

"No." She shook her head and smiled unhappily. "I am sorry, massa, they say they from embassy – "

He put his hand on her shoulder. "Don't worry, I'm sure they were." The embassy was a world far removed from Sarah's and infinitely powerful in her eyes; she had never seen it. In reference to this world any oddity of character or event was at once inexplicable and acceptable since its causes and meanings were wholly elsewhere. In any case, it was still possible that Sir Wilfrid or Clifford or Miss Teale had arranged for the removal of Whelk's possessions without bothering to tell Patrick. "You did the right thing, Sarah."

She ceased her unhappy smile but looked embarrassed. "Massa, you are wet."

"Ah, yes." He picked at his clammy shirt. "I've been in a swimming-pool."

"With your clothes?"

"Yes. It was an accident." She nodded solemnly. He wondered if she were afraid to laugh at him. "I fell in backwards," he added, with a smile.

"You fall in?" Wide-eyed behind her thick spectacles, she began to laugh with a high delighted giggle. She clutched his arm, pushing it roughly backwards and forwards and shaking her head. She wobbled the whole of his upper body. "Oh massa, massa, sometimes you do damn silly thing."

He steadied himself, laughed and gripped her hand. "Yes, Sarah, sometimes I do many damn silly thing."

"I make you tea." She let go of him and straightened her apron.

"No," he said. She looked surprised. He had never before refused tea. "I have to get changed and then I must rest. You carry on with your rest."

"Yes, massa."

He turned away, then stopped. "Did they – as a matter of interest – did they leave enough things to make tea with, or coffee?"

She counted on her fingers. "They leave one plate, five cup, one fork, one knife, one saucepan, two frying-pan, one teapot, three kettle, four tray and one spoon."

"Good. Well, I'll have to get some more things some time."

"But your things are coming from England?"

"Of course. I'll find out when they're due."

"I have some things I can bring."

"No, no, it's all right. I'll get some later. We don't need them now. You carry on with your sleep."

"I done my sleep, massa."

"Oh, well, have some more, there's plenty of time."

She nodded obediently but looked puzzled. "Thank you, massa."

He told Joanna that the embassy had sent the packers without informing him. It was typical.

She looked at the bare kitchen. "But where are your own things?"

"Somewhere on the high seas, I think."

"What have you got?"

"Cutlery and plates, that sort of thing."

"Are you really as helpless as you sound or are you just playing for sympathy?"

"Both." He opened four cupboards rapidly, all bare. In the fifth were tins, packets and jars. "I can produce coffee, look."

She pushed gently against his shoulder with the tip of her finger. "Why don't you go and dry and get changed. I'll make the coffee and bring it through. Where's the kettle?"

"I don't know."

"Is there one?"

"There are three."

She glanced at him disbelievingly and began searching.

He was relieved to find that the extra large PSA double bed, to

157

which he was not entitled, was still there. He stripped and had a shower. He was drying himself when he heard Joanna call out that the coffee was ready. He hesitated, telling himself that there was nothing to lose whilst knowing in his heart that there was everything. He called back, "Bring it up here."

There was no reply. He stood poised between the bathroom and the bedroom, listening. If she didn't he would simply get dressed, go down and carry on as if he had not said it. For a second or two his own breathing seemed loud, but then he heard her boots on the stairs and the rattle of cups on a tray. He wrapped the towel round himself and went through the bedroom, reaching the door as she paused at the top of the stairs to gaze at the rape-gate.

"What on earth is this?"

He was embarrassed by it. "It's a rape-gate."

She laughed but carefully because of the tray. "Who do you think's going to rape you? My God, the vanity of it."

"It's to stop thieves. They're compulsory for insurance purposes. Don't lots of people have them?"

"Lots of diplomats, maybe. What a life. In your case, though, there's not much left to steal, is there?"

She edged the gate open wider with the toe of her boot and walked into the bedroom where she put the tray on the bare dressing-table. There was only one cup, a discouraging sign. He stood by her, his heart beating rapidly. As she straightened he put his hands lightly on her arms and kissed her on the lips. She at first permitted herself to be kissed, neither refusing nor responding, then pushed gently against his shoulders and pulled back her head. "Aren't you even going to shut the door?"

He did so and then led her by the hand to the bed where, still standing, he began to undress her. He kissed her again as he took off her blouse and she responded carefully, her eyes half-closed and her hands moving slowly over his body. As their lips touched, images of the embassy, where he should have been, suddenly filled his head and for some seconds he was unable to rid himself of the picture of Philip Longhurst crouched protectively over a file and nibbling a sandwich.

The boots were difficult. She sat on the bed laughing as he struggled with them. Then, still wearing her white jeans, she went to the dressing-table and began to unpin her hair. He lay naked on the bed, watching, his hands behind his head. He felt warm and relaxed. He had never seriously imagined making love with her for fear it would not happen; he had simply wanted her. Now that he was about to, though,

158

he wanted to stop, to think about it, to enjoy the anticipation. Her hair fell to her shoulders and she paused, looking at herself then at him in the mirror. When their eyes met she smiled very slightly, stood and walked over to the bed. She took off her jeans and knickers and lay down beside him. Her body was soft and shapely, tanned except for the bikini'd parts. They entwined and kissed for a long time. The time lengthened. They kissed again.

"Sorry about this," he said eventually.

She laughed and bit his ear. "You sound so English."

"Perhaps this is what they mean by the English disease."

"Maybe the coffee will help."

He fetched the cup and they lay side by side, sharing it. "Why didn't you bring yours up?" he asked.

"I was going to drink it on the veranda."

"You really were?"

"I really was."

One of her legs was slung across his and he ran his fingers along her thigh, slowly and deliberately. In bed her features were no longer taut but had a softness that in normal conversation was held in check. She kept pushing her hair away from the coffee. He wanted very much to make love with her and blamed Philip Longhurst, hating him silently. He took away the coffee, leaning across her to put it on the floor, and began kissing her again.

"This has never happened before," he said after a while, thinking of the occasions when he wouldn't have minded.

She stroked him and said nothing.

He felt he had to keep talking. "It's probably just a question of time. I've never known it before."

She smiled. "I believe you: you don't have to insist. After the three kettles I'll believe anything."

"P'raps it's the drink."

"Or nerves."

"Why nerves?"

She laughed and rolled on to her back. "You shouldn't take it so seriously."

"I'm not."

"Of course you are. It's that that's stopping you." She kicked him.

They rolled in mock combat from one side of the large bed to the other. He breathed deeply, his whole body heavy with desire. Still nothing happened. "Let's get between the sheets," he said.

"Don't you have to go back to work?"

"Yes. Get in." In bed it was luxurious and affectionate, no longer urgent. They both slept. His last thought, several times repeated, was that all would no doubt be well later.

The sound of the rape-gate creaking on its hinges woke him. Then he heard footsteps on the landing. He reached the door as Sarah knocked, grabbing the handle so that she couldn't open it. He cautiously opened it himself, keeping his body out of sight. She wore a clean apron and cap, her hands clasped before her, and looked serious. She said something about Snap which he had to ask her to repeat.

"You lock him in de kitchen for a reason, massa?"

"No, I didn't – why?"

"He make de chocolate cake."

"Chocolate cake?" Not all of his brain was awake. He heard a suppressed giggle and looked round to see Joanna curled in the bedclothes and biting the pillow. He looked back at Sarah's solemn face and understood. "Oh dear, Sarah. I'm sorry."

"I have cleared it up but I want to know if it is all right for Snap to go out now."

"Yes, quite all right. There was no reason for him to be in. It was an accident."

Her face brightened. "I think so too, massa. Usually he do it on Deuteronomy's heap. Would you like tea?"

"Yes, thank you, tea would be good. I'll come down." It would be better to introduce Joanna downstairs as if she had just arrived.

Sarah nodded. "For two, massa?"

"Oh – yes, for two, I think, yes." There was more muffled giggling from the bed.

"For two only, Massa?" Her hands were clasped before her and her tone was matter-of-fact. He had never known her ironic.

"Yes, for two only, Sarah."

"I see a handbag in de kitchen and I do not know how many people."

"Just one."

She paused by the rape-gate and looked round demurely. "Would the other person like biscuit?"

Patrick smiled. "Yes, I think the other person would." He shut the door and leant against it. Joanna lay on her back laughing helplessly, her hand on her stomach. He went to her.

"No," she said.

"There's time."

"Of course there isn't. She's making the tea."

"It doesn't matter if it gets cold."

160

"It does, it's rude. And if you have to think about the time there isn't time. Anyway, how do we know how long it would take?"

"It's better now."

She stood and briefly kissed him. "Too late."

When he got downstairs he considered ringing the embassy but it was gone five and there was no point in going in. He wondered if he'd been missed. No one had rung, which was a good sign.

Sarah brought tea with unmatched cups and a plate of ginger biscuits to the veranda. When Joanna appeared he introduced her and they shook hands. Joanna said something in Swahi and Sarah, delighted, held up her hands and laughed. They spoke for some minutes with much mutual laughter. Patrick stood by, feeling awkward, then sat and munched a biscuit. At the end of the conversation Sarah curtsied, then walked away chuckling and swinging the empty tray.

"What was all that about?" he asked, aware of sounding slightly gruff. The tightness of Joanna's white jeans and her suggestive silk blouse were gratuitous reminders.

"Your lack of household goods. I said I didn't think you had a clue what was needed and you'd never had to look after yourself and she said that so long as you had a cup of tea and a chair to sit in you wouldn't notice if the rest of the house fell down around you. She said you needed a wife."

"Did she?" It was a novel thought. He assumed it reflected a peculiarly African attitude. "At least she doesn't seem too worried about it all."

"Of course she's worried. She wants to do her best for you and she can't with an empty kitchen." She smiled as she poured the tea, which he had ignored. "She's very fond of you, you know. I told her how terrified you were when you thought she was going to see us in bed and how you left it like a scalded cat. That's what made her laugh so much."

"You told her that?"

"Don't worry, she wasn't shocked. Nothing you could do would shock Sarah. You're white so you're completely different. You can't be moral or immoral, you can only be a good or bad massa."

"Where did you learn Swahi?"

"My husband had a farm, among other things. I went down there a lot and stayed after I'd had Belinda. My maid taught me Swahi but really I spoke Zulu better because that's what most of the Africans spoke. I spent a lot of time with them. There was nothing much else to do." She reached across and put her hand on his arm. "Why are you looking so serious?"

161

He smiled and took her hand. "I didn't know I was." In fact, he was wondering if she would again agree to go to bed with him or whether this had been a spontaneous opportunity which, not having been properly taken, would not recur.

She finished her tea and said something in Zulu, rapid sounds interspersed with the clicking-tongue noises that people often make to horses. "That's thank you for tea and hospitality. Now I must go and see my little girl."

"Is she better?" He had forgotten to ask earlier.

"Yes, much. I've got my sister and her husband coming for dinner this evening. May we go?"

The Battenburg rush hour lasted only about thirty minutes and they were in any case driving against it. Patrick recalled Jim's parting remark. "Did you tell Jim we were having lunch?"

"Yes."

"Did he mind?"

She looked straight ahead. "I think he does but he wouldn't try to stop me."

"What if he knew what we did after lunch – or, rather, didn't do?"

"He might shoot us both." She looked at him. "It really matters to you whether we did or didn't, doesn't it?"

He tried to sound casual. "Well, yes and no. I mean, obviously it's not all-important but on the other hand I wish we had."

She pushed her fist against his shoulder. "You shouldn't mind that much."

He dropped her at her car. She searched her handbag for her keys. "When?" he asked.

"You're the man of business. You tell me."

"Tomorrow night? The night after?"

Her manner became brightly and chillingly social. "No, look, ring me when you've got some things for Sarah to cook with." They kissed fleetingly. "Thank you for a lovely lunch."

He drove wretchedly back, convinced that she was no longer interested in him. When he arrived Sarah was feeding Snap, something he normally did because Sarah seemed to feel that feeding a dog was degrading.

When she saw Patrick, though, she clasped one of his hands in both of hers and pressed it. "I must thank you, massa, for the lady speak Swahi."

He joined his other hand to hers. "Did she speak it well?"

"She speak very well. It is nice for me to hear Swahi. She is very good

162

madam, I think." They discussed dinner. There was no shortage of food, only the wherewithal to cook it. She would fry steak. As he was leaving the kitchen she took an envelope from her apron pocket. "Oh, I forget. A man bring this."

It was his cheque to Jim Rissik for the bakkie, torn in half. There was no note. "Did you see him?" he asked.

"He was the policeman who come here before. I did not speak to him. He put it through the door."

"When?"

"When you were upstairs with the madam." She smiled. "He did not wait. I think he is frightened of Snap."

13

Patrick drank wine and sat up late that night. Every tone, remark and gesture he recalled, even the most affectionate, was overwhelmed by pessimism. When he went to his bed the width and comfort of it reminded him cruelly of her. Nevertheless, he slept.

It was Snap's barking that woke him. He groped for the truncheon beneath the bed. Whoever packed Whelk's belongings had missed it because it came reassuringly to hand. However, a ring at the doorbell indicated lawful callers. He pulled on his trousers, then fumbled the key at the rape-gate, dropping it so that it bounced a couple of steps down the stairs. He had to lie on his stomach and stretch his arm through the railings to reach it. The bell rang again.

The spy-hole showed the caller to be Jim Rissik. Patrick stood the truncheon against the wall and opened the door, holding Snap back by his studded collar.

Jim wore jeans and a crumpled white T-shirt. His arms were folded and there were drops of sweat on his face. The night was oppressively warm. "I want to talk," he said quietly.

The hall clock said ten past one. Patrick quietened Snap and opened the door fully.

"I'm not sober. I won't stay long."

"D'you want another drink?"

"If you're having one."

They went into the living-room and Patrick poured two whiskies. Jim looked round. "I heard you had a clear-out."

"I thought you might know something about it."

"I've only just heard."

Patrick tried to sound businesslike. "Sarah thought they were from the embassy. They told her they were. She didn't see the van, though. But it suggests Whelk's alive, doesn't it?"

"Why?"

"They knew what to take. He must've given them a list."

"I reckon he's done a bunk, as I said before. Kidnappers wouldn't

164

have done this and thieves wouldn't have known what to leave behind."

"Unless they were trying to make it look as though he'd done a bunk."

Jim shook his head. "I'll get descriptions from Sarah. Someone will have seen the van."

There was a pause which Patrick was anxious to fill. "Was the letter about Chatsworth all right?"

"Fine, fine." Jim looked at the wires running from the radio on the mantelpiece across the back of the sofa to the window. He stepped carefully over them, opened the window and stood staring out. "I don't like it when it's close like this. Gets at you. It'll rain soon, though. I like the rain."

"You look as if you've been running."

"That's the drink. I must be sweating neat alcohol by now. Fine state for a policeman to drive in." He raised his glass and looked at it before drinking carefully. "Have you changed your mind yet about the way we do things in Lower Africa?"

Patrick leant against the mantelpiece. He doubted that this was the purpose of the call but the more Jim talked and the more he drank the farther they might get from his real purpose. "No, I haven't changed my mind. I don't think it's right." Jim shrugged as if he had nothing more to say. "I don't know how I'd go about changing it," Patrick continued, "I suppose I'd start with education. See that all races have as many opportunities as the whites. That would take some time but it would be peaceful and universal. It would be a real change."

"We have a great hunger for approval. All the time we want approval in everything. Maybe we're so hurt when we don't get it because we don't really approve of ourselves." Jim spoke quickly and continued to stare out of the window. "The point is, any serious change would mean giving up our way of life and we're not going to do that. Would you give up yours simply because the rest of the world says you're wrong? It's not as if they're innocent. Give me a few million blacks to dump in sanctimonious Sweden and I'll give you racist Sweden. What's more, this country feeds Africa. The blacks can't get their crops in in time, can't plant in straight lines, can't harvest properly. Only the African could starve in Africa. Any other race would grow enough to feed half the world. We'd be feeding you if we were running it but if we had what you call a moral system we'd be starving with the rest of them."

Jim held up his hand as if to stop Patrick arguing. Patrick had made no move. "Imagine if overnight you had a majority of West Indians in Britain outnumbering you three or four to one and a system of government that kept you on top. Most of them would be apathetic so long as they were comfortable but some of them would hate you because they'd sense that you hated them. A lot of my countrymen, the working class ones, hate blacks – really, simply, completely hate them. It would be the same in your country. How many whites would vote themselves out of power and a black majority in? If they did the civil service, the police force, the army – maybe not the airforce and the navy because blacks aren't too hot on technology – would all be black. And the government would be completely black because blacks vote for blacks like whites vote for whites. People want to be ruled by their own kind. Do you want to be ruled by a bunch of West Indians? If you think you do, take a look at the West Indies. Who would you vote for?"

Jim moved into the middle of the room and faced Patrick. He held his glass in both hands. Patrick did not want an argument but wanted even more to avoid more personal topics. "It's not a question of who I'd vote for. It's a question of the blacks having the same right to be represented as I have. That's an absolute right; it's not dependent upon consequences. It's the same with your blacks here. They have equal rights to your freedoms, or should have."

Jim waved his hand. "Of course they should have, and they know it, those that think at all. But that's not the point I'm making. You don't see what I'm saying. You're like all these liberals, you talk in theory. I talk about what is."

"Theory shapes fact. Liberal values are no more theoretical than the system here. I mean, you claim a theoretical basis, naturally or divinely ordained, for white supremacy."

Jim slapped his glass, spilling some of it. "That – all that's shit. You might find a few who still say that but it's just an excuse so that they can dress up their loathing for blacks. That's what it is, you see, loathing. It is universal. Even the Indians and Chinese. They've been here for generations – longer than some of the blacks – they hate them too."

"Why?"

"Why?" Jim raised his eyes. "I don't know why. I could list all sorts of reasons but they wouldn't matter. Why don't dogs like cats? Because they're different."

"But we're not dogs and cats."

"True, but we're not so far from them that we're never like them. I don't know why other races don't like blacks. Maybe because blacks are more physical, because they've got beautiful strong bodies. Envy and fear. Maybe that's why."

Patrick still spoke slowly, trying to sound relaxed. "Then if people didn't think of themselves simply as bodies they wouldn't envy or fear other bodies."

"But they are bodies, aren't they? Very much so." Jim spoke quietly. He emptied his glass and pointed at the bottle on the table. "May I?"

Patrick nodded. "You're wrong, nonetheless. It's unjust and injustice is wrong. Everyone yearns for justice, you included. That's why you talk about it so often, to appear justified. Even the great slaughterers – Stalin, Mao – try to appear justified."

Jim replaced the bottle heavily on the table and turned awkwardly. "Sure, but you're still missing my point. We know what we ought to do. We don't do it because we don't want to. It's easy for you. You're not going to bring up your children here. We are and we're going to keep it as it is."

He moved to the other end of the mantelpiece and leant against it. He put his arm along the top and turned his glass slowly in his hand. He looked relaxed.

Patrick turned to face him. "You're still wrong, even leaving aside the moral issue. You're wrong because you're doomed, because it can't last. The world has turned against what you stand for. You'll be forced to change."

"Who by? The Russians maybe. Sure, they've got the political will and muscle but they wouldn't be doing it for moral reasons. They don't give a damn about blacks. They'd only do it for their own advantage. You and your kind, you'll never force us. You're not going to kill hundreds of thousands just so that you can make a moral point when the immorality is no threat to you. You're never going to do that, are you? Eh? How many deaths is a moral point worth?" His dark eyes half closed. He drank again and moved closer along the mantelpiece, then held up his free hand in an exaggerated, stagey manner. "Look – we're born, we live – comfortably if we're lucky – and we die – not too uncomfortably if we're lucky. What else is there?" He closed his eyes and lowered his head. "When I speak like this I wonder why I feel about Joanna as I do. It's funny to have feelings and beliefs so different."

In the pause that followed Patrick could hear the hum of the fridge from the kitchen.

"I know about it," Jim continued. "She told me."

Patrick swallowed some whisky. "What did she tell you?"

Jim looked up. "When she told me she was going to have lunch with you I knew." He held up his hand again. "Don't misunderstand me. She doesn't go jumping into bed with everyone. It's just that when she said she was going to have lunch with you I knew – I just knew immediately – how it would end. I saw her this evening and I knew I was right. She didn't lie to me. I didn't ask her. There was no need. She knew I knew. We didn't even talk about it."

Patrick felt like telling him that nothing had happened, as if that would make a difference, but he was ashamed of the idea.

"I knew you hadn't gone back to the embassy and I guessed why."

"How did you know?"

"My job. I told you, we look after you people."

"Check on us?"

Jim drank again. "Was she here when I brought your cheque back?"

"Yes."

Jim nodded very slightly. "Funny, you set out to do one thing when all the time there's something else going on which makes what you do seem completely different – afterwards, when you know about the other thing."

Patrick again heard the hum of the fridge. He had nothing to say. To apologise would be insulting and insincere. Being brazen would be the same. The pause lengthened. He saw there were tears running down Jim's face. He hoped at first that it might be sweat but knew that it was not. Jim looked past him rather than at him, making no effort to wipe his tears.

"Why" – Patrick swallowed at the wrong moment and had to clear his throat – "why didn't you try to stop her?"

"You can't change people, you can't make them different. It's like all that I was saying earlier. People do what they want first and then justify it. She wanted you. I hope she enjoyed it." He spoke quietly and looked again at Patrick, the water standing in his eyes. "No, I don't. I hope she didn't enjoy it. I hope she didn't like it."

Patrick still said nothing.

Jim gulped his whisky. When he spoke again his voice was lower and thicker. "Only she'll come back to me, you see. She always will. I'll be here and she'll be here when you're gone. You've got her on loan, that's all."

He held up his empty glass for Patrick to fill then leant both shoulders against the mantelpiece with his arms spread along it. "I don't know why she chose me. We're unlike in a lot of ways and she

168

doesn't agree with much of what I think. Not on the surface, anyway."
He looked up and grinned but did not take the glass that Patrick was
offering. "Anyway, loan I said and loan I meant, okay?"

He put his right hand on Patrick's shoulder, as in a comradely
gesture. Patrick never knew whether Jim planned it or whether it was
simply the feel of his rival's body that provoked him. He was suddenly
and violently bent double, his head so firmly locked against Jim's hip
that he nearly passed out. Both glasses fell to the floor by his feet but he
did not hear them. His lips were crushed against the seam of Jim's
jeans and he could taste blood. His neck was twisted at an ever more
painful angle as Jim dragged him towards the centre of the room.

His first thought was that Jim was going to run the top of his head
against the wall or through the window. Forgotten practices of schoolboy rugby came to his aid; he caught Jim by his legs, and pulled his
knees together at the same time as pushing forward. When they hit the
ground Jim's grip was momentarily weakened. Patrick pulled his head
downwards but could not completely free it. He humped his body and
pulled again, pushing his elbow in Jim's crotch.

His head was free and his ears ringing. He hesitated and was kicked
sideways. Jim's arm locked around his neck again. They rolled against
the sofa and then away. Their feet tangled in wires and the radio
crashed to the floor.

Jim's personality was his body, concentrated now, no longer dif-
fuse as in social dealings. He was strong and determined but not
cunning and not vicious. Patrick, weaker and at one disadvantage after
another, was obdurate. He could never achieve an ascendancy but was
never so subdued that he could not escape from a position that was
becoming critical to another not yet critical. They wrestled and kicked
but they did not hit and they did not bite. As Patrick's flesh weakened
the warmth and strength of Jim's seemed to increase. Patrick's
movements became desperate and ineffectual though as both bodies
became slippery with sweat he could wriggle out of Jim's holds more
easily.

The end was sudden and undeclared, like the beginning. They
almost sprung apart after Patrick got his elbow beneath Jim's sternum
and pushed with all his strength to free his head again. For a few
seconds they lay panting and quivering, watching for a resumption but
both reluctant to make it. Patrick's muscles trembled and he felt
drained. Jim's T-shirt had risen to his armpits and his tanned skin
glistened with sweat. The dark hairs of his abdomen were matted and
wet. He rolled on to his back and let his arms lie by his sides.

"You're a slippery bastard," he whispered as his chest rose and fell.

Patrick stared at the ceiling. A vein in his throat pumped wildly. They lay in companionable silence and for a while their breathing was in time, as in the aftermath of gratified desire.

Jim reached across and let the back of his hand fall heavily on Patrick's shoulder. "I could do with some water."

Patrick got up slowly and went to the kitchen. His thighs were still quivering and he felt dizzy. Snap was still in his basket. When he returned with two glasses Jim was sitting cross-legged on the floor fiddling with the radio.

"Can't get a squeak out of it. I'll get you a new one."

"Wait till I see what's wrong. It may be repairable."

"Have you got a licence yet?"

"No."

"Then it isn't. I'll get it done for you. Trust a policeman."

Patrick slumped on to the sofa. He drank half his water then lifted his head and poured the rest over his face. It ran over his bare shoulders and down his chest and back with shocking, delicious coldness.

"Mind if I piss in your garden?" Jim walked slowly out on to the veranda, straightening his T-shirt and rubbing one of his shoulders. "You ought to do something about that pool of yours," he said when he came back.

"I've done everything the instructions say you can do to a pool."

"Couldn't be any worse if I pissed in it. Get a firm in."

"One day when I've had a good night's sleep."

Jim grinned as he picked up the two glasses. "At least it's only a government carpet." He put them on the mantelpiece. "I hope you won't think it's unfriendly of me if I go now."

Patrick went with him to the door. "I've got a cheque for you."

Jim stopped but did not look round. "Okay." Patrick wrote it slowly because his hand was still unsteady. Jim put it in the back pocket of his jeans without looking at it and stared at the sky. The night was more oppressive than ever and the air still. The clouds on the horizon reflected a constant dance of lightning. "It'll rain tonight."

"I hope so."

"You like the rain?"

"Yes."

"So do I."

Patrick locked the door and picked up the truncheon, thinking he might have done better to keep it with him. He felt physically tired but mentally restless. He would not sleep for some time. His neck ached and there was a pain on the right side of his ribs which hurt whenever he breathed deeply or turned incautiously. He decided to have a shower and had just got under it when the telephone rang.

"Are you all right?" Joanna's voice was low and urgent.

"Yes, I'm all right." He hesitated. His mind was more on Jim. It was not that he had forgotten about her so much as that Jim had snatched dramatic priority. It was impossible to think of her without thinking of Jim.

"I was afraid that Jim might come and see you," she continued quickly. "He was here earlier and stayed for dinner with my brother and sister-in-law and just sat there and made himself drunk. When they'd gone he hardly spoke, he just sat. And then he suddenly got up and went. I couldn't sleep because I was sure he was upset about you and me and I kept thinking he might come and beat you up or something. I mean, he didn't say anything but I could tell. After he'd gone I rang him but there was no answer. He might have gone drinking with some of his friends or gone back to work. He does that sometimes when he feels like it. He'll just go and work all night whether he has to or not. Then I lay in bed and couldn't sleep. I kept looking at the lightning and thinking: what if he's gone to see you and taken his gun or something awful? The more I thought the worse it got. You must think I'm really stupid. I am sorry to have woken you but I really was worried. I am sorry." She laughed nervously.

Patrick felt as elated now as he had been depressed earlier. "You haven't woken me. I was in the shower."

"In the shower?"

"Jim's just left."

"Patrick, what's happened? Tell me."

He basked in her concern. It was the first time she had used his name. "Well, we had a talk and then we had a sort of fight, a wrestling match, really. We're both okay. He's gone now."

She said she would come over straight away. She would wake Beauty and tell her she was going out. Belinda was asleep, anyway. Patrick said that there was really no need but then quickly added, in case she changed her mind, that he would like to see her. He offered to come to her. She asked several times if he was sure he was unhurt and stopped only when he told her to bring plasma.

He returned to the shower and stood with his forehead against the wall so that the hot water streamed over his stiff neck.

Her hair was loose when she arrived. She did not step straight in but

171

remained on the doorstep looking at him. She smiled only when he did. "I am sorry," she said.

"For what?"

"For Jim."

"I'm not." He took her hand and led her upstairs, leaving the rape-gate open.

"I only came to talk," she said, "and to see that you really are all right." Her tone was more resigned than determined. He shut the bedroom door, held her and kissed her. She broke off, pushing with her hands against his shoulders. "I want you to tell me what happened."

He undressed her as he spoke. She was more interested in what Jim had said than in the fight. He knelt to take off her shoes and at one point she laughed as she had to put her hand on his head to balance. When he stood and held her to him he felt in her lips, in her moving hands and in the pressure of her body the beginning of her passion.

"Fighting must be good for you," she whispered.

Outside the first rain dropped heavily on to the veranda roof, spattering against the bedroom windows. It fell slowly as if delaying its full effect so that there was time to anticipate. Heavy single drops became a regular beating, the beating became a drumming, and the drumming a torrent. Soon the rushing, gurgling and spluttering of water was all-enveloping and the room was the only dry, hidden and secret place.

Her long hair spread across the pillow and was damp with sweat. She breathed gently. They lay side by side, as he had lain with Jim. When dawn approached the sky brightened enough to show the falling grey rods of rain. It had continued unabated throughout the night. Patrick turned his head to look at her. He almost wished himself alone though without wishing her away. He had had a glut of impressions which could be properly assimilated, and so fully experienced, only in recollection. While she was there the flow continued like the rain and he could stop or separate nothing.

She opened her eyes. "What did he say about me?"

He had thought her asleep and was resentful that she should have been thinking about Jim. "He said that you would go back to him, that I had you on loan." The rain emphasised the silence that followed. He felt his heart beginning to quicken. "What are you going to do about him?"

"Do?" She turned her head. "What do you mean?"

172

"Aren't you going to – well – explain things to him?"

"There's nothing more to explain. He knows already. I don't have to say anything. It wouldn't do any good to go on about it." She rested her head on his chest. "He's – it's not what you might think. We've known each other for over four years now."

He carefully removed some of her hair from his mouth. "Has he ever asked you to marry him?"

"Yes, often."

"Why don't you?"

She turned over on to him and pressed her chin between his upper ribs. "You're not very diplomatic, Mr Stubbs. There are some things which might not be good for you to know and they're none of your business anyway."

He hugged her and they rolled over. "I thought you came here to talk."

She stretched her arms behind his head and pulled him to her. "Tell that to the marines."

The rain was gentle when she left. It made countless disappearing rings in the dull water of the pool. The trees dripped and the air was fresh. Scents he had never noticed rose from the garden. She had to be back before Belinda awoke.

He held the car door. "Tonight?"

"Won't you want some sleep? You've hardly had any."

"I can do that too."

"Come to dinner. Don't stand there, you'll get wet."

"I'm getting used to that."

She drove off, waving twice. He was tired but too exhilarated to be sleepy. He skipped over a puddle, then another that was not in his way, then decided to skip all the puddles between the house and the garage. Whilst doing this he saw a movement from inside the garage, which he had left open. He stopped short, causing one foot to get wet. His first thought was that someone was trying to steal the bakkie and that he had left the truncheon indoors. As he looked he made out a young black standing just inside. He was tall and thin and wore a checked shirt with faded jeans. He held a red plastic sack on his head and shoulders, clutching it beneath his throat. He was very wet. The whites of his eyes showed up in the gloom of the garage. He stared with sullen wariness at Patrick's approach.

The fact that the boy did not try to run away reminded Patrick of Sarah's son. "Are you Stanley?" he asked. The boy nodded. Patrick stepped forward and held out his hand. The boy hesitated, then came out of the garage and shook it limply. "Does your mother know you're here?"

"No." Stanley breathed the word, barely moving his lips.

"She'll be pleased. She was very worried about you."

"Yes."

"How long have you been here?" Stanley did not reply. Patrick wondered if Jim had spotted him. "Have you been here long?" Still he did not reply. "Have you been walking in the rain all night?"

"I have been walking."

"You must like walking." Patrick's smile was not reciprocated. He thought he must sound like a caricature of some colonial official but could do nothing about it. He also felt awkward because Stanley was considerably taller than him. "Your mother was telling me you've left your school?"

"Yes."

"What are you going to do?"

"I must be a doctor."

"A doctor?" Patrick did not mean to show surprise. "Yes, well, that's a good idea but it will take many years at school and college. Where would you like to train?"

"Yes."

The rain fell softly around them. Patrick was beginning to feel wet. He was aware of speaking loudly with an enforced heartiness. He hated to sound patronising but still could do nothing about it. "A good idea, yes. But you must go somewhere to learn. Where would you like to go?"

Stanley lowered his eyes. When he spoke the words tumbled out but he did not look up. "I do not know. It is difficult in Lower Africa because there are not many colleges for black people and I must have qualifications which I do not. I must go to a small college first."

Patrick was encouraged. "That might be a good idea. Which one?"

"I don't know."

"Can you get qualifications if you go back to school where you are?"

"I don't know. Perhaps."

A door opened. They looked round to see Sarah standing in the entrance to her quarters. She was awkwardly putting on her glasses with one hand and with the other clutching her faded blue dressing-gown across her stomach. When she saw Stanley she uttered a cry and let go of her dressing-gown, revealing a pink nightie. She made to step out into the wet, hesitated briefly because she had no slippers on, then stepped out anyway. She ran with her bare feet slapping on the wet concrete, half speaking and half wailing in Swahi. Stanley looked sullen and embarrassed. She held up her arms to embrace him, moaning in a quiet, high voice. When she touched him, though, she changed as if discovering she was deceived into embracing the wrong person. She shook him by the arms and spoke crossly. He bent his head and permitted himself to be pushed, shaken and railed against. He spoke once as she led him away. She replied sharply and he let go of the red plastic that covered his head and shoulders. It fell to the ground where he would have left it had she not spoken sharply again.

As he picked it up she turned to Patrick. "Massa, I am very sorry for this. He has been a bad boy and I tell him. I am sorry he wake you."

"He didn't, Sarah, I was awake anyway."

"Still I am sorry, massa." She spoke to Stanley and he walked slowly across the yard towards her quarters, dragging his plastic sack.

"It's good he's been found," said Patrick.

"Oh yes, I am very pleased." She pushed Stanley's back as he went in through her door. "You want early breakfast, massa?"

"No, no, the usual time."

She nodded and went inside.

There was no question of sleep. He washed and dressed, straightened up the living-room again and tried to get the radio to work. He had some success but it crackled and would not stay tuned for more than a minute or two. He picked up the local early morning news, the main item of which was the 'good rain' that had fallen on Battenburg and the high veldt during the night. It had been long awaited and there was hope of more to come. Reservoir levels were still low and grazing was poor. The rain had not reached the northern area where there had been a drought now for eighteen months.

He walked in the dripping garden. Snap sniffed everywhere and rooted amongst the undergrowth. Patrick ended his walk by standing once more by the pool. He did not so much think of the events of the night as permit them to float and settle in his mind like great sea animals which it was wise not to disturb by questions or proddings. The biggest of the animals was Jim Rissik, but he was no longer frightened of him. Now that they had fought there seemed nothing more to be frightened of. He knew him better now and liked him better too; but he was still the biggest animal. Of Joanna he was reluctant to think directly, preferring to keep her for later like the knowledge that he would see her again that night, a warm reassuring certainty, unthreatened by analysis.

175

The rain had thickened rather than cleared the pool's murkiness. Deuteronomy called it a "bad pool" and said there was nothing to be done. Patrick would have believed him but for the thought of how it had sparkled under Clifford's care. The memory of that reminded him of Sandy. She began that morning to seem more attractive to his mind's eye. It was a disturbing reflection, implying unaccustomed promiscuity. He went back into the house.

During breakfast he asked Sarah about Stanley. She twisted her apron in both hands. "He will not say where he had been, massa. Last night he walk all night but he do no good, I am sure of that. I am worried that he is with bad boys in Kuweto. Never was he like this before, not ever, massa. I tell him he must go home, he must go back to school. I will take him to the coach. This morning I will find out when it go. There are two every week to my home."

When she brought the coffee-pot through she lingered, needlessly adjusting the lid. "Massa."

"Yes, Sarah?"

"The black people like me who are in England, do they live in the city or the village?"

"Mostly in the cities, Sarah. Nearly all."

"They are not in the village?"

"Very few, I think. It's nearly all white people in the villages."

"Oh?" She opened her eyes wide and stopped fiddling with the lid. "Here is different. Here is nearly all black people in the village. Many of them want to come to the city but cannot. Sometimes they are moved from the city back to the village."

"In England people like to live in the villages."

She put down the coffee-pot. "In England is different, I think, massa."

"Yes, Sarah, I think it is."

She left the room, nodding seriously.

Before Patrick finished his coffee there was a telephone call from the police headquarters informing him that Mr Chatsworth was awaiting collection. He had not anticipated having to do this himself but there was clearly no alternative. Not yet, anyway. Perhaps the ambassador would suggest Chatsworth should be put up in the residence.

He drove in before the rush-hour. The clouds had cleared and the morning haze that normally hovered over Battenburg had either lifted or had not been there that day. The white tower blocks stood out with misleadingly pristine freshness against the blue African sky. There were few whites about but the streets were busy with blacks who had to travel early to work.

Chatsworth was waiting in the entrance to the headquarters. He wore a regimental blazer, cavalry twill trousers and a regimental tie. He had two suitcases. Patrick had to sign for both him and them, undertaking to return all to police custody whenever asked and to report immediately if any went missing. The two passports were withheld.

They shook hands and set out across the car-park with the suitcases – both large and very heavy. "What've you got in here?" asked Patrick.

"Oh, nothing much. Things I might be able to flog, some stuff I've bought. Bits and pieces, you know."

"Legal stuff?"

"If it isn't I'm sure those bastards will have had it." He frowned. "D'you know what they did? Told me at the prison I couldn't have breakfast because it was too early and I'd get some here. When we got here they said it was too late. I had half a mind to kick up a stink. I expected you to come for me last night, by the way. I'm famished now. Have you got plenty of scoff at your place?"

"Lots of food but not much to eat it with."

"Well, cut off its horns and wipe its arse and I'll have it as it is." He looked at the sky and the tall buildings. Some of the windows dazzled in the early sun. "Must say, it's good to be out. You didn't do too badly. Chap in Rio took as many days as you took hours. Much worse prison, too. Hope I can do the same for you one day."

"Thanks."

"Trouble is, I'm skint. Flat broke. I'll have to sponge off you or the embassy until L and F cough up. I s'pose you're on allowances? No problem, then. Don't like doing it, all the same." They loaded the suitcases into the bakkie. Chatsworth tapped it approvingly. "I like these things. Chap in prison was always on about them. He had four when he was caught – only one with him, of course. He put up a good fight – helicopter chase across the veldt. Why does it have to be bloody Nippon, though? I mean, one look and you can tell it's a winner. We'd never come up with anything so popular and obvious. I wouldn't say no to a spin in it one day."

Patrick wondered which arguments he should use to persuade the ambassador to look after Chatsworth. It would not be easy. However, Chatsworth was too pleased with the world as a whole to notice a lack of response in any part of it.

177

"Know what those police sods did?"

"What?"

"Pinched my pornography."

"It was probably illegal."

"That wasn't why they pinched it. Know where I can get any?"

"No."

"No cutlery, no pornography, you're in a bad way. Have you got a maid?"

"Yes, but not for you."

"Keeping her for yourself?"

"She's not suitable and wouldn't want to."

"Pity. Never mind." Chatsworth opened the window and rested his elbow on the door. The wind lifted his hair. "You know, I've a feeling this place is going to be all right for me from now on. I owe you a debt of gratitude. Don't forget it." He stared at the distant hills. "It's God's country, seen from the right side of the bars. Why are you holding your head like that?"

"I've got a stiff neck."

"Try sleeping without a pillow – or don't you have one of them either?"

Let loose in the house, Chatsworth went from room to room like an eager dog. He chose as his den the double bedroom at the far end of the upstairs corridor. He found his own way to the kitchen where he was introduced to Sarah after he had already opened the fridge.

He patted his stomach and grinned. "The biggest breakfast you can make, Sarah."

She laughed. "I always make big breakfast for Mr Patrick."

"Mr Patrick has only one tummy. I have two. A very big breakfast, please."

She laughed again and waved her hand. "Yes, massa, I make you very big breakfast." She went into the larder, chuckling and shaking her head.

He ate five eggs, toast, cereal and all the bacon. He had four cups of coffee. Patrick wondered if he could claim an extra allowance for him. When Sarah was out of the room he explained why the house was so bare. Chatsworth then suggested – and, it being his own suggestion, was immediately convinced – that this meant that Whelk was alive and well and had defected to the Lower Africans.

"What for?"

"So that he can stay here."

"He can do that anyway. He doesn't need to defect."

Chatsworth shook his head and swallowed some toast. "It's something like that. Bound to be. I'll get back on to his trail as soon as I've got a base."

Patrick decided that firmness now would be better than firmness later. Besides, hints and subtleties would probably be as effective against Chatsworth as musketry against a tank. "Not if you want to stay free, you won't. They'll have you back inside in no time if they think you're up to anything. The ambassador would be furious and you wouldn't get out again because he wouldn't answer for you. In fact, he doesn't know you are out. Neither does London, come to that."

Chatsworth compressed his lips and nodded sorrowfully. "I know what you mean. Never trust those in authority. They won't ever take responsibility when something goes wrong. Always ditch you tomorrow because you do today what they begged you to do yesterday. That's been my lesson. Just the same in the Army. Pity, I thought your ambassador was all right." He got up and looked out on to the lawn, his hands behind his back. "It's peace that does it, you know. Too much peace. No one has to struggle, to face up to consequences. Country goes to the dogs. Not enough spunk."

"Funnily enough, the ambassador once said something very like that."

Chatsworth again nodded sorrowfully. He appeared to relish the role of sage. "Probably has the right instincts, as I suspected, but won't act on them. He can't. He's a bureaucrat. If he stands out he suffers."

"You've had a lot of experience of this?"

"The dead hand of bureaucracy, I know it well. It's almost impossible now to be a hero. The man of parts cannot get on. He's not wanted. The trail of the slow-worm, Sir Richard Burton called it."

"Was he a hero?"

"Of course."

When Patrick finally left for work Chatsworth was squatting on the ground outside Sarah's quarters whilst she showed him how she prepared her mealie-meal. Patrick realised he had taken no such interest. Deuteronomy arrived and Chatsworth, amidst laughter, demonstrated how Sarah's large wooden spoon could be used as a reflex-tester.

14

There was almost open warfare at the embassy that morning. A four-day-old copy of *The Times* was found when it reached registry to have been mutilated by a member of the public who had visited the embassy library. The court and social column was torn and the crossword filled with obscenities.

This brought to a head the lengthy and bitter argument as to whether the British papers should go to the library first before being passed to registry for distribution, or whether they should go to the library last before despatch to Kuweto. It was a question of whether British passport holders who used the library but misused the papers should take precedence over embassy staff. Only the ambassador, who was unaware of the dispute, and Patrick, whom Miss Teale had not put on the distribution list, were neutral.

The registry clerks protested at this latest outrage and Miss Teale triumphantly took the evidence to Clifford. Clifford had been in since eight that morning. In his opinion only intellectual snobs did the crossword and only social snobs read the court and social column. It served both lots right, he said. It so happened that Miss Teale's birth had featured in the court and social column of an older and better *Times* and also that Daphne, who was in Clifford's office, sometimes got fairly near to finishing the crossword. Both took affront. Clifford shouted at Miss Teale. The commercial officer heard the row and joined the argument. The defence attaché, sensing battle, left his office and sided with the commercial officer.

Clifford slammed a file on to the desk and knocked a cup to the floor. He would hear no more. Everyone was stupid, idle and selfish and Miss Teale was a spinster. They were all to get out of his office and no one was to say any more about the papers until he had discussed the matter with the ambassador. The debaters dispersed to form a mutinous, muttering group in registry.

Philip, though siding in principle with Clifford, remained at his desk rather than joining in. "I wish I had time to read newspapers," he said with a doleful smile.

Patrick sought refuge in the consular department. He was waiting for a chance to tell the ambassador about Chatsworth and about the disappearance of Whelk's possessions. There were no DBSs that morning, only a small number of peaceful visa applicants. He began to think about Joanna.

The first sounds of panic in chancery were slamming doors and hurrying feet. Soon voices were audible, particulary Clifford's. Patrick paid no attention until Daphne came into the office. Her eyes were wide open and her cheeks quivering.

"Guess what!" she exclaimed, adding, before Patrick could react, "Guess what's happened to Clifford!"

Patrick imagined an apoplectic seizure, spontaneous combustion or a crippling electric shock from a massive accumulation of static.

"The minister's coming next week instead of next month!" said Daphne. Patrick waited. She realised she would have to explain. "Clifford is beside himself and no one knows where Sir Wilfrid is. Nothing's been prepared. London are calling for a revised programme and they haven't even had the first one yet. I thought Clifford was going to explode when he heard. Serve him right if he had. It's a punishment for being so nasty about the papers."

Clifford did not so much sit or stand in his office as undergo a kind of bureaucratic fission. His desire to be everywhere and do everything was such that he was unable to sit still, did not know where to go, wanted everyone to be available and at the same time to be doing something and wanted above all to reproduce himself a dozen times and perform a dozen different functions. He shouted contradictory and inappropriate instructions: Philip was sent to fetch files, a registry clerk to tell the responsible MFA desk officer of the change of plan, the defence attaché to find the ambassador's diary and the commercial officer and librarian with two receptionists to search the streets for Sir Wilfrid.

He pointed his finger at Patrick and shouted: "Get two cars for everyone in the party – every group, I mean, split them into groups – every car must have a back-up and make sure the drivers know where they're going. Do it immediately."

Jean, the ambassador's secretary, ran in. "We can't find the official visits file anywhere. Registry say you've got it."

Clifford put both hands to his head. "Of course I haven't got it. If I had it I wouldn't want it."

Jean stared. "But it's marked out to you. You must have it."

Clifford shook his fists and contorted his red face. "How can I have it if I haven't got it? Go and search Philip's cupboard. Don't let him go

181

anywhere till it's found." Jean ran out. Clifford turned to Patrick. "What are you waiting for?"

Anger in others nearly always made Patrick feel calmer. "Where do you want the drivers to go?"

"Jesus Christ!" Clifford kicked his chair away and almost ran from the office. "Follow me!"

When Patrick caught up with him in reception Clifford explained in short sentences that the minister was now to call on Lower Africa on his way to rather than from the Far East. London believed that this way it would be easier to present the visit as a low-key courtesy call by a junior minister. Informal talks might eventually lead to formal talks at the United Nations. This was the matter of border disputes that Lower Africa had with all her neighbours. There was hope of 'movement' since the disputes were thought to be bad for relations generally. More particularly, they made British economic links with Lower Africa embarrassing.

But now the ambassador had disappeared. He wasn't at the residence; he wasn't visiting the MFA, where Jean thought he was supposed to be; he wasn't at the editorial offices of the main English language newspaper, which was where Philip thought he was supposed to be; neither was he at the Battenburg Dog Show, a function held to raise money for a new black hospital. Clifford was exasperated. It was bad enough with the ambassador around, interfering and whatever, but worse still when he wasn't at the one time you wanted him.

They walked quickly along the corridor. "Perhaps he's been kidnapped," said Patrick.

Clifford stared determinedly ahead. "This is no time for facetiousness, Stubbs. You'll find, if you continue in the Service, that some things are important and have to be treated as such. It's a lesson you'd do well to learn."

He turned off abruptly into the unmarked loo. Patrick had assumed they were going to look at a route map for the drivers. Clifford fumbled with his flies. "Bloody buttons. Always on at Sandy to put zips in but she doesn't take a blind bit of notice. Same with everyone else round here. Feel I'm speaking to a brick wall sometimes." He became calmer as he talked. "We'll need two official cars to meet him at the airport, two for his visit to the gold mine, two to the MFA, two to the meat-packing station, two to the formal dinners and two for his wife to go to Kuweto if we can arrange it. That's assuming the programme is accepted and we haven't heard yet because we haven't sent it. 'Course, the whole bloody thing might change."

182

Patrick finished first. Clifford continued. Just as talking calmed him, so giving instructions fuelled his imagination. "I hope you've taken all that on board. You're going to have your hands full trying to keep all these transport balls in the air. As for your own posture during the visit, I think a low profile would be about right. Hull down but antennae up in case the Lower Africans try to bowl any fast ones, logistically speaking. Also, make sure London don't slip anything through the net on the run-in. 'Course, Miss Teale thinks all this ought to be in her parish, really, and so it should in a sense but horses for courses. I mean, she's mad so you'll just have to have a light touch on the tiller where she's concerned. Keep her briefed by all means but don't let her run with the ball. I'll be long-stop in case there's real trouble but I don't want to have to take flak unless I have to. I shouldn't say this but I must be about due for an award – you know, something in the honours list – and so I don't want the minister walking into any trip-wires and us all ending up with egg on our faces."

"Roger," said Patrick.

Clifford changed his mind about the transport arrangements whilst walking back down the corridor. As they were absolutely vital it was better that he should keep a grip on all the reins himself. Patrick should concentrate on liaison with the Lower Africans and with the police about the Whelk business. Sir Wilfrid wanted the minister to discuss that with his opposite number.

"Any more happened?" he asked.

"Hard to say at present. You didn't by any chance order anyone to take Arthur's furniture away?"

"No. Why, has someone?"

"Yes."

"But they left yours?"

"I haven't any."

"That's all right, then. Have you told Sir Wilfrid?"

"Not yet."

"I should, if I were you."

"Thanks, I shall." Patrick returned to his and Philip's office. Philip had just called for twenty-three files, cancelled a dinner with the American first secretary and made arrangements to work during the weekend. The commercial officer's wife later told everyone that Philip's wife had told her in confidence that she and Philip would sleep in separate rooms until after the birth of the ministerial brief he was writing.

"Anything I can do to help?" asked Patrick. He was determined not to give up his dinner with Joanna that night but confident that Philip would refuse the offer.

A guarded, awkward expression grew slowly in Philip's eyes. He looked at his files. "Jolly kind of you to offer but I think I'll have to cope myself. It's really second secretary stuff, you see. Many thanks all the same. Much appreciated."

"Well, let me know if there is."

Patrick's telephone rang. It was a woman asking for Clifford. It was a moment before he and Sandy recognised each other. "Hang on," he said, immediately self-conscious because of Philip's presence. "They've given you the wrong number. I'll get you transferred."

Her voice sounded unnaturally close. "Don't bother. Just tell him I rang. He was trying to get me when I was out. Can't think why. Probably some great panic about his shoe-laces."

"It was his buttons he was complaining about just now."

She laughed. "Was he now? Very uninhibited for him. He must be in a real flap about something. Wouldn't normally mention that department. How's your love-life?"

"Very good."

"Mine's a graveyard."

Patrick pressed the phone hard to his ear, hoping that Philip couldn't hear. "Perhaps you should do something about the buttons, then."

"I might as well sew them up for good for all the difference that would make."

Patrick wasn't sure what to say.

"Why don't you come up and see me some time?" she continued, in an American accent.

"Well, I'd like to but – "

"But you're busy? Typical. You're getting like the others already. I'll have to come and see you, then."

He tried to sound encouraging but she cut him short. "Don't worry, love, I was only joking. Tell him I rang. Be nice to her. Bye."

Sir Wilfrid strolled past the door. Patrick followed him to his office, for once unguarded by Jean because she was elsewhere searching. Sir Wilfrid threw his jacket on to the armchair, stretched his arms above his head and then rubbed his hair vigorously with both hands. He did not seem surprised to see Patrick. "Ever played golf?"

"No, sir."

"You should, you know. Very relaxing. Restores perspective. Took a round off the American ambassador this morning. Very good. Winning is good for you, too, now and again." He stopped rubbing his hair and put his hands in his pockets. "Now, what've you got for me? Some new horror, I suppose?"

Patrick described the removal of Whelk's possessions and the release of Chatsworth. Sir Wilfrid was pleased by what he took to be signs of Lower African complicity. He put the radio on the desk and switched on the pop music just as Jean put her head round the door. She started to speak but he turned up the music and waved her away. He and Patrick took up their usual positions and he shouted into Patrick's ear. "Thing to do is to let Chatsworth sniff around by himself – see if he can flush out anything. If they try to stop him it's a sign we're getting warm and we can brief the minister to raise it with them. The minister's very keen, as you know, and now the Lower Africans are in it with us we don't need to worry about their making a scandal of it. Also, it could be useful for the minister – stick to beat them with."

Patrick doubted that it was safe to let Chatsworth do what he liked. "We're responsible, sir. Me particularly. I signed for him. And you did say we mustn't risk anything that could upset relations during the visit."

Sir Wilfrid nodded impatiently. "I know that, I know that. You don't have to tell me what I said. But they're in it with us now, like it or not, and as long as he just sniffs around and doesn't do anything stupid nobody can complain. He struck me as a sensible sort of chap. Wouldn't do anything out of the ordinary."

"Well, he did get himself locked up, sir."

"Yes, yes, I know that too. But that can happen to anyone in this country."

"Does he have to stay in my house?"

"Why not? You must have room, haven't you?" Sir Wilfrid switched off the radio. Patrick realised it was a mistake to put the question so directly. Sir Wilfrid's point was unanswerable. Patrick changed the subject to the ministerial visit, saying it had been brought forward. Sir Wilfrid shrugged. "Oh, well, sooner over. Ever met him? Wretched little man. Blows with the wind. I was hoping he'd stay long enough for us to take him up north and show him the drought. Cattle and people dying all over the place. He ought to see it. I want to propose that we donate a water pump from official funds, you see, and the embassy budget is exhausted. After all, the French and Germans are building a dam, so we should be seen to do something. Clifford knows about the visit, does he? Good. Hope he's had the sense to get on to the MFA himself."

185

Patrick left the room as Clifford rushed in to announce the news. Through the closing door Patrick heard Sir Wilfrid say, "I know that, I know that. Why are you carrying all those newspapers?"

Jean gave him a hostile glance. "What do you two do in there – kiss each other?"

Patrick smiled and raised his eyebrows. She went on with her typing.

The avenue to Patrick's house appeared to have been subjected to one of Battenburg's freak storms of small circumference but great intensity. Yet he noticed that although the road was wet the trees were dry; then that the road was wet only as far as his house. Water bubbled up from beneath his garden wall and surged across the grass verge before streaming down the road.

He left the bakkie in front of the garage and ran towards the house. The front door was open and there was a dead rat on the hall floor. From the veranda he saw that the bottom third of the garden, all that was below the pool, was flooded. The pool itself was two-thirds empty, the pump motor was running and there was dark green water gushing from the large pipe that led from the pump. The flower beds were flooded out of sight and there was an ominous swirling where the water ran away beneath the wall. He ran down the lawn towards the pump. The grass that looked dry was wet. He slipped as he turned and for an instant saw his feet in the air before he landed on his back and skidded into the slush. He felt like remaining on his back and howling his rage but after a few seconds of silent fury he got to his feet and stood in three or four inches of water to turn off the pump. He was wearing his nearly-new dark suit, having got the new lightweight one wet in the roof restaurant the day before.

"What did you do that for?"

The cheery voice came from the compost heap at the top of the garden. Chatsworth leant on a garden fork. His shirt-sleeves were rolled up and he wore a pair of corduroys that looked familiar. Next to him Deuteronomy leant on a broomstick. On the wall behind stood a number of beer-cans. Snap was energetically digging into the heap, ignoring Deuteronomy. Deuteronomy grinned and waved his hand as if Patrick were far away.

"What d'you think I did it for? It's flooded all over the bloody road." It was a pleasure to give vent to anger by shouting but it meant that he became more aware of it and so was in fact less angry.

Chatsworth was unabashed. "Doesn't matter, it'll drain away."

"It's undermined the bloody wall and washed out all the bulbs and plants." Patrick was not sure what was in the flower-beds but knew that Deuteronomy spent some time there. "The wall will collapse now."

"Well, it's not yours, is it? PSA, you said. Public property, therefore everyone's, therefore no one's." Chatsworth pointed his fork at the pool. "Someone had to drain that malarial mess. Look at all the green gunge it's left on the sides. Bloody disgrace, letting it get like that."

It was true that the sides of the wall were horribly stained and that the remaining water looked evil. There was no doubt that he would have to get the contractors in now. His anger subsided rapidly into resignation.

There was a bark from Snap. Chatsworth hit at something with his fork. Deuteronomy yelped, jumped and disappeared behind the heap. Snap emerged amidst a great flurry of leaves shaking a small object.

"That's five this afternoon and one I got with the fork," shouted Chatsworth. "There's a nest here, or was. He's good for a big dog. Small ones are usually better. Ever shot coypu?"

Patrick trudged up the lawn, his shoes squelching. "No."

"You want to try it. South America's the best place but Norfolk's not too bad. They're nearly the size of him." Snap tore at the mangled rat. There were sounds of ripping skin and snapping bone. "He does that to the ones that nip him. Hates them. Breaks their necks, crushes their ribs and tears them apart." He patted Snap, who glanced up obligingly. The rat's tail hung from his mouth.

"There's a dead one in the hall," said Patrick.

"Is that what he's doing with them? I put them in a heap but they kept disappearing. Thought they must be resurrecting themselves or being eaten by the live ones that were brave enough to creep out. They eat each other, you know. We can eat them, too."

"Can we?"

"I was talking to Sarah about it. Might try one whilst I'm here." He frowned at Patrick. "Did you know you've got wet and filth all up your arse?"

"Yes."

"Take a tumble?"

"Something like that."

"Bit early in the day to be that bad. All those allowances, I suppose. If you're not careful you'll end up like Deuteronomy." He indicated the beer-cans on the wall. "Found them inside. Hope it's all right. Hot work, rattin'. Had to get a few down Deuteronomy before he'd even come into the garden with Snap. Bad relations, I'm told. Okay this

187

afternoon, though. Snap takes no notice of him as long as there are rats around."

Deuteronomy crawled round from the other side of the compost heap. He got unsteadily to his feet by starting to crawl up the heap and then straightening himself. There were leaves in his hair and bits and pieces of garden rubbish stuck to his green overalls. He grinned blissfully and took Patrick's hand in both of his. "Mmmm-massa," he said, caressing it.

"Hallo, Deuteronomy."

"Mmmm-massa." He bowed over Patrick's hand as if to kiss it.

Patrick tried to withdraw but Deuteronomy would not let go. They all three walked towards the house, Deuteronomy still clasping Patrick and gazing admiringly into his face.

"He seems to have taken a shine to you," said Chatsworth.

"He's drunk."

"That's when it shows."

Patrick freed himself at the kitchen door, leaving Deuteronomy still grinning and bowing.

There was another dead rat behind the sofa in the living-room and two more by the rape-gate. For the rest of their time together in the house Chatsworth competed with Snap in what he called "kills". Snap was always ahead but Chatsworth's score was respectable, achieved with fork, stick, boot, and once a well-aimed wine bottle. He frequently complained that he would do much better if he had his pistol.

"Couldn't help noticing you had company last night," he remarked over tea.

Patrick's first thought was of the fight with Jim. "What do you mean?"

"I helped Sarah make the bed. Blonde hair on the pillow."

"Observant of you."

"How about an explanation?"

"In due course, maybe."

Chatsworth laughed. "I like that. 'In due course.' Very Foreign Office. I shall take it as a challenge to find out."

There was a letter for Patrick on the hall table. He had one every week from his mother in Chislehurst but otherwise letters from England were rare. This was from Rachel. His guilt at not having written to her as promised was replaced by alarm as he read the letter. She wrote on television notepaper in breathless telegraphese to the effect that she'd got a grant to do some research for a documentary and if she added her own money to it she could come out and stay with him – "Safer 'cos diplomatic protection" – and get some material on Lower Africa for the film. The theme was the connection between capitalism and racism. She would not say more in case LASS intercepted his letters but would send a telegram to let him know when she was arriving. It would only be for a few days, anyway. Maurice sent regards.

He wondered if it would be possible to move in with Joanna.

"Upper middle class leftie with a conscience as big as her boobs?" said Chatsworth from behind him.

"What?"

Chatsworth repeated what he had said. "Your correspondent. I'm guessing. Couldn't help noticing the letter over your shoulder. Am I right?"

"D'you always read other people's letters?"

"Only when they hold them up so that I can't miss them. Don't you?"

"No."

Chatsworth frowned. "Don't you really?"

Patrick hesitated. "Well, if I really couldn't help it – "

"There you are, then." Chatsworth began walking up the stairs. "I'm right about her, am I?"

"More or less. Were you wondering if she's seducible?"

"Everyone's seducible. Thought you'd have learnt that at university. Mind you, students are priggish, aren't they? My experience, anyway. All the guff about sincerity. What's her man like?"

"Quiet, pleasant. He's going to be a barrister."

"Is he wet?"

"Maybe by your standards."

"They met at university and now they're living together?"

"Yes."

"Must be, then." Chatsworth disappeared at the top of the stairs.

"D'you think she'd fall for you?" called Patrick.

"Time and place," shouted Chatsworth. "Like the rest of us."

Whilst in his bath Patrick considered what to do with Chatsworth that evening. He did not dare think of the longer term. There was no question of taking him to Joanna's; but to leave him entirely to his own devices would be asking for trouble. When he came downstairs Chatsworth was raiding the fridge. He told him that the ambassador had said he could go out and look round – sniff around – provided he didn't do anything.

"How?"

189

"You can take the bakkie." This had not been an easy decision. "Go and explore Battenburg for the evening. I'm going out to dinner but I can get a taxi."

"With 'in-due-course'?"

"Yes."

"Has the bakkie got plenty of petrol? Much as I'm looking forward to having a go in it . . . "

"It's over half full. You won't be going far, anyway."

"But I'll need some money just in case."

Patrick gave him some.

"Make a note of this," said Chatsworth, pocketing it. "Don't want to end up owing you."

It was already dark when Chatsworth left. Patrick was upstairs about to ring for a taxi when he was called by Sarah.

"Massa, you come down please." She stood in the kitchen. "Deuteronomy has bad cut."

Patrick assumed that he had returned to his other employer, with whom he lived, to sleep off the effects of ratting. "Where is he?"

"Here, massa." She pointed outside.

Deuteronomy stood in the white courtyard beneath the outside light, his head on one side and his hand pressed against his cheek and ear. There were dark streaks of blood on his overalls, while blood trickled between his fingers and down the back of his hand. There was a cut from beneath his cheek up towards his ear. The flesh was open like meat on a slab. Deuteronomy's dark eyes gazed sorrowfully but when he saw Patrick he smiled with the right side of his mouth, bowed his head and mumbled.

Patrick did not know how to cope with any injury. "Let me see." He took Deuteronomy carefully by the wrist and moved his hand. The cut ran right to the top of the ear and the exposed flesh was slightly whitened where it had been pressed against the cheek-bone. It reddened quickly when the pressure was off. Patrick pressed Deuteronomy's hand back on to it.

"Come inside and sit down." He led him to the kitchen. Deuteronomy was limply obedient and stumbled on the step. He smelt strongly of beer. Patrick sat him down and told Sarah to bring a bowl of cold water and a flannel. When she returned he removed Deuteronomy's hand and pressed the flannel hard against the cut, every so often taking it away, soaking it again and putting it back. He wasn't sure that this was the right thing to do but remembered having it done to him as a child. "Is there any first-aid kit, any bandages?"

"I don't know, massa. I think madam that was here before has taken them with her." Sarah went from cupboard to cupboard with a slow haste, her sandals flopping on the tiled floor. She found a few strips of Elastoplast which were too small.

"What happened?" Patrick asked.

Deuteronomy attempted another half smile. Sarah addressed him sharply in Zulu and he made monosyllabic replies, ending with a short sentence.

Sarah turned back to Patrick. "A man in the beer hall cut him with a big knife. He drink with bad boys at a place for black people and they take his money and cut him. He come here because it is closer than his home. He say he is sorry." She clasped her hands and stared disapprovingly at Deuteronomy, then at the blood on the kitchen floor.

"We'll have to take him to a hospital. You hold the flannel."

Sarah held the flannel against Deuteronomy's face. She said something sharp to him which he did not answer.

Patrick rang Joanna and asked if it would be quicker to get a taxi to the nearest hospital, wherever it was, or to ring for an ambulance. She said it would be quicker if she came in her car.

She arrived with cotton-wool, bandages and antiseptic. "Get something to put on the car seat in case the blood starts again. And get Sarah to make some sweet tea whilst I'm bandaging him. You look as if you could do with some, too."

He found the red plastic bag that Stanley had used in the rain. He had forgotten about Stanley. Sarah was happily busy now making tea and so he did not ask her what had happened.

Joanna tended to Deuteronomy with the crisp efficiency of someone who knew what she was doing but did not know the patient. She bent over him from behind the chair, her hands moving confidently as she applied the bandage. Patrick was pleased to see her so capable. He wanted to say something personal, as if to reassure himself of their intimacy. "How long were you a nurse?"

"Not long." She did not look up. "You're pale. Why don't you sit down?"

"I'm not used to blood. Pathetic, isn't it?"

"Men all over."

He drove and she sat in the back with Deuteronomy. The white bandage round his face covered one ear completely and combined with his lugubrious expression to make him look like a clown who had done something wrong and was being taken off to be punished. Joanna

191

gave directions and soon they were approaching a large hospital.

"Turn in here?"

She shook her head. "Whites only."

"But what about accidents?"

"Only white accidents."

Another ten minutes' drive brought them to a clinic which was the only one in the area for blacks. It was a squat, square building with a walled backyard and an area of earth at the side that served as a car-park. It was lit by a single high floodlight from one corner of the car-park and had a sign in big letters saying that evening surgery was open. There was a queue of blacks, mostly women, stretching round the walls of the backyard and out into the car-park. A few stood but most sat on the ground.

"He'll be here all night," said Patrick. "When do they close?"

"I don't know. These people have probably been here all day and if they're not seen tonight they'll come back tomorrow. But we'll be all right. Bring your wallet."

She led the way past the queue and into reception. The waiting people gazed placidly at them, apparently neither hostile nor curious. One woman crouching near the door stared unseeingly. Her black skin was tinged puce-grey.

At the counter sat a middle-aged, balding Indian. He wore several large gold rings and was writing slowly. Joanna went ahead whilst Patrick followed holding Deuteronomy by the arm. Deuteronomy was like a frightened prisoner, reluctant and silent.

"This is Mr Stubbs's gardener who needs urgent treatment," said Joanna. "He's lost a lot of blood. Could he be seen immediately?"

The Indian looked at her. "The doctors are busy."

"Have you something on which we can write the details?"

The Indian pushed across a form and sat gazing past them at the queue, slowly turning each of the rings on his fingers. Joanna wrote Patrick's name and address and Deuteronomy's name. She took a banknote from Patrick's wallet, folded it in the form and pushed both across the desk to the Indian.

He unfolded it as if lost in thought, removed the note and put it in the breast pocket of his shirt. He then got up and walked unhurriedly down the passage. A short while later he returned and said, "This way."

The doctor was an elderly white with crinkly grey hair and side-whiskers. He had with him an attractive young coloured girl in a white

192

coat. He bade Patrick and Joanna good evening and sat Deuteronomy on a chair whilst he undressed the wound.

"This needs stitching. It'll take a little while. D'you want to wait?"

"Yes," said Patrick.

The doctor motioned to them to sit on a bench at the side. Deuteronomy eyed Patrick piteously as they moved out of his range of vision and Patrick feared for a moment that he might find his hand clasped again. The doctor moved Deuteronomy's head to and fro with one hand whilst he dabbed at the wound with cotton wool. "Someone stick a knife in him?"

"Yes, and robbed him."

"Lucky it missed his eye."

He cleaned the wound, gave a local anaesthetic and put in fourteen stitches. Deuteronomy made a number of soft, high-pitched whimpers indicating that the anaesthetic might not have had time to take effect properly, but the job when done was neat and clean. Joanna watched calmly whilst Patrick stared with fascinated horror at the way the flesh was tugged and pulled.

"He's your gardener?" the doctor asked.

"Only part-time. He lives with his main employer." Deuteronomy stood meekly by the door tentatively touching his new bandage.

"That's who should be paying for him."

"I'll pay."

"No, I'll send a bill. It's simpler. Tell him to come back on Tuesday to have the stitches out. No need to bring him, just send him. Make sure his regular employer knows he's to bring his medical card with him. I must have that."

The Indian barely glanced as they passed him on the way out. The people in the queue, stretching round the courtyard and out into the car-park, simply gazed.

The other employers lived behind high wrought-iron gates in a very large house. They were out and so Patrick left Deuteronomy with a note. Deuteronomy, still touching his bandage and smiling with evident pain, mumbled his thanks several times. He seemed to want to say something else but nothing came. Eventually they shook hands and Patrick again found himself held for a long time.

Joanna drove. He felt relieved and affectionate but her purposeful driving inhibited him from demonstrating his affection. He became talkative instead. "What would've happened if the clinic had been closed?"

193

"We'd have had to take him to a hospital in a black area."

"Or if he hadn't had someone to bribe for him?"

"He'd have waited with the others."

"Terrible, isn't it?"

She shrugged. "Paying is the only way to avoid waiting in Africa. All over the continent people spend most of their time waiting."

"It's still terrible."

"Look, anywhere else in Africa he wouldn't have got proper treatment at all." She sounded aggressive and irritable as if he had been making a personal criticism. She held up her hand. "All right, it's wrong, I agree, I'm not arguing with that. I mean, I don't like having to bribe people. But what do you do about it? It's not going to change peacefully because people don't want it to change and if you try to change it violently who suffers most? All the Deuteronomies. And not just at the time of change either. In the long run as well. Unless he had family in high places his kind would always be hungry in black Africa. They are everywhere else and they would be here."

Patrick wished he had not begun. He had as yet no wish to explore their differences and did not like the hardness in her tone. He tried to sound conciliatory but knew it would fail because he was unable to capitulate. "Yes, okay, but I'm not talking about the future or about the rest of Africa or anything general. It's only particulars. I keep coming back to particulars. It just seems to me that it ought to be possible to arrange things so that Deuteronomy gets the same kind of treatment as you and I. I mean, simply in terms of resources."

"Yes, it ought to be." She drove on in silence.

Patrick silently blamed Chatsworth for having got Deuteronomy drunk.

They were greeted at the door of Joanna's bungalow by Beauty, the exquisite miniature maid. Beauty looked solemn. "Madam, there are many dead people."

Joanna stiffened and clutched Patrick's arm automatically, which made him feel instantly better. "What do you mean? Belinda – "

Beauty took her hand with irresistible simplicity. "Come, I show you."

Patrick followed them into the sitting-room. He was slightly ashamed to realise that his main concern was that the evening seemed to be going from bad to worse. Beauty pointed to a glass cabinet in which were painted china figures in eighteenth-century costume. Most had fallen over.

"Belinda did this before I put her to bed. I am very sorry for her, madam."

Joanna put her forehead against Patrick's shoulder for a moment. He took her hand. "Don't worry, Beauty, I'll put them up again. They're not broken."

"I am very sorry, madam."

"It's all right. Nothing has happened. You can go to bed now."

"Thank you, madam." She glanced demurely at Patrick and glided from the room.

Joanna put her arms around his neck. "I'm sorry, too."

"For what?"

"For being so awkward."

"You weren't. You were helpful."

"D'you fancy burnt cottage pie?"

He kissed her. "I fancy you."

"Instead?"

"Before and after."

She bit his neck. "Instead would be too good to be true."

15

He took a taxi to work from Joanna's the next morning. In the car he gazed out of the window, in the office at the files; in each case without seeing. Philip was drafting and again wanted no assistance. Clifford was seeing the MFA about the ministerial visit, having left an instruction that the last memorandum on transport arrangements was to be disregarded. Patrick was to make no further arrangements without further conference. He filed the last instruction, ready for its resurrection.

He felt drenched in Joanna. His senses had become conditioned to her presence and he was constantly wanting to touch, to turn, to speak to her. Although he had showered he could still detect the smell of her skin on his, elusive and tantalising. It reminded him of pine-needles. Presumably it was something she wore.

The first sentence of the previous year's review of trading trends between the UK and Lower Africa spoke of a possible upturn although, after allowing for inflation, it was equally possible that the overall context was that of a downturn. He read the sentence seven or eight times, musing on whether or not he was in love.

His eye wandered across a couple of pages of trading statistics. He took a sheet of drafting paper from Philip's pile and made a simple calculation. Assuming that there were roughly four thousand million people in the world and that roughly half of those were women, about a quarter – five hundred million – should be within the age range within which he might reasonably expect to fall in love. Most people, he knew, chose their mates from a very small sample, usually no more than the lower double figures, and most people considered themselves to have been in love with their mates at some time. Even if he assumed, therefore, that he was likely to fall in love with no more than one in a hundred – a more stringent selection than was common – this still left him with the possibility of falling in love with five million women. And even if he divided this figure by ten there were half a million women he could fall in love with. It seemed unreasonable to settle upon one, especially the first. He drank his coffee, doodled on the drafting paper and concluded that if he could think about it in this way he could not be in love.

Nevertheless, it felt as though he were. At least, his feelings accorded with other people's descriptions of their feelings. Perhaps everyone was wrong. Reception rang through to say that two policemen were asking for him.

They stood by the desk, pale and burly with cropped hair and sullen faces. He assumed it was something to do with Whelk.

"Are you Patrick Stubbs?"

"Yes."

"Are you the owner of a red Toyota four-wheel drive vehicle?"

"Yes."

"Can you account for your movements yesterday evening?"

Everyone in reception was listening whilst pretending to work. "Well, I was having dinner with a friend."

"What time did you go to dinner?"

"At about seven-thirty or eight."

"What time did you return?"

"Well, I was out all night, I think, yes." He wondered if Jim had set this up. "But I wasn't with the Toyota. I didn't drive it at all last night."

The policemen looked disappointed. Someone driving the said Toyota had caused a riot in Kuweto the previous evening. The police had made arrests following a robbing and stabbing incident and a crowd had gathered outside the police station. They were dispersing peacefully when the red Toyota appeared. Driven from the first in a reckless manner it then began to chase the crowd, making several runs through them and charging any who remained. No one was killed but one of the arrested men had escaped and a policeman lost both his shoes trying to get out of the way. The crowd later re-formed and, believing the incident to have been the work of the police, stoned police premises and vehicles for most of the night until pacified by police reinforcements.

"Do you have any idea who might have driven your vehicle, sir?"

Patrick spent most of the next thirty minutes or so on the telephone, first to Chatsworth, who was not up, then to Jim, who was not in, then to Jim's superior who said that if Chatsworth's release conditions had been breached – as it seemed on the face of it that they had – he would be locked up again.

Chatsworth was finally roused by Sarah at the third attempt. He was unrepentant. "Stopped the riot, you mean," he said, "not caused it."

197

"That's not what they say."

"You can't trust them. They're policemen. Biased."

"They're talking of locking you up again."

"Typical. Try to help the buggers and that's what they do to you."

"You'd better give me a full account before I talk to them again and before the ambassador finds out."

They met in an Austrian coffee shop near the embassy. It was run by a morose Viennese who practically never spoke but would leave his customers to sit all day over a newspaper and a coffee. Chatsworth was late. He parked the bakkie half on the pavement and came in wearing Patrick's corduroy jacket.

"Sarah said she'd never seen you wear it and it's cooler than mine. I'll put it back, don't worry. Found a packet of Durex in the pocket. Is that what you use with 'in-due-course'?"

Patrick could not remember when he had last worn the jacket nor for whom the unopened packet had been intended. This was not how the conversation should have started.

Chatsworth helped himself to sugar. "Can't use them myself. Instant deflation. It just won't take them. Sarah had never seen any before."

"You showed them to her?"

"Filled one with water to demonstrate. She could hardly stand for laughing."

Chatsworth's account of the evening, when it came, was rambling and incomplete. He confessed that his memory might be hampered by the effect of Lion beer, a brand popular with blacks, but insisted that his interpretation of events was correct. He had deliberately gone to Kuweto knowing he was not allowed but assuming, rightly, that the bakkie's new diplomatic number plate would ensure that he wasn't stopped. There was, after all, a chance that Whelk might be there; he could've gone native. He had known a chap in the Army, chap called Peters, who had gone native in Borneo after an exercise. Turned up three years later with seven wives. Anyway, after driving around for a while without seeing much that looked like action he went into one of the beer halls.

"I was the only white bloke there. They all looked as if they'd never seen one before. Felt a bit out of place, to be honest. I wasn't going to stay for more than a quick one but then there was a bit of a shindig in one corner and a chap got knifed so I thought I'd stick around. They were still giving me some pretty odd looks so I bought a few drinks. Must say, once they got used to me they were all very friendly. Quite

198

pleasant once you get to know them. I had to keep nipping outside to see if the bakkie was okay and then it occurred to me to get a couple of them to sit in it and guard it, with me keeping them in drink. That worked all right. They were very willing.

"Anyway, I bought a few more drinks – don't forget I owe you, by the way – and got talking, which was pretty difficult because they don't all speak English. Most of them aren't even Lower African. They come from black Africa to work. I didn't know that. Well, you know how one thing leads to another sometimes – perhaps you don't – d'you ever get pissed?" He broke off and looked at Patrick with an air of serious enquiry.

Patrick remembered going backwards into the restaurant pool. "I get a bit tipsy sometimes."

"That all?"

"Yes. Being drunk is like being ill."

Chatsworth looked at him as at one who thinks that Buddhism consists merely in shaving one's head. "Well, I can assure you that one thing does sometimes lead to another and this time I ended up offering lifts home to a few of them. I suppose you'll say I shouldn't have but it seemed a good idea at the time. In the end, what with the bakkie guards who'd got some of their mates in and this other lot, there must've been about twenty of the buggers crammed into the back, all singing and dancing and what-have-you. There were also a few in the cab with me. It still stinks a bit, actually, but I'll clean it out.

"So, off we set and I thought to myself, why stick to the roads when you've got a cross-country vehicle with good headlights? It does it good to do what it's designed for now and again, like the rest of us. Also, they lived at every bloody point of the compass so it was handy to cut about a bit. 'Course, it then turned out that they were as clueless as I was about where they lived. Fortunately, we lost a few overboard otherwise I'd still be delivering them. But it was all okay, no problem, until this to-do with the police."

He leant earnestly across the table and held up his spoon. "You may get another story from them but I can't help that. What I'm telling you is what happened so far as I'm concerned. Now, what they'd done was arrest these blokes for something or other and they'd made a bog-up of it. There was a sort of demo going on outside one of their forts. Demo – riot, really, just beginning. They hadn't got a grip of it and they weren't going to, I could see that straight away. Seen a lot of that sort of thing in Belfast. If you don't get a grip straight away you lose control. Anyway, I'd dropped off or lost all my passengers by then so I thought I'd give the police a hand. I mean, imagine it – fort surrounded by a couple of hundred murderous natives running up and down, all pissed as rats and howling for the blood of the defenders. Rourke's Drift all over again. And then you pitch up with the cavalry. What do you do? You'd do what I did, wouldn't you? You'd charge 'em." Chatsworth's thin face was eager and his eyes were bright with the memory. "It was a wonderful sight. Solid mass of rioters in the headlights, great black wall because they thought I was going to slow down. Then they were all arms and legs and teeth scrabbling all over the place, trying to get out of the way. Some of them jumped right up in the air like grasshoppers. Must've landed behind me. Then I reversed through them, then forward again. Did it four times altogether. Wasn't anyone left after that so I waved goodbye to the defenders and came home." He shook his head. "Goes to show you can't trust the fuzz, doesn't it? No matter where you are. When you first said they'd reported it I thought you meant they wanted to pass on their thanks. I was ready to let you share the credit, too. Would it help if I went to see them, to sort things out, you know?"

"No."

"S'pose you're right. Don't know why it is but this sort of thing nearly always happens when I try to be helpful. No gratitude. What's more, I caught one hanging around the house when I got back."

"One what?"

"Black. Young chap."

"That was Stanley, Sarah's son."

"Is he supposed to be here?"

"Not really, no. He's going soon."

"Just as well, then."

"What's just as well?"

Awkwardness was rare in Chatsworth but it showed clearly this time. "Just as well I saw him off."

"You what?" Patrick heard the sharpness in his own voice.

"Saw him off. Well, he was skulking around the garage looking as though he was going to nick something. You were still out enjoying yourself with 'in-due-course' so there was no one I could ask. I went for him with a shifting spanner but he got away."

Patrick did not hide his anger. "That was bloody stupid. If you'd stopped to ask him what he was doing there he'd have told you. You'd better apologise to Sarah as soon as you get back."

"All right, all right, I'll apologise. I've no objection to apologising.

200

Lot of people can vouch for that. But what I'd like to know is what was he doing skulking around there at twenty past one in the morning? I bet Sarah didn't know he was there. He'd been up to something. I could tell. He was shifty."

"It's hardly surprising with you chasing him with a spanner."

"No, no, before that. It was his manner. He was definitely up to something. Also, he'd been boozing more than was good for him. Couldn't hold it. He'd been sick behind the garage."

Patrick was not able to feel wholeheartedly angry. What Chatsworth said about Stanley was worrying because he was the kind of man to know shiftiness when he saw it. He rang Sarah when he got back to the embassy and asked about Stanley. He repeated then that he didn't mind her son being around but he could tell from her voice that she thought he was complaining. In fact, it was Stanley's absences rather than his presence that worried him.

She spoke hesitantly and loudly. "On Friday I try to take him to the buses depot, massa. I try but he is bad boy and we are late. It take two and a half hours to get there and we miss the bus."

He softened his tone as much as he could. "Why did it take so long, Sarah? What was the difficulty?"

She hesitated again. "My fault, massa, I get the wrong bus and then we have to walk and there is no other bus for a long time. But we go again tomorrow afternoon. I get the bus right then, massa."

"What time does it go?"

"At half past two."

"I'll come home for lunch and I'll take you both to it."

"That is kind, massa. Thank you."

Jim Rissik rang a few minutes later. He had heard about the Chatsworth incident and had talked to his boss about it. Patrick gave Chatsworth's version, with which Jim did not bother to argue. "For Christ's sake and his, make sure he doesn't do anything like it again. I had a hell of a job persuading them not to get on to the MFA and make a protest. It was only because of the visit of your minister that they didn't. You owe me a favour there, Pat."

Patrick spoke with forced jocularity. They both laughed at the idea of Chatsworth in the beer hall, then discussed Jim's so far unsuccessful efforts to discover who had removed Whelk's effects.

"How's Joanna?" asked Jim, with no change of tone.

Patrick felt himself stiffen. "All right, well."

"Is she at home at the moment?"

"As far as I know, yes."

201

"I rang earlier but there was no answer. I wondered if she was with you."

"No, no. She might have been shopping."

"Yes, something like that."

He recognised the affected unconcern in Jim's voice, sensing the same in his own. They rang off with cheerful goodbyes.

He told Sir Wilfrid about Chatsworth. There was a good chance that Clifford would come to hear of it anyway and he did not want to be seen keeping a secret from the ambassador. Sir Wilfrid pursed his lips. "It was a bit injudicious of him, I admit, but he's naturally not aware of diplomatic niceties. It's up to you to make sure he understands, Patrick. He struck me as a very level-headed sort of chap and I'm quite sure he wouldn't have done anything like that if he'd had any sort of inkling of the embarrassment he could have caused. It's your responsibility to make sure he does have inklings in future. Goes to show they're keeping tabs on him, though, doesn't it? They must be in it up to their necks."

"But they thought at first it was me."

"Of course they did, it's your car. They're probably keeping tabs on you, too. Where were you at the time, by the way?"

"I was seeing a friend."

"Well, why not take Chatsworth along with you in future? He's probably bored and rather lonely. It's up to you to take care of him and he's not the sort of chap to get in the way, I'm sure."

The day before the minister was due to arrive his visit was downgraded yet further to a 'private fact-finding mission'. It was to be announced to the press that the minister was to have no formal contacts with the Lower African government. It was known within chancery, though, that he was to have an informal meeting with his 'opposite number'. In a lengthy immediate telegram London gave the reason for the downgrading as HMG's imminent refusal to recognise the so-called independent homelands that Lower Africa had created for large numbers of rural blacks. London's argument was that if the decision were conveyed during an official visit both countries would be obliged to assume unhelpful public postures, leading to a worsening of bilateral relations. Such relations, though they existed only in the minds of a very small number of officials, were believed by governments to apply to entire peoples, and they were sustained in this belief by the very officials in whose minds such relations existed. The telegram also argued that an unofficial visit might be a more 'viable' forum in which to persuade the Lower Africans to be more flexible on the question of the disputed Northern territories.

"Frankly, I don't believe it," said Clifford, tossing the telegram on to Philip's piled desk, from where it fluttered to the floor. Philip had to pick it up. "London have known this all along. Why are they suddenly trotting it out at the last minute? Either because they don't trust us – for which they have no reason because we haven't let them down yet – or because someone wants the visit to pass off as quietly as possible so that we don't get any credit for any success. There's been plotting, mark my words. It's that man Formerly again, trying to do us down."

"He didn't strike me as a plotter," said Patrick. "He didn't seem sufficiently interested."

"How long have you known him?"

"I've only met him once or twice."

Cliifford shook his head. "You'll find as you go on, Patrick, that the Service is full of plotters and schemers at court, ambitious men who won't hesitate to do you down. Formerly is one of the worst, a real smiling assassin if ever there was one. Personally, I detest such ambition."

Philip looked pained and weary. "Is that really so, though? I know I haven't been in the Office as long as you but I honestly haven't found it thick with assassins. Most people are conscientious and on the whole decent. Perhaps Formerly is a little more relaxed than he should be but he's not dishonest and when he does do something he does it rather well. You must admit, his drafting – "

Clifford waved his hand. "Oh, his drafting, yes, his drafting's very good. But we can all draft well or we wouldn't be here, would we?" He waited for a response. "No, it's his integrity I worry about. It's corrupted by his passion for self-advancement."

When Clifford had gone Philip picked up his pen again. "*Scribo ergo sum*. Other men need enemies."

Sir Wilfrid had a different explanation. He tapped his copy of the telegram with one of his longer pipes. "I detect the Prime Minister's hand in this. No doubt just been reminded that the visit is taking place, can't trust a junior minister like Ray Collier to get anything right so it's turned into a damage-limitation exercise to try to stop him doing anything at all. Collier would be quite incapable of introducing such subtlety into one of his own visits. I heard from Hugo Loveless in Cairo that his trip there a few months ago was devastating: export orders cancelled, Arab money withdrawn from London, Middle East

203

peace hopes set back, all that sort of thing. Ever met the man?"

"No." said Patrick. This was the third time in two days that Sir Wilfrid had asked the question.

"The least internationally-minded of anyone I've met in government, which is saying a great deal. I hope his plane crashes." He smoothed his hair. "Actually, we don't need knowledgeable ministers. We just need ministers with real political determination – 'boot' or 'bottle', I believe the phrase is now. It's our job to know about foreign countries. All they need is to know what the national interest is and then to tell us to get on with it. As a Service we often reflect the interests of the countries we deal with rather than our own. We achieve reasonable relations, negotiations or whatever when it might actually be in the national interest to be unreasonable. It's up to the ministers to see that. We can't help it, we're diplomats." He paused again. "You'd better not repeat this, Patrick."

"No, sir."

Ray Collier, his private secretary and his wife Sheila were to arrive at six-thirty in the morning. They were to be met by Sir Wilfrid, Clifford and Philip and not, now that the visit was unofficial, by any Lower African representatives. The afternoon before, though, Philip was taken ill once more with the unspecified virus infection. He had worked on his brief throughout the weekend and during the evenings, manning his desk through dizziness and nausea. He cared a great deal about getting it right whereas Clifford cared only about the inconvenience of not having Philip do it.

As Philip was helped from the office, pale and shaking, Clifford said that Patrick would have to take his place at the airport the following morning. Philip shook his head weakly. "It'll be all right by tomorrow. I'll go. No need for Patrick."

"Rubbish. It's no good meeting the minister looking like death warmed up. Anyway, supposing you didn't last the night – if we hadn't made other arrangements we'd be left high and dry. Patrick must come." The redeeming feature of Clifford's insensibility was that it was so obviously impersonal. "And even if you did make it you might infect the minister and then where would we be? Old Formerly would be cock-a-hoop. It would be round the Service in no time. Better Patrick than you with the plague." Clifford turned to Patrick. "We'd better have another meeting on transport arrangements. We'll need a big car for tomorrow morning. Draft proposals and come to my office at four."

"We'll only need one car, won't we?"

204

"That's as maybe but it still needs to be properly organised. Do a memo."

"A big one?"

"What?"

"I'll bring it at four."

The parked aeroplanes were sharp and bright in the early morning sun. A few cleaners and mechanics wandered contentedly about; nothing was happening.

Besides Sir Wilfrid, Clifford and Patrick there were two other waiting groups in the VIP lounge. They comprised dark-suited men, official and quiet. Each group kept as far away as possible from the other two. Sir Wilfrid sat in an armchair in the sun. He fidgeted for a while, then turned to Clifford. "D'you know Harry Potts?"

"Head of Southern European Department?"

"High Commissioner in Ghana. People used to speak of him as a future permanent under-secretary. Ever hear why he didn't get it?"

"He had an affair with the wife of the Home Secretary."

Sir Wilfrid shook his head. "Legal sex never harms any career except a politician's. In fact, it can make it. People take notice of you. No, what went wrong with Harry was that he got a bit shirty with the then PUS during a meeting with the Foreign Secretary. Told him he was talking rubbish about the Common Market, which he was, and that the country would suffer if his advice were followed – it was and it did – but that sort of thing just doesn't do, you see, especially not in front of the minister. The Service hates disagreements. Thirty years of assiduous graft thrown out of the window by five minutes' plain speaking. The PUS never forgave him. Saw to it that Moscow went to Eric Wilson, who was everybody's yes-man and as wet as the Spanish armada, and New York to Herbert Simpson who'd been dead on his feet for years. They actually put him in the ground last year but that was a formality. Brain death set in at about the time of Suez. Doesn't do to disagree with your superiors, you see, as I've learnt to my cost. Never say what you think till you've thought what you ought to say. It's the most important thing to remember in this business."

For a moment it seemed that Sir Wilfrid would expand upon the lessons of his own career but he turned his fine features towards the sun, closed his eyes and dozed. Patrick read the book he had been given in the Kuweto library. Clifford paced up and down, his hands behind his back.

"What are you reading?" he asked in an undertone. "Never heard of it. The minister's our only hope."

"Hope of what?"

"Saving our allowances. We've got to get it across to him that if they're cut by the twenty-seven per cent people are now talking of we'll all be on the bread line." He glanced at the other groups. "Laughing stock of Battenburg."

The airliner landed and disgorged its load of tired and untidy passengers. A tall silver-haired man carrying a slim black briefcase was ushered into the VIP lounge. Sir Wilfrid, awake now, remained where he was and gazed at the distant hills. Clifford braced his shoulders, put his hands to his sides and stepped briskly forward to the silver-haired man.

"Minister, good morning," he said.

The man looked faintly surprised but shook hands. "Good morning," he said in careful, heavily accented English. "Might I have the pleasure of knowing whom I am addressing?"

Clifford bent over the man's hand, which he still held. "Clifford Steggles, head of chancery. Permit me to introduce the ambassador." He turned and, seeing Sir Wilfrid still sprawling in the armchair, called sharply to Patrick, "Call Sir Wilfrid, will you?"

One of the other groups converged suddenly upon Clifford and the silver-haired man. They looked anxiously possessive, fingering their cuffs and ties. The man recognised one of them. There was humourless laughter, explanations, apologies, further explanations. Clifford went red in the face. The man was a leading Swiss banker who handled a great deal of Lower African business, a connection which neither the Swiss nor the Lower Africans were keen to advertise. He was escorted away by worried government officials.

Clifford put his hands behind his back again. "You might have said something instead of waiting for me to go ahead. Nearly made a fool of myself."

Meanwhile a pale, podgy man with sparse carroty hair and a shiny blue suit stood by the door trying to get his lighter to work. He had sandy eyebrows, a mobile fleshy face and a jowl that looked about two decades more developed than Clifford's. He had to make way for the Swiss and his escort. Sir Wilfrid shook his hand.

Mrs Collier stood by her husband clutching a bulky red handbag. She gazed through oversize glasses at the third group of people, who were sitting down with two swarthy men. Her small mouth was tightly shut. She was short and round and wore a dress that made her look like

206

a tea-cosy. Next to her was the private secretary, a pale neat young man with short brown hair, gold-rimmed glasses and a slim black briefcase like that carried by the Swiss.

The minister looked displeased. He stared after the departing banker, now escorted by a shoal of minor officials, then turned back to Sir Wilfrid. "You knew I was coming, didn't you?" he asked crossly. He was still trying to get his lighter to work.

"Yes, minister, that's why we're here."

"Who was that bloke?"

Sir Wilfrid looked at Clifford, who said, "A Swiss banker, minister."

A stab of flame from the lighter caused everyone to draw back. The minister adjusted it and lit his cigarette. "A Swiss baker? What's a Swiss baker doing in the VIP lounge?"

"Banker," said Sir Wilfrid.

"I told you to get that thing seen to before we left," said Mrs Collier.

"I didn't have a chance, did I? All that rushing about." He shook the lighter a couple of times.

"Should've got it done before we came. I told you."

Sir Wilfrid stooped to the level of the minister. "The car is waiting. Would you and Mrs Collier prefer to freshen up here or at the residence?"

"At the what?"

"At my house."

The minister turned to his wife. "Want to have breakfast here or at the house?"

"Oh, at the house. We might get a decent cup of tea there, I hope." She turned to Sir Wilfrid. "Let that muck they gave us on the plane settle first."

"This is going to be a bad trip," Anthony, the private secretary, said to Patrick as they followed the group. "Your boss and mine crossed swords in London."

"About the Common Market?"

"Very likely. Anything foreign is likely. He hates it. Hates travelling, too. He looks upon trips as fault-finding missions. The first thing he disliked was the plane. He particularly hates travelling with his good lady. Her whole life is a fault-finding mission."

The main hall was crowded and sunny. Automatic glass doors led to the parking area reserved for diplomatic and official cars. Before they reached them Patrick heard a woman's voice call his name. He knew it

207

but could not place it. There was no one he recognised. A couple of yards ahead the minister and Sir Wilfrid came abruptly to a stop. There was a scuffle and then a woman wearing jeans and jumper and holding a weighty rucksack in both hands stumbled between them. She let go of the rucksack with one hand and waved at Patrick. The rucksack knocked against her knees and then against Mrs Collier's, who grabbed Clifford for support.

"Patrick!" squealed Rachel. "Fantastic! How did you know?"

She brushed her long hair aside and hugged and kissed him with a fervour quite foreign to their friendship. Her rucksack rolled on to Anthony's feet. The whole party stopped and stared.

"God, I thought I was going to have to get a taxi to your place and I thought it's bound to be miles and I stupidly haven't got any Lower African money and I could imagine this really awful scene, you know." She held his jacket sleeve as if to make sure he didn't escape. "I didn't send a telegram because it was all sort of last minute but I did ring twice but there was no answer. It's fantastic that you're actually here – how did you know? D'you have contacts with the airline or what? Did Maurice ring you and tell you?"

Patrick smiled and glanced at the others. "No, neither. I was here meeting someone else."

Clifford frowned and tried to get Mrs Collier to move on but she stood staring through her thick glasses at Rachel.

"So it's just coincidence?"

"Yes."

"Fantastic." Rachel looked about. "Who are you meeting?"

The minister and Sir Wilfrid moved away. Anthony disentangled his feet from the rucksack straps and stepped gingerly round. Clifford put his hand on Mrs Collier's arm and nudged her forward.

Patrick hesitated so as to give them all time to move. "Mrs Collier and her husband," he said quietly, but not quietly enough because, hearing her name, Mrs Collier stopped and smiled. She held out her hand.

"How d'you do. Were you on that flight? Wasn't it awful? All them children, you could hear them from the first class; just as well we weren't paying for it ourselves. Mind you, it's the parents I blame. There's no discipline these days. Let them do just what they like. Look at all them football hooligans."

"Are you staying with Patrick as well?" asked Rachel.

Mrs Collier looked at Patrick. "I don't know. Are we?"

"No, you're staying with the ambassador," said Clifford. "They've reached the car now. We must join them."

Rachel turned to him. "Are you Mr Collier?"

Mrs Collier laughed loudly and briefly, like a squawking chicken swiftly strangled. "Oh, fancy that, that's quite a compliment, that is. Mr Collier's twice his age if he's a day. Mind you, I sometimes wish anyone else was Mr Collier especially when we go away. He's like a bear with a sore head, he really is. I used to think it was the water but now I think it's him, you know, it's what he's like."

"D'you go away a lot?" asked Rachel.

Mrs Collier had no chance to reply. Clifford took her firmly by the arm, saying, "The minister is leaving," and walked her off towards the car. He looked crossly over his shoulder and said sharply, as if to one of his children, "Come along, Patrick."

"Funny friends you've got," said Rachel. "D'you work with them?"

"Some of the time," said Patrick. "I've got to go now. I'll explain later. Ring my house and reverse the charges and you'll find a man called Chatsworth. Tell him you're a friend of mine and he'll come and pick you up in my car. I'll be back at lunchtime."

Rachel's pale face was puzzled. "Who is he?"

"He's a friend of mine."

"What's his christian name?"

"I can't remember." Patrick backed away, seeing that Mrs Collier had been eased into the Rolls and that it was about to leave. "Great to see you." Rachel stared. "I mean it. Explain later."

He jumped into the car, shutting the door on the flap of his jacket. It was a limousine and so everyone, apart from Simon, the driver, sat in the back. "I'm sorry about that. An old friend. Unexpected meeting."

The minister ignored him and Sir Wilfrid looked as if he didn't know what he meant.

"That's nice," said Mrs Collier.

"Not a journalist, I hope?" asked Clifford.

"No, not quite."

The minister asked why the Swiss banker was in Lower Africa and whom he was meeting. No one knew. "If I'd realised who it was I'd have made myself known to him," he said.

"I'll find out, minister," Clifford volunteered.

They were overtaken by a bright yellow Datsun with two blacks in it.

"Who were they?" asked the minister.

Sir Wilfrid leant anxiously forward. "I'm sorry?"

The minister pointed so that his cigarette was nearly touching

Simon's face. "There – in that yellow car – who are they? Is it some-one important? That's what I'm asking."

Sir Wilfrid looked at all the cars on the motorway. "Someone important?"

The minister waved his hand and sprinkled ash. "That yellow car is being driven by two black men. Who are they? Does it mean they're anyone important? That's what I want to know."

Clifford leant forward. "No, minister, it doesn't."

"Blacks are allowed to drive?"

"Oh, yes."

"In new cars?"

"Yes."

The minister looked disappointed. "But do they own it?"

Clifford looked again at the car. "I'm afraid I don't know."

The minister cheered up. "Well, there you are. There's the rub."

Sir Wilfrid now understood. He asked Simon who the men were, perhaps thinking that a black man might know other black men. Simon did not know.

"How many blacks own new cars?" continued the minister. No one knew. He released the strain on the middle button of his jacket and sat back. "Well, that's significant, isn't it? That says something. I thought you diplomats would know all about that sort of thing."

"It was a Japanese car," said Clifford.

"So?"

"The Japanese do a lot of business with Lower Africa."

The minister snorted. "The Japanese do a lot of business with everyone."

As they turned off the motorway a red bakkie sped the other way. Patrick glimpsed Chatsworth's fair hair in the cab. The bakkie was travelling very fast.

At the roundabout there was the familiar advertising hoarding show-ing a giant jar of Marmite with the grinning head of a black man beside it. Mrs Collier nudged her husband. "At least they've got Marmite."

16

Back at the embassy Clifford once again briefed everyone who was to meet the minister on what they were to say and where they were to be. He told each person individually what everyone else was supposed to be doing "in case the pass is sold and you have to come in to the line." He ordered that visa applicants and British subjects visiting the consular section were to be kept to a minimum and on no account should they be visible to the minister. The section was to close early.

"Patrick, I want you to oversee the where and whom of everything," he said when they were alone in the corridor. "You should be familiar with all the arrangements. Miss Teale needs a particularly close watch. I've told her that she's to wait in the garage and hold the lift for ten minutes before the minister and party arrive. She's to telephone me in my office – I've given her the number in writing in case she forgets in the heat of the moment – so that I can be at the lift to meet them when it gets up here. There's no need for you. Your job is simply to keep everything else out of sight and tamped down. A general low profile everywhere but for God's sake keep your eye on the ball. Five minutes before the visit is due to end Miss Teale will summon the lift again and hold it at this floor so that no one is kept hanging about. D'you understand?"

"Yes."

"Your first task is to ensure that she understands."

"You've already told her, haven't you?"

"Yes, but there are times and people with whom one has to make doubly or trebly sure. I trust your girlfriend is now under control."

It sounded as if Joanna had done something public and extravagant. "Under control?"

"That woman at the airport. No more extraordinary interruptions I hope?"

"Oh, no. She's not my girlfriend."

"What was she doing throwing her arms round you in front of everyone?"

"We're just friends."

211

"I see."

Miss Teale was so incensed at having received her instructions five times in two days (twice in writing) that she was friendly to Patrick. She told him that Sandy had rung Clifford in a rage because Clifford had taken the car when she thought she should have it. She was threatening to walk out. Clifford would have to take the car home during the day if he wanted her still to be there in the evening. Miss Teale had also heard that Philip had risen from his sick-bed and set out for the embassy so that he could present his brief to the minister in person; but he had been sick in the car and had returned home.

The minister and Sir Wilfrid were late. Clifford stood by his telephone but twice came in to Patrick to check watches before telling him to ring the residence to see what had happened. It was gone eleven and Patrick was still delaying ringing when Clifford rushed past the door towards the lifts.

A few moments later there was a sharp click of heels on lino. It was Daphne from the consular section. Her mouth was mobile before she spoke. "He's here."

"Yes, I know. Clifford's run off to greet the lift."

"No, not him. McGrain." Patrick's immobility probably made her think that he had forgotten. "You know, the DBS you threw out. The one who's always after Arthur."

"Better keep him out of sight." Patrick still did not move.

"He's in a bad way again."

"At this hour of the morning?"

"He wants an interview with the minister."

They went to the consular section. Neither his previous triumph nor his fight with Jim had in any way prepared Patrick for more fights. A brawl in the embassy coinciding with the minister's arrival was unthinkable – at least to the Foreign Office mind; it was all too thinkable to Patrick's.

Daphne's cheeks wobbled as before. "I was sure we wouldn't get through the visit without something happening. There's nearly always a DBS waiting round the corner to sabotage anything important. It was just the same in Tripoli."

McGrain stood as before at the counter, this time clutching a newspaper. There were no other visitors. A frightened consular girl was trapped behind the counter and a nervous male clerk hovered by the door. He disappeared when Patrick arrived. Patrick adopted what he hoped was the appearance of calm bureaucratic inexorability. McGrain turned, his blue eyes focusing slowly. His bloated face had a

212

bluish tinge. He held the rolled newspaper to his fist and stabbed at it with his thick forefinger.

"I wanna see the minister."

"I'm afraid he's not here." Patrick cleared his throat because his voice sounded unnaturally high.

McGrain drove his finger into the paper. "It says here he's coming to the British embassy today."

"He won't be here till four." That was when the minister was due to visit the meat-packing station. McGrain might by then be too drunk to return.

"I'll wait here till he comes then." McGrain settled solidly against the counter.

"I'm sorry, we're closed."

"I'll wait here till you're open."

"You can't do that."

"Who says I can't?"

Patrick's armour of bureaucratic implacability felt thin. "The rules."

McGrain shook his head. He seemed to have difficulty bringing his words out. "Ah'm a British subject. I wanna see my minister."

"Come back later." For a few moments McGrain's eyes became lugubrious and thoughtful. Patrick felt more confident and became more conciliatory. "If you have a message for him I'll do my best to pass it on." McGrain nodded and said nothing. Patrick put his hand on his shoulder and stepped towards the door. McGrain turned unsteadily and lumbered off.

"I wanna tell him about Arthur Whelk," he said. "I wanna tell him Whelk owes me."

"What does he owe you?"

"He owes me my cut."

"Well, I daresay he'll pay it." They negotiated the double doors after McGrain had lurched against the closed one. He smelt of whisky. "What exactly does he owe you?"

"It's not right for diplomats to owe. It's takin' advantage."

"When did you last see him?"

"He must come here sometimes? He must come to work?"

"He doesn't work here at the moment."

"He's not done a bunk, has he?" McGrain turned his face towards Patrick. He looked angry.

"No, no," said Patrick hastily. "He's just not here."

"Where is he, then?"

McGrain was now more perplexed than angry. There was a note of helplessness in his tone. Patrick found himself wanting to be helpful. "Look, I don't know where he is. I'm sorry. If I could help you I would. But if you have a complaint about him or anything that you want passed on to anyone tell me and I'll do my best. The problem is that until you tell me what he owes you and why I'm even more in the dark than you are."

McGrain allowed himself to be led along. Patrick felt like a boy holding a bull's tail. Clifford was at the lifts. He looked directly at Patrick but did not appear to notice McGrain.

"I don't understand what's going on down there. Miss Teale rang over five minutes ago and they're still not here. Hope to God they're not stuck." He pointed to the indicator board. "She's supposed to have summoned number four but it's been in the sub-basement now for ages. It got up to ground once before going down again, then up to seven, then all the way back down one at a time and that's where it's stayed. I should've supervised this myself. You can never trust other people." He looked at his watch, smoothed his thinning hair and looked at McGrain, looked away and looked again. Apprehension and incredulity struggled for mastery in his expression.

Patrick smiled more confidently than he felt. "This is Mr McGrain. He's just on his way."

Number two lift arrived. The minister was flanked by Sir Wilfrid and Anthony. McGrain stretched his hand as if to hold open the door and the minister shook it. Sir Wilfrid and Anthony stepped out as Clifford stepped forward to intervene. McGrain said something and the minister said he was very pleased to meet him. Clifford raised his arm and took another step forward, addressing the minister. McGrain, perhaps thinking he was being shown into the lift, advanced right into it and blocked all view of the minister. The door closed and the lift descended.

For a moment no one moved. Patrick felt the delicious sense of irresponsibility that sometimes accompanies complete loss of control. He imagined how he would describe it to Joanna. Sir Wilfrid looked at where the lift had been. Anthony looked at Clifford and Clifford, his face reddening, turned to Patrick.

"Now look what you've bloody done, Stubbs. You've ruined everything."

Sir Wilfrid raised his eyebrows. "Patrick, have I met that man? He looked familiar."

"He's a DBS, sir, called McGrain."

Sir Wilfrid looked pleased. "A DBS? What did he want?"

"He wanted to see the minister."

Clifford pointed at the lift doors. "Well, he's seen him now, hasn't he? He's probably throttling him."

Anthony smiled thinly. "Now there are two DBSs."

Another lift came. "Perhaps you'd better go and find them, Clifford," said Sir Wilfrid.

Clifford was alarmed. "Me?"

"I'll come with you," said Anthony.

By the time the doors closed the indicator showed that the minister's lift had reached the basement. Clifford's dithered between the fourth, third and second floors as if reluctant to go right down and see.

Sir Wilfrid clasped his hands behind his back. "I hope the minister gets lost. He was a perfect brute over breakfast. Kept on about the Lower Africans as if they're the mongol hordes. I may have little love for what they stand for but I flatter myself I do have a little understanding. That man knows no more of Africans white or black than how to tell them apart. He simply wants to curry favour with his own party. If he reappears I shall be in my office."

Patrick kept his finger on the lift button. An empty one came and went. The minister's went from the first to the top floor without stopping, then descended to the seventh. It crept up one floor at a time and opened but was empty. Clifford's lift appeared, also empty, and the service lift went rapidly upwards with what looked like the face of Miss Teale at the window. Eventually one came down from the twelfth containing McGrain and the minister. McGrain was bent over the minister in a confiding manner and whispering something about gold mines, tapping his thick forefinger on the minister's shoulder. The minister was nodding and interjecting with, "Is that true? How much? Foreigners as well?" On seeing Patrick he put his hand against the door to stop it closing but did not leave the lift until he had again shaken hands with McGrain. The doors closed and McGrain ascended.

The minister walked briskly with Patrick through reception. "Those lifts were all over the shop. If it hadn't been for that bloke I'd have ended up on the bloody roof. Who is he?"

"His name's McGrain, sir."

"Scottish?"

"Yes, sir."

"He's a good man. Knows a lot about the gold market here. What's his job – economics?"

"He doesn't actually work here. He's just visiting."

"Visitor, eh? That's why he's not as stuck up as everyone else. More natural. How people should be. Man to man. Said someone here owes him money. D'you know anything about that?"

Patrick's diplomatic evasiveness deserted him. To explain McGrain meant explaining Whelk, which was what the ambassador wanted to do.

"Better look into it," the minister continued quickly. "I said I'd find out about it for him. Tell whoever it is to pay up. Bad enough with the country in debt the way it is without all you diplomats sponging off the locals." His eyes sought out the girls in reception. "Are all these local?"

"Yes," said Patrick. He wasn't sure but felt it better to be definite.

The minister grinned for the first time since arriving in Lower Africa. "You don't do yourselves badly."

Patrick left him with Sir Wilfrid. As he closed the door he heard the beginnings of questions about the market.

In the corridor he met Anthony, who observed, "Your head of chancery's going berserk. Keeps dashing from one lift to the other and changing his mind about which floor he wants. He's convinced the minister and the ambassador are stuck somewhere and he's blaming you. I just changed lifts once and stayed there. Last time I saw him he was having an argument with a strange woman I thought was the lift attendant, though she seemed to think otherwise. Anyhow, she's something to do with the lifts and they're arguing hammer and tongs. I must say, this promises to be one of the very worst visits."

Patrick took Anthony into his office and gave him Philip's weighty brief. Anthony turned the pages slowly. "This looks very good. Clear, comprehensive and concise. A model of Office drafting, I should say."

"He put a lot of work into it."

"I'm sure he did. This is the Service at its best. Philip will go far." He put the document in his black briefcase. "The minister won't read a word of it, of course. Far too long. He hates reading. I'll take it back and give it to Formerly."

"Will he read it?"

"Shouldn't think so but at least he'll know where to file it. Then it'll be safe."

Patrick went home to lunch so that he could take Sarah and Stanley to the bus depot that afternoon. He was glad to have no immediate

216

further part in the visit, especially as there was now Rachel to cope with. He hoped she wouldn't want to interview him.

There was a small lorry in the entrance to his drive. Thinking it might be more mysterious removals men he hastily paid the driver, leaving a much larger tip than intended, and ran up the drive. The garden gate was open and through it he saw a bearded energetic white man in shorts working with two black labourers on the swimming-pool. They had drained it into the sewer, scrubbed it clean and were now refilling it. Snap was chained to the railings by the house and barked when he saw Patrick.

"What are you doing?" asked Patrick.

"What's it to do with you?" The man's manner was as bristly as his beard. Patrick explained what it had to do with him. The man pointed at the pool as if Patrick had perpetrated an outrage in it. "That there is a rogue pool," he said. "A rogue pool. We'll get it right when it's full but it won't stay right. No use you thinking it will. It leaks."

"Ah, yes. Someone said that before."

"There's a crack in the bottom and it seeps away. That could be your problem. Upsets the chemical balance. That accounts for the disgusting state of it."

"Could you repair it?"

The man put his hands on his hips and nodded vigorously. "'Course we could, 'course we could, but you don't want that, do you?"

"I wasn't asked."

The man pointed at the house. "There's a guy in there says you don't want it repaired. It's expensive and he says you wouldn't want to pay for it yourself if the British government wouldn't. He says you'd rather top it up with a watering-can every day."

Miss Teale had told Patrick that his pool allowance was exhausted. He would have to pay for all maintenance himself in future. He nodded. "He's probably right. Was he the man who sent for you?"

"The very same, yes. Anything wrong with that?"

Patrick shook his head resignedly. "No, nothing wrong with that." He took Snap indoors. Chatsworth was sitting on the stairs sharpening a broken spear with a flint.

"Found it in the back of the garage. Thought I might as well get it in working order. You never know."

"I've just been talking to the swimming-pool contractors."

"Pretty efficient, aren't they? I rang them as soon as I got back from the airport and they were here inside thirty minutes. Didn't wait till you got back because the pool was in such a putrid state and I thought you'd want it cleaned up in time for Rachel to have a swim. She's upstairs, by the way, sleeping off the effects of British Air. I was right about her."

"What do you mean?"

"She will."

"With you?"

Chatsworth paused in his sharpening. "Nothing so odd about that. Others have."

"How d'you know she will?"

"You can always tell. She knows, if she's honest with herself. No one ever really fools anyone. We always know whether we would or wouldn't, straightaway." He resumed sharpening. Snap sniffed at something in the cupboard under the stairs. "I've put her in the room next to mine, by the way. I locked the one next to yours and told her you never let anyone in there. Anyway, you've got 'in-due-course'."

"That's very thoughtful of you."

"Also, I've got Deuteronomy in to help Sarah with the lunch. He couldn't do much in the garden with those blokes swarming all over it."

"Is she pleased about that?"

Chatsworth looked puzzled. "Shouldn't she be?"

Sarah was cooking in the kitchen. Deuteronomy, looking very self-conscious in a white jacket, peeled potatoes. The scar on his face was healing well. He grinned sheepishly on seeing Patrick and lowered his eyes without looking at Sarah. She greeted Patrick with prim correctness and glanced crossly when Deuteronomy dropped a potato.

Chatsworth slapped him heartily on the back, causing him to drop it again. "You're doing well, Deuteronomy. We'll make a waiter of you yet."

Deuteronomy smiled and nodded. "Yes, massa, I make a big waiter."

Sarah rarely used the serving hatch that led from the kitchen to the dining-room but on this occasion Chatsworth had opened it. "It will impress the madam," he explained to Sarah and Patrick. He rapidly explained to Deuteronomy how it should be used, illustrating by passing an empty plate through it, running round to the dining-room to pick it up himself, then passing it back and returning to pick it up. Deuteronomy nodded continuously and said "Yes, massa," several times.

Patrick went to the living-room to read the paper alone. He did not object to Chatsworth's attempts to run the house, provided there was no serious interference with Sarah and Deuteronomy. The centre of gravity of his life was shifting increasingly towards Joanna and he spent most of the time when he was not with her trying to distil the essence of the times when he was. Her absence excited in him a hunger which her presence, so far from satisfying, only sharpened. He could not define what it was; she seemed always to suggest something beyond whatever she was doing or saying, perhaps beyond herself. It was a question of the extent to which that was a quality of hers or of his own imagination.

Chatsworth prepared drinks. "You look miserable. You need a drink. I'll do one for Rachel, help wake her. I'll take it up, don't you worry. You could go and see how they're getting on with the pool."

Patrick glanced out of the window. He was not miserable but having been told he looked it irritated him. "They can fill it with earth as far as I'm concerned."

"Too much 'in-due-course', that's your trouble. You ought to have a few away fixtures with an alternative. Restores the sense of proportion. You could call her 'now-and-again' if you're still worried about revealing names."

"I'm quite happy as it is." Patrick sounded prim to his own ears which further irritated him.

Chatsworth took Rachel's drink upstairs on a tray and reappeared some time later. "She's still on course."

"Is that her name?"

Chatsworth sighed and sat down with the spear again. "I must say, I don't like sponging off you like this, Patrick. It's boring. It'd be okay if only they'd let me get on and find that bugger Whelk. It's what I came for, after all."

"It's better than prison, isn't it?"

"Yes, better than prison." Chatsworth drew his thumb slowly across the blade. "Chap called Jim called to see you."

"What did he want?"

"A chat, I s'pose. Seemed a decent bloke. We had a talk about guns. He's got an old water-cooled Vickers on his farm, he was telling me. Wonderful weapon. Perfect for riot control. How d'you know him?"

"He sold me the bakkie."

"He said he was a friend of your girlfriend's."

"He actually said that?"

"Something like it. Asked if I knew her. I said you wouldn't even tell me her bloody name. Nor did he."

"She was his girlfriend. He's a policeman."

Chatsworth stopped fingering the blade. "I knew he was keeping

219

something back. Still, there are one or two good ones. I used to have an arrangement with one in London."

"He's in charge of the Whelk case. I think he knows more than he's letting on."

"'Course he does. He wouldn't come here just to hear your voice or to check that all's well with 'in-due-course'. Could've been after young Stanley, of course. He's illegal, isn't he?" He held up the blade to the light. "Chipped on one side. I reckon Deuteronomy's been digging the garden with it."

"His face has healed well, hasn't it?"

Chatsworth nodded whilst squinting along the blade. "They patch up quickly, these black buggers." He went outside to talk to the pool contractors.

Rachel appeared wearing clean jeans and a clean T-shirt. Her hair was tied up at the back and her face looked thinner than Patrick remembered. She was cheerful and enthusiastic. He introduced her to Sarah, who was laying the dining-room table, and found they'd already met.

"We had a talk early this morning, didn't we, Sarah?" she said.

Sarah smiled politely and bowed her head. "Yes, ma'am."

"*Rachel*, Sarah, my name's Rachel."

Sarah looked apologetic. "Oh, madam Rachel."

Rachel clutched Sarah's arm. "No, no, not madam Rachel – Rachel."

Sarah gave a small embarrassed smile and nodded.

Rachel followed Patrick back into the living-room. "God, it's awful, all this sir-ing and ma'am-ing and bowing and scraping. It's so humiliating. Why d'you allow it?"

Patrick realised it was some time since he had noticed. "It's what's expected."

"You should change their expectations. You're contributing to the oppression by letting them call you 'massa'. That keeps them in their places and you in yours."

"They wouldn't like it if I started changing the rules when no one else did."

"Oh, that's everyone's excuse for oppression – they wouldn't understand, they like it the way they are and all the rest of it. No mention of choice for them. Can't you see how humiliating it is?"

"D'you really think Sarah is humiliated by being my servant?"

Rachel flopped on to the sofa and put up her feet. She enjoyed argument. "That's balls, Patrick, absolute balls. You've gone over to the other side and now you're trying to justify it. The Foreign Office has corrupted you, if you weren't secretly corrupt all along. Come on, admit it."

Patrick poured her another drink. It was disconcerting that she seemed much more attractive than before. He had imagined that when a man fell in love as he now thought he had, other women became less attractive. Instead, he now found that all women were more so. He would have preferred to discuss that with Rachel but did not wish to appear flippant. "You're picking on the wrong things. It's not whether a black servant should call her white master 'massa' that's important but whether she would be allowed to employ a white servant and be called 'ma'am' if she wanted."

Rachel shook her head. "More balls. You're making it impossible by keeping her in her place. Don't you see how the system works? Perhaps you can't when you're at the top. If you'd seen it from the underneath and inside and suffered in it like Chatsworth you might understand in the way he does."

"Like Chatsworth?"

"Yes, he's seen it from the real inside, from in prison. That's where you really learn about Lower Africa, he was saying." She lit a cigarette. "What is his first name, by the way? He just introduced himself as Chatsworth."

Patrick sat. "I can't remember."

"But he's a friend of yours, isn't he?"

"Yes, but no one ever uses his other name."

"He probably got used to that in prison. I admire people who are prepared to suffer for their beliefs like that, don't you?"

"Well – yes. I'm not quite sure what his beliefs are, though."

She smiled. "Shame on you, Patrick. You always were lazy, weren't you?"

"Was I?"

"Yes, and now you're living the life of Riley you don't take any interest in the other ninety-eight per cent."

Lunch was announced. Rachel stubbed out her cigarette, tipping the ash-tray so that some of the ash went on to the carpet. "Thank God for that. I'm famished."

Chatsworth threw himself with relish into the role of host. He was cheerful, energetic and attentive. He poured the wine with a flourish of the wrist that meant he poured it from over the back of his hand whilst standing to attention and facing the top of the table. He insisted that Rachel should try it first.

221

"I never drink Lower African wine. I always refuse on principle."

"Quite right, quite right. But this stuff is different. Grapes crushed by the feet of Deuteronomy's relatives. Without this there would be nothing for those feet to do. Isn't that right, Deuteronomy?"

Deuteronomy's head appeared in the serving hatch. "Massa?"

Chatsworth bent his head to Rachel's. "There, you see, listening to every word. He's watching to see if you like it, poor fellow. Be very hurt if you turn it down. It's the same as turning him down."

Rachel sipped her wine, turned towards the hatch and told Deuteronomy it was good.

Deuteronomy grinned and nodded. "Ma'a'am," he said, dragging out the word as he did when calling Patrick 'massa'. He continued to grin and nod until Chatsworth waved him away.

"Did you learn to pour in that extraordinary way in the navy?" asked Rachel. "Something to do with the roll of the ship?"

"No, no. From a barman in Belfast."

"The navy?" asked Patrick.

Chatsworth, unabashed, shook his head. "No, not there. Definitely not there."

"When were you in the navy?" continued Patrick, ruthlessly.

"Learnt it from a chap called Long John, so called because he had a parrot. One day someone threw a bottle – a full bottle – of Guinness at it and knocked it off his shoulder. Straight off the perch and on to the floor. Stone dead. Long John killed the bloke with a crate of Mackeson. Hell of a mess. He got life for it but he's probably out now. They get fifty per cent remission in Northern Ireland."

"Were you in prison there as well?" asked Rachel.

"No, I was helping alcoholics. Lot of work in Belfast."

There was scrabbling, grunting and wheezing from behind. Deuteronomy was coming through the serving hatch. He had one leg and one arm through and was holding a plate of roast lamb precariously before him. His small body was bent so much that his head was twisted beneath his extended arm. His teeth were bared in a determined grin.

Patrick got up and took the plate. "Thank you, Deuteronomy. You go back the way you came and we'll bring the next plate another way."

Deuteronomy was too constricted to speak. Still grunting, he began slowly to recede through the hatch. From behind him Sarah said something shrill and angry in Zulu. Patrick feared that Chatsworth would guffaw and was going to tell him not to but there was no need. Chatsworth leant towards Rachel, his hand on her arm, and said

222

quietly, "Poor chap's keen to impress because you're here. Probably still thinks you might throw his relatives out of work by not drinking."

Patrick was summoned by the telephone before he could witness more of Chatsworth's new image. It was Joanna. Jim had appeared at her bungalow the night before, drunk and maudlin. "He kept talking about how when you've gone he and I will get back together again. You're not going, are you?"

He remembered how he had felt on the day of his arrival that he would not be long in Battenburg. He could recall the very part of the motorway that he and Clifford were at. "Not for at least two years, they told me."

"He seems to think you're going soon."

"Maybe he knows something I don't. But I can't think what."

She sounded flat and unhappy. Her voice, normally quick and provocative, was slow and distant. He told her about the minister's arrival and about Rachel, then that he had discovered from Miss Teale that he was permitted to bring a guest to the garden party at the residence the following afternoon. "If you could come we could go off and have dinner afterwards." She agreed with more liveliness but still without great enthusiasm. "You sound hesitant."

"I was thinking about what to wear. How smart is it?"

Patrick had never been to a garden party. "Quite smart, I think."

"Gloves?"

"Possibly."

"Hats?"

"Possibly not."

"You haven't got the faintest idea, have you?"

"Not really."

She laughed. "Will your guest be there – the man who's staying with you? I'm dying to meet him."

"He'll be there if the ambassador invites him." He thought it unlikely.

"You sound bored," she said, sounding more cheerful herself.

"I'm sorry, I was thinking."

"Well, stop it if that's what it does to you. You sound horrible."

"It's the telephone. It emphasises the wrong things. Can I see you tonight?"

"I'm going out to dinner, I told you."

"I could come round afterwards."

"It might be late."

"Now you sound bored."

"No, I'm not, it's just that" – she laughed again – "it's just that I keep thinking it shouldn't be too easy, you know, as if it's tempting fate. It's so stupid because I do keep wanting to see you."

"I'll come round, then."

"Good."

Later when he went to find Sarah he saw Rachel talking to Stanley by the garage. Stanley was slim and elegant in a clean white shirt. He clutched a holdall in both arms, nodding and replying briefly to Rachel's questions. She several times pushed hair back from the side of her face and gesticulated excitedly. Stanley's self-conscious reticence became more sullen and wary as Patrick approached.

Rachel turned to him. "Why didn't you tell me about Stanley? He's terrific. He's been to Kuweto, he's in touch with people, he knows the activists and he wants to stay and get educated and you're sending him away."

Patrick did not want to have to talk about Stanley in his presence. "If he doesn't go back he'll be arrested."

Rachel put her hand on his arm. "Look, I want to tape him. He'll be great on tape. He'll be able to talk about things that only a black can. It fits my project perfectly. Can't you hang on?"

"He'll miss the bus."

"He can get the next one."

"That's next week."

"But the police aren't after him now, are they?"

Patrick recalled what Jim had said. "They know about him."

"Shit. We'll have to do it somehow. Perhaps I can come up and see you." She looked at Stanley. "Is that possible?"

Stanley shrugged. Sarah's door was half open and Patrick went over to tell her they were ready. She wore her best grey suit, a red hat and glasses. Rachel said something to Stanley and handed him a note, which he put in the back pocket of his jeans. He glanced at his mother.

Rachel smiled. "Just making sure we keep in touch. Are you going down in your car? Can I come?"

Patrick was annoyed with her. "You can if you like but there are only three seats in the front."

She held up her hand and turned away, smiling. "All right, don't worry, I get the message. We'll still be in touch. Bye, Stanley."

Sarah prodded Stanley and he got in. He sat silently between them throughout the journey, his holdall on his knees. The depot was in a black area and swarmed with people who clambered on to buses, were herded off them, clambered on to others and greeted every new bus

224

jovially. There was a great deal of talk, laughter, shouting and confusion. Sarah argued with Stanley in Swahi as to whether she and Patrick should wait to see him off. He insisted with sudden vehemence that he could put himself on the bus and eventually she agreed. He submitted reluctantly and passively to her embrace and kiss.

As Sarah was getting into the bakkie Patrick shook hands with him again, no less awkwardly than before. "Good luck, Stanley."

Stanley looked down, presenting his eyelids and his smooth brown forehead.

"How long will the journey take?" Patrick continued. Stanley mumbled something. "Your mother is worried. Telephone the house from your post office when you get there. Reverse the charges. She will be very pleased to hear from you."

Stanley's dark eyes flashed once before he picked up his holdall and turned towards the throng.

On the way back Sarah sat upright with her handbag on her lap, clasping it tightly in her horny brown hands. "He is heavy pull, that one," she said. "My daughter is difficult because her boyfriend is a bad boy and she want to marry him and I tell her he will be bad husband. These young people do not listen any more. It is not like before. But she is not difficult like Stanley. She is not secret."

"What about the little one?" asked Patrick.

She shook her head and laughed. "Oh, the piccaninny, she is too little for big trouble. Perhaps later. But she is not like Stanley." She stopped smiling and nodded a couple of times. "All his life he has been hard. He is never happy, that one, not once. Everything I do with him is heavy, heavy pull."

17

The radio news in the morning reported a small explosion in Kuweto. This was the latest indication of unrest in the township following Chatsworth's excursion, though there was no proven causal link. Bombs on the railway line, such as this, were a way of registering protest. They carried little risk to the bombers and simply inconvenienced the thousands of blacks who used the line daily, many of whom would lose pay for not being at work. The track was repaired within two hours.

Patrick had spent that night with Joanna, escaping his responsibilities as host.

"D'you think they slept together?" she asked.

"I could ring and ask."

"You can't do that."

"Chatsworth will tell me, anyway."

The atmosphere of panic in the embassy that morning indicated that something had already gone wrong. As Patrick reached for the buttons to open the chancery door Clifford opened it and grabbed him by the arm.

"Where's the ambassador?"

"I don't know."

"You haven't seen him?"

"No."

Clifford rushed on. It turned out that the minister and Sir Wilfrid had become separated. The minister was waiting in Sir Wilfrid's office. The panic was not only because no one knew where Sir Wilfrid was but also because the minister wanted to change his programme so that he could accompany his wife to Kuweto that morning. On behalf of the British government she was to present an electric sewing-machine to the cultural centre.

"I must see those people," the minister announced. "It's important that they shouldn't feel isolated."

Clifford appeared in the doorway of Patrick's office and pointed at the telephone. "Ring the police!" he shouted.

Patrick reached for the phone.

"Get an up to date report on the situation. We could be walking into a minefield."

Patrick realised that he was referring to the bomb in Kuweto. He discovered from the police that following the explosion there had been a security operation involving house-to-house searches. These had provoked rioting which had been quickly put down. This aspect of the affair had been censored on the news. The police advised that the area was now quiet, and there was no reason why the minister should not accompany his wife provided the visit was low-key and there was no attempt to publicise it.

He was relieved that he had not had to speak to Jim but a few moments later Jim rang back.

"Sorry I was out just now. I hear you want to go sightseeing. It should be okay. If there's trouble it won't be large-scale and it won't be anywhere near your little outpost."

They made conversation for a while about Whelk and how there was still no news until Patrick suddenly said, "Joanna's okay." He regretted it instantly. He did not know why he had said it.

There was a slight pause. "Yes, I saw her this morning. She seemed fine. See you."

Patrick replaced the receiver slowly. Clifford reappeared in the doorway. "What do they say?"

"They say it's okay."

"Damn. Have you seen the ambassador?"

"No."

"Damn."

A little later Patrick overheard the minister talking in the corridor. "Bombs or no bombs, these people need assistance and it's my job to see they get it. We'll go without the ambassador if he's not here. I don't see it makes any difference."

He rang Sarah to say he wouldn't be back for lunch. The phone was answered by Rachel. "Can't I come to Kuweto with you?"

"No, it's only the official party."

"Look, I really want to go there. Can't you fix it, say I'm your secretary or something? It'll be great for my project if I can go back with tapes from the heart of Kuweto."

"Can't be done."

"God, you're a stick-in-the-mud, Patrick. You weren't always like this, were you? Perhaps you were. Look, how about you taking my tape-recorder and switching it on if there's anything interesting? It would fit in your briefcase or whatever you have."

"I won't be carrying one. Anyway, we won't be talking to people in the way you want. It's an official visit to present a sewing-machine."

"That sounds pathetic." She paused and made the silence sulky. "I suppose I'll have to look round Battenburg instead."

"Good idea."

"I can't because you've got the car."

"Get a taxi in with Chatsworth. He'll show you round."

"That sounds expensive."

"He's got plenty of money. Mine, actually."

"It might be traumatic for him, going back and seeing that police headquarters where they tortured him."

"He'll live."

"God, Patrick, you're so bloody callous." She put down the phone.

The ambassador wandered past. "Seen the minister?"

"He was in your office, sir. Clifford was talking to him."

Sir Wilfrid made his habitual gesture of running his hand through his hair. "All the way to the barbers and they were closed. Moved to the other side of the railway lines or somewhere. I'll have to find a new one."

"The minister wants to go to Kuweto this morning, sir."

"Really? Is it open after the explosion?"

"Yes."

"Damn."

Later Philip walked into the office. His dark clothes and black hair combined with his pallor to make him look an embodiment of the Reaper in modern dress. He moved slowly and spoke hoarsely. "Did the minister get my brief?"

"Yes, he did." Patrick stood in case Philip needed supporting.

"What did he say?"

"I don't know, I wasn't there. His private secretary was very impressed. He said it was a model of its kind. You all right?"

"The minister said it was a model?"

Patrick did not disabuse him.

"Is it true he's going to Kuweto this morning?"

"In about five minutes."

"Are you going instead of me?"

"I think so. I'm waiting to hear from Clifford."

228

Philip leant against the desk with his fingers outstretched. "I'll go. Where is Clifford?"

"He's looking for the ambassador, who's in his office. Are you sure you're all right?"

Philip turned and made for the door as if he were about to topple. "I'll be in the loo."

He was still there fifteen minutes later when the party assembled for the lift. In the meantime his wife had rung to say that she too felt ill and was going to the doctor. She wanted Philip to go home before she left. Patrick left a note.

Having made a fuss, altered his programme and generally inconvenienced people the minister was in good enough humour to joke with his wife as the Rolls waited in the Battenburg traffic. "Ever worked a spinning-jenny before?"

Mrs Collier's huge eyes blinked at him through her spectacles. "It's not a spinning-jenny, it's a sewing machine. An electric one. Spinning-jennys went out years ago."

"Same difference. Anyway, there's nothing wrong with a jenny."

"I never said there was."

"Puts people out of work, though, you've got to remember that."

They passed a number of police and army vehicles on the way to Kuweto but there was no sign of tension until they reached the township itself. The barricade that was normally open was closed and manned by police armed with carbines. Pedestrians and vehicles were searched, and many of the latter turned back. Anyone without a document of identity was taken to a flat-roofed building at one side. Such activity seemed incongruous in the friendly warmth of the sun, as if it were not really serious.

The Rolls waited in the queue. It was not air-conditioned and Anthony discreetly lowered the front window. Mrs Collier peered out. "I don't think I like this," she said.

Sir Wilfrid craned his neck to see what she was looking at. Clifford leant forward. "It's all right, they'll let us through. It's only because of the bomb this morning."

"Oh, was that here?" Mrs Collier turned to her husband. "Did you hear what he said? This is where that bomb was."

The minister sat four-square, his chubby fists on his knees. "It's gone off, hasn't it? Won't hurt anyone now."

Mrs Collier shook her head. "That's all very well but I still don't like it. All those guns poking at you. Look at them."

229

"They're not poking at us, are they?" The minister looked bullishly about. One of the policemen searching the vehicle in front had his carbine pointing carelessly over the top of the Rolls. "They'll be careful once they know who we are. Anyway, if there's trouble we might be able to help."

The police captain saluted smartly. He was scrupulously polite. There was no trouble in any area at present and no parts were forbidden to accredited British officials and their guests. However, he advised that they should avoid large groups if they saw any gathering.

They drove slowly through the rows of squat, red-roofed bungalows, past barricaded shops and beer halls and dawdling, indifferent people. Nothing seemed sinister or dangerous. The minister looked at the bare gardens. "Why don't they grow anything?"

Everyone followed his gaze. "They don't seem to go in for gardening," Sir Wilfrid said in a puzzled tone. "Perhaps it's not part of the tradition."

"Are they starved of water?"

Clifford sat up. "Plenty of water, sir, and eventually they'll all have electricity, too. About forty per cent have it at present. It's behind schedule partly because the company putting it in had to sign a contract agreeing to use manual labour for digging all the holes and trenches so as to create employment."

"More jobs, then?"

Clifford was encouraged. "There was also a suggestion that the work should be done with bare hands but it wasn't adopted."

"You can't have it both ways."

"But the company now say they can't finish the project unless they're allowed to use machines. They can't get the labour because the workers don't like that sort of job."

"Do they pay enough? Strikes me that's the problem."

There was a pause, the embarrassment of which was felt by all but Clifford, who shook his head. "No, I don't think so, minister. Not wholly. The problem is partly that in many African tribes the men think it's demeaning to do manual work. It's not part of their tradition. In the rural areas and the homelands you can see brand new roads all hand-built by women."

"Go on," said Mrs Collier, wonderingly.

"It's the duty of a woman, you see, to rear children, to look after the home, to tend crops and to earn money if there's any to be earned. The duty of a man is to talk and drink."

Mrs Collier was wide-eyed behind her spectacles. "Well I never." The minister said nothing.

Sir Wilfrid pressed the tip of one finger against his chin and looked worried. "But is it really so, I wonder? It's certainly not universally the case and I wonder sometimes whether it might not be one of those curious self-validating myths that appear to be true but for reasons quite other than those we commonly assume. For instance – "

Clifford's face shone with the pleasure of holding forth. "It's just the way they are. Not necessarily worse than us, of course, but different. Just different."

"Not worse at all," Sir Wilfrid replied emphatically. "Perhaps not even very different. After all, many men – "

"Sounds to me like they're no better than they should be," said Mrs Collier.

The minister looked irritable. "That's no reason for not giving them light bulbs, is it?"

"No, no, it's just indicative," said Clifford.

"Indicative of what?"

Sir Wilfrid looked out of the window with an expression of saintly renunciation. Clifford looked at the minister, who looked back. Patrick looked at his shoes.

"If you ask me they don't know no better," said Mrs Collier.

"Whose fault is that?" demanded her husband.

"If they don't know no better they don't expect no different," she snapped in a tone of confident finality. There was puzzled silence for the rest of the journey.

Mr Oboe greeted them at the door of the cultural centre. He was accompanied by both his wives and six or seven of his children, the latter ranging from languid adolescents down to a baby not yet old enough to crawl. Some of the younger ones were playing in the dirt when the Rolls drew up and it was their clamour that brought out the others. The mothers scolded the dirty ones and Mr Oboe deftly and discreetly cuffed one of them before advancing towards the car, his arms outstretched. He wore a double-breasted pin-striped suit with wide lapels and baggy trousers that were too long. There was some confusion as the party tried to debus without treading on their hosts. The children, knowing they were to greet someone but not whom, made for Sir Wilfrid as the tallest figure. Their father compounded the error by shaking Sir Wilfrid's hand with elaborate formality. Grinning with pleasure, he said, "Sir Wilfrid, I and my family greet you."

231

Sir Wilfrid thanked him and looked vainly for the minister, who was hidden behind one of the Mrs Oboes.

"You and your family are extremely welcome," continued Mr Oboe, still holding Sir Wilfrid's hand.

Clifford stepped forward. "The minister is here," he said to Mr Oboe, indicating no one. Mr Oboe smiled again and shook Clifford's hand. Clifford tried hard to assert priorities but eventually the whole party had to shake hands with the entire family before Mr Oboe and the minister finally met. Mr Oboe then led the minister by the hand into the library.

They crowded into the little room. The young readers who were there were hustled out by Mr Oboe, who then opened the door of the side room so that the minister could see all the old British newspapers stacked to the ceiling. Each of the party in turn squeezed into the doorway to look at them.

Sir Wilfrid described the function of the library. Mr Oboe again took the minister's hand and smiled slyly. "Minister, I must give you a book."

The minister shook his head so that his jowl quivered. "No, no. No need for that. I've got lots, thanks very much."

Mr Oboe squeezed the minister's hand. "You can have another one."

Anthony leant forward. "This may be a presentation copy, minister."

Mrs Collier turned to Sir Wilfrid, who had stopped speaking in order to permit his interruptors to be heard. "I've got an aunt at home who loves reading, you know. Real bookworm, she is." Sir Wilfrid raised his eyebrows and looked politely interested. Mrs Collier nodded firmly, as if she'd been contradicted. "Oh, yes she does, you know. Simply loves it. Won't go anywhere without a book. She even reads at the tea-table, but I think that's going a bit far, myself."

Mr Oboe had meanwhile handed a red book to the minister. "Please, you must have this book."

The minister took it warily. "Thank you very much."

Mr Oboe beamed. "It is yours."

"Yes, thank you very much."

"A gift from the British cultural centre."

The minister glanced at his wife and Anthony as if afraid he might be laughed at. "I know, yes, thank you very much."

Mr Oboe nodded, still beaming. "The British are very big in Kuweto."

232

Anthony took the book from the minister and held it up to Patrick as they filed out. It was Henry James's *Portrait of a Lady*. "He won't be able to put it down," he whispered.

The sewing-machine was on the table tennis table. Half a dozen methodist ladies stood in a line on the far side of the table. They wore black stockings and skirts, red blouses, white hats and sailor's collars, the uniform Sarah wore to church. They clapped as the party entered the hall. Mr Oboe introduced the ladies by name and once again everyone shook hands with everyone else. The ladies smiled, curtsied and gave most of their attention to Sir Wilfrid.

Mr Oboe nodded and smiled. "Very good," he said. Everyone smiled back. There was a pause, then Mr Oboe took a deep breath and burst into prayer, declaiming, "Oh Lord, oh Lord, oh Lord," in a voice that filled the room.

Mrs Collier was shaken but the minister clasped his hands and looked solemn. When the noise of the prayer died down the methodist ladies sang a hymn. During this the local ambulance driver came in and sat on the sewing-machine box whilst he ate his sandwiches. He grinned happily and with one hand tapped out the rhythm on the side of the box.

By the end of the hymn Mrs Collier had recovered herself sufficiently to look as though she were in church. There was then another, longer silence. No one was in charge. Clifford looked angry, the minister purposeful but undecided. Mrs Collier looked at the man eating the sandwiches.

Eventually Sir Wilfrid stepped forward. He thanked Mr Oboe and his family and made flattering remarks about the methodist ladies. He then indicated the sewing-machine and said that Mrs Collier had come all the way from London to meet the people of Kuweto and that she, like himself, everyone else there and the people of the United Kingdom who could not be present, was delighted to be making this gift. All the ladies smiled and there were murmurs of thanks from the two Mrs Oboes who stood, broad and smiling, by the door. Sir Wilfrid concluded with, "I am sure Mrs Collier will now wish to declare this machine open, or launched, or ready for the needle or whatever is appropriate." He smiled, inclining his body elegantly. "Mrs Collier, would you care to . . . "

Mrs Collier stared at Sir Wilfrid. Her husband nudged her forward. She stopped by the machine, stared at it, then looked helplessly round. There was another silence. "Thank you very much," she said, in a small, high voice.

233

"They're not giving it to you, you're giving it to them," whispered the minister loudly.

Mrs Collier blinked and addressed Clifford. "I hope you get a lot of pleasure from it."

The minister pointed to the heap of green cloth on the table. "Feed it in," he whispered.

Mrs Collier picked up the cloth. It was unwieldy and began falling off the table. Clifford and Mr Oboe stepped forward. There was confusion as to which was the right end. After two or three attempts a piece was fed into the machine. Mrs Collier stood back, clutched her handbag and waited.

"Switch it on, then," said the minister, no longer whispering.

Mrs Collier dithered at the back of the machine. Clifford pressed a button, with no result. The minister stepped forward. "That's the stop one. Here, let me." He moved them both aside and pressed another button.

"I'll check that it's switched on, sir," said Clifford. He got down on all fours and followed the white flex under the table. It ended in three coloured wires. "No plug," he said.

"Where's it made?" asked the minister.

Clifford examined the machine. "Britain, sir."

"That's typical, that is," said Mrs Collier, rounding on her husband. "If it was made in Japan or Hong Kong or one of those places it would have a plug, wouldn't it? Bound to." She nodded and looked at everyone. "It would work then all right, I'm sure it would."

The minister turned to Sir Wilfrid. "Fine advertisement, I must say. What's the use of me traipsing around the world on behalf of British industry when they can't even produce plugs? No wonder no one lets us build their power stations any more. Might as well stay at home."

Sir Wilfrid's long, lined face was patient and understanding. "My sentiments entirely, minister."

"There might be another one attached to something else," said Clifford. He began moving all the chairs that were lined up against the wall, pushing them aside with a great deal of noise and bustle.

The ceremony ended with another loud prayer from Mr Oboe. He gave thanks for food, water, the sun, the earth and the English sewing-machine. He prayed for a plug, and smiled. The methodist ladies then sang another hymn, possibly the same one as before. They sang it with gusto, and the ambulance driver again tapped out the rhythm.

234

"That was embarrassing," Clifford said to Patrick as they shuffled out. "The plug should have been checked. It is British, after all. Remind me to speak to the commercial officer."

Outside, Simon was using a short stick to keep the children off the Rolls. Everyone milled around and all hands were again shaken. Sir Wilfrid was applauded.

Simon took a route that led downhill towards one of the beer halls. The earth was parched and the air dry enough to crack lips but the road outside the beer hall was wet and covered with mud, as if a pipe had burst or a water-tanker had unloaded in the wrong place. A crowd of twenty or thirty men spilled over the road. They kept moving, shouting, cheering, sometimes jumping aside. As the Rolls approached it became clear that two of them were fighting. They rolled and splashed in the mud with almost comical desperation.

A small open-backed lorry, packed with people, some clinging to the roof and sides, one on the mudguard, made its way lop-sidedly down the opposite hill. It veered off the road and back again. Simon braked to avoid the fighters. When he saw the lorry he reacted suddenly and with unnecessary violence. He swung the Rolls hard to the left and then, feeling it lose grip on the muddy road, hard to the right, accelerating at the same time. The car lurched off the road, scattering the bystanders amidst a shower of mud. The lorry wobbled and continued on its way, its cargo waving and laughing.

The Rolls came to rest with its front wheels on the road and its rear in the mud. Clifford was flung to the floor with his head between Mrs Collier's knees, and Mrs Collier and the minister slid along the rear seat into Sir Wilfrid. Anthony banged his head on the front side window. Patrick fell off the occasional seat.

Clifford picked himself up. Mrs Collier uttered little moans and gasps and tried to replace her glasses which had fallen on to her shoulder. The minister, finding himself in a near embrace with his wife, hastily detached himself. Sir Wilfrid was powerless to do anything except gaze with mute surprise at his oppressors. Patrick decided it was easier for the time being to stay where he was.

Some of the crowd moved towards the car, good-naturedly holding up their arms to show how muddy it had made them. Simon abruptly pushed the accelerator right down, the car jumped, then slid again, and the approaching men were showered with more mud. They dodged, slipped, shouted and banged angrily on the roof. One opened the passenger door, where Anthony sat clutching his head, and shouted at him. Simon said something shrill in Zulu, jumped out of the car and fled, leaving the engine stalled and his chauffeur's cap upturned in the mud.

Another man banged on the rear window. The noise inside the car was frighteningly loud. Sir Wilfrid tried to move but couldn't because Mrs Collier was leaning heavily upon him, clutching her husband, who winced each time a fist hit roof or window. Clifford was on the floor again trying to get up. Patrick, who had stayed on the floor, rose and tried to open his door. Someone was pressing against it. He braced himself against the occasional seat and pushed. The man stepped back and Patrick almost fell out.

He looked at the crowd and they at him. Most of the spectators had left the fight and were gathered round the car. One of them wore a jacket with a torn sleeve. He kept waving and shouting something. Patrick knew that at least some of the words were English but could not understand them. He felt mentally intact but for the memory of words, which appeared to have forsaken him entirely.

It was probably no more than a second or two before he pointed at the car and said, "We're stuck – can you push?" He made a pushing motion with his arms, as Sir Wilfrid had done when they had been stuck before. It had seemed absurd then but now seemed natural. "Can you push?" he repeated, gesturing vigorously.

Several of the faces near him smiled. There was more incomprehensible speech. He smiled back and others grinned and laughed. There was general movement towards the car. The door had been left open by Simon and so Patrick got in and tried to start the engine. At first nothing happened because the automatic gearbox was still engaged. Patrick disengaged it and the engine started at once.

Anthony looked at him as if he had trouble focusing. "Are you all right?"

"I am. Are you?"

"I'm not sure."

"I don't think you are."

"You may be right." He remained staring at Patrick.

The glass division was lowered and Clifford's fleshy face was thrust between them. He spoke in an urgent whisper. "Do nothing, don't move. You'll only make them worse. Stay as you are. They might lose interest and go away."

The minister's face appeared alongside Clifford's. He breathed rapidly and his eyes bulged. "Get the police!" he hissed to Anthony. Seeing no reaction he turned to Patrick. "Get out and talk to them.

Make them stand back. Keep them talking. Tell them we're from the British government."

"It's all right, they're helping us." Patrick engaged the gears and accelerated slowly, turning the front wheels so that they pointed down the slope. The big car was light and responded with almost alarming ease. There was pushing and heaving from outside. More black faces appeared at the windows, causing Mrs Collier to whimper. The car edged forward and there was a great cheer.

At this point Sir Wilfrid opened his door and stepped out. His shirt-tail showed from under his jacket, his hair was ruffled and his tie askew. He stood with one hand in the air, like mad Lear in a suit. "This is the Brit-ish ambass-ad-or. Do you un-der-stand? The Brit-ish am-bass-ador." He shouted over the startled faces nearest him as if addressing multitudes ranged over the hills. He raised his voice still more. "We have visit-ed your cultur-al centre. We are visit-ors. We mean no harm. There is a Brit-ish govern-ment min-ister – "

Those at the back were still pushing. As the spinning rear wheels reached firm ground near the road the car jerked forward. The open door caught Sir Wilfrid on the shoulder and toppled him gently into the mud. Patrick braked suddenly, fearing he was about to run over his ambassador.

"Look out, they've got him! They've got him!" Clifford shouted from the back. The minister knelt on the floor, put both hands to his head and bellowed, "Police! Police!"

Patrick put the car into neutral and smiled.

The police came. They were in open lorries and wore riot helmets. The whites had carbines or pistols, truncheons and shields. The blacks had truncheons and shields. They debussed and laid into the helpers swiftly and precisely. Those with carbines took up positions alongside the road whilst the others ran amongst the fleeing helpers. Some who had seen the lorries approach escaped in time but others were too late and became embroiled in mud and confusion, stumbling, slipping, sometimes yelping before they were hit. Some ran into the beer hall but most tried to get away between the bungalows. One of the two who had been fighting sat bemusedly at the roadside, holding his head. He was hit across the shoulders, knocked sideways and dragged by his feet back to one of the lorries. Others were beaten as they fell. Some howled and some were suddenly silent, blood streaming from wounds to the head and face. As one was dragged unresistingly away his shirt rode up to his shoulders and his trousers slipped down his thighs.

Two policemen, one white and one black, ran to Sir Wilfrid. He was already on his feet. He held up his arm again. "Stop! Stop! Stop all this!"

Clifford got out and held the ambassador by his other arm. Sir Wilfrid took no notice. The minister and Mrs Collier watched the beating and dispersal of the helpers from within the Rolls. Two of the younger ones stopped at a safe distance, picked up some stones and threw them. A policeman knelt and aimed at them with his carbine.

Putting the Rolls into gear and accelerating were actions performed unthinkingly and completely. They were obvious and once taken seemed inevitable. The car moved sharply on to the road, causing two policemen to jump aside, and pulled up in front of the kneeling man so that his aim was blocked. It missed the barrel of the carbine only because the policeman lifted it at the last moment. The stone-throwers ran off.

The young policeman's face was thin and freckled, pale with anger.

"I damn near shot you, man!" he shouted in a Lower African accent. "What the hell d'you think you're doing?"

Patrick switched off the engine and got out. He felt suddenly weary. "I was stopping you shooting."

"How did you know I was going to shoot?" The young policeman came close.

"I saw you aiming."

"How do you know I wasn't aiming over their heads?"

"I hope you were."

The policeman moved closer still. "And what is it to you whether I was or wasn't?"

"I saw you doing it, that's what it is to me." Patrick stared stonily into the policeman's hard eyes. He felt both angry and unsure of himself. The policeman raised the butt of his carbine to waist height.

The captain who had stopped the car on the way into Kuweto stepped between them and said something sharp in Lower African. Without hesitation the policeman turned and walked away, his carbine at his side.

The captain smiled disarmingly. "Was he rude to you, sir? My apologies if he was."

"He was about to shoot someone for throwing stones."

"You mean he was pointing his gun? It was more likely he was just taking precautions."

"It didn't look like that to me."

"It wouldn't, though, would it?" The captain shook his head and looked in the direction of the young policeman. "You should know,

238

sir, that not long ago that officer faced eight hundred rioters out for his blood and kept them at bay for twenty minutes until help arrived. He's very committed when he goes into action. Like the rest of us. It's not always easy for other people to understand."

"I understand you perfectly." Patrick's anger subsided into a dull core which he feared would express itself in petulance and petty resentment. It was all too easy to imagine how the scene might have appeared to those already expecting the worst: the ambassadorial Rolls spattered with mud and stranded outside the beer hall; an excited, drunken crowd; one of the men who had been fighting sitting by the road with blood on his face; in the mud by the Rolls the body of the British ambassador. Nevertheless, he wanted to say something. "Why don't you use plastic bullets?" he asked, knowing that that was not it.

The captain nodded whilst he gazed at the prisoners being dragged towards the lorries. "We'll use plastic bullets when they throw plastic stones."

The minister had got out of the Rolls and was talking to Sir Wilfrid, Clifford and two policemen. There were a dozen or so prisoners, mostly bowed and bleeding, but no other helpers in sight. The police returned to their lorries, talking and laughing as they tapped their truncheons against their thighs. The captain turned to go.

Patrick felt he hadn't finished. "There wasn't any trouble, you know. We'd got stuck and they were pushing us out of the mud. That was all."

"That wasn't how it looked to me."

"You didn't wait to see."

The captain faced him. "To be plain with you, sir, if it wasn't for people like you poking around trying to do good for something you don't understand there wouldn't have been any trouble here anyway. If you'd seen one half of what I've seen in this place you wouldn't wait to see more. You'd just act, like I did, then you'd know that's an end to it."

The captain walked back to his lorries. Patrick tried to think of a reply, but he too had acted without waiting to see.

Personalities began to reassert themselves. Clifford gave the police a long description of the missing Simon, necessarily repetitive since he could remember only that Simon was small and black. He pointed to the cap in the mud as evidence of abduction. Sir Wilfrid talked earnestly and at length to the captain, on the one hand apologising for being the unwitting cause of the incident and on the other condemning the brutal effectiveness of the police operation. He named people in the Ministry of Foreign Affairs to whom he would speak; the captain was polite and unyielding. The minister strutted about before being properly noticed and then, having secured the attention of most of those near, offered to intervene between the police and the local community.

"I'll be the go-between," he said. He looked round to see if there were any blacks he could approach. "They're more likely to talk to a third party. I'll come back and let you know their demands."

The captain looked puzzled. "Demands?"

"Yes, you know, what they want. I'll go and find out. I'll go on a walkabout."

A small old man was creeping warily back towards the beer hall by a circuitous route that took him well away from the police. The minister strode purposefully towards him. The man scampered away. The minister turned back. "See what I mean? Your men have frightened them. They were quite approachable before you charged in. This will look bad in the press, I'll tell you that for nothing now."

The captain shrugged. "You won't find any press here, sir."

"Can we go now, Ray?" Mrs Collier called from inside the Rolls.

The captain walked away. The minister ignored his wife and picked on Clifford. He repeated what he had said to the captain. Clifford energetically agreed.

Patrick leant against the car with his arms folded. When Sir Wilfrid came over to him he neither stood up nor composed his features in their usual expression of respect.

Sir Wilfrid's shirt hung out, his tie was still loose, there was mud down his right side and his hair was wild. He shook his head and looked towards the lorries. "I am assured that the prisoners will now be well treated but I'm not sure I believe it. I shall take it up with the MFA when we get back. This would happen when the minister's here, though I must say he seems to relish it. It's just rather unfortunate when we are indebted for our rescue to the Lower African police."

"Are we?" asked Patrick.

"Of course we are. What would have happened if they hadn't come when they did?" He poked his head through the car window and spoke reassuringly to Mrs Collier before turning back. "One thing I must say, Patrick – and I'm not complaining, you must understand that – but one thing I must say is that I thought you behaved a bit rashly. I expect you know what I'm talking about. There's really no need for me to say

240

it. It was that moment towards the end when the police had arrived and the rioters had dispersed and you suddenly shot the car forward. I don't mean when I fell over, I mean after that. I saw you do it. In fact, you very nearly hit my foot. Perhaps you didn't mean to? Perhaps it was an accident?"

Patrick felt the same dull anger as with the police captain. He kept his arms folded and stared straight ahead. "No, I did mean it. It wasn't an accident."

"You very nearly hit one of the policemen, Clifford was telling me."

"Yes, I very nearly did."

"I'm not blaming you, mind, it was a very tense time for all of us. But I must say I think you overreacted."

Clifford joined them, holding Simon's cap. "Everyone panics at some time or other. Don't let it upset you. No harm done, though when you shot forward I got a nasty bang on the head from the minister's knee."

"I didn't know that." Surprised by the violence of his inner reactions Patrick had no wish to defend himself. The police captain would have been easier to talk to than his own colleagues. There had been a sudden widening of the gap he had always felt between himself and others in the embassy, though where precisely he or they stood he could not have said.

"Never mind," continued Clifford. "As I say, no harm done. The thing is to keep cool in future."

By the time they left, the minister was in good enough humour to ask his wife how she was. "No doubt in my mind the police went over the top," he said, whilst she was still replying. "We could've talked them round if the police hadn't gone in like that. But that's not the point. The point is the original grievance. Why were they rioting in the first place? That's what's got to be rooted out and put right." He looked challengingly about him.

Sir Wilfrid smoothed his hair and said reluctantly, "It's oppression come to boiling point. The particular cause was probably incidental and unimportant."

"Drink," said Clifford firmly. "They'd been on the beer."

"They weren't rioting," said Patrick.

The others looked at him. There was a pause and then they turned away again as if embarrassed. The minister shook his head. "If only the police had waited until we'd got a dialogue going. If only they'd held off for that. That's what's wrong with this country – no dialogue. You must have dialogue. Everywhere. Same the world over."

Patrick drove the Rolls back. Anthony had a headache and said nothing. Simon's house was in another part of Kuweto and it was generally agreed – at least, confidently asserted by Clifford and not disputed by anyone else – that he had not been abducted but had fled there. He would probably turn up for work as usual the next day.

Despite the anger, which remained with him like a tolerable ache, Patrick enjoyed driving the Rolls. It was big, stately and surprisingly responsive. He felt that perhaps he would prefer Simon's job to his own. Musing on this reminded him that there was still no news of his car; Miss Teale's last report, blithely delivered, was that the ship bringing it and his baggage was overdue.

They reached the embassy an hour or so before the minister was to have his informal talks in the MFA. He bustled about with cheerful brusqueness, exhorting Anthony and the press section to get the newspapers interested in what had happened. He announced two or three times that the time had come to abandon his low profile in the interest of "eyeball to eyeball dialogue throughout the whole of Lower Africa".

Various versions of the story later appeared in British and Lower African newspapers. The one that most appealed to the minister had a picture of him alongside a picture of Mrs Acupu, the Kuwetan community leader who was visiting Britain and whose excess baggage was being transported in Patrick's freight. The picture was captioned, 'British Minister Begins Black Dialogue', and the article described how the minister had intervened in a confrontation between blacks and the police which had begun after a car was driven at a policeman. After calming the crowd, the minister was cheered out of Kuweto. Mrs Acupu, the article concluded, was visiting Britain.

The story that went round the embassy, spread during frequent confidential disclosures by Clifford "within these four walls", was that Patrick had panicked and run over the ambassador at the critical moment, provoking the crowd to riot.

Patrick's principal concern, the moment he got back, was to find out what had happened when Jim had called on Joanna that morning. He also wanted to talk to her about the events in Kuweto. In fact, he wanted to talk to anyone not connected with them but particularly to her because she would be warm and sympathetic and would take his side. Instead he got Beauty, who said that Joanna had come back from shopping and gone out again. She had gone to have coffee with someone whose name Beauty could not remember. Beauty giggled as she apologised.

242

He had hardly put the telephone down when Jim rang. He had heard what had happened. "Your people all okay?"

"No problems," said Patrick. "A pair of dirty ambassadorial trousers, that's all."

"I guess I should've advised you not to go. It'd be my head on the block if anything went wrong."

"There was no trouble anyway. There wasn't a problem until people thought there was, and that made it one."

"Your people or my people?"

"Both. They both got it wrong."

Jim chuckled. "That's the way it is round here. You're learning."

"It was all completely unnecessary. It needn't have happened."

" 'Course it's not necessary, but it happens just the same." Jim broke off and gave an instruction to someone else in the room. "We should have a beer and a chat some time."

"We should, yes, I'd like that." Patrick did not have to pretend; even this conversation was a relief. A talk with Jim would be refreshing. They would at least be discussing the same thing.

"Yeah, well, I'll ring you." Jim's voice was curt, as if he felt he had gone too far. He rang off without saying goodbye.

18

The minister was to discuss Arthur Whelk at the MFA, amongst other subjects of which Patrick was not informed. The ambassador suggested that Chatsworth should come to the reception later in the afternoon in case the minister wanted to meet him.

"Nothing to hide by then. We'll have had it out with them one way or another, for good or ill. And your man will be able to report on any progress."

"There hasn't been any."

Sir Wilfrid put his hand on Patrick's shoulder. "Don't be negative. One of the curses of the Service. Don't let it grip you so soon." He bent his head. "Shouldn't dwell on the morning's business if I were you. No one blames you and it'll be forgotten in no time. Bring young Chatsworth along. He's presentable and he'll be company for you."

When Patrick got home at lunchtime he found that Rachel had gone off in a taxi to do some interviews. Chatsworth sat in one of the wicker chairs on the veranda, his feet on another. He was sharpening the spear again. "One for you on the table."

"Thanks."

He pointed with the spear at the pool, which was clean and brilliant. "Had a dip with Rachel this morning. Bit sharp round the balls but all right. Ordered some more chemicals."

"Who's Rachel interviewing?"

"Haven't a clue."

"She didn't say?"

"Not to me."

Chatsworth's tone sounded more definite than the apparent offhandedness of his words but it was clear no more would be learned from him just then. "The ambassador's invited you to this reception to meet the minister this afternoon," said Patrick.

Chatsworth nodded as if this were no more than he had expected. "'Fraid I won't have much to report. Got a telegram from the office this morning asking all sorts of damn fool questions about what I was doing and wanting answers by yesterday. Rang them back and gave them a piece of my mind. Pointed out they were lucky I wasn't still in clink and that I wasn't getting any benefit from my salary here anyway. Then they tried to ask a lot of stupid questions about Whelk and I had to shut them up. You'd think they'd never heard of security. Thick as a wet fog on a Sunday, some of these people in business. And I thought when I left the army I was joining a world of sanity and reason." He sipped his drink. "I owe you for that call, by the way. Don't forget it." The telephone rang. "If that's them again, tell them I'm wrestling with gorillas."

Sarah came out and said quietly that it was for Patrick. Her manner was subdued and he could tell immediately that she was troubled by something. The caller was Joanna. She wanted to know what time she should appear at the reception; also, whether he had learned any more about what people were to wear. Hearing her made him realise how much he wanted to speak to her. All he wanted to say about the events in Kuweto that morning threatened to gush out but he was constrained by the businesslike nature of the conversation; also, he was learning that things came out wrongly on the telephone. "What did Jim want?" he asked. He had not meant to ask so blatantly.

"What? Oh, he just wanted to talk. He wasn't horrible or anything. I gave him a cup of coffee and he talked about Belinda. He only stayed about fifteen minutes."

Patrick did not want to appear jealous and knew he should not go on. "Does he often do that?"

"Well, sometimes, not often. He just drops in."

There was now a slight defensiveness in her tone which he knew he had provoked. He resolved to show more interest in Belinda in future and changed the subject to Rachel and Chatsworth.

"D'you think they have?" she asked.

"I don't think so because he hasn't said anything. Shall I ask him?" She laughed. "Yes, go on. No, no, you can't."

He put down the phone and walked out on to the veranda. "Have you seduced Rachel?"

Chatsworth looked up. "Not yet. Don't want to rush it. The sooner it's over with the sooner I'll get bored. Why, have you got a better idea?"

"No, just wondered." He went back to the phone.

Joanna sounded shocked. "He actually said that? God, how arrogant. I hope you don't talk about me like that."

"No, no, he doesn't even know your name. You'll meet him this afternoon, though."

"I'm not sure I want to."

The conversation ended better than it had begun. He went cheerfully into the kitchen to see why Sarah was troubled. She was sitting on a chair by the oven and was reading slowly from a bible in her lap, forming the words with her lips but making no sound. The bible reminded Patrick that she had the evening off. She was to go to church and stay all night for a twelve-hour festival of prayers and hymns. She had been very excited about it.

"Are you getting ready for tonight?" he asked.

She put her finger on the page and smiled dolefully. "Tonight I have to read out loud in church. It makes me nervous."

"Which part do you have to read?"

"I cannot say in English, massa. The bible is Zulu."

"May I have a look? I've never seen a Zulu bible."

She handed it to him. "I have a bible in Zulu and Lower African but not in English."

Patrick turned the pages, able to observe only that the book was well kept and leather-bound. "It's a very nice bible."

"Thank you, massa."

"Do you have to read about Jesus?"

"I read about the God who send Jesus to earth for us."

"That's the important bit." He smiled. She nodded solemnly as he handed back the book. "Read loudly and slowly, Sarah."

"Mr Chatsworth tell me to read soft and quick. That is what he would do, he said."

"He'd get someone else to read for him."

She laughed. "He is fine man, I think. It is good he is here."

"Yes."

"Before with one massa there was not enough work. I worry that I do not do enough for you. But now there is plenty. Mr Chatsworth make much work. Also your ladies. They make work, too. That is good." She looked thoughtfully at her new blue slippers. Snap had stolen one the day before and Sarah, outraged, had beaten him with the other.

"Is your slipper all right?" asked Patrick.

"Yes, yes, is all right, thank you, massa." She nodded, closed her eyes and made a sound like a hum cut short. "But I worry about Stanley."

"Why – hasn't he gone?"

"Yes, but still I worry."

"He hasn't telephoned?"

"No."

He saw again the blacks scattering before the police and the bleeding prisoners being dragged back to the trucks. "I'm sure he must be back in Swahiland."

She nodded obediently. "Yes, massa."

"Is there anyone you can telephone?"

"There is only one telephone to the chief of my village but he will not speak to it. Maybe his wife, she will speak."

"Ring her. You can use this phone at any time." Chatsworth's abrogation of this privilege to himself made Patrick determined to extend it to more deserving cases.

She brightened. "I can ring tomorrow, perhaps."

"Ring now."

"Tomorrow, massa, definitely."

He paused as he left the room. "Will you wear your special clothes at church?"

"Yes."

He smiled. "Very smart."

She laughed. "Thank you, massa, thank you very much."

Staff had to be at the reception before guests. It was held on the residence lawn. Waiters busied themselves around a long drinks table and on a smaller table there were tiny quantities of food. The blue sky was beginning to cloud over and a cool breeze, more purposeful than playful, fluttered the ladies' dresses. The minister and his wife were in the house, where it was thought Sir Wilfrid was, but the minister had twice had to come out looking for him. The embassy staff stood in an uneasy huddle on the lawn, the usual enmities silenced.

Clifford was gloomy. He had tried to discuss the threatened cut in allowances but the minister had not been very understanding. He had not realised that diplomats had such large allowances: how much were they and what were they for? Clifford had spent an uncomfortable ten minutes explaining that the ambassador had a tax-free entertainment allowance almost as large as his salary, of which he was obliged neither to spend nor to return a penny; he had finally to confess that his own total income, when his children started school, would be larger than the minister's. The minister said that it was not his business to interfere with the work of the inspectors.

Patrick detached himself from the group and wandered off in the direction of the pool. He would have dinner with Joanna that evening and would describe what had happened in Kuweto, the suddenness of it all, the misunderstanding, the beatings, the realisation that none of it was new and that there was no apparent end. He felt he had to talk to someone about it. Until he did the memory would remain undigested.

"This is going to be awful." It was Sandy. She walked down the lawn wearing a flimsy pale-green dress, rubbing her bare upper arms with her hands. "I'm so cold I've been hiding in the loo. It's going to be short on booze and food, too. They always are, these big do's. Last Christmas we were limited to a glass and a half of sherry each. Can you believe it?" She pouted and put on a cockney accent. "There's bleedin' Christmas spirit for yer."

"You look cold."

"So would you be if you were wearing this." She flounced her dress with her fingers. "Nice, though, isn't it? Is it see-through?"

"Not in this light."

"It's meant to be. Clifford was shocked. Tried to stop me wearing it. Not that there's anything to see, anyway."

It was always hard to refuse invitations to gallantry. "You've no need to be so modest."

"I don't mean me, I mean underclothes. I'm not wearing any. Now you're wondering why I'm telling you this. You always look as though you think I'm trying to seduce you and you're about to run a world record mile. How's Joanna?"

He smiled. "She's very well."

"D'you love her?"

He maintained his smile. Sandy's eyebrows were delicately raised and she gazed evenly at him.

"Don't reply," she continued. "Whatever you said would be less than honest. You can't help it. I don't think you know what you feel, if you feel anything."

"How do you know what I feel?"

The sudden hardness of his tone was reflected in her eyes. She was startled and stared as if waiting for more, slightly frightened. When he said nothing her gaze softened. "Sorry, love, have I touched a raw nerve? I shouldn't keep on about her. It's only that I'm a bit jealous."

"It's not Joanna."

"Who is it, then?"

He looked away, trying to rid himself of the vision of howling blacks being clubbed to silence. "It's what I saw in Kuweto this morning."

"This country getting at you?"

"Something like that."

"It does now and again. You have to fight back."

"That's all right for those that can."

"Same with everything." She smiled and flounced her dress again. "Anyway, I thought men were supposed to find underclothes more erotic than nakedness? If that's true I can't see why Clifford should get so angry about me not wearing any. Don't s'pose he knows what's erotic, that's the trouble."

Clifford hurried towards them from the group. Patrick felt a little guilty and almost raised his hand in greeting. Sandy stared at her approaching husband. "I knew it wouldn't be long. He's jealous too, you see."

"The guests are arriving and the official party will be out soon," said Clifford. "It's time you started hosting and circulating, Patrick."

"I need to host some gin to circulate my blood before I do anything else," said Sandy. "Are they serving any?"

"Yes, yes, of course they are. Patrick, will you help Miss Teale make sure that people get a drink as soon as they come on to the lawn? I'll look after the ministerial party."

"I can't see any drinks," continued Sandy.

Clifford became less officious and more irritable. "Well, go to the table and get some but don't finish it before anyone else gets any."

Soon the minister and his wife appeared, Sir Wilfrid following like a thoughtful stork. Clifford hovered round the party, bringing forward various guests to be introduced and then dispatching them with too little ceremony. Sandy and Mrs Collier stood next to each other, silently. The minister clasped a glass of white wine in his podgy fist and looked belligerent. Patrick talked to an architect and his wife from Crawley, a maker of scientific instruments and his wife from Wolverhampton and a bank manager and his wife from Ballymoney.

He looked for Joanna. Philip and Claire Longhurst appeared on the veranda. Claire held a baby and stared combatively about her. Philip, looking no better than he had that morning, drooped behind her with the appearance of one who is beginning to realise that perhaps the whole of life will disappoint him. They gazed towards the minister, who now stood apart from the others talking earnestly to Sir Wilfrid. The two were attended by a servant with a tray of drinks. There was only one other tray circulating and several people looked about with unease that bordered upon desperation. Several times the servant attempted to offer his drinks elsewhere but each time he was recalled by the minister. Eventually the servant gave up trying to escape and stood respectfully a few yards away, stepping forward every so often to replace the minister's empty glass with a full one. Whilst this went on Sir Wilfrid's gaze passed over Clifford's watchful head, traversed Philip and Claire, settled on Patrick a moment, left him and returned with sudden recognition. He beckoned.

He put his hand on Patrick's shoulder. "Minister, you know Patrick Stubbs, my third secretary. He's dealing with the Whelk business at this end, liaising with the – "

The minister stared at Patrick without shaking hands. "'Course I know him, he was at the airport."

Sir Wilfrid held up his hand. "Yes, of course, minister – "

The minister turned to Sir Wilfrid. "In fact, he's the one who nearly ran us all over this afternoon."

Sir Wilfrid nodded with closed eyes. "A moment's panic, that's all. He's new here."

"He's not as new as I am." The minister reached for another glass. "Anyway, least said, soonest mended. I spoke to my opposite number about Whelk this afternoon. He didn't want to know at first, said he'd only heard about it yesterday or some such daft excuse. I put it to him straight: told him we wanted him back or there'd be trouble." He suppressed a belch and drank. "Anyway, what he said convinced me that whatever has happened to Whelk the Lower Africans aren't behind it. In fact, they're as keen to find him as we are. He came clean with me and said they'd been watching us and the investigator who's still out here to see if we knew more than we were letting on. That's why they let the investigator out of gaol. But now they believe we're not up to any monkey business they're prepared to pull out all the stops to help us."

Sir Wilfrid rubbed his jaw. "All the same, I can't help feeling that at the very least they know more than we do. They're quite capable of being duplicitous. Why, for instance, are they so keen to find him?"

The minister shook his head dismissively. "No, no, this was straight, man to man. He knew who he was talking to. It was the same when we discussed the border question. I let him have our position straight from the shoulder. Told him what we'd say at the UN – "

Sir Wilfrid leant forward. "Minister, Patrick hasn't been party to the confidential discussions on the border question and I rather think our UN position – "

The minister held up his hand. "And then he said that if we recognise the independent homelands, starting with Bapuwana, they'll be flexible on the border in return. I told him it was more than our

250

reputation with the Third World was worth. We'd be the pariahs of the UN, just like they are now."

Sir Wilfrid gave up trying to interrupt. He nodded. "Quite so. In no time at all."

"'Why give a damn about the Third World?' he said. 'What does their opinion matter? If the boot were on the other foot they'd be kicking us all round the globe. They wouldn't give a damn about our opinion.' I told him that wasn't the point."

Sir Wilfrid nodded again. "Indeed it isn't. Even if that were true the moral point remains. It's the moral point that's crucial."

"He may be right, of course, but it's not only up to us, that's the trouble. It's not that simple. We've all got to pretend we like the Third World. Myself, I don't even like calling them that. It's all one world, and either you make your way in it or you don't. It's not up to me, as I told him."

Sir Wilfrid looked pained. He asked the minister if he would like to meet Chatsworth and whether the Lower Africans would now agree to Chatsworth's being quietly put on a plane home.

The minister emptied his glass. "They'll agree, no doubt about that. I'll thank him for his efforts and send him on his way."

Patrick was dispatched with instructions to introduce Chatsworth at a convenient time. The smooth lawn seemed springier than hitherto. There were daily flights to London.

Clifford and Sandy talked to Philip and Claire, ignoring the guests. There was no sign of Joanna. Patrick was pretending not to have noticed the architect's welcoming look when the familiar knock of a diesel-engined taxi caused him to glance at the entrance. Chatsworth got out, followed by Rachel. She wore yellow jeans and a white T-shirt, through both of which she bulged. Chatsworth wore flannels and a blazer that Patrick recognised as his.

"Got any cash for the cab?" Chatsworth called. "I'm right out. Put it on the ledger."

Heads turned and there was a lull in the chatter. Patrick made his way through the guests, paid the cab and led the pair towards Clifford's group. He felt safer with people he knew, however disapproving Clifford might be.

"Hope you don't mind my coming along," said Rachel to the group at large.

"'Course they don't," said Chatsworth, grinning. "I was invited. You're my guest."

Patrick introduced them as friends who were staying with him

251

Other guests stared. Sandy brightened, Philip smiled wanly, Claire perfunctorily held out her free hand and Clifford indicated to Patrick to step aside.

"Was he really invited?"

"Yes, the ambassssador asked him. He's to meet the minister."

"You shouldn't take everything the ambassador says literally. Keep them out of sight, save embarrassing everyone else. Why is she dressed like that? Doesn't she know the form?"

Patrick shrugged. "She knows the form." The more he experienced Clifford's displeasure the less he minded it. They both watched as Chatsworth secured the only visible waiter by taking his arm as he was serving another group and leading him away. Glasses were replenished and Chatsworth called for beer. The waiter said there was none. Chatsworth said there must be. The waiter smiled in embarrassment and said there wasn't. Chatsworth took him by the arm again, saying, "Take me to your leader." They disappeared into the house.

No one in the group spoke for a few moments. Rachel looked at the guests who were looking at her, then turned to Patrick. "God, those frightful hats. Really really awful. Trust you to end up in this sort of scene."

"You'll find this is standard form in diplomatic circles," said Clifford with quiet pomposity.

"That makes it even worse," said Sandy. "I agree with Rachel. It's awful. They all think the sun shines out of their whatsits and they're all nobodies."

"D'you mean to say you really like it?" Rachel asked Clifford. "Is this how you like to live?"

Clifford looked skywards as if assessing various ways to live. "It's a great deal better than some. And it's a matter of what you're used to."

"Used to it or not it's absolutely bloody, I think. It's almost as bad as one of my parents' garden parties. All champagne and tittle-tattle by the lake."

"I could handle the champagne," said Sandy.

Philip and Claire looked warily interested. Clifford was clearly waging an inner struggle. "Your parents have a lake?"

Rachel gazed at the other guests. "What? – oh, yes. Only an artificial one. It's two hundred years old and it leaks like Patrick's pool. Bloody nuisance, actually."

"Nothing artificial about this," said Chatsworth, returning with a pint of beer. "It's funny, you know, I've never been to a place where there's absolutely no beer. Just find the right bloke and you can find

252

beer, even if there's no water. Same all over the Sahara. When I was in Chad people were dropping off like flies for lack of water but even there I found a crate of Guinness that had come up from Nigeria. Bit sour but that's how they like it. You always have to ask, though. No one ever offers it to you. Cheers.''

They discussed the geographical regions of Lower Africa. Clifford was didactic about what should and should not be seen. Chatsworth claimed to have been to several of the same places but seemed to have seen different things. Philip began a remark about the politico-socio-economic structure of extinct nomadic tribes in the west but was unable to finish it because of a coughing fit. Someone mentioned Sin City, a newly-built gambling centre in Bapuwana. It was famed for relaxations not permitted in Lower Africa. Chatsworth, Rachel and Sandy said they wanted to go there. Claire abruptly changed the position of the baby in her arms, waking it, and said she thought the place sounded boring. Chatsworth looked at the baby and grinned.

"D'you know what I'd like to do with your baby?"

Claire smiled for the first time. "He is awfully cuddly, isn't he?"

"I'd like to eat him. They look so succulent when they're very young. Those lovely plump little limbs and rosy cheeks. Don't they make your mouth water?"

Claire glanced at her husband, then back at Chatsworth. "I think that's disgusting."

"Come on, you must admit they'd be a delicacy if they weren't human babies. They even smell nice when they're clean."

Sandy giggled and Claire turned away, muttering to her husband. He nodded faintly and, with a smile of goodbye, led his wife back towards the house.

"What else would you like to eat?" Sandy asked Chatsworth.

It was Joanna's gesture rather than her face or her blue dress that caught Patrick's eye. She had her hair tied back but a stray piece fell forward and, with the habitual movement he had first noticed in the airport lounge, she quickly pushed it into place. He left the others and walked over to her. "I'm glad you came."

"Did you think I wouldn't?"

He touched her hand and felt an answering pressure. The sky had now clouded over completely and the breeze was cooler still but he was sure he was physically warmed by her presence. "We must leave as soon as possible."

"But I've only just got here."

"I know. In fact I can't leave before the ambassador or the minister. It's not allowed. But we'll go as soon as they do."

"Will I meet your lodger?"

"Yes, and his intended." He introduced her. Chatsworth told her she was known as 'in-due-course' and then told everyone else why. Joanna laughed, as did Patrick, but he was suddenly aware of her Lower African accent amongst all the English and, tense and defensive, waited to see if Rachel would get at her in some way. But Rachel was pleasant and was in any case more interested in knowing who all the other guests were.

She turned to Patrick. "I'm going to talk to some of them. Don't introduce me. This is so awful it's actually quite enjoyable. I've had a good day today."

"What else have you done?"

"I've got some super stuff on tape for this trial programme."

"What sort of stuff?"

"Oh, just background stuff – what you'd expect me to get." She smiled and accepted another drink from the servant procured by Chatsworth. "Don't worry, I haven't got a mike down my cleavage."

The ambassador beckoned and Clifford left the group, only to return and say gruffly that the ambassador wanted Patrick and Chatsworth. He told Sandy to circulate more.

The ambassador was still with the minister and his wife, their area of lawn having been purged of guests. The minister was still talking about his meeting in the MFA which had apparently ended with him giving his unsolicited views on Lower Africa's racial problems.

"They tried to tell me I should go and wash my own back doorstep. Bloody cheek." He looked at Sir Wilfrid. "Lower Africans are obstinate."

Sir Wilfrid nodded gloomily. "We've worked for years to establish reasonable relations with the possiblity of influence. We're in no position to bully and any other pressure has at best no effect and is at worst counter-productive. It's a very long job. It requires patience."

"Maybe, but they appreciate straight talking, these people. They're like that themselves. They understand it." He noticed Chatsworth. "Where d'you get that beer?"

Chatsworth's expression had the solemnity of an oath. "I'll get you one." He walked off and reappeared with another pint. The minister tasted it. They discussed small breweries in the north of England. Chatsworth said that two more pints were on their way.

The minister wiped his lips with the back of his hand, then wiped his hand on his chins. "I wish you wouldn't," said his wife.

He turned confidentially to Chatsworth. "How d'you reckon on handling these Lower Africans?"

Chatsworth's manner was serious, determined and crisp. "No good messing about."

"Exactly what I say. You've got to put it to them. Make sure everyone knows where they stand."

They gazed approvingly at each other. Each drank deeply from his pint. Chatsworth gave an account of his arrest in short, punchy sentences, leaving out the reason for it. Patrick caught his eye and grinned but saw only sincerity and purpose. The other pints arrived.

Sir Wilfrid sighed, turned away and gazed at the darkening sky. "He has probably put back British-Lower African relations by a good ten years," he said quietly to Patrick. "He wouldn't let me come with him to the meeting, an unheard-of procedure. Now I know why. We've probably less chance of influencing them than we've ever had. Perhaps it's as well I wasn't there. Normal diplomatic relations can go on as I wasn't associated with it."

The major event of the party was the arrival of Mrs Hosanna Anna Acupu, the Kuwetan lady councillor whose excess baggage was included with Patrick's. She was six feet tall and very nearly as wide. Her body was wrapped in a red sari and on her fat black arm, which Patrick judged thicker than his own thigh, she carried a small white leather handbag. She beamed at everyone.

Following his experience of Kuweto the minister greeted her as one comrade-in-arms to another. Hands were shaken, Mrs Collier was shaken and Mrs Acupu displayed a mouthful of teeth like new tombstones. Sir Wilfrid escorted and introduced her courteously.

She and Patrick shook hands vigorously. He said how pleased he was to meet her.

"I thank you for your condolences," she replied. "The plight of the black people is truly bad."

"Appalling," said Chatsworth as a way of getting himself introduced.

"They are trodden beneath by racist Lower Africans," continued Mrs Acupu.

"We saw enough of that this morning," said the minister. "I did what I could but I can't answer for what happened after I left."

255

Mrs Acupu continued to beam. "Your country was very well when I was there and many people are interested in the plight of the black people of Lower Africa but your government is mean. I do not understand them. I do not know why that is."

"Very often the new immigrants are the worst offenders in Lower Africa, the most repressive and racist," Sir Wilfrid put in quickly. "There's a great deal of Italian money here."

"Much for the Italians but not for the black people."

"Always the same with Eyeties," said the minister.

Chatsworth gazed at Mrs Acupu with an expression of shocked concern. "I am appalled that you should have been treated meanly."

"So am I," said the minister quickly. "Make sure we take the details. Someone will look into it."

Mrs Acupu bent her head and sighed. "When I come to take my baggage – "

Sir Wilfrid interrupted. "Your excess baggage has come with Patrick's baggage. It's all here."

Mrs Acupu turned to Patrick with a huge grin. "You have my baggage?"

"Well, no, not as far as I know. Certainly, it wasn't there when I left."

Sir Wilfrid shook his head. "Miss Teale told me it was to be delivered this afternoon. Perhaps she forgot to mention it to you. There's some problem about your car, though. You'd better speak to her."

"You have a car?" Mrs Acupu was delighted. "You can deliver my baggage please."

Sir Wilfrid said that the embassy would deliver it for her. The Jaguar would be put at her disposal.

"I thank you," said Mrs Acupu.

More drinks were served, with more beer for the minister and Chatsworth. There was some inconclusive talk about sanctions which was brought to an end by Mrs Collier, who had been staring at the pool.

"What makes the water so blue?" she asked.

Everyone looked at the pool.

"The colour of the sky," said the minister. Everyone looked skywards but the clouds were now inky black. One or two heavy drops of rain fell.

"Chemicals," suggested Sir Wilfrid.

"It is the natural colour of the water," concluded Mrs Acupu. Everyone nodded.

"I'm frozen," said Mrs Collier.

The onset of rain was expected but unprepared for. In the absence of a lead from Sir Wilfrid no one liked to suggest moving tables, chairs and people inside. Sir Wilfrid himself could not be relied upon to notice the change in weather. The rain fell suddenly and massively with a fury that was almost personal. Even so there was a moment's hesitation before the stampede to get into the house under the veranda. It both finished and made the party. People huddled away from the edge of the veranda, laughing and wet, while the rain spattered venomously on to the concrete. Clifford pushed his way here and there trying to organise something. Patrick kept out of his way and sought Joanna, but found the minister. He was in a corner of the veranda, huddled protectively round his beer and unnoticed by the taller people crowded over him. He seemed not to mind.

"Good man, that Chatsworth," he said. "He's gone to get some more and lock the rest away so this mob don't get at it. I told him he should stay on here for a few more weeks. You never know, he might be able to pull something out of the bag. Strikes me the embassy could do with someone like him around. He's staying with you, I'm told? Good. Well, give him all the help you can and don't worry about the cost. We're paying the firm's fees. I'll square it with the Lower Africans. Oh, and by the way." He held Patrick by the arm. "That fat black woman, the one who's on the make. What does she do here?"

"She's a councillor, that's all I know. Sir Wilfrid knows much more."

"No matter, no matter. Just humour her. Important we're seen to get on with her sort."

"Why?" Joanna had joined them. She stood with hunched shoulders because of the crush and stared challengingly at the minister. "Why is it important to be seen to be getting on with people who are on the make?"

The minister looked uncomfortable. "Well, it's not the fact that she's on the make – if she is. I didn't mean she necessarily is. No, it's because she's representative – "

"Black, d'you mean?" Her voice was sharp and her grey eyes were fixed firmly on the minister. She did not look at Patrick.

"No, no, I mean representative. It doesn't matter whether she's black or white."

257

"Is it important to be seen to get on with white people on the make?"

The minister looked bewildered and angry. He glanced round as if for assistance. "It is simply a question of representation. No more than that. She represents – "

"Herself. She's no more representative of Kuweto than you are. There's a whole group of them who live off people like you."

Patrick had never seen her like this. She almost glowed with resolution. He wished only that she could have chosen someone else, such as Clifford. "Joanna, this is the minister of state, Mr Collier. Minister, this is – "

"Yes, yes, I know," she interrupted, still without looking at him. "You must think I'm very rude. It's just that a lot of people come to our country and talk to a few token blacks or coloureds and think they know it all and then tell us how to live when they get safely back to their own countries. They're not really interested, they don't really want to find out anything. They just want to be confirmed in their views so they can look good back home. If you really want to talk to blacks you'd be better off with your servant or your driver. I bet you don't even know his name."

The minister was plainly disconcerted. He had begun to say that he fully understood and sympathised when Chatsworth thrust himself between them with more beer.

Patrick led her away. "I don't suppose that's done your career much good," she said. "I'm sorry."

"No, no, he's only the minister."

She shook her head. "I've seen so many people come here with that sort of attitude, it's so irritating. They're just out to do good for themselves and they use us as the whipping-boys. It wouldn't be so bad if they were sincere. They're always so smug and yet if they lived here they'd be just like us. That's what gets me." She smiled. "I'm sorry, it must've been embarrassing for you."

He put his hand on her arm. "Let's have dinner. No one will notice if we run away now."

"I'll get my jacket."

Chatsworth rejoined him. "I think the minister's onside. Seems to approve of me."

"I don't think he approves of me any more."

"No. Had to distance myself from you a bit. He was on about your performance in Kuweto this morning. Then said you'd introduced him to some harpy. I didn't say anthing too bad."

"I'll give you my side of it later."

"That's what I've been saying all my life. No one ever wants to hear it, that's the trouble."

Patrick thought of his own domestic responsibility. "Did you also explain how Rachel came to be here?"

"No need. I introduced her to the giantess and they went nineteen to the dozen on how injust it all is. Inequality, freedom and all that. I think the minister fancies her. That helped."

"Where is she now?"

"Taking her tights off."

"For him?"

"For me. I asked her."

"That's a little premature, isn't it?"

"I just wanted to see if she'd do it when I asked her. I said I wanted her to give them to me."

"I never knew you had a nylon fetish."

Chatsworth glanced over his shoulder. "Don't shout it round the houses. Anyway, I don't. It's the exercise of power. Getting her to do something she doesn't normally do, just because I ask her. It makes her feel desired and adds excitement for me. You only ever do it with a woman you haven't had, of course. Just to see. No point if you know she will."

"I wouldn't have thought Rachel would like to be regarded as a sex object."

Chatsworth shook his head impatiently. "Everyone wants to be regarded as a sex object. All the problems start when they think they're not. Anyway, I'm a hero of the coming revolution, remember."

Joanna reappeared. "Joanna's been getting her jacket," Patrick said to Chatsworth. "Didn't want you to get the wrong end of the stick."

"What do you mean?" she asked, suspiciously.

"Tell you later," said Patrick. Chatsworth grinned and looked round for something else to do.

They ate an uninteresting meal in an expensive French restaurant in the city centre. All food in Battenburg tasted very much alike whatever its alleged origin, but there was at least plenty of it. As it was, Patrick hardly noticed that he was eating and Joanna ate little. He was voluble and self-indulgent; she listened, laughed, sympathised, questioned. She was horrified by his description of the beating of the helpers in Kuweto, but seemed more so by his account of Chatsworth.

"But he was so nice," she said, pained. "Quite charming, really. You make him sound awful."

"Can't he be both?"

"How long is he staying?"

"Indefinitely."

Later she said, "I wish you were more often like this. You're usually so tense and restrained, as if you're watching me. It's horrible sometimes." She smiled. "It's interesting too."

They decided they should go to the coast together for a few days. She had some friends there with whom they could stay and she could leave Belinda with other friends. Jim had a part-share in a plane that went there and back nearly every week. They could go down in that free.

"Wouldn't he mind?"

"No. If he did he'd say. He's very straight, you know, Jim. And he likes you."

A thunderstorm broke as they came out of the restaurant. They ran to the car through pelting rain. The thunder rolled back and forth amongst the tower blocks and sheet-lightning rent the night. Water ran down the gutters of the hill so deeply that it covered the exhaust pipes of cars. The bakkie was high enough to escape trouble but even so it was difficult to reach because of the surge of foaming brown water.

Patrick drove slowly, the rain bouncing on the bonnet. They were in a white area, allegedly the most violent in Battenburg, and to Patrick the lightning, the hammering rain and the overflowing gutters were symbolic of a Battenburg that had finally burst apart. He felt heavy with foreboding but not of anything he could express. Joanna was cheerful and positive, enjoying the storm, but he was quiet. Once, as he nosed the bakkie across a junction where the robots had failed, they saw a motorbike on its side, the front wheel still spinning, and in the road a shoe. Two cars were slewed across the pavement and people were just getting out. Patrick considered stopping but decided there were enough people around to help. Farther on, outside a hotel notorious for its stabbings, there was an ambulance and three police cars. His sense of foreboding increased.

When they got back the light was on in Sarah's quarters. She was in her room with two women with whom she usually went to church. They were sitting and talking, all in their church uniforms. Sarah made to get up but Patrick prevented her. "I'm sorry, Sarah. I thought you'd gone to church and I wondered why the light was on."

"No, massa, it is raining so we are not going."

"You don't go in the rain?"

260

She shook her head. "The rain makes much mud. It is not good."

"Is the church outside then?"

"No, but the way there is muddy. Also, there are bad boys near that church and it is easy to get lost."

"I'll give you a lift." He regretted it as he spoke because they would not all fit into the cab and because Joanna was upstairs.

The three women conferred in Zulu, then Sarah shook her head again and smiled awkwardly. "Thank you, massa, but we do not go. It is not good in the rain."

He could not prevent them all from standing and thanking him again.

Before they slept Joanna described the house on the coast where they could stay. It would do him good to get away, she said. Also, they had never seen each other outside Battenburg and Battenburg was a strange place; it made people tense, distorted them; the rest of Lower Africa was not like that. There was a public holiday that weekend. It would be a good time to get away.

He was woken by the sound of the rape-gate being closed with accidental force, followed by excited whispering and laughing. He had left it open for Rachel and Chatsworth. They could not lock it because he had the key. He heard them go down the corridor, presumably to the same bed, and considered getting up to lock the gate. But Joanna snuggled closer, muttering something, and he stayed where he was.

He was next woken by the sound of the gate opening. The clock showed two in the morning and he lay tense and still, straining to listen. Hearing nothing, he disengaged himself, got up, wrapped a towel round his hips and cautiously opened the bedroom door. The rape-gate was half open, the shadow of its bars thrown across the landing carpet by the downstairs light. He slipped through and went softly down the stairs.

Chatsworth, also clad in a towel, sat on a chair in the kitchen. His elbow was on the table and his head was in his hand, as in a rough imitation of Rodin's Thinker. The fridge door was open and a half-finished glass of milk was on the table before him.

He looked up when Patrick entered. "It must be the beer. It's the only thing I can think of."

"It's made you ill?"

"I suppose you could call it that."

It was some seconds before Patrick understood. "You mean you can't do it?"

261

Chatsworth shook his head. "After all that build-up. She was practically frantic."

"D'you think the milk will help?"

"I don't know. It's refreshing. Does you good when you're tired. At least it's not beer. I blame the minister, of course, but that doesn't cut much ice with Rachel."

Patrick tried not to smile. "It happened to me once."

Chatsworth stared. "Good. I'll tell her that. She'll feel much better."

"You'll probably be all right if you go and have a sleep. Have another go afterwards."

"Don't s'pose she'll have me back in the bed. Not that it would be worth it anyway. Never is. Our bodies are simply programmed to want to keep on doing it, whether we like it or not, that's all. But now that I want to do it, my body doesn't. Typical."

There was not much else to say and so Patrick turned to go. "Don't worry about locking the rape-gate. Just push it to."

Chatsworth lifted his chin from his hand for the first time. "If that was meant to be funny, it was pretty poor taste."

When Patrick got to the top of the stairs he noticed that Sarah's light was still on. She was alone, still in her church uniform, and sat staring at something out of sight, or at nothing. As he watched she got up wearily and walked to the window. Her movements were slow and her features heavy. She looked up but did not see him. She pulled the curtains together with a weighty finality.

19

The minister left the following day. "An example of how low-key political contacts can be constructive," Clifford read aloud from one of the papers. "Both governments now understand each other better and the minister's disaster-averting diplomacy in Kuweto has shown how dialogue, patience and human contact can help in even the most difficult circumstances." He folded the paper and dropped it on the desk. "Nice that someone appreciates our efforts. Too much to expect of old Formerly, of course."

Though still not well, Philip went to the airport rather than Patrick. "You don't mind if I see him off?" he asked.

"Of course not," said Patrick truthfully.

"It's just that after all that work I'd like to see something of the man." He smiled. "Not that I expect great enlightenment."

Patrick's baggage had arrived the previous afternoon, as Sir Wilfrid had predicted. The garage was now nearly filled with boxes and crates, none of which he at first recognised as his own. After rooting about with Chatsworth, Sarah and Deuteronomy, to the accompaniment of frustrated barking from Snap who was locked in the house, three battered boxes were dragged out and identified as his. Sarah unpacked them with growing disappointment.

"Massa, is this all your things?"

Patrick capitulated immediately. "We'll buy some more, Sarah."

"I make a list?"

"Yes, please, make a long list."

A couple of large boxes were claimed by Rachel as the teaching materials that she and Maurice had asked Patrick to include in his baggage. She had them pushed to one side. "Lucky I was here when they arrived. Saves you having to find the schools they're going to. I'll get them to pick them up. Don't bother opening them now." She was cheerful and business-like. Her manner towards Chatsworth was friendly though slightly offhand. He was helpful, solicitous and subdued.

263

The embassy Jaguar arrived with Mrs Acupu. She beamed and then spoke sharply to Sarah and Deuteronomy. She insisted on checking the contents of her boxes. They contained an abundance of brightly-coloured clothes, several dozen pairs of mens' and womens' shoes and several rolls of cloth. Patrick had been told that the kind of shoe worn was an important status symbol amongst blacks and he noticed that most of the shoes were large and ostentatious. The Jaguar would have to make several trips; Deuteronomy was detailed to help.

"Is there much to be made from clothes?" Chatsworth asked Mrs Acupu. They walked away from the house to continue the conversation. She made expansive gestures and accompanied her words with a number of high-pitched exclamations.

"She's some sort of racketeer," Chatsworth said, when she went. "Or her husband is. Whatever it is, it's pretty good. I'm told Kuweto is run by a lot of gangland bosses and he sounds like one of them. Worth keeping in with her. She thinks I own this place. I didn't disabuse her but don't worry, I shall if necessary." He looked at Patrick for signs of appreciation.

"What was she talking to you about?" asked Rachel. She had opened one of her boxes, then closed it again.

"Extortion."

"God, how awful. Is there much of it?"

"Heaps."

Sarah came out to say that there was someone on the telephone for Rachel. Chatsworth looked sadly after her. "I didn't realise she was flying back to London this afternoon. Now I'll never get the chance to redeem myself. She'll spread it all round London."

Patrick tried to look sympathetic. "Do you have many friends in common?"

"You never know. Anyway, it's the thought that's hurtful." He trod on a piece of wrapping paper and turned his foot till the paper was torn. "This means I'll have to continue in the role of victim, playing to her sense of mission and guilt. They all have it, these trendies."

Patrick leant against the wall and folded his arms. There were moments of enjoyment in talking to Chatsworth, no matter what else was going on. "Tell me, why d'you call her a trendy? Many people might see her as normal and reasonable. I mean, just because she makes a fuss about being anti-racist – "

Chatsworth shook his head. "But that's not normal. Nearly everyone is racist at heart. We all look down on other races. Every race does that, even if only subconsciously. That's what's normal. It's just that a few people like me admit it and a lot of others like her sense it and don't."

Rachel appeared at the door. "I'm going to get a cab into Battenburg and use up the rest of my tape. Be back this afternoon."

"I'll give you a lift," said Patrick. "I'm going into the embassy."

"No, it's all right. I'm not ready yet." She disappeared inside.

"Probably thought I might come," said Chatsworth gloomily.

Patrick took her to the airport later that afternoon. He missed her farewell to Chatsworth, who was not much in evidence.

"I've arranged for some guys from the school to come and pick up the teaching materials," she said. "It's been really sweet of you to put up with me. You've been great. Thanks."

"Which school?"

"A school in Kuweto. They'll be up some time, there's no need for you to do anything. They were really grateful."

He asked if Chatsworth had mentioned when he might return to London. He hadn't.

"He's a funny guy," she continued reflectively. "Sometimes I think he's not what he seems at all but when you've been through what he's been through, in prison and all that, I s'pose it alters you. He's very sensitive. He goes about things in a funny way, sort of indirectly, and when it comes to – " She lit a cigarette and opened the window. "No, but they did some terrible things to him in prison and it's left him psychologically scarred. It just comes over him every now and again. He was telling me about it last night."

Patrick was slightly tempted to tell her about Chatsworth but there was too much to explain. Anyway, it didn't seem fair on either of them – although he was a little surprised to find himself applying the concept of fairness as readily to Chatsworth as to others. Perhaps it was more deeply ingrained than he had realised.

He accompanied her through immigration, as his diplomatic status permitted, and she enthused about how her recordings would help on her course. Her contemporaries would have recorded the socially deprived in the inner cities or at best immigrant communities but she had real stuff from real people in Kuweto. It might be good enough to turn into an actual programme instead of just a mock-up. Daddy would throw a fit if he knew what he'd coughed up the air-fare for.

When she'd gone he rang Joanna from an airport call-box. If he had waited until he had got back to the embassy he would have had to ring in the presence of Philip.

265

"You must be telepathic," she said. "I've just rung you."

He did not believe he was telepathic. "Why?"

Beauty had been caught gambling again. She had gone off to the park with some other women and the police had arrested them. Joanna heard the wailing and went out and pleaded with the policemen, eventually bursting into tears. "I felt awful because it was partly deliberate, you know, but not completely. I mean, it was also because Jim had been round again and I was a bit upset and it was just one thing on top of another. It wasn't just because of Beauty. I know I'd be lost without her and it was horrible seeing her being taken away though she deserves it, the little monkey. If I've told her once I've told her a hundred times but all the same I'd hate to think of her in prison." She laughed. "You know, I cried my eyes out, all over his uniform, and all the time I knew I could've stopped if I'd wanted. Wasn't that awful? And both the policemen got so embarrassed they let all the women go. They shouted, 'Run! Vamoose!' and you should've seen them scamper off." She laughed again.

She wanted to talk. He asked questions and she went on for some time. Eventually he asked what had happened with Jim.

"Oh, nothing happened. He just talked, you know. He told me he's arranged everything with the plane for the weekend."

"Are you sure he doesn't mind?"

"No, he doesn't, really. He likes helping people, anyone, even you and me." She hesitated. "It's just that I do get a bit upset when he comes round because – well, not because he's awkward or anything but he's very vulnerable, you know, much more than he might seem. I mean, I know he's unhappy but he doesn't complain about it and that makes it worse in a way. He still keeps saying how much he likes you and he still keeps calling you the 'temporary boyfriend'. You're sure you're not going away?"

"Yes, quite sure." There had never been any suggestion that he should leave, but he still felt dishonest in being so definite. The feeling of transience had not decreased during his time in Lower Africa.

"You're quite, quite sure?" she asked, perhaps sensing uncertainty in his tone.

"Quite, quite, quite. I'll come and see you after work."

She laughed. "That's what I've been trying to get you to say. I was thinking I was going to have to say it myself."

Work on the report of the minister's visit began immediately. It was an important document and would go out under the ambassador's signature. Clifford delegated it to Philip.

266

Philip achieved a major coup by going to the MFA desk officer concerned with British affairs. The man was indiscreet and over lunch gave an oral summary of the Lower African view of the visit. This was that it was neither successful nor unsuccessful, that the British position on all major issues was as predicted and that the minister, though tactless and ill-informed, had an instinctive grasp of political realities which the Lower Africans respected.

"Didn't they say anything better than that?" asked Clifford.

Philip looked puzzled. "Well, no, but isn't it important that we know what they really think rather than what they say to the press? I mean, it's pretty unusual, getting the other side's view of a ministerial visit." He smiled. "In my career it's unique."

"Fact-finding mission, that's all it was," said Clifford. "Anyway, we can't say in writing that the minister's ill-informed and tactless. Reflects badly on us. You'll have to leave that out."

Patrick saw the draft before it went to Clifford. It was succinct, truthful and detailed, but Clifford was no better pleased. "I don't like all this stuff about our positions being predictable."

"But that's what they thought," said Philip. "There were no surprises."

"Can't you say it lived up to expectations?"

"But that's not what they meant. It conveys a false impression."

Clifford frowned. "I'm not sure it does, you know, not really. You see, this is as much a report on us as on the minister. Let me have your draft. I'll do the necessary."

The final report was flattering, self-congratulatory and misleading. Sir Wilfrid was surprised that the Lower Africans had been so pleased.

Philip raised his hands in the air. "There is corruption amongst honest men. I feel the waters closing over my head."

"Is corruption essential?"

"I'm beginning to think it might be."

"Why don't you leave?"

"Mortgage, school-fees, allowances. It would be easier for you."

"Would you in my position?"

Philip smiled. "To be honest, I enjoy being a bureaucrat. I'd just like the chance to be a good one now and again."

After persuasion from Patrick, Sarah eventually rang her village to hear if Stanley was back, but no one had seen him. She was less worried than he had thought she would be. "He will come back, I think. He always come back."

Patrick took her shopping farther into town than they normally

267

went. They parked on one side of a main road and shopped in the hypermarket on the other. It was not as good as their usual one. "We do another shop for the meat," said Sarah. Also, they had to go to a chemist where every fortnight he bought her tablets for high blood pressure. It was, he had discovered, his duty to pay for his servants' health care.

Laden with bags, they crossed the road on the way back. It was illegal in Lower Africa to cross against a red signal or to cross in towns at anywhere other than junctions. The busy one-way street was clear because the traffic was held up by another robot fifty yards to the left. They crossed with half a dozen others, although the robot indicated that pedestrians should wait. At the far side a policeman stepped out from behind a parked car and stood in front of Sarah.

"I'm fining you for making an illegal crossing." He pulled out his notebook. "Let me see your identity card."

The others who had crossed were white. They glanced at what was happening and walked on. Sarah looked frightened and guilty. The policeman prodded her with his notebook.

Patrick put down his shopping. Sarah was fumbling in her handbag. Her fear and guilt in the face of authority communicated itself and his first instinct was to dissociate himself from her. He knew he would stay, though, and seeing the policeman prod her awakened in him an anger which he also knew he should not show. "Why have you picked on her?" he asked slowly. "We all crossed, me with her."

The policeman was young, like the one in Kuweto. He had a new and uncertain moustache. "This is not your business. If you take my advice you'll make yourself scarce."

"If she's in trouble, I should be in trouble. I'm her employer and I crossed with her."

The policeman stepped back as if making room to draw his pistol. "Let me see your life certificate."

Life certificates were a compound and detailed document of identity which the law said all Lower African citizens should carry. They were not yet issued to blacks, who had pass books or identity cards. Patrick showed his diplomatic identity card. Sarah clutched her handbag in both hands and looked down. Her shopping lay at her feet. Whilst his card was being examined Patrick put his hand on her shoulder and told her not to worry. She did not look up but remained mute and unmoving, like a rabbit that hopes danger will pass if it only keeps still.

"Are you a diplomat?" asked the policeman.

268

"Yes." Patrick sensed that this was where the battle could be won if he were prepared to stop fighting. The policeman was hesitant, probably did not want trouble and was prevented only by his pride from walking away from it. If Patrick offered to take Sarah home and see that she didn't do it again, apologising for himself at the same time, all could still be well. But the sight of her bowed head hardened the stubbornness within him. "You singled out this lady because she's black. If you arrest her you must arrest me, too."

The policeman hesitated no longer. "I'm taking her to police headquarters. If you want to come you can." He pulled out a pair of handcuffs.

"You're not going to use those on her?"

"I use what I like." He pulled Sarah's wrists together and handcuffed them. She still clung to her handbag and did not notice Patrick's attempt to relieve her of it. His face as he did so came very close to the policeman's. He was younger than Patrick and did not look strong. Patrick wanted to hit him. Instead he picked up Sarah's shopping and walked alongside them.

The headquarters was a few hundred yards away. The policeman guided her by the arm, forcing her to walk quickly. People who saw them looked hurriedly away, pretending not to notice. Sarah's handbag knocked against her knees. Patrick felt angry, ridiculous and impotent. "Don't worry, Sarah, nothing's going to happen," he said, loudly enough for the policeman to hear. Neither responded.

They went through the entrance he had used when visiting Jim Rissik to a room on the ground floor where four men, three black and one white, sat handcuffed on benches. A group of policemen stood smoking and talking in the middle of the room, at the far end of which was a reception desk and a door through which prisoners were taken. Several were led back through it and out into the corridor. All the police were smart and the one guarding the door had his boots and holster polished to a high gloss; the atmosphere, though, was of bureaucratic indifference, impersonal and slow. Sarah was put on the back bench and Patrick sat next to her. He put down all the shopping which he then had to move to make way for an escorted prisoner.

The young policeman went forward to the reception desk and spoke quietly to the desk officer. They were joined by an older man and all three turned twice to look at Patrick. They seemed unsure and reluctant. Patrick decided to attempt to gain the initiative. He went to the counter and said that Sarah's high blood pressure could be worsened by anything such as handcuffs that restricted her circulation. He did not know if this was true but neither did they and the handcuffs were removed.

No one seemed to know what to do next. "If you want to hold me you'd better notify the British ambassador," Patrick said.

The senior man shook his head. "We're not holding you, sir. You are free to leave at any time. You came here by your own choice, as I understand."

"And what about my servant?"

"In your case, would it not be more appropriate for us to inform the consul?" asked the desk officer.

Patrick wondered whether this was an ironic reference to Whelk but there was no trace of irony in the policeman's tone or expression.

"The consul is not here. I am the acting consul. Perhaps you'd like to tell Captain Rissik I'm here. He knows me. Tell him who you've arrested and tell him that her employer, who committed the same offence at the same time and in her company, is here too."

A telephone call was conducted in Lower African and shortly afterwards Jim appeared, his uniform buttoned and gleaming, his belt creaking faintly as he moved. His regular features were set and serious. He smiled briefly at Sarah, who did not respond, and indicated to Patrick to follow him to a side office. They both remained standing. Jim put his hands in his pockets and faced Patrick squarely.

"He's a young policeman, nervous and a bit keen. I can see it might annoy you, especially because it's you and especially because it's Sarah, but you shouldn't have done it like that. Your own people would dislike it as much as we do. Your ambassador wouldn't like to ruffle feathers following the minister's visit and Clifford would go up the wall. But no matter, nothing's going to happen; they'll let her go." He spoke quickly and formally. His dark eyes were serious and impersonal.

Patrick felt like a schoolboy being ticked off. His anger now seemed adolescent and self-indulgent. He could've done it differently and achieved the same result without the fuss. But still it was wrong. "I'm sorry about the trouble. All the same, it shouldn't have happened."

"It does, though. These things keep happening, you keep forgetting that."

"They wouldn't if everyone protested."

"But they don't. They don't want to. You forget that too."

Patrick said nothing.

Jim looked down at his polished toecaps. "Two other things have happened, three in a way. I wanted to talk to you anyway. First, your

270

friend Rachel, whom you saw off yesterday." Seeing Patrick's raised eyebrows he smiled slightly. "Well, we check everyone going in and out of that airport. Rachel's been having a nice time in Kuweto with young Stanley. Did you know that? She's been tape-recording him and his activist friends. That's who they are, you know, that's who he's been seeing when he should've been safely back at school. People connected with that railway bomb the other day. Communists, infiltrators, terrorists, call them what you like. We don't mind her taping them. She can get their propaganda line just as easily in London but she was useful to our anti-terrorist boys. She led them from one contact to another. That's why we let her continue. They were quite upset when she left."

Patrick half sat on the desk and folded his arms. He watched Jim's face, which was softer now and more thoughtful.

"Of course, this is none of my business. I'm not in the anti-terrorist squad and I shouldn't be telling you. I'm doing it to help you because there are people in this building who think you're a real bad guy whereas I think you're – well, you're no worse than me, only different." He smiled and stepped closer. Patrick remained leaning against the desk. "The point is, it's one thing your harbouring commie agitators and kidnap investigators, or even keeping anti-state literature on your premises – that's what's in Rachel's boxes but we don't mind that, we'll pick up the stuff and the people who'll come to collect it in time – but it's another thing when it comes to Stanley. I know you let him stay at your place and I know you tried to help him return home but take my advice and don't have any more to do with him. He's in trouble now, too far in for you to help. Keep him away."

They stared at each other. Patrick did not know what to say. He was not frightened but his heart beat faster. It would take some time to digest this new perspective on himself and his activities. He was already wondering what to say to Sarah. "Where is he now?"

"I don't know. As I said, it's not my department." Still with his hands in his pockets, Jim walked over to the window and looked out. "Stanley and anti-state literature, that's two of the three. Guess the third."

Patrick was about to say Joanna but Jim continued quickly. "Whelk, dear old Arthur. We know where he is. He's in Sin City." He turned and grinned.

Patrick relaxed. "What's he doing there?"

"Don't know. Go and see for yourself. We've got no authority, you must know that. It's outside our law. That's why he's up there, I reckon."

"How do you know?"

"I suggest you go up this weekend. Strike while the iron's hot. But I wouldn't want our mutual friend to be upset by not having her trip to the coast. Specially not after I've fixed the plane for you."

The sarcasm was new. It sounded forced and unnatural. Patrick stood. "Thanks for everything."

"Don't thank me." Jim spoke the words slowly and very clearly. "For two pins I'd knock your teeth down your throat." He remained by the window, his face paler and his features hard. His dark eyes stared unflinchingly but his concentration seemed to be inward. "It's not that I don't like you," he continued. "It's just that I would like to hurt you. I would like to break your hands."

Patrick said nothing.

Jim shrugged and moved away from the window. "You don't give much away, do you? I hope you're being nice to her."

"I try to be."

Jim put his hand heavily on Patrick's shoulder. "You'd better be."

Sarah seemed unable to understand that she had been released. "I have never been in no trouble before, massa," she repeated. "I am very sorry."

After a while he gave up trying to reassure her and said, "Sarah, we must find Stanley. He may be in trouble."

She nodded and smiled. "Yes, yes, always in trouble, that one."

"But really in trouble, Sarah. I think the police are looking for him. We must find him and send him home."

"Massa, how can we find him when we do not know where he is?"

"He is in Kuweto."

"But Kuweto is very big and I don't know those people there."

"We could go and look for him."

She said nothing to this suggestion. Kuweto was bigger than Battenburg. "Before, he always come back even when it is longer than this. When he come I take him home."

Patrick was not content with doing nothing even when there was nothing to be done. Eventually he thought of something he could do. Rachel would not be back in London immediately, since she was to stop in Nairobi; he would ring when she returned and ask how she had kept in touch with Stanley.

272

He saw the ambassador at the residence. He was watching cricket on the television. "You weren't a blue or anything?"

Patrick remembered Sir Wilfrid's misconception as to which university he'd been to. "No, sir."

"Play for your college?"

"No, I didn't play cricket."

"Funny. Something about you reminds me of college sport."

Patrick had still not found a way to return the tie. Perhaps Sir Wilfrid knew and was being ironic. He nearly confessed.

"What did you play?" continued Sir Wilfrid.

"Football."

"Which ball?"

"The round one." Patrick went on to tell him what had happened during the afternoon. He did not like talking about it. He felt he did not come out of it well and that Sir Wilfrid would probably disapprove. But the news about Whelk had to be explained in full.

Sir Wilfrid sucked noisily on an empty pipe. "Well, whether they knew all along where Arthur was or whether they've really only just discovered makes no difference. I must say I'm delighted he's alive and in one piece – assuming there's nothing your friend forgot to tell you. The important thing now is to make contact with him and find out why it is they want him, since they're not disposed to tell us. Of course, it may simply be that he only thinks they want him but there must be some reason for that. My guess is that there's nothing definite. Anyway, it's clear that you must go up and see him and you must go as soon as possible – tomorrow or the day after. That's the long weekend, isn't it? You'd nothing planned, I hope? Pity. Still, you can see the coast at any time. Sin City is by all accounts a bizarre place and I shall be interested to hear what you think of it. What poor Arthur finds to do up there I can't imagine. You should plan on spending a night or two but whatever you do don't do anything that could be interpreted as diplomatic recognition. To all outsiders this must be a strictly private and unofficial visit. In fact, I think it's best that no one else in the embassy even knows you're going. Not even Clifford. Just go."

Sir Wilfrid filled his pipe whilst Patrick sat in silent desolation. Joanna had staked a lot on their weekend at the coast. He could not think how to explain unless by lying and saying he had to be embassy duty officer. He did not want to lie to her. "One thing I will say, Patrick," continued Sir Wilfrid, shaking his match out, "is that your escapade with Sarah today was sailing a bit close to the wind. I

273

understand your feelings and applaud your motives but you must not take advantage of your representative position. It's a responsibility as well as a privilege and it can work only as long as it is not abused. What you did could have caused trouble and we don't want that. Remember we're still dependent upon their co-operation to get Whelk back, as well as to keep young Chatsworth out of gaol. In fact, I think it would be an idea to take Chatsworth with you. Often useful to have a steady hand on the tiller and it was after all what we paid him to come here for. But I must stress – absolute confidentiality."

He pointed his pipe at Patrick to emphasise the point but his expression was kindly. Patrick nodded agreement. There was no point now in voicing doubts as to Chatsworth's reliability and judgement. He was in any case preoccupied with what to tell Joanna.

Sir Wilfrid saw him to the door. "So what did you do in the summer?" Patrick did not at first understand. "If not cricket, you know – what did you play?"

Patrick recalled one or two hours spent on the Reading municipal putting green but that wouldn't do. He had played tennis at home when his family lived for a year near some courts.

"A bit of tennis."

Sir Wilfrid nodded.

"Now and again," Patrick added hastily. "Were you a cricket blue, sir?"

Sir Wilfrid took the pipe from his mouth. "Lord, no. Couldn't bat a ball to save my life. Never played. Just assumed everyone else did, that's all – you know, young chaps like yourself. No, I'm just a listener and a watcher, I'm afraid."

Chatsworth was pleased with the news. "Good. Always wanted to go there. 'Course, they may be having us on about Whelk – just trying to get us up there so that they can help us out of the country and not let us back in. Have to keep our eyes peeled. Anyway, should be fun, Whelk or no Whelk. Might even get the chance to do what I didn't do with Rachel. Restock the old male pride."

Patrick did not believe there was any trick. He could see no point in one. "The condition is that no one should know why we're going."

"No problem about that. Everyone knows people go to Sin City for gambling and sex. They won't look for other explanations. Probably wouldn't believe them anyway. Which reminds me – I may have to touch you for a bit more of the ready. Trust you're keeping a book."

Joanna was out when he rang that evening. He wanted to tell her in person but it was more important she should know soon. In the end he had to leave a message with Beauty. He made her repeat it three times in case she forgot to add that he would go round the next day to explain.

He half expected Joanna to ring the next morning but she didn't. He went round as soon as he could and Beauty answered the door. Joanna was in her bedroom packing.

She wore her white jeans and had her hair tied back. He felt her anger as he entered the room. Her features had a cold sculptured firmness and her movements were quick and decisive. She glanced up and immediately looked away. Beauty did not linger.

"I'm sorry," he said.

"If you can't go you can't go." She continued to pack.

"Are you going anyway?"

"Someone ought to. The pilot could have gone down this morning otherwise. He delayed specially for us. And my friends there have not gone away for the weekend, specially for us."

He stood awkwardly by the door. "It's something I have to do for work. I'm not supposed to say what it is now, though I hope I shall be able to next week. I know it sounds inadequate but there's nothing I can do."

She carefully folded a tartan skirt, then threw a blue bikini on top of it. He watched in growing despair. "Jim was telling me that Stanley's on the run in Kuweto and is getting into trouble. I was at the police station with Sarah yesterday. And Rachel left a whole lot of illegal literature in my garage." He did not know why he said that.

"I thought you would have approved of all that."

"I'm worried for Sarah's sake."

She pushed her suitcase closed, opened it again, threw in a tin of talcum powder, then closed it by kneeling on it. Her way of ignoring him and her brisk movements made him want her.

"Let me give you a lift to the airport."

"I'm taking my car. I'll leave it there."

She went into Belinda's room and spoke to her.

"Are you taking Belinda?"

"Yes."

He put his hand on her. "Look, I know it's horrible but I can't do anything about it."

"And if you could tell me you would – right?"

"Right."

She sat down at her dressing-table, unpinned and repinned her hair.

"I only heard about this thing I've got to do when I was with Sarah yesterday."

"Sod Sarah," she said quietly. She looked at him in the mirror, her hands raised to the back of her head. "Yes, that's what I said. When it comes to helping some poor black you seem to have unlimited time and concern. It's fortunate that all this important work you can't talk about doesn't get in the way of that."

He sat on the bed. "It's nothing to do with it. Anyway, you help people. You helped Beauty when she was arrested and you helped Deuteronomy."

She tugged at her hair. "I'm sorry if my sympathies don't seem to match yours any more. Perhaps they never did. I suppose you'd like me to go around saying we ought not to keep the blacks out of our lives. But it so happens we do and so do you in your country. There are fifty million Bangladeshies who would come and live in Britain if you didn't lock them out. You're lucky. We feel just the same only you've got the advantage of distance so no one notices. They could all have come if you hadn't changed your laws to stop them. Now you come here and preach about it."

"What has that to do with anything between us?"

"It has to do with everything between us."

"But why now? Why are you suddenly – "

She put both hands on the dressing-table and leant forward slightly, her shoulders hunched as if she were trying to hold the table down. "Because if I don't argue about something with you I shall scream," she said quietly. "Please go."

When Patrick got home that evening Chatsworth said, "'In-due-course' rang just after you'd left this morning."

"I've seen her." He did not want to talk.

Chatsworth did, though. During dinner he spoke about the number of times he'd had to invent stories to conceal whatever he was doing. "In my line of business, I mean. You get so used to it after a while that wherever you go you automatically dream up some reason for being there apart from the real one, even if you're innocent. Teaches you to think on your feet which is often handy, like with 'in-due-course' today."

"What d'you mean?"

"Well, she rang wanting to know why you couldn't go away with her

276

this weekend. Put me on the spot, bearing in mind what you'd said about the need for secrecy."

Patrick put down his knife and fork. "What did you say?"

"Did the decent thing by you. Took it on myself. Said I wanted to bugger off to Sin City for a bit of variety and you'd kindly offered to take me."

"You said that?"

Chatsworth nodded, his mouth full. "I didn't say you wanted the variety. I said I did."

Patrick ran to the telephone in the study. Beauty said that madam had gone. He slammed the receiver so hard that the plastic case splintered and bits flew across the room. It left the guts of the telephone exposed. Surprisingly, there was still a dialling tone.

Chatsworth looked in, still chewing. "Did I get it wrong?"

"You did."

"Wrong emphasis?"

Patrick nodded.

Chatsworth made to go and stopped. "They never leave you, you know, just for treating them badly."

Patrick swung the receiver to and fro on its cord. "That's not the point."

"Does the phone still work?"

"Seems to."

"Good."

Chatsworth went to his room. Patrick remained sitting in the study for some time before slowly picking up the bits of shattered case. Later there was angry barking from Snap. "Some men are come in a car, massa," said Sarah.

"What men?"

"Black men. I don't know them."

There were two of them in a battered Ford estate. One was half out but paused when he saw Patrick. They looked anxious and resentful. Snap hurled himself against the garden gate.

The driver explained, not very clearly, that they had come to pick up some things of Stanley's, some boxes. They were not the men for Rachel's boxes, as Patrick had assumed.

"Where is Stanley?" he asked.

The man looked sullen. "I don't know."

"You must know if you're taking boxes to him."

"They are not to him."

"But are they his?" He was aware of sounding angry.

"Yes."

"Do you know where he is?"

"He is in Kuweto." The driver started the engine. Both men now looked nervous.

Patrick told them to wait while he fetched Sarah. She spoke to them in Zulu but they did not say much. She wiped her hands repeatedly in her apron. They drove off abruptly whilst Patrick was telling her to ask more.

Sarah seemed less concerned than he was. She shrugged. "They say they know him but they do not know where he is. They say he keep moving with other people. I tell them he is to come and get the boxes himself. Then I will take him home."

Chatsworth joined them. "Better take him in the bakkie, tied down in the back," he said.

Sarah laughed. "Tie him like a goat." She shook her head and dabbed with her apron at the tears on her cheeks.

There were two small boxes at the far end of the garage that Patrick decided must be Stanley's, though no one knew when or how he had put them there. They were partially shielded by Rachel's. He opened the nearer one. It was filled with black consciousness and anti-Lower African leaflets. Sarah put her hands to her face. "Oh, massa, this is big trouble. He will go to prison."

"We'll burn them when we come back from the weekend," said Patrick. "Meanwhile, keep the garage locked so that no one can come in and get them."

"I can move them so you can get the car in better," she said anxiously.

"No, don't worry." He realised she thought he was irritated with her.

"But I can do it. Is easy job. I can clean the garage."

He put his arm round her shoulder. "No, Sarah, you clean the house whilst we're away. Get rid of all the noo-noos."

Chatsworth shifted the other box a little. "No trouble. Not too heavy. They'd go on top of the others."

"There's no point in moving them now. Leave them."

"Why?"

Patrick turned on him. Everything angered him now. He felt like shouting but kept his voice quiet. "Just leave them."

Chatsworth shrugged and went back into the house.

20

It was hot when they set off. At first Patrick thought of nothing but Joanna. He went over their conversation of the day before and rehearsed imaginary alternatives resulting in reconciliation and happiness. What gnawed at him most was being unable to ring and explain. Chatsworth was inclined to talk but gave up in the face of Patrick's unresponsiveness.

After a couple of hours, though, the exhilaration of the drive across the high veldt, the sun, the fresh air, even the gleaming red of the bonnet made themselves felt. Patrick's spirits lifted. He began to feel slightly guilty at having been unfriendly to Chatsworth, though he had not yet forgiven him.

"Miss Teale tells me that my car, the one being shipped out from England, is at the docks. I should be able to pick it up after the holiday."

Chatsworth nodded cheerfully. He did not bear grudges. "That's right, she rang about it yesterday when you were out somewhere. She said you should've been at work but she couldn't find you. Apparently there's some problem about the documents. The customs say the car's been imported illegally and they've impounded it. She wanted you to see her about it. I forgot to tell you."

There was another silence. Patrick felt less guilty.

Chatsworth added, "You'll know Whelk when we see him, will you?"

"No, I've never met him."

"But you've seen photographs?"

"No, I assumed you had."

"I haven't." There was a pause until Chatsworth laughed and slapped his thigh. "I love these cock-ups. They're delicious. You've got to laugh at them otherwise you'd despair. Colonel Sod is everywhere. Very meticulous staff officer. The only way to get your revenge is to anticipate the next cock-up."

"What do you think that will be?"

"Haven't the faintest. I reckon he's keeping all his options open."

The realisation that neither would be able to recognise Whelk did in fact make the journey more cheerful. It added a sense of irresponsibility.

The route lay across a dam famous for being the only large expanse of water within a day's drive of Battenburg. It was popular with sailors and anglers and there were traffic jams where the road wound in single lane through blasted rock. After this they passed several small villages but only one town, a long strip of hamburger bars, supermarkets, car showrooms and petrol stations. Bakkies were drawn up on both sides of the broad street with their noses towards the buildings as if tethered like horses.

After this the road led through vast fields of crops. Occasionally there were dirt tracks leading off with signs pointing to farmhouses several miles away. There was no livestock apart from a few distant cattle. Now and again a lone black man could be seen standing motionless on the veldt, or slowly walking, seemingly from nowhere to nowhere.

"Kaffirs," said Chatsworth, using a word which Sir Wilfrid had once sent an assistant military attaché from his dinner-table for using. "They walk for miles in the bush. Don't seem to know where they're going half the time but that doesn't matter. They just go walkabout."

Patrick drove at a steady speed, his elbow resting on the opened window. He knew the sun was scorching his forearm but the wind cooled it. The puncture occurred not long after they passed the entrance to some distant platinum mines. It was in the nearside rear wheel and he knew it when he felt the bakkie drag heavily on a bend.

The spare wheel was in the back but both the jack and the wheel-brace were missing. "Colonel Sod," said Chatsworth. "It's because we didn't anticipate this."

"Or didn't check before we left."

Chatsworth shook his head. "Would've been something else if we had. That's two things. They come in threes."

Car after car swept past, leaving dust and sudden disturbance in the hot air. The entrance to the platinum mines was only half a mile back but there were no buildings nearer than some miners' houses, their red roofs shimmering in the sun on a hillside about half a day's march away. Many of the cars that rushed past were new Mercedes or BMWs. Chatsworth tried waving one down and just escaped. He swore at it. "They don't like helping people in this bloody country. Have you noticed they never smile, never say 'please' or 'thank you' in the shops? That BMW probably lives round the corner from you, too."

"Nothing to be done," said Patrick, with a certain satisfaction.

"That's a pretty constructive attitude."

"Well, we could toss a coin to see who lies down in front of the next one. It's the only thing that might stop them."

"It wouldn't. People are taught not to stop for bodies in the road in Lower Africa. It's a favourite robbers' trick. The body has some vertical mates in the bush and they all jump out and slug you."

They sat for another ten minutes or so, occasionally waving at the speeding cars. The sun was hot and there were smells of tar and dry grass. If it weren't for the puncture it would have been a pleasant enough way to pass the day. "All I can say is Sin City must be a hell of a place to bring all this lot and at that speed," said Chatsworth. "There's nowhere else they can be going. I mean, no one goes to Bapuwana itself."

What did stop was a small Ford lorry, open-backed and crammed with black farmworkers. The farmer was white. He had a lean craggy face and blue eyes permanently screwed up against the sun. He wore a broad-brimmed khaki hat and was grim and unsmiling.

He preferred grunts to speech and the few words of English he permitted himself were warped by his Lower African accent. When the problem was explained to him he spoke quickly in Lower African to his workers. They jumped out of the lorry and stood chatting excitedly round the bakkie whilst he got a spanner from his cab. When he was ready they lifted the back of the bakkie and the wheel was changed.

He pointed at his workers with his spanner. "I have a high jack that would do it but it's quicker to use them." Patrick thanked him and shook his hand. "We always help travellers, those of us who live here." The words came reluctantly as if he either had difficulty in choosing them or was loathe to speak at all. "It is the law of our land because you never know when it might be you. You always help the traveller." He waved his spanner again. "But you two are plain stupid to travel without tools and water. How are you for petrol?"

"We're all right for that," said Patrick.

"Just remember the garages closed at noon today for the whole holiday, just like they do on Saturdays for the weekend. It's the government trying to save petrol. You're not allowed to carry any spare, remember that. If you haven't enough to get you where you're going you should turn back now. Where are you headed for?" When they told him he pulled at the brim of his hat and turned away. "Well, that's your business. The laws are different there. You'll get fuel and everything else you want, I daresay." He climbed into his lorry and rejoined the stream of Mercedes and BMWs.

The border with Bapuwana was marked only by a signpost, like county boundaries in Britain. Although the landscape was the same on both sides, everything immediately became more haphazardly African. The road worsened, the bush looked somehow less tidy, there were mud-huts and people. Most squatted or stood near the road gazing at the cars. There were also wandering cattle – high, skinny, hump-backed beasts with wide horns.

The green and brown hills that concealed Sin City rose abruptly from the plain. It had been built by Lower African businessmen in collaboration with The Lion of Bapuwana whose personal wealth, as well as that of his relatives and friends, was said to have benefited enormously from the project. It was a popular boast that the city would one day out-Vegas Las Vegas.

The winding road led through a gap in the hills into a wide green bowl, rimmed by more hills. The city was a large complex of casinos, hotels, bars, restaurants, sports and shopping facilities, with more being built. It dominated the entrance to the bowl like a great white fortress, built deep into the hillside and tapering outwards in a curve like the horns of the Bapuwana cattle. The concrete gleamed in the sun and six storeys of darkened windows reflected a dazzling gold. Trees and shrubs grew in profusion on the terraces and balconies, giving the effect of something constructed in a vast hanging garden. There was a large swimming-pool and beyond that palm trees, tennis and volleyball courts and bowling greens. An eighteen-hole golf course, startlingly green, stretched the length of the valley floor. To one side was a man-made lake.

It was big, brash and successful. Patrick, somewhat to his surprise, was impressed. With more enthusiasm than knowledge he told Chatsworth that the valley had been landscaped with a boldness and vision not seen in Europe since the end of the nineteenth century.

Chatsworth rarely complimented anything without denigrating something else. "Anywhere else in Africa this would be hailed as a masterpiece. It would've taken twenty years to build with scores of millions of foreign aid and then it wouldn't have worked. Here it's taken for granted. Only the Lower Africans could do it."

After the long drive in the bright sun it seemed when they entered the building that they walked into near-total darkness. To the right were rows of illuminated fruit-machines. They could hear but not see them being operated continuously. There were sounds of people moving about. After a few moments their eyes adjusted well enough for them to make out darkened mirrors and strange reflecting surfaces the colour of dull gold. There were no windows at all but high in the blackness there were lights, some of which moved. Others, they slowly realised, were reflections of reflections.

The large central area was on at least three levels connected by lifts of darkened glass, the corners edged by beads of light. In the centre was a mass of gambling machines, illegal in Lower Africa. They stood in rows being played by scores of people. In a glittering ring around the central area were casinos, bars, restaurants, cinemas and strip clubs.

They made their way to two armchairs not far from the reception desk, intending to sit until their eyes were fully acclimatised. Patrick felt for the arm of the chair and lowered himself into it. There was a powerful squirming convulsion beneath him. He leapt from the chair as a small black boy clambered over the arm and scampered off into the gloom.

Chatsworth slapped his thighs repeatedly as he laughed. "All I could see was the whites of his eyes, then he was off like a rabbit. You shot up as if you'd got a snake up your arse."

"I thought I had."

"I like this place already. We're going to have fun here."

They took a lift to a veranda bar where the daylight was dazzling. After a beer each they descended a flight of stairs to a restaurant overlooking the valley. It was too late for lunch and too early for dinner, but they were hungry. They were served by a pretty black waitress whose name-tag announced her as Gift.

Patrick looked for anyone resembling a British diplomat in disguise.

"He's short, isn't he?" asked Chatsworth.

"And dark."

"Had a moustache."

"Yes, but he might have shaved it off before he went missing. No one can remember. You know how unobservant people – we – are."

"What d'you think he's doing here – running a brothel?"

"Or playing golf."

"Could do both. Lot of people do. Does he play golf?"

"No idea. There weren't any clubs amongst his things."

A couple of tables away were three whites. One was a fat, dirty-looking girl with blotched skin and lank brown hair. The two others were men, one obese. His belly bulged over his belt. He had dark curly hair and bloated, brutal features. Twice he sent back his steak, bullying the frightened and silent Gift. The other man was thin and

283

pock-marked and had a crushed bitter expression that became cruel when he smiled. He offered a flick-knife when the fat man was having trouble with his steak.

"D'you think they're British?" asked Patrick.

"Yes."

"Why?"

"Because the British are ugly."

"But *are* they British? They look more than ugly."

Chatsworth walked over to the balcony and stood near their table looking out. "Lower African working class," he reported when he came back. "Poor whites. Backbone of the system. I suppose I ought to approve but it's hard to love faces like that. The blacks are more pleasing to the eye."

Gift took their orders with her thighs pressed against their table. Patrick asked her what the three had said to her. She smiled and looked embarrassed. "They don't like the meat. They want it blue but there is no blue meat. I don't know why they must eat blue meat."

"I want to eat black meat," said Chatsworth. "You."

She giggled and put one hand to her face. "Then you would be sick."

"Why?"

"I am not cooked."

Chatsworth put his arm round her waist. The group at the next table stared. "I will make you very warm."

She laughed again but did not move away. "Please, I must be working now. Will you have a bottle of whisky?"

Chatsworth smiled. "We haven't eaten yet. We'll have wine with our meal."

"But if you have a bottle of whisky it is more money for me."

"If I buy a bottle of whisky may I eat you?"

"Maybe, if you like."

The three whites still stared. "Don't let me cramp your style," said Patrick when Gift had gone.

Chatsworth looked wistfully after her. "Would be nice, wouldn't it? It's certainly there. I'd have to borrow the money from you, though."

After their meal they walked outside, past the pool and on to the golf-course. There was no proper twilight in Lower Africa and the dark was closing in fast. "Might as well walk round with illuminated placards saying, 'British diplomats report here'," Chatsworth gloomily observed. Patrick asked if a Mr Whelk were booked in at the hotel but was told there was no one of that name staying. They considered putting a call over the public address system but decided to leave it as a last resort in case it frightened him off.

Chatsworth made enquiries in the restaurant for Gift but she too was not to be found. "Someone's got her already, I bet."

"She might be off-duty."

"That's probably what they call it here."

They took a lift to what was called a floating bar. It was firmly fixed, windowless and charged for entrance. A white pianist sat at a white piano and sang badly. The barman did not know how to make Chatsworth a Pimms. Chatsworth then ordered Irish coffee but after a long search the barman announced there was no cream.

Chatsworth turned to Patrick. "Are you on expenses?"

Patrick had not thought about that. "I could be. I suppose I'm on duty, though no one's supposed to know that. Perhaps I can claim it from my entertainment allowance."

Chatsworth ordered a large whisky.

They went next to an indoor balcony which looked down on the people swarming round the gambling machines. One of the many security guards, a young and diffident black, tried to move them on: non-residents were not allowed on the balcony.

"What makes you think we're not residents?" asked Chatsworth.

The guard smiled in embarrassment. "If you are not you must go, please."

"We'll come to that in a minute. Why d'you think we're not?"

Patrick was embarrassed for the guard. "Come on, let's go."

"Not until I know why he assumes we're not guests."

The guard repeated that non-residents must go, Chatsworth repeated his agreement and asked why he was thought to be one. Both men smiled whilst they spoke. The guard looked nervously over his shoulder. Chatsworth several times assured him, with a smile, that he really did not want to make trouble and the guard, also with a smile, several times nodded his agreement and said, "I know, I know, sir."

Patrick recalled his own brushes with authority when with Sarah. It was different with Chatsworth; nothing ever seemed entirely serious. Nevertheless, he did not want the guard to be embarrassed. "Let's go," he said.

Chatsworth held out his hand to the guard. "We are friends."

The guard shook it. "I am pleased. My name is Gladstone."

Chatsworth introduced Patrick, who also shook his hand. "We are not awkward," continued Chatsworth. "Just interested."

Gladstone apologised again, and so did Chatsworth. Gladstone said his white boss had told him to keep non-residents away from the balcony. It was a rule. He did not know why. Chatsworth said he understood. Throughout his life he had been troubled by rules and bosses. It was the same for Gladstone. Chatsworth said that he and Patrick were from the British embassy in Battenburg. Gladstone shook hands with both again. Chatsworth asked how Lower Africans treated black people in Sin City, there being no race laws.

"It depends," said Gladstone cheerfully. "English white people have more patience with black people because they live with them in other parts of Africa. Lower African people are not patient; they do not like black people."

He lived with his sister in a nearby village. Nearly everyone in the villages now worked in Sin City. He wanted to save money to go to boarding school so that he could become a scientist. He was sixteen. Many people from Bapuwana made much money from Sin City but only the bosses and relatives of the Lion were paid well. If he did not become a scientist he would become a lawyer.

Chatsworth asked which was the best casino to visit.

"Raffles," said Gladstone, promptly.

"Which has the most gamblers?" asked Patrick, remembering what Jim had said of Arthur's tastes.

"Raffles. It is very expensive but I have some tickets for you which are very cheap." He produced a fistful of tickets from his pocket. They could have them at half price. He was always pleased to meet Englishmen. When more people came up the stairs towards the balcony he glanced uneasily over his shoulder. "I must go. People are coming. I am pleased to meet you."

They bought two tickets. Gladstone and Chatsworth shook hands but after the first grip they angled their hands upwards and gripped each other round the base of the thumb. Patrick did the same, thinking it must be a convention on parting, and Gladstone left them with a broad grin.

"What did that mean?" asked Patrick.

"Freedom handshake. It's the one the terrorists use."

"Where did you learn it?"

"In prison."

"Surprising thing for you to do, wasn't it?"

Chatsworth shrugged. "He was a nice bloke."

The man on the door did not want to see their tickets. There was no entrance fee to the casino. "Not just a nice bloke," said Patrick.

He had never seen a casino before. The murmur of voices and the

286

click of roulette balls contributed to an undercurrent of tension which made the place seem exciting. "D'you gamble?" he asked.

"Used to but I got bored. It's like sex: initially interesting but after a while you need something else, you need conflict. I ceased to care whether I won or lost."

"That doesn't sound like you."

"It wasn't my money."

It was mostly roulette and blackjack. Patrick knew no more how to play than to knit but Chatsworth spoke with authority. Patrick listened but was more impressed by the atmosphere, the ritual murmur of the croupiers and the beguilingly unfamiliar jargon. Most of the croupiers were women whom Chatsworth said were recruited or trained in London. An unwise management made them wear black one-piece swimsuits to which bits of white fluff were stuck like rabbits' tails. They were supervised by slick and bored-looking men who walked from table to table with their hands behind their backs, intervening whenever misunderstanding threatened.

The liveliest table featured a big noisy woman in her forties, who was gambling heavily. She had dyed red hair and her neck and wrists were festooned with gold. Her ample body was squeezed into a white shoulderless dress and the freckled skin of her arms and shoulders was burnt a dirty brown. She kept up a constant backchat with the male croupier who flattered her and took her money. Behind her stood her escort, a dull-eyed stupid-looking man. His shiny black shirt was undone almost to his waist, revealing a heavy gold pendant that reached below his chest to his belly.

"White trash," said Chatsworth. "Let's have a drink."

They were served by a blowzy big-breasted blonde. The natural bad temper of her features was emphasised by heavy make-up. 'Slack Alice', Patrick christened her. They drank and stood looking at the other customers. None were black although there were one or two wealthy-looking Indians.

"I think we should go," said Patrick. "It's a waste of time. We wouldn't recognise him anyway."

"It's not wasting time if you're enjoying it."

"I'm not. It's boring."

"That's your fault." Chatsworth smiled at Slack Alice who ignored him.

A short man in a white dinner-jacket approached them. One of the croupiers stopped him and asked something. He nodded authoritatively. Slack Alice made herself less slack. The man walked slowly but his eyes moved quickly, never resting anywhere. "Are you two from the embassy?"

They introduced themselves. He held out his hand with a quick grin. "Whelk, Arthur."

"Told you," said Chatsworth.

21

Arthur Whelk had crinkly black hair and a tanned, lined face. He still
had his neat moustache. His manner was crisp. "Sent you to find me,
have they? Thought they'd hear where I was some time. Doesn't
matter. I'm safe enough as long as I keep in with the people who run
the place." He turned to Patrick. "You're the one living in my house?
Sorry about the sudden removals. Had to be done like that. Trust they
took nothing of yours?"

"D'you work here?" Chatsworth interrupted.

Arthur Whelk smiled. "I run 'em. The casinos, that is." His eyes
quickly surveyed the bar and two or three gaming tables. "I think we
all need more drink, don't you?" A table was found and a bottle of
champagne produced. Arthur lit a cigar with a gold lighter. "Daphne
coping with the visas in my absence? I was sure she would. She'd cope
with the whole bloody embassy if they let her. Clifford still faffing
around?" Patrick told him about McGrain. Arthur laughed briefly.
"Poor old sod. I'll tell you where he fits in. Tell me first about Sarah,
Deuteronomy and Snap."

Finding Arthur was neither surprising nor momentous. Once it had
happened it seemed normal. Patrick tried hard to see something
remarkable or different in him but he was merely plausible, like a
competent salesman, easy on the ear and eye. He was entertaining too,
even jovial in a foxy sort of way. He sat back and crossed his legs and
waved his cigar as he spoke. The champagne bottle was emptied rather
quickly and another produced. Chatsworth was enjoying himself, as
would Patrick had he been better able to concentrate. Champagne
made him heady. He didn't particularly like it but it slipped down
easily.

"I'll keep it simple," Arthur said after various preliminaries. "No
harm in people knowing now. In fact, it may help. I was involved in a
bit of playing – gambling – myself when I was in Battenburg. You
may know that. Strictly illegal, of course, but lots of people do it and it
supplemented the allowances, paid for the booze and so on. The main
thing was, it added a bit of spark to life. Living death in the embassy,

don't you think? Old women of both sexes fussing around, worrying about what the whole world thinks when in fact no one gives a damn. Frankly, I decided some time ago I was through with the Service. It gets harder to take seriously as you get older. I admit it's been good to me one way or another but I've done it a few favours too – not always appreciated, mark you. Also, all that's left for me is another London posting or maybe a European one. Don't want either. Africa's the place for me. A man can still breathe here."

"Do you play much?" asked Chatsworth.

Arthur exhaled smoke and watched it curl away. "Mug's game. Why are the casinos rich? No, I used to organise it, lay on facilities, look after the banking and so on. Well, the long and the short of it is that the Lower African security people got to hear of it – LASS, you know, the lot everyone always makes a fuss about. Actually, if the two they sent to see me are anything to go by they're quite charming. I mean, it takes something to be charming when you're trying to blackmail some-one."

Chatsworth nodded. "It does."

"Especially as I didn't want to do it."

"Do what?" asked Patrick.

Arthur's eyes flickered. "Well, it's a bit of a shaggy dog story. Not worth going into now but it boils down to the Lower Africans wanting to round up a terrorist network they reckon they've discovered. Actually, it's more criminal than terrorist. White gunrunners bringing arms in for blacks, paid for by other whites abroad. Some of it from church funds, they reckon. Anyway, one or two of my player-contacts turned out to be peripherally involved and LASS wanted me to implicate them. Set them up, in fact." He relit his cigar. "Lots of things I would do but that ain't one of them."

"Bad for business," said Chatsworth.

Arthur turned to Patrick. "What really did for me was that they wanted me to finger poor old McGrain. That stuck in my throat a bit. He's a loyal old dog and he just takes messages. Doesn't even know what they're about. So I played them along for a while, kept them talking whilst I thought it over. If I refused outright they'd do me for playing which would mean I'd be kicked out, back to London in disgrace, never to return. On the other hand if I confessed all to the Office it would be the same only less public. Posted double-quick.

"Well, I like this place. Lower Africa suits me. I reckoned the best thing was to lie low and let them find some other way of rolling up the villains then they wouldn't bother me any more. Most likely they'd

290

leave McGrain out of it, with me gone. I had one or two contacts here, knew there was a job going and so I did a bunk." He smiled. "Very nice bunk it is, too. Sorry you've been left with McGrain. I owe his wages for the last two sessions. Now you've found me I must do something about getting them to him."

"He'll be glad of that," said Patrick. "So shall I." He noticed his glass was empty again. Arthur refilled it.

"Look after you nicely, do they?" asked Chatsworth.

Arthur smiled. "Very. Money's good, work's a pleasure, one's needs are well catered for. Only thing is, it would be nice to be able to pop back to London now and again. There's a chance of acquiring some business interests there but I can't do it without travelling through Battenburg. Also, wouldn't mind doing something about my pension rights. Still, I can't complain that people have bothered me. No one's even looked for me until you two. Beginning to feel quite unwanted." He raised his glass. "Cheers."

Chatsworth asked about the financial side of the business; Arthur asked Chatsworth about his own line. It was soon agreed that they would both profit from further discussions. Patrick said little. There was some sort of filter between himself and his perceptions. He suspected he was seeing and hearing things a little later than usual.

"Did Jim Rissik and the police know about LASS and all the rest of it?" he asked abruptly. His speech sounded loud. The others looked at him.

"Don't know," said Arthur after a slight pause. "No idea what they tell each other, if anything. They could've been hand in glove all along but my guess is they weren't. If LASS ask someone to work for them and he doesn't they're not likely to broadcast their failure."

Patrick leant forward rather too quickly, losing his thought on the way. He had to wait for it to return. "It was Jim Rissik that told me you were here."

"Well, they all have their contacts." Arthur drained his glass. Chatsworth did the same. Patrick put his on the table without spilling it. "Come on, let me show you round. I'll introduce you to some ladies later. We have some very charming girls – not the rubbish you see now."

"Too early for the good ones?" asked Chatsworth.

Arthur smiled. "You're learning, my boy. Follow me." He took them from table to table, occasionally whispering some snippet about a punter. Some of them greeted him. The croupiers were invariably respectful. He smiled and nodded as he spoke, his eyes darting from

291

person to person. Chatsworth asked many questions. Arthur was eventually called to attend to some matter in another casino. He said he would be back. Another bottle of champagne awaited them at their table.

"I knew I'd like this place," said Chatsworth, pouring. "We've done what we came to do, we've met a nice man who can help us in our careers – mine, anyway – we're treated like princes, we've got the run of the whole joint and the night is young. Aren't you glad we came now?"

Patrick was not glad. He wanted to talk to Joanna, he wanted to go and he wanted not to be drunk. Somewhere in the back of his mind, somewhere not yet beyond reach, was a question he wanted to ask Arthur. It had to do with whether or not Arthur was coming back and with what he should tell the ambassador, but it was difficult to formulate. His glass was in his hand again. He raised it to his lips and put it down untasted. Slack Alice from the bar looked as if she was about to lean over and engulf him.

"You all right?" he heard Chatsworth ask.

"Yes."

Slack Alice loomed. She was saying something and Chatsworth was answering. She pointed back towards the bar. Some people there were looking at them. One of them was Jim Rissik and one was Piet, the policeman he had brought to Patrick's house one night. The others looked familiar; after a few moments he recognised them as the ugly trio from the restaurant. Slack Alice was saying that he and Chatsworth were invited to join them for a drink. Chatsworth was suggesting they should share the champagne.

Patrick stood at the bar with everyone else. There were introductions. The ugly trio was known to Piet. They talked excitedly, except Piet who talked slowly and pedantically. Only Jim said nothing. He leant against the bar and watched. Patrick was very aware of Jim. He turned with difficulty so that he faced him. The thin man of the trio had just asked him something and he did not like the thin man. He did not like any of them. The woman had a horrible, abrupt laugh and her mouth was stupid. He had just said something to someone about mouths. To talk to Jim he had first to close his eyes, think what he wanted to say then quickly say it.

"I've drunk too much," said Jim.

Patrick recognised the brutal heaviness of his features from the time they had fought. "Me too," he said. He told Jim he had found Whelk. Jim knew, he had seen them talking. Patrick asked how Jim knew where Whelk was. Word had got around. He asked what Jim was doing there.

"Chasing tail!" bellowed Piet, and everyone laughed.

"What are you going to do about Whelk?" asked Jim.

"Nothing. He wants to stay here." Patrick thought he must be getting better. "I'm glad you're here. I wanted to talk."

Jim's dark eyes glistened. "I thought you'd be down at the coast. I didn't think you'd come."

"I wasn't. I was. I was going." Patrick mentioned Joanna and stopped. He was filled with feeling but there were no words. Instead, he asked Jim if he'd been told why Whelk had left Battenburg. Jim had. LASS had heard that the police had discovered where Whelk was and had come clean.

"We've no more excuses to talk," said Jim, grinning. "Now we're just rivals."

Patrick took it seriously. "We can still talk."

"Can we?"

Patrick raised his glass. "We can drink." He didn't want to drink.

They drank. Jim put his arms round Patrick's shoulder. "This is the guy who pinched my girl," he announced. Patrick could feel Jim's breath on his cheek. He concentrated on trying to remain steady on his feet. "He should've been with her this weekend. But, look, now he's drinking with us instead." They touched their glasses at the second attempt. Patrick looked at the faces before him. They were individual but he was unable to respond individually. Chatsworth said something to Piet.

"Now you come chasing black tail in Battenburg," said the fat man.

"Is that what he did?" asked Jim, in mock surprise.

Patrick shook his head. "No, no."

"They did. They were mauling the waitress. They couldn't keep their hands off her." The fat man gulped his beer and dribbled. He said something in Lower African and the others laughed.

"They did, you were telling us about it before," said Piet. "You were talking about it. You said so."

"That's a mean thing," said Jim quietly.

Patrick turned to him. He was serious and angry now. "It's not true. I wouldn't do that to Joanna."

The fat man stretched out and grabbed his collar. Piet said something but the fat man ignored him. His face seemed larger than before and twisted with disproportionate passion. "Are you calling me a liar?"

Patrick stepped back but the man still had hold of him. He looked at the bloated white features. He felt an unassailable disdain. "Yes."

He did not see the blow, nor feel it precisely. He knew it as a stunning shock inside his head, a flash and a kind of soundless bang. There was a great pain in his nose and he couldn't see. He bent nearly double and someone hit him on the side of the head. Next he was on the floor with his head in his arms. A kick in the kidneys made him gasp. He lashed out with his legs and was kicked again. He remembered that the thin man had a flick knife. He tried to roll but someone was on top of him. Very soon he was too comprehensively battered to distinguish individual blows.

He was helped to his feet. His mouth was full and he was coughing. The pain in his nose had expanded to the whole of the middle of his face. His eyes streamed and he couldn't keep them open. There was talking and shouting. He was led through a press of people and then there was somewhere white, empty and echoing. There were only one or two voices, unnaturally loud. Someone held him by the hair and bent him over. Someone else pulled his hands from his face. There was a gleaming white wash-basin before him, spotted suddenly with blood.

"You bled like a pig," said Chatsworth afterwards. It was a gratuitous observation as the blood was all over Patrick's clothes.

Chatsworth said it was the fat man who had hit him. Patrick had gone down with Jim though whether Jim was fighting him or trying to protect him was hard to say. Everyone fought everyone else. The thin man hit the girl. Chatsworth was punched on the ear by someone, then he punched the fat man on the side of the head. He noticed no effect beyond hurting his own fist but was not displeased by that. The affray lasted only some twenty or thirty seconds before bouncers and security guards materialised as though from the walls. Piet and the fat man unwisely tried to fight them and were beaten with truncheons. Jim was last seen nursing an injured hand that someone had trodden or stamped on. Everyone had been arrested. Chatsworth had agreed to come quietly, under the circumstances.

"If you'd told me you were going to start a fight I might've been able to help you," he said.

They were in a gents' lavatory watched over by two black guards, both with truncheons. Conversation was permitted. It was evident that they were pacific and that Patrick in particular was incapable of posing any threat to anyone. They were accorded none of the rough treatment they could hear being meted out to others in the corridor.

"Like being on exercise waiting for interrogation," continued

Chatsworth. "Except that we're not sitting in the snow with our hands tied behind our backs."

It was hard to be grateful for this small mercy. The pain in Patrick's kidneys worsened whenever he breathed deeply or moved. His lips were swollen and still seeped blood. One eye was closed and throbbing and his nose felt as if it might gush again at any moment. He touched it gingerly, trying to determine whether it was broken. He sat against the wall, shifting carefully in vain attempts to avoid pressure on his tender coccyx.

"What gets me is that they were drinking our champagne when it happened," said Chatsworth.

Arthur Whelk came in, one hand in the pocket of his white dinner-jacket and a cigar in the other. He nodded at the guards, who left. He looked angry. "Gets the place a bad name, this sort of thing. That's why we jump on it straightaway. Very rarely happens, fortunately. You're a mess, Patrick. Why d'you pick on that crowd?"

They explained as best they could. Patrick did not mention his and Jim's link through Joanna and hoped that Chatsworth would not. Arthur puffed at his cigar, exhaled forcefully and cut them short. "Doesn't really matter who started it or who was drunk and who was sober. What does matter is that the group here has an arrangement with the Lion and his police force. We deal with trouble makers in the first instance, then hand over to them. They lock 'em up and give 'em a hard time to make sure they don't come back in a hurry. No messing about with trials and courts as there would be in Lower Africa. African justice. Works well."

"I don't fancy African justice," said Chatsworth.

"Don't blame you, old boy. Neither would I in your position."

"What's going to happen?" asked Patrick.

"I don't know. You're in a spot. Plenty of embarrassment potential, as the Service would have it. Could even be a minor international incident – diplomat imprisoned and all that. Doesn't matter about Chatsworth because he's only a British subject; Britain doesn't recognise Bapuwana and so there's sod-all anyone's going to do about it. Bad for business all the same."

"Thanks a bunch," said Chatsworth.

"Don't thank me. You got yourself into it, you'll have to get yourself out. Like the rest of us."

"Except that you're not in trouble. You're all right."

"I'm not all right. Look, either it's official and there's a big fuss or they think you've been kidnapped and there's an even bigger fuss. The

Lower Africans will get the whole story and they'll use it in some way to suit themselves. The group don't like that kind of publicity, which is bad news for me and could cost me my job. Meanwhile, you two will be languishing in African justice."

Arthur flushed the stub of his cigar down one of the toilets. There was a tense pause.

"It's not that I'm trying to be unhelpful," continued Arthur. "I want everyone to be happy. After all, we're in the same tribe, more or less."

Chatsworth readjusted his tie. "If you could make us happy maybe we could make you happy when we get back. You mentioned pension rights and whatever."

Arthur's quick eyes were still whilst he lit another cigar. "The way to an ageing civil servant's heart." He relaxed enough to smile very slightly. "Patrick?"

Patrick dabbed at his lips with his handkerchief. He was not up to long sentences. "I don't know."

"What we need is a deal. The group like trade-offs. More sensible than conflict. Also, the Lion is here tonight. Could be very bad for you unless we make it good."

"How much?" asked Chatsworth.

"Not money. If it were it would be a lot more than you could lay your hands on. But there's something else that might interest them." He watched the smoke of his cigar. "Hang on here and don't show your faces outside the door."

It was an unnecessary warning. When Arthur returned he was obviously more relaxed. He smoothed his moustache with his thumb and forefinger. "It's fixed, conditional upon a personal appearance by both of you. Before the Lion, you know."

"Like the Christians?" asked Chatsworth.

Arthur laughed. Patrick soaked his handkerchief in cold water and held it against his lips. "Will we have to speak?"

"Just apologise. You any good at apologising?"

"I am," said Chatsworth. "Lot of experience. Plenty of grovel."

"Grovelling's what's needed. I'll brief you in a moment but first we've got to get you looking respectable. Can't appear before the Lion with blood on your clothes. I'll fix you some others. Also plaster for you, Patrick. Don't want blood on the carpet."

"Wouldn't the grovel look better if we were bloody and bleeding?" asked Chatsworth.

"The Lion wouldn't like it in his suite. Just stick to what I say." Whelk paused, his eyes flickering from one to the other. "Let's make

296

sure we understand each other. I get you off, you discuss my pension with the ambassador and he fixes it with the Lower Africans so that it's okay for me to travel to and fro."

They agreed.

Arthur took their clothes and reappeared a while later with dress-shirts, trousers, bow-ties and dinner-jackets. "Bow-ties are clip-on, I'm afraid. Here's some plaster, Patrick. Can't do much about the swellings, I s'pose? Pretty ugly. I should stand back a bit, keep in the shadows."

Patrick straightened himself with difficulty and looked at his battered face in the mirror. His swollen left eye was blue verging on black and his lips were split and bulging. He looked like an actor whose make-up was so grotesquely and clownishly overdone that he had wept about it ever since. Standing straight and looking in the brightly-lit mirror made him feel dizzy and slightly sick.

"Your face looks lived-in now, more than before," said Chatsworth. He put an unnecessary bandage around his fist. "Wounded in action. Always impresses."

In the corridor they squeezed silently past Jim, Piet, the fat man and the thin man. The four prisoners were propped against the wall on their outstretched arms. They stood on their toes and their heads hung down. Four guards with batons stood behind them. No one moved and no one spoke. Jim was at the end of the line, supporting himself on one hand only. The other he held close to him. His shirt-collar was torn and bloodstained and he breathed noisily. Patrick wanted to speak but there was no time.

They were led along corridors to a private part of the main hotel, plushly carpeted and quiet. They stopped at a white door. Patrick felt weak and sick. "What do we do?"

"What I tell you," said Arthur. He pulled nervously at his cuffs and knocked.

A suite of rooms led to a double bedroom from which sliding windows led on to a balcony which formed part of the hanging gardens. The Lion of Bapuwana was the kind of leader beloved in a continent where starvation was common and age respected. His girth suggested prosperity and years of good living; his face was wrinkled, weathered and dignified. He wore a flowing white robe and had large red, green and gold rings on his fingers. Around his head was a band of red cloth.

The regal effect was vitiated by the fact that the Lion sat propped up with pillows in the middle of the double bed, his legs splayed. He looked like a giant brown baby. He had a glass of whisky in his plump hand and laughed at something said to him by a big black lady sitting on the far side of the bed. She was swathed in bright green and she rocked backwards and forwards, rippling all over as she talked and laughed. The bed sagged. A slimmer and younger black woman sat upright on a stool, smiling and saying nothing. She had high cheek bones and a calm expression. She shook her head slowly when she smiled, showing perfect teeth. Her large gold earrings swayed a little. She was elegant and beautiful. Patrick's good eye dwelt on her until he had to move his head.

Outside on the balcony some men were talking and drinking. Three were white and middle-aged, one a plump and prosperous-looking Indian and the other a handsome young black in a white robe.

Arthur inclined his head. "Your Majesty, these are the two British officials who were set upon by the mob." He spoke slowly and carefully and still seemed nervous.

The Lion nodded and smiled. The group on the veranda got up with a scraping of chairs and came in, glasses in hand. One of the whites whispered something to the Lion who stopped smiling and addressed Patrick in a deep voice, "You bring fighting to my country."

Arthur half turned towards Patrick. "Say you're sorry," he whispered.

Patrick was still uncertain about sentences. He tried to focus on the Lion but the young black in the white robe was easier to see. He could feel Arthur beside him, tense and impatient.

"Say you're sorry," hissed Arthur.

Patrick turned his swollen eye away from the Lion. He afterwards suspected that this must have made him look ineptly sly and devious. "I am sorry," he said, through swollen lips.

Chatsworth stepped forward. He gazed with passionate devotion upon the Lion. "We have great respect for Your Majesty's beautiful country. We apologise. We did not come to fight."

The Lion nodded slowly. He addressed the woman next to him in his own language. The white man tapped him on the shoulder and whispered again. The Lion looked puzzled. One of the other whites spoke in an undertone to the young black, who then sat on the bed next to the Lion. He moved one long hand in elegant circles to the even music of his words.

The Lion asked a question, nodded and turned to Patrick and Chatsworth. "You like my country?"

"It is a wonderful country, Your Majesty. We have always liked it," said Chatsworth eagerly.

Patrick thought he would feel better in a cooler room. Arthur

298

nudged him. Patrick knew what was expected but couldn't for a moment speak. He nodded.

"Say it!" hissed Arthur.

Patrick nodded ponderously, almost bowing.

The Lion grinned and held out his hand. "That is good. I am pleased. Welcome to my country."

Arthur led Patrick by the arm so that he shook hands with the Lion. The two women stared at his swollen face and the Indian photographed him with a flash from one side. Chatsworth came forward, his eyes brimming and his head inclined as if exposing his bare neck for the Lion to bite. He kissed the Lion's hand. The Indian took another photograph. One of the whites muttered something and the others laughed. "Your Majesty is most kind, noble, beautiful and good," said Chatsworth. The Lion nodded and smiled.

"He liked that last bit," Arthur whispered as they stepped back. He was less uneasy.

"What about letting us go?" whispered Chatsworth.

"Wait."

The Lion talked to the young man in white again, then raised his hand. "Go now. Please come to my country again."

"Say thank you," whispered Arthur.

Chatsworth said thank you. The other two turned to go but Patrick did not move. There was something wrong but he was incapable of seeing what. There was also something else, something he had to say. Arthur pulled his arm but he remained facing the Lion. Everyone looked at him. He remembered it was Jim. Yes, it was not Jim's fault. Jim was all right. Joanna would not like Jim to be hurt. He formed his words very carefully. "Your Majesty, please, what will happen to the other people?"

He could feel Arthur's hand tighten on his arm. There was a pause until the Lion laughed deeply and generously. "Do not worry, there is much justice in my country. They spend long time in prison. They will remember well."

"Come on," said Arthur. "Shut up and come on."

Patrick stood his ground. It was getting easier now that he knew what to think about. "Two of them are policemen. They were trying to stop the fighting. They will leave immediately."

The Lion frowned. "But that is less justice."

Arthur muttered something urgent and inaudible. The other men stared coolly at Patrick. He focused on them rather than the Lion. "They are Lower African policemen."

The men exchanged a few words. One of them again whispered to the Lion. The Lion looked puzzled and fretful but then nodded. He turned to Patrick. "They go in the morning."

Patrick bowed as far as his pains permitted. "I thank Your Majesty."

Arthur turned to him when they got out into the corridor. "You cut that fine, Stubbs. Nearly sank the whole damn issue. What's so special about Rissik and his friend?"

Patrick limped along behind the others. He felt stronger now. "It wasn't their fault."

Arthur was anxious and hurried. "I'll get your clothes and you can hop it fast before the group change their minds. They're quite capable of it and then you'll be here for the duration."

Patrick's head was clearing. "Why did you describe us both as officials?"

"Well, you are. You're on official business aren't you? Sort of. Chatsworth as well. Sounds better too. Come on, quick."

They changed in one of the hotel bedrooms. "We're damn lucky, no thanks to you," said Chatsworth. "You should've kept your mouth shut."

"Like you?"

"Yes, like me. I've had enough of prisons."

"But Jim and Piet are as innocent as us."

"That's their lookout."

Patrick sat on the bed trying to put on his shoes without bending.

"New role for you, isn't it – moralist?" continued Chatsworth, hurriedly doing up his tie.

Patrick looked at him but said nothing.

Arthur saw them to the bakkie. He had once more recovered his humour. "Come again, gentlemen both," he said cheerfully. "Give me notice next time and I'll see you meet the right sort of company."

"I will," said Chatsworth.

Patrick did not feel up to driving. Chatsworth readily agreed. They asked about petrol.

"Round the corner here," said Arthur. "I'll come with you so you can get it on the house. Trust you'll both get credit for finding me. Let me know if you need a letter to back it up." He laughed. "Remember me to Sarah and Deuteronomy – and Sir Wilfrid. He's a sweet old thing, really. Means well. Forget the rest of them. But don't forget pension and passport." He waved goodbye.

300

22

The holiday, a Jewish festival, was not yet ended when they returned. Battenburg was for once quiet. Patrick drove himself to the residence. He preferred to talk to Sir Wilfrid alone, anticipating difficulty.

There was none. Sir Wilfrid was delighted that Whelk had been found, saddened but unsurprised by the poor fellow's involvement in gambling and pleased that LASS had confirmed his suspicions – albeit not in the way he had expected. He looked forward to writing to London about the whole business.

As for Arthur, there should be no problem about his pension. He had only to submit his resignation in the normal way and it would be accepted. The rather unusual manner in which he had left the Service would be overlooked in the interests of not rocking the boat. His passport and freedom of travel through Battenburg were not really matters for the British authorities; after all, he had his passport, it was his. Whether or not the Lower Africans permitted him to use it for travelling to and fro was up to them. It was unlikely that they would interfere; Arthur had not after all done them any harm and he was clearly not exactly unsympathetic to their own attitudes. This both saddened and surprised Sir Wilfrid. He had liked Arthur. He was jolly glad he had not after all come to a sticky end.

"Been in the wars?" he asked. "Or is it too many late nights?"

Patrick had forgotten about his face. He explained briefly.

"Just as well you had Chatsworth with you. You seem rather prone to fall into these scrapes, left to yourself. He's earned his keep, that man. I shall write to his firm and tell them what a good job he's done. We could do with one or two like him in the Service."

Patrick went straight from the residence to Joanna's. She should have got back that day. He still did not know what he would say to her. He did know he wanted no awkward telephone calls. Perhaps the simplest would be best; there was no longer any need for secrecy and so he could explain why he had had to go to Sin City and hope she believed him. If necessary Chatsworth could be produced as a witness. Or Jim, if he were free.

301

He scoured Battenburg for flowers but nearly every shop was closed and he ended up with a box of chocolates, dusty and probably stale. He drove confidently to her bungalow but her car was not there. It had not occurred to him that she might stay on at the coast.

Beauty would know but he did not want to ask. He drove slowly away.

It was as he turned on to the main road home that he saw her car turning off it. She saw him and stopped. After turning the bakkie clumsily, because it hurt to twist in his seat, he pulled up behind her. She waited in her car. "Patrick, your face," she said, as he approached. "And your clothes."

The concern in her voice made him feel confident again. "I had a fight. Shall we go back to your place? I'll tell you about it there. I'm all right."

She had been to her brother's. Belinda was at home with Beauty. He did not say he had already been there. "How was the coast?"

"Beautiful. How was Sin City?"

"Pretty awful."

She started her car. "It looks it."

Once in her bungalow he talked quickly, nervously and too much. He had hoped she would laugh at the misunderstanding about why he had to go to Sin City but she did not. Once or twice he was facetious but soon stopped. She poured drinks, listened – sometimes distractedly – and asked questions. It was as if she were weighing what he said against a different version she had heard from someone else. He had never felt less at ease with her.

She several times interrupted abruptly, going back to something he had said and ignoring what he was presently saying. "But I don't understand how Jim got hurt if they didn't hit him."

"Neither do I. I was at the bottom of it all. It may have been accidental or he may have been protecting me, I don't know. It could've been the guard afterwards."

She asked twice more about Jim's injuries. "I mean, they weren't as bad as mine," Patrick said eventually.

She looked at his face again. "Are you sure they'll let him go?"

"Not sure, no, but they said they would let us go and they did. Also, they'd bring trouble on their own heads if they locked up Lower African policemen."

She fidgeted with the tassles of a cushion, saying nothing.

"Shall I open some wine?" he asked.

She nodded. He debated whether he should ask to stay the night or say nothing and simply not go. She went to the kitchen and began

302

preparing dinner. During the meal she was friendly but gave no sign of affection.

"It's good to see you," he said after a pause.

She ignored the remark and talked about her friends on the coast. He felt increasingly lonely. However, she laughed when the chocolates turned out to be mouldy. "That's so typical of you. I knew they would be before I opened them."

He sat on the sofa and put his arm around her. He felt ridiculous and gauche, as in the early stages of courtship, and more estranged than if they had never made love at all.

She carefully removed his arm and moved herself farther along the sofa. "Are you on a one-way ticket?"

"What do you mean?"

"Will you go away and not come back?"

For a moment he was irritated. "Why do you keep on about my going away? You always mention it."

"I just have this feeling that you will. I can't believe you'll stay. You always seem like someone who won't stay."

"I've no plans to go away."

"D'you have any plans?"

"No, not really. Everything can change in a week, anyway. What should I plan?"

"You live for the moment, do you?"

Her expression was taunting and her tone slightly bitter. He disliked the cliché and the assumptions that went with it. He put his head in his hands.

"I thought of you all the time in Sin City. I'd been round here looking for you when we met."

At first she did not react but then she smiled and stretched her leg along the sofa, prodding his waist with her bare foot. "I hoped you had but I thought you'd never say so."

They made love that night with a passion neither manufactured nor feigned. Afterwards she wept and would not be comforted. He felt hopelessly distant and unwanted. Eventually he offered to make tea, the most comforting thing he could think of. She shook her head.

"Glass of water?" he asked. She nodded. When he returned with it she sat up in bed and dried her eyes. She sipped the water and said nothing. The brightness of the light, the crumpled bed and their clothes strewn where they had fallen made everything seem tawdry and hopeless. He lay on his back and closed his eyes.

"Have you ever loved anyone?" she asked.

He looked at her. The love of which people spoke so familiarly found no corresponding reality within himself. When he thought of her he could convince himself it did but faced with her he did not know what it was. "No."

After a while she put out the light and they lay together in the darkness. She turned restlessly two or three times, then switched on the light and sat up.

"Please go." She pushed the hair back from her face. Her mouth was set hard, showing little lines where she normally smiled.

He felt willing to say whatever she wanted if it would make her fond once more but instead he sat up. "D'you really want me to?"

"Yes. I can't sleep and I – I'd just rather you weren't here."

He dressed in silence, then went in search of his shoes which he had kicked off by the sofa. She followed him in a blue dressing-gown and stood by the mantelpiece. Her arms were folded beneath her breasts.

He hesitated by the door. He knew he would fully experience what was happening only in retrospect when he ran and reran it over in his mind. Whatever happened he would see her tomorrow. He would not tell her that now. "Goodbye, then." He felt absurdly British.

"Goodbye."

He opened the door and stepped out. He surprised himself by reflecting with complete detachment that this was what it was like to be finished with. It had never happened as definitively before.

As he walked down the gravel path he heard her gasp as if in pain, then begin to cry. He stopped. The moonlight cast a sharp-edged shadow from the inevitable jacaranda.

He had left his jacket behind. That did not matter, of course. He could collect it the following day or not at all if she refused to see him; it was only a jacket. What did matter was that he should have made her so wretched. Perhaps there was something evil in him or some lacunae in his moral and emotional responses which he could only guess at by other people's reactions. Her sobs were loud enough to be heard in the street.

She might in any case send the jacket on and now was perhaps the worst time to try to comfort her. She might not want to be seen until she felt stronger. On the other hand, perhaps she most needed comfort when she was most wretched and if he went back later he might reopen a wound which had already begun to heal. He stood at the edge of the shadow. Then went back.

She bent as she sobbed, holding on to the mantelpiece with one

hand. She shook her head at him. "You shouldn't have come back."
She half ran across the room, her hand over her face, and pressed her
head into his shoulder.

They were awoken very early by the doorbell. Joanna got up
immediately, as if she had been expecting it. She put on her blue
dressing-gown and was gone for some time. Patrick could hear voices.
When she returned she smiled. "Jim's here."

"Here? Now?"

"He's come to see you. Come on."

Jim still wore the clothes he'd worn in Sin City. One of his teeth was
missing. "I went to your house. Guessed where you must be. Sorry
about the interruption." He grinned. "You look worse than me, even
if you have kept your teeth."

"Did the guards do that to you?"

"No, they were all right – just. I don't know who did it. It was
someone's boot. I was on the floor with you – trying to protect you, for
God's sake, you bugger." He laughed and held out his hand. "We
should shake on that, you know. We fight together, we fall together. I
was saying to Joanna, it's not only her we have in common."

She smiled at him. "Shut up, Jim. I'll make some coffee."

Patrick felt disadvantaged by Jim's early morning vigour and cheeri-
ness. Joanna moved briskly about the kitchen despite her admonitions
to them to be quiet and not wake Belinda.

"I hear it's thanks to you that me and Piet got off lightly," said
Jim. "That almost makes up for getting into trouble in the first
place." He held up his hand. "No, no, I know it wasn't your fault,
you didn't cause it. It's just that it wouldn't have happened if it wasn't
for you. Trouble happens round you, Patrick. You come through all
right."

"Who were those people, the ones you were with?"

"Friends of Piet's. Bums. Talk about them later." They sat at the
table. Joanna offered toast but neither wanted it. She said she'd make
it anyway and both accepted.

"I didn't come here to thank you," Jim said. "I'm doing you a
favour. I'm breaking rules."

Patrick waited.

"Sarah's boy was arrested in Kuweto yesterday with a lot of others.
They're in headquarters. They might be brought to trial, they might
not. They don't have to be. I don't know what he's in for, it's not my
department. But he's there and they're talking to him." He buttered
his toast. "I'm telling you so that if Stanley's left anything he shouldn't

round your house or in Sarah's quarters you can get rid of it fast. If they turn the place over and find just one propaganda sheet there'll be trouble. Burn it before they get there. Don't think they won't come because it's embassy property. You're all right with diplomatic immunity – the worst they'll do is kick you out. But they'll lock up Sarah for a long time."

Joanna glanced at Patrick when Jim mentioned his being kicked out. Patrick did not respond. He thought instead of Stanley's two boxes in the garage. "I'll have a look. I'll talk to Sarah."

"Don't tell her they've got him. The only way you could know would be through me."

"How long have we got?"

Jim shrugged. "Could be any time. They've had him since yesterday. He'll talk quickly. They always do."

"Will they interrogate him?"

Jim dipped toast in his coffee. "Something like that."

"You mean they'll beat him, torture him?"

Jim put the toast in his mouth. "It's not exactly unknown in this continent. Anyone arrested in Africa expects a beating. We'd have all got one last night if Arthur hadn't wanted to do a deal with you. It's how we live here. It's how you'd live if you came from here. But you come from somewhere else."

His manner was relaxed, cheerful and heartless. Patrick wondered whether it was assumed in order to annoy him or to hide embarrassment. "Thank you for the favour."

"Don't bother. It wasn't for you."

"More coffee?" asked Joanna. She seemed to regard the conversation about Stanley as none of her business.

"I'd better go," said Patrick.

At the door he started to say he would ring or come round later but she clutched his arm. "You've forgotten your jacket. It's in the bedroom. I'll get it."

When she returned Jim came to the door. He had his hands in his pockets and was still munching toast. He looked at Patrick. "They won't do much. It doesn't take much."

Patrick climbed into the bakkie feeling that he, not Jim, was the interloper.

As he drove into the garage he saw that Stanley's two boxes were still there, at the back.

Sarah came out of the house, smiling and wiping her hands on her apron. "Mr Chatsworth said you not come for breakfast, massa."

"He was wrong again, Sarah."

"He is still in bed."

"I'm not surprised."

She laughed. "But I got food for you." He left the boxes and walked in with her. She put her hand to her mouth. "Oh, I forget. The embassy ring and say you must go straight away. The ambassador want to see you. I am so sorry, massa. Some days I forget everything."

He said he would not stay for breakfast but nevertheless stood stroking Snap's head whilst she laid the table. She wore a clean blue maid's dress with white apron and cap, all neatly pressed. "Sarah, does Stanley have things in your quarters?"

"No, massa, only his things in the garage."

He would see the ambassador as quickly as possible, then come back and tell her about Stanley. After that they would get rid of the cases, if necessary. He would also see if Jim could find out more. "Please ask Mr Chatsworth to stay in until I return. I'll be back later this morning."

"Yes, massa."

The garden glistened in the morning sun. He let Snap out. "It's a beautiful morning."

"Yes, massa."

"I won't be long."

"Yes, massa. Massa?" She frowned and looked at him sideways. "What has happened to your face?"

He touched his eye. "Ah, yes. Well, I met some bad men in Sin City."

She turned to him. "In Sin City? That is a bad place, massa. Did they beat you?"

"Yes, but not badly. It'll soon get better."

She shook her head and put her hand on his arm, tugging it to and fro. "Massa, sometimes you do damn silly thing. Now the embassy will beat you for going to bad place."

He took her hand. "I'll come back before they catch me." She laughed and went back to the kitchen, still shaking her head.

Patrick paused at the door of his office. Clifford was sitting on his desk and was reading aloud from a newspaper, swinging his legs. Philip, slumped in his chair, smiled a sympathetic greeting and raised his hands in a gesture of helplessness.

" 'The establishment of official links with Bapuwana is a decisive and courageous step by Britain in the face of predictable United Nations

307

wrath,'" Clifford read. "'The decision was no doubt a result of the recent visit by the British minister, Ray Collier, who achieved an excellent understanding with our government. There is now said to be a closer identity of view between the two governments across the whole range of African questions than at any time during the past twenty years. This includes agreement on the crucial border question which is shortly to be the subject of UN debate. Britain's momentous step is particularly well timed.'"

Clifford looked up. "You really have made a name for yourself. Listen." He read the final paragraph of a leader in another paper which said that Mr Stubbs would be based in Battenburg for the time being until quarters were ready for him in Sin City.

Clifford's fleshy face was relaxed, almost benign. "Frankly, this must be the end. It's almost as if you did it deliberately. It could only be worse if you were caught *in flagrante* with the wife of the president."

"I doubt HMG would mind that so much," said Philip. "It wouldn't involve the UN."

"No, but this does," Clifford added with gratuitous relish. "All very public, this. No government could possibly ignore it."

There had been little other news that holiday and the subject was given considerable prominence. The photograph of Patrick shaking hands with the Lion was on all the front pages. His face was shown from its less damaged side. There were one or two photographs of Chatsworth kissing the Lion's hand but he was unnamed and his features blurred. One headline read, 'Britain Establishes Links with Bapuwana', another, 'Queen's Envoy Meets Lion'.

Clifford sighed. "HE told me what you were doing up there. Bound to go wrong. Alway does, this off-the-cuff stuff. Said so all along. Didn't you realise what was happening?"

"I'm afraid not."

"You must've been half asleep."

"I was."

"Who hit you?"

"A fat man."

"Just goes to show." Clifford walked contentedly from their room, the papers under his arm. "HE wants to see you now."

Patrick noticed Jean glance at his face as he entered the ambassador's office. Sir Wilfrid was calm. "Of course, you'll have to go. London will be outraged, HMG will have to apologise at the UN and there'll be problems with the Third World for years to come. Because, of course, no one will believe us." He searched in the clock for a pipe-stem to replace the one he said he had bitten through whilst reading the papers that morning.

Patrick once again recalled Whelk's evasiveness during and after the audience with the Lion. No doubt everyone else was delighted; it was free publicity for the backers of Sin City, the Lion would enjoy having his photograph in the world's press, British denials would give the Lower African government the pleasure of righteous indignation at Britain's inability to control her own diplomats, and Arthur had no doubt secured his permanent position. In short, HMG would be embarrassed, the rest of the world amused and no one any the worse. Except himself.

Sir Wilfrid fitted another stem. "They won't sack you, there's no question of that. You're a civil servant. But your career is another matter. My own is over anyway after this posting but yours" – he paid particular attention to filling the pipe – "might have been all right. They'll probably keep you in London for a few years, then send you somewhere harmless like Moscow. The Russians will look after you. They follow you around all the time so that you can't go anywhere, do anything or talk to anyone without supervision. I know it's not entirely your fault but London will need a scapegoat. They always do." He lit his pipe. "One thing I must say, though, is that young Chatsworth comes out of this rather well. He's not even mentioned. I had hoped he'd be a restraining influence but I suppose he wasn't to know you'd get into a fight."

Patrick was remote from London's displeasure. He was more concerned with what Joanna would say to the fulfilling of her prophecy that he would leave soon. Perhaps she wouldn't mind so much now. "Should I go and pack, sir?"

"No, no, don't be precipitous. Looks bad. Wait till I've explained to London. Clifford will get something off this morning." He stared out of the window, one arm folded across his stomach and the other holding his pipe. "Bit of a mess, isn't it? Like everything else in this country. Not that we can talk."

Sir Wilfrid gazed down into the shopping area where a young black woman sat alone on a bench. She was elegant and slight. She wore a red and black robe beneath which her red sandals just showed, and there was a large bundle on the ground beside her. She sat poised, still and upright. Her brown neck was slim and straight, her features in repose, expressionless and beautiful. It seemed that no amount of looking was sufficient to absorb her grace and stillness.

"What was Sin City like?" asked Sir Wilfrid.

Patrick stared at the young woman, thinking of Slack Alice behind the bar and of the red-haired lady punter. "Pretty ugly. A lot of people enjoy it, though."

"That's the point, I imagine." Sir Wilfrid turned away from the window and put his hands in his pockets. "The trouble is, you see, many countries are going to think we really did establish links with that tinpot regime in Bapuwana and then backed down because of all the fuss. The only respectable way out would be for us to claim that the whole thing was a put-up job by the Lower Africans. That would carry conviction because people would want to believe it but it would do irreparable damage to bilateral relations." He looked seriously at Patrick, then added quietly, "You must accept, Patrick, that because of this you may never get a Third World posting. You may not be welcome in black Africa."

"I hadn't thought of that, sir."

On his way out Jean said that Clifford wanted him. She was almost friendly, as if he were ill.

Clifford was back in his office, no longer benign and beginning to revel in the businesslike bustle of someone else's misfortune. "It was clear to me from the start that this chasing after Whelk would lead to no good. All that secrecy and getting into bed with the Lower Africans and having that mad convict staying in your house at the same time as living in sin with your airport girlfriend. It all adds up, you know. It'll be very hard to say anything in your favour to London. Of course, Whelk's part in the whole affair is thoroughly reprehensible too. Never did like the man. I'm told he retains full pension rights and his desertion is going to be treated as resignation. Scandalous, considering he's almost as involved as you."

"Rather more, surely. He was the cause of it."

"Unwitting."

"So was I."

"You should've known better. Besides, if you hadn't picked on Jim Rissik's girlfriend as well as your own you wouldn't get involved in brawls. You seem to spend a lot of time with the ladies." The telephone rang. Clifford answered brusquely and his tone changed to puzzled irritation. "He's here now." He held out the telephone. "My wife. She wants to speak to you."

Sandy sounded brittle and nervous. "Hallo, Mr Celebrity. Just thought I'd ring and say well done while you're still around to be spoken to."

"Thanks. I'm not sure I deserve all the credit." Clifford pretended to busy himself with the telegram he was writing. Patrick felt he must sound as brittle as Sandy.

"You mean to say it wasn't deliberate?" she asked.

"Not on my part."

"You disappoint me."

Having established that he didn't know when he was going back she rang off. He put down the telephone feeling he had something to hide.

"You'd better discuss the organisation of your work with Philip," said Clifford. "Let me have something on paper later."

There was nothing to hand over. Philip was sympathetic and helpful. "Of course you'll suffer damage but it needn't be lasting. The ambassador likes you. He'll give you a good report."

"I'm sure we'll meet again," said Patrick when later they shook hands.

"I hope it works out for you," said Philip, with greater honesty.

Patrick decided not to tell the ambassador of Stanley's arrest, preferring to dispose of the boxes first so that he could then honestly say that there was no scope for further embarrassment. He rang Chatsworth to warn him about what was happening but got the number-unobtainable sound. The switchboard told him that the line was out of order. He rang Joanna to see if she would have lunch but she was out. He decided to go home anyway.

On the way out he met Miss Teale. She smiled. "You've done very well for yourself, I must say. Not a very flattering photo, but still. I didn't know we were going to establish links with them. Very important task for a third secretary. Well done."

She had been friendly since the minister's visit, seeing in Patrick an ally against Clifford. "There's a bit more to it than that," he said. "I'll explain later."

She closed her eyes. "No need, no need. I know how confidential you people in chancery have to be sometimes. It's a jolly good thing your car's here. The paperwork came through this morning. You can pick it up whenever you like."

The first sign was the paper that littered the avenue adjoining his own. A dozen or so pieces fluttered along the normally tidy road, whirled into the air by each passing car. One stuck in the branches of a jacaranda, another against the trunk. He pulled up and by leaning across saw from the bakkie that it was one of Rachel's propaganda leaflets. In his own avenue the trees were festooned. Leaflets lay as thick as leaves on the verges. Two policemen were slowly collecting them. Outside his house were police cars, a fire engine and an ambulance.

He approached with a growing blankness, a turning down of feeling. The drive was crowded with people and littered with glass and débris. Windows were blown out of the house and tiles were missing. The garage and most of Sarah's quarters were wrecked. Charred timbers and unidentifiable bits lay strewn about. He passed unnoticed among the police and firemen. The space where the garage had been was cordoned off with white tape and some men were crawling over it on their hands and knees.

He saw Jim, uniformed now, talking to other policemen. Near the garden gate Chatsworth was with some reporters. He was paler than usual and talked quickly. When he saw Patrick he broke off and came over.

"Bloody nearly got me. I was in the upstairs loo and it went off right when I flushed. Thought I'd done it at first. They reckon it was that other box of Stanley's, the one I was going to shift, but they don't know what it was. Must've been incendiary. Nearly burnt the place down." He paused and looked at Patrick. "Didn't you know about it – doesn't the embassy know?"

"No."

"I thought that's why you were here." Chatsworth rubbed his hands. He was awkward and nervous. He looked round. "Snap's okay. I've tied him to the tree by the rubbish heap. Most of the house is all right. No structural damage."

There was a stretcher on the forecourt. A grey blanket covered something, but one brown leg, wearing a blue slipper, protruded.

"She must've been trying to move it," Chatsworth continued. "She was right over it. Wouldn't have known anything."

Jim came over. "It was old stuff. Unstable and already primed. It exploded when shifted. The lab boys will tell us exactly what it was." He looked down, then at Patrick again. "If we'd known about these boxes we could've done something."

Patrick did not want to speak. The grey blanket, much larger than the small heap it had to cover, was still in his range of vision. It was an effort not to stare. "I thought you were warning me to move them."

"If you'd said there were boxes like that I'd have told you not to touch them."

"Stanley didn't tell you then?" His voice sounded harsh.

"They hadn't started on him. They will now. If they had he'd still have a mother." The gap in his teeth showed when he spoke. His voice

312

was quiet but there was an edge to it. "Your friend Rachel didn't help. She told Stanley he could hide the boxes here and pretend they went with hers. One of his friends confessed this morning, a little reluctantly. They told her they were leaflets. She arranged for them to be picked up by her friends who were coming for her propaganda stuff. Pity they weren't."

He walked back towards the stretcher. Patrick turned away.

Deuteronomy was laconically picking up debris in the garden. "You can go home," Patrick told him. "Come again tomorrow when there are fewer people and help clear up then."

"Ma-ass-a." Deuteronomy smiled his usual smile and nodded slowly. Ten minutes later he was still there, working nearer the house. Patrick remembered then that it was his pay-day. He paid him.

"Ma-ass-a," said Deuteronomy, smiling and nodding. He pocketed the money and went.

There was dust on the surface of the pool and one or two bits of debris floating in it. "We'll hook those out and filter it," said Chatsworth. He still sounded nervous and anxious. "The police have looked all over the house. There's nothing else. They reckon it's habitable."

Patrick nodded. Chatsworth continued to look awkward and unhappy. "Good," Patrick added. "I'm glad it's habitable."

Sir Wilfrid was brisk. "You must leave immediately. With leaflets and bombs on top of this other business the Lower Africans would be forced to make an issue of it. Then they'd png you. You must leave before anything is announced. First flight in the morning. Before anything else happens." He ran his hand through his hair. He looked suddenly tired. "I never met Sarah but I imagine you must be very upset. And to be killed like that by her own son. Poor lad, how he must feel. He'll spend the rest of his life in prison. What a dreadful comment on this country it all is." They shook hands. "I hope we meet in London. I'm sure we shall. I don't have much longer to serve and it would be nice to talk things over in more relaxed circumstances. Chatsworth is still in the house, is he?"

"Yes."

"Good. He can look after it for a day or two until we sort something out. Goodbye, Patrick, and God bless." He held Patrick's hand for a moment longer.

Clifford was in an ecstasy of administration. He appropriated the commercial officer's secretary to supplement his own, shouted at Miss Teale and ordered Philip to prepare a paper on the possible threat to

313

diplomats arising from the subversion of domestics, including the families and friends of domestics.

"Sarah was killed outright, wasn't she?" he asked.

"Yes."

Clifford wrote something in his notebook. "Much damage to the house?"

"Nothing structural."

"I'll get on to the PSA about repairs. Probably take years. Miss Teale was in here just now talking nonsense about it not being insured unless the front door was locked at the time the explosive was put there. You can't answer that, I s'pose?"

"No."

"Never mind. The important thing is to get the bureaucracy working. Just as well I've kept the wheels oiled. Internationally, the repercussions are only just beginning. Italy, France and the Americans have already made enquiries about establishing links with Bapuwana. Their ambassadors have been on to HE this morning. They think we've done it in exchange for mineral rights and they won't take no for an answer. As if we'd be so smart. London have put out a statement saying that your action was a purely personal initiative, taken without authority, and that you were being recalled. There's already talk of a censure motion at the UN. What about the inventory of what's in the house? You can't leave without signing that."

"Chatsworth will sign."

He reached Joanna's house as she was leaving to collect Belinda from play-school. She listened in silence. "So you are going back?"

"Tomorrow morning."

She turned her face away. At one moment she looked upset, at another stonily determined. "I don't mind going," he added, "except for you. It's only you."

She did not look at him. "What about Snap? Who's going to look after him?"

"I haven't thought about that."

"I suppose I could have him. I haven't got a dog."

"Yes, yes. Shall I bring him round?"

"I'll collect him when you've gone."

He swallowed. "You'd rather I didn't stay the night, then?"

She looked at him. "Yes, I'd rather you didn't."

He felt like asking her to go with him but he knew she wouldn't. His request would not be serious. He could not believe he really wanted her yet his heart beat faster and when he tried to speak he had to swallow again. "What's happened?"

"You're leaving."

"I wasn't always leaving."

"You were never really here. I thought you were at first but you weren't. You were always neutral. You can't be neutral here."

He grabbed her by both arms. "I was never neutral. I tried to give this place a chance. I was never neutral about you. You know that."

She neither resisted nor yielded. "It seemed neutral to me."

He was aware of gripping her too tightly and had to stop himself from shaking her. "Look, all along I've tried to be honest. I do have feelings, more than I want. I feel for you. But feelings have limits and they change and so I keep trying to be honest, that's all. I have to know what I really feel. I can't just ignore myself."

"It's not enough." She was calm and implacable. He let go of her.

His desires narrowed to the single one of keeping her talking. "Will you go back to Jim?"

She looked sullen and annoyed as she turned towards her car. "It's not like that. You don't understand."

"Tell me what it is like, then."

"It's not what you think." She sighed and looked away again. "Jim and I are friends. We were before and we still are. The rest – it's not everything. Can't you understand that?"

"Did you go on sleeping with him?" He hated himself for asking.

Her grey eyes met his. "You don't understand at all, do you? You never have." She opened the car door. "I must go, I'm late for Belinda."

He grabbed her arm again and pulled her towards him. Her eyes suddenly filled with tears. "Please let me go."

She drove off with unnecessary revving and untimely gear-changes, which he could not help observing. As he climbed slowly into the bakkie Beauty waved from the living-room window. Immediately and unthinkingly he smiled and waved back.

He had to spend some hours at the police station going over all he knew about Stanley. They told him that Jim had gone off duty. He thought all the time of Joanna. It was dark when he returned to the house. The tape around the cordoned-off area showed white in the moonlight. Debris had been pushed to one side of the drive and a start had been made on clearing the remains of Sarah's quarters. A note from Chatsworth said that he had gone out and would be back later. He too had been interviewed. Snap had been fed and was locked in the kitchen.

There was electricity but not all the lights worked and there was still no telephone. Despite the broken windows the air in the house was heavy with dust from the rubble outside. He opened all the doors. Plaster was cracked, an outhouse wall bulged, a lavatory door was blown off, and there was a hole in the kitchen roof. He walked from room to silent room, glad to be alone. He allowed himself to think of nothing but what he would pack and what leave to be sent on. His heavy baggage would be returned unused. Practical thoughts, such as whether he'd be able to stay in the same flat in London and when to ring his mother, washed to and fro in his mind with a lot of flotsam – that it was lucky for Arthur Whelk that his possessions had gone before the blast, that Sarah's daughter would now be free to marry her unsuitable man, that Snap would find Joanna's garden small and lacking in rats.

At the top of the stairs the rape-gate hung lop-sidedly on its bottom hinge. It opened and closed but swayed precariously. It could no longer be rattled in the mornings.

The light in his bedroom did not work but that on the landing did. It was whilst he was packing his big suitcase in semi-darkness that he heard footsteps on the stairs. He started, then saw that it was Sandy. She stopped the other side of the rape-gate.

"All the doors were open so I walked in. It's awfully spooky, isn't it? I was beginning to wish I hadn't. May I come in?" She walked forward hesitantly. "I'm a little drunk, so don't ask. You know what it does to my walking but that's the only thing. I've come to see you to say bye-bye." She sat heavily on the bed.

Now that there was someone with him it was comforting not to be alone. "Would you like a drink?"

"In a minute. Don't stop packing. I'll watch. I just thought you might like company."

He smiled. "You were right."

She sat silently for a short while then crossed her legs and put her hands around her knee, leaning forward slightly. She wore a jumper and a pleated skirt. "How is it with Joanna?"

"It isn't any more."

"Are you upset?"

"Yes."

"Is she?"

"I think so."

316

"Of course she is." She watched for a few moments more. "Will you kiss me?"

He stopped what he was doing. She smiled a little sadly, though it was hard to see her features clearly. Now that she had asked he wanted to. He sat on the bed next to her and she uncrossed her legs with a susurration of nylon. "What I really mean is will you make love with me?" she said.

A few minutes before he would not have believed he could make love with anyone other than Joanna but now he felt a sudden over-whelming comfort and pleasure in being wanted, however superficial-ly. They undressed each other hurriedly. She laughed as he fumbled with the clip on her skirt. "You don't know how much I've been thinking about this. It's been so long."

"Very long?"

"I'm married, don't forget. It's almost like being celibate. You'd've found out if you'd succumbed."

"What makes you think that?"

"Because the urge that attracted you to Joanna is the same one that would make you tire of her quite quickly and would make you want other women. You may be fond of someone, you might even love them, but the old hormones go on churning and they always point elsewhere." She laughed again and caressed him. "Like yours now. You may be in love with her, you may be horribly up-set but the hormones go their own sweet way, don't they? Look at them."

He stopped. "It'll be no good if you're going to be serious."

She smiled and put her bare arms round his neck. "Don't worry, love."

Afterwards she asked for a big gin with a small tonic. When he returned with it she was sitting on the bed, dressed. "I must get back to my husband soon. He'll be suspicious."

"Where does he think you are?"

"Here. I told him I was coming to say goodbye to you."

"You'll tell him we talked, will you?"

"Yes, and went to bed and made love. That'll wake him up a bit." She smiled. "I wonder what he'd say? One of these days I'll say that when I haven't, just to see."

"How long d'you think you'll stay married?"

"Now who's being serious? And naive. One reason I made love with you tonight, my love, is that you're leaving. I wouldn't have if you'd been staying. That's the difference between me and Joanna. And I'll

317

probably stay married until I'm too old to do anything else. Come on, help me with this drink."

She put her arm through his as they went downstairs. "D'you feel better?"

He grinned. "I'm afraid I do."

She squeezed him. "Good. I thought you'd be lonely and upset. It takes the edge off it, doesn't it?"

"Blunts the sensibilities."

"It's done me good, too. I think it really is good for you."

At her car they kissed tenderly. "Bye-bye, love. Look after yourself. Have a good life. Think of me sometimes."

On the way upstairs he switched out the landing light and paused again by the rape-gate. It was still slewed at its drunken angle and the moonlight threw shadows of its bars diagonally across the wall. He thought of Stanley, Sarah's heavy pull, and undressed again slowly. He left the gate open and all the doors unlocked, and slept well.

Chatsworth drove him to the airport next morning. He was cheerful. "Spent yesterday evening with Jim and Piet and a few of their cronies. A good crowd. It's a pity you're going. As you are, though, you might get on to my firm for me when you're in London and tell them they owe me a month's salary plus expenses. Then I'll be able to pay you back what I owe. Hope you've kept a bill."

"Pay what you think," said Patrick. "What should I tell your firm you're doing here?"

"Don't tell them anything. Just say I'm winding up my affairs, tying loose ends and all that. In fact, I'm going to resign and stay on but I don't want them to know until I've got my money. I like this place. Jim was telling me last night about a new anti-terrorist unit the army is setting up. Seems to think I might be able to join it. Sort of work I like. Apparently, my record won't count against me if I join the army. If not, I'll see if Arthur could fix me up with something at his place. I want to keep in touch with him anyway. Useful bloke to know."

Chatsworth willingly undertook to do battle with Miss Teale about the inventory and about sending back Patrick's belongings. He was confident of convincing Clifford or the ambassador that he should stay in the house as a caretaker until all the repairs were effected, which would be several months at the very least.

"Do you want the bakkie?" asked Patrick. He had put off thinking about its disposal until his final drive.

"I was going to ask. How much?"

"Have it."

"I thought you liked it?"

"That's why I'm not selling it."

"Thanks. I'll pay you back one day. What about this new Ford that's arrived? You must let me give you something for it at least."

"That goes back at taxpayers' expense."

"Bloody scandal. No wonder Britain's the way it is."

At the airport it appeared that one of the priorities was to make it difficult for people to leave the country. There were complicated formalities. Chatsworth got bored and Patrick was by then happy to do without his assistance. They shook hands. "I'll look you up when I'm passing through London," said Chatsworth. "I'll come and stay."

"Anything you want me to say to Rachel?"

"Tell her about the explosion and say I've had to go underground. I've got her address and I'll see her in London if I make it across the border."

There was no one from the embassy to see him off. Clifford had said it would "look bad"; besides, it was the early flight. It was not until he was past the barrier that he saw Joanna and Jim. Jim's pass must have got them through. There was no time for awkwardness.

"Will we see you back?" asked Jim. "No reason why not. Come for a holiday." He grinned.

"How's Stanley?"

"He's okay."

"Have you seen him?"

"That's what they tell me." Jim put his hand on Patrick's shoulder. "Really, I think he is. But he'll stay away for a long time. Nothing you can do."

Joanna had her hair tied back. On a thin gold chain round her neck she wore the bullet. He shook hands with Jim but not with her. They looked at each other and she wished him a good flight.

His last view of Battenburg as the aeroplane climbed into the early morning haze was of the hundreds of blue and green swimming-pools glinting in the sun. The plane was nearly empty and he sat alone at the back. A stewardess struggled up the aisle with the drinks trolley, complaining of the heavy pull; but he wanted nothing.